DISASTER

The ferret pointed to a reddy-orange glow illuminating the sky beyond the headland. It took a moment for realization to sink in, then the pirate stoat let out an agonized wail and began tearing at his braided beard, the clumsy wooden clogs clicking together as he performed an anguished jig on the shore.

"Whaaaagh! The slime-coated villain's burnin' me ship! Yarrggh! Me luvverly *Seascarab*, pride o' me 'eart! Badrang, yer rotten foul-nosed worm, stinkin' screwtailed stoat, warp-eyed snotty-snouted shark!"

The corsair crew looked on in dismay as their Cap'n gave full vent to his spleen. Hurling himself at the gates, he hacked with his cutlass, kicked with his clogs, even gnawed savagely at the woodwork with his teeth as he yelled between mouthfuls of splinters, "I'll rip yer liver 'n' lights out an' feed 'em to the crabs. I'll cut off'n yer 'ead an' throw it in yer face. I'll string up yer tripes fer riggin'. I'll pickle yer tail in burnin' brine!"

THE REDWALL BOOKS

Redwall
Mossflower
Mattimeo
Mariel of Redwall
Salamandastron
Martin the Warrior
The Bellmaker
Outcast of Redwall
The Pearls of Lutra
The Long Patrol
Marlfox
The Legend of Luke
Lord Brocktree
Taggerung
Triss
Loamhedge
Rakkety Tam
High Rhulain
Eulalia!
Doomwyte
The Sable Quean

The Great Redwall Feast (picture book)
A Redwall Winter's Tale (picture book)

OTHER BOOKS

Seven Strange and Ghostly Tales
Castaways of the Flying Dutchman
The Angel's Command
The Tale of Urso Brunov (picture book)
The Ribbajack and Other Curious Yarns
Voyage of Slaves
Urso Brunov and the White Emperor (picture book)

A tale of REDWALL
Martin the Warrior

BRIAN JACQUES

Illustrated by Gary Chalk

FIREBIRD

AN IMPRINT OF PENGUIN GROUP (USA) INC.

Dedicated to a true friend,
Patricia Lee Gauch

FIREBIRD
Published by the Penguin Group
Penguin Group (USA) Inc., 345 Hudson Street, New York, New York 10014, U.S.A.
Penguin Group (Canada), 90 Eglinton Avenue East, Suite 700, Toronto, Ontario, Canada M4P 2Y3
(a division of Pearson Penguin Canada Inc.)
Penguin Books Ltd, 80 Strand, London WC2R 0RL, England
Penguin Ireland, 25 St Stephen's Green, Dublin 2, Ireland (a division of Penguin Books Ltd)
Penguin Group (Australia), 250 Camberwell Road, Camberwell, Victoria 3124, Australia
(a division of Pearson Australia Group Pty Ltd)
Penguin Books India Pvt Ltd, 11 Community Centre, Panchsheel Park, New Delhi - 110 017, India
Penguin Group (NZ), 67 Apollo Drive, Rosedale, North Shore 0632, New Zealand
(a division of Pearson New Zealand Ltd)
Penguin Books (South Africa) (Pty) Ltd, 24 Sturdee Avenue,
Rosebank, Johannesburg 2196, South Africa

Registered Offices: Penguin Books Ltd, 80 Strand, London WC2R 0RL, England

Originally published in Great Britain by Hutchinson Children's Books Limited, 1993
First published in the United States of America by Philomel Books,
a division of Penguin Putnam Books for Young Readers, 1994
Published by Firebird, an imprint of Penguin Group (USA) Inc., 2004

7 9 10 8

Text copyright © The Redwall Abbey Company Ltd, 1993
Illustrations copyright © Gary Chalk, 1993
All rights reserved

THE LIBRARY OF CONGRESS HAS CATALOGED THE PHILOMEL EDITION AS FOLLOWS:
Jacques, Brian.
Martin the warrior / Brian Jacques.
p. cm.
Summary: Captured and enslaved by the corsair stoat Badrang, young mouse warrior Martin vows to
end the evil beast's plundering and killing.
ISBN 0-399-22670-2 (hc)
[1. Mice—Fiction. 2. Animals—Fiction. 3. Fantasy.]   I. Title.
PZ7.J1537Mas 1994 [Fic]—dc20 93-26434 CIP AC

ISBN 978-0-14-240055-5

Printed in the United States of America

MARSHANK

Prison Pit

Main Gate

Stockade

Longhouse

Broadstream

Cherry Orch

Inlet

Outle

R.

Northwest Coast

Badrang's Ship Scuppered Here

Caves of Luke's

Lizards and Warden
of Marshwood Hill

Gawtrybe

ed's
nnel

Pygmy Shrews

Eastern Sea

South Cliffs

Seascarab

Marshes

Marshank

North Hills

n
v
a
l
e

Broadstream

N

"Amid the deep white winter snow,
Sleeps Mossflow'r until spring,
While snug in Cavern Hole below,
All Redwall's creatures sing.
Old autumn gave us plenty,
Our harvest did not fail,
No plate or jug is empty,
There's good October ale."

Three young creatures, the otter twins Bagg and Runn, accompanied by Grubb, their molefriend, hauled a small beech log between them along the path to Redwall Abbey. The intrepid trio kept stopping to clear away the snowdrift building up in front of the log as they dragged it through the snow. Singing lustily, they pelted each other with snowballs, their breath rising in white plumes as they ran around the beech log.

"Yaow! You'm a drefful villyun, Baggo, leggo oi!"

"Hahah! I'll save you, Grubb. Take that!"

"Missed me! You couldn't hit the Abbey gate if you was stooden in front of it, Runn!"

"Ho, couldn't I then? Well, 'ave some of this, mate!"

The young otter flung the snowball, Bagg ducked. Unaware that two travellers were coming along the path from the north, they hurled snowballs wildly at each other.

"Oof! Great seasons, go easy there!"

One of the travellers, a large sturdy hedgehog, had been struck by a snowball. He wiped snow from his snout with the edge of his cloak. The three young ones stopped throwing and hung their heads sheepishly. Grubb took it on himself to apologize.

"Hurr, us'ns turrible sorry, zurr. Be you'm 'urted?"

The hedgehog's travelling companion, a very pretty mousemaid, stifled laughter at the sight of the three delinquent snowballers.

"Oh, I'm sure Bultip will live. He's had worse injuries."

Grinning, the big hedgehog nodded. "I have indeed, mates. Come on, I'll help you with your log. Where are you bound with it?"

Bagg curved his mittened paw as he pointed. "Jus' round that bend, sir, to Redwall Abbey. We live there."

Bultip nodded at his companion as he took the tow-rope in strong paws. "I told you we'd find the Abbey on this path. Right, you three terrors, sit up on the log and I'll give you a ride. You too, Aubretia, rest your footpaws."

There was little doubt the hedgehog was a mighty beast. Tossing the rope across his shoulder, he trudged off through the snow, hauling the log and its passengers behind with no trace of effort.

Redwall Abbey stood backed by the vastness of Mossflower Woods, its front facing the path and open flatlands to the west. Capped with snow, the beautiful building resembled a vast frosted cake, walls, battlements, belltower and Abbey fringed with icicles hanging over its red sandstone towers and turrets.

Abbot Saxtus folded his paws into wide habit sleeves, gazing up at the main building. Beside him old Simeon the blind herbalist leaned on a hawthorn stick, sniffing the cold air.

"Looks beautiful, doesn't it, Saxtus?"

Knowing his friend's uncanny knack of sensing every movement, the Abbot nodded. "Remember what our old friend Abbot Bernard said before he passed on: No matter what the season, Redwall always looks marvellous."

Simeon sniffed the air again and held up a paw. "Somebeast is coming this way. One, maybe two—it's hard to tell."

They stood out on the path by the open main gates. Saxtus watched until he saw the party approaching.

"I might have known. It's Bagg, Runn and Grubb. They've brought company, two travellers."

Simeon tapped his stick on the snow eagerly. "Oh good, we'll have some fresh tales in Cavern Hole tonight!"

Old Friar Cockleburr hurried along with the preparations for a Midwinter Mossflower Feast, helped by his assistant, Alder. Both mice worked furiously, putting the finishing touches to dishes as they called out orders to the Redwallers on kitchen duty.

"Brush more honey on that pie if you want a good shiny crust!"

"Pass those chopped nuts and greensap milk, please."

"Quick, pull those pasties from the oven before they're too brown!"

"Durry Quill, will you stop loading hotroot pepper into that soup!"

"Ohhh, leave me be, soup's gotter be 'ot t'be any good."

Paws on hips, Cockleburr glared at the hedgehog. "I wish you'd go back to your cellars and see to the drinks with your Uncle Gabriel. Go on, be off with you!"

Durry popped a candied chestnut into his mouth and spoke round it. "Drinks're all ready, 'tober ale, elderberry wine, strawb'rry cordial an' fizzy dannelion cup—nowt to do in cellar. Old Nuncle Gabe, he's takin' a nap afore feastin', restin' 'is stummick."

Aubretia and Bultip had been shown round the Abbey. They gaped and marvelled at the great structure, expressing their admiration for it at every opportunity. Later they had been shown to their rooms by a Foremole.

Now rested, washed and garbed in warm old green habits, they came down to the place called Cavern Hole to attend the feast. Aubretia smiled at the gallant young male mice who flocked about her, each one trying to outdo the other as they saw to every need of the pretty stranger in their midst.

"Sit here, Miss Aubretia, next to me."

"No, sit here, it's more comfortable. Here's a cushion."

"You must have travelled far. Let me get you some food."

"Perhaps you'd like to try some elderberry wine. It'll take the chill of your long journey away, Miss Aubretia."

Abbot Saxtus looked over the top of his spectacles, wagging a paw. "So much help for one traveller! Aubretia, come and sit here with Bultip and Simeon. Here, I'll push up a bit so you'll be next to me. Why shouldn't a venerable old Abbot have the pleasure of a pretty mousemaid's company?"

Aubretia curtsied and smiled. "Why not indeed, Father Abbot!"

Bultip had a massive appetite. Scarcely had grace been said when he was munching away, sampling this and that as he allowed old Gabe Quill to fill his tankard. "Redwall October ale, finest in Mossflower. Try it with some nutbread an' yellow sage cheese, young 'og."

Aubretia sipped from her beaker and shuddered. "Whoo! Taste's lovely, full of tiny bubbles too. What is it?"

Simeon pushed a large confection toward her. "It's called fizzy dandelion cup. Very nice with snowcream pudding and damsons—fill your plate. My nose told me today when we met that you are a healer. Am I right?"

Aubretia looked surprised at the blind mouse's keen perception. "Yes, you're right Simeon. I am a healer."

Simeon reached out and took hold of Bultip's hefty paw. "And you, sir, I don't think you are a healer somehow."

"I'm no healer," the stout hedgehog chuckled, "just a travellin' companion protectin' Aubretia."

The blind herbalist felt the strength of Bultip's paw as he flexed it. "I imagine you do it very well. Woe betide the beast who stands in the way of this paw!"

Laughter and merry chatter rose to the rafters of the big room beneath the Abbey. There was warmth there, good companionship and good humour. Dishes went this way and that from paw to paw, snowcream pudding, hot fruit pies, colorful trifles, tasty pasties, steaming soup, new bread with shiny golden crusts, old cheeses studded with dandelion, acorn and celery. Sugared plums and honeyed pears vied for place with winter salads and vegetable flans. Aubretia and Bultip joined in the merriment, enjoyed the food and basked in the legendary hospitality of Redwall Abbey.

It was late night. Sleepy little ones had been carried off to their dormitory beds and fresh torches placed in the wall sconces. Bultip nibbled on his fourth pastie. Draining a tankard of October ale, he looked about at the still chattering Redwallers bantering with one another across the tables.

"Does nobeast ever sleep in this place, Simeon?"

The herbalist shrugged. "Are you tired, friend?"

Bultip blew on a bowl of hot soup. "Not me, I'm wide awake now."

The Abbot watched the soup disappear. "Good, that's the spirit! None of us has to rise early and work tomorrow. It's winter, and there's not a lot to do save eat and sleep, so we eat when we're hungry and sleep when we feel like it. How does that suit you, Aubretia?"

The mousemaid sat back contentedly. "It suits me fine, Abbot. What happens now we're finished feasting?"

Foremole looked up from his turnip 'n' tater 'n' beetroot pie. "You'm travellen beasts, may'ap you'm gotten gudd stories to tell us'ns, mizzy. We'm 'eard all our tales ten 'undred toimes o'er."

Cushions and chairs were set in a half-circle round the big fireplace, fresh logs placed on the fire, damped down with snow-soaked herbs to give a sweet aroma to the air. Every Redwaller who did not want to sleep took a seat. Aubretia and Bultip were installed in carved highback chairs. The audience settled down, watching the two travellers eagerly.

"Today as we walked through your beautiful Abbey we saw a tapestry," the mousemaid began. "I immediately recognized the mouse pictured there, Martin the Warrior. As I understand it he is the guiding spirit of this place and one of its founders. Do you know much about him?"

Abbot Saxtus sighed, shaking his head slow. "Martin has always been here to guide us in times of trouble. His presence was felt when two of our young ones, Dandin and Mariel, were here. Unfortunately they have been gone a season and a half now. Martin's presence has not been felt since. We know too little of our Abbey Warrior. I dearly wish we knew more."

A faint smile hovered about the face of Aubretia. She leaned forward and looked at the Abbot and his Redwallers sitting in the flickering firelight.

"Then you shall, for I have a long and great tale to relate to you. . . ."

It is said that Badrang's dream was to be Lord of all the Eastern Coast. A former corsair, he ceased plundering the high seas to carve out his own empire on land. He chose good territory, facing the Eastern Sea, with hills to the north, cliffs to the south, marshes to the west and wild forests beyond. Secure at the edge of the shoreline the battle-hardened stoat could defend his position from any attack. There he set about making his dream become reality, a fortress of timber and stone.

Marshank!

Badrang was Chieftain of a horde: weasels, ferrets, foxes and rats. He did not trust other stoats, considering his species to be the most cunning and resourceful of all creatures. Scuttling his crippled ship on the northwest coast, Badrang had set out overland, striking for the far coast where corsairs and searats seldom sailed the grey-blue waters of the great Eastern Sea. As he travelled, the vicious stoat ravaged the land, killing those he could not conquer and enslaving those he could. It took two long seasons until he finally arrived triumphant at his destination, laden with plunder, backed by his ruthless horde and driving a long chain of wretched slaves before him.

Badrang set his slaves to work, forcing them to carve a rock quarry and commence building his fortress. The work went well, and soon a living quarters was erected, followed by a perimeter guard wall with its gates facing the shoreline.

He scanned the open sea each day, for he had made enemies among his own kind when he was pirating. Fortunately there was never a sign of sail or ship on the horizon. However, he bullied and drove both slave and hordebeast to have the fortress fully built and established. Only then could he rule completely, burning and killing his way in all directions until he was absolute ruler of all he surveyed. Tyrant! Badrang loved the sound of the word. . . . Tyrant!

BOOK ONE

The Prisoner and the Tyrant

1

He was only a young mouse, but of strong build, with a glint in his eye that proclaimed him a born fighter. A creature of few words who never chattered needlessly. The early summer sun of the Eastern Coast beat down pitilessly on his unprotected head as he carried and stacked chunks of rock beside the masons who would shape it into blocks that would enlarge Fort Marshank.

A weasel Captain named Hisk swaggered up, cracking his long whip threateningly, looking for an excuse to cut loose on the slaves who toiled in the dusty heat around him. His eye settled on the young mouse.

"You there, liven yourself up! Come on, stir yer stumps. Lord Badrang will be round for an inspection soon. Get movin' or y'll taste my whip!"

The mouse dropped the rock he was carrying and stood staring levelly at the bullying weasel. Hisk cracked the lash viciously, the tip flicking the air a fraction from his victim's face. The young mouse did not move. His eyes hooded over as he stood in silent defiance.

The weasel Captain drew the lash back to strike, but the bold, angry eyes of the young slave seemed to challenge him. Like all bullies, the weasel was a coward at heart. Averting his gaze from the piercing stare, Hisk snapped his whip in the direction of some more timid creatures.

"C'mon, you worthless idlers, no work, no food. Move your carcasses. 'Ere comes Lord Badrang!"

Flanked by his aides, Gurrad the rat and Skalrag the fox, Badrang the Tyrant strode imperiously onto the site. He waited while two hedgehogs hurriedly built him a makeshift seat from stone blocks. Skalrag swiftly covered it with a velvet cloak. Badrang sat, gazing at the work going on around him.

The stoat Lord addressed Hisk: "Will my fortress be finished before summer is out?"

Hisk waved his coiled whip about at the slaves. "Lord, if the weather was cooler an' we 'ad more creatures . . ."

Badrang moved swiftly in his anger. Seizing a pebble, he hurled it, striking Hisk on the jaw. The weasel Captain stood dumbly, blood trickling from his lip as the Tyrant berated him.

"Excuses! I don't want to hear complaints or excuses, d'you hear me? What I need is a fortress built before autumn. Well, don't stand there snivelling, get on with it!"

Immediately, Hisk got to work, flaying about with the whip as he passed on his master's bad mood.

"Move, you useless lumps! You heard Lord Badrang, Marshank must be ready before the season's out! It'll be double the work an' half rations from now on. Move!"

An old squirrel was staggering by, bent double under the burden of a large rock. Hisk lashed out at him. The whip curled around the aged creature's footpaws, tripping him as he dropped the rock. The weasel began laying into his victim, striking indiscriminately at the old one's frail body.

"You worthless layabout, I'll strip the mis'rable hide off yer!"

The lash rose and fell as Hisk flogged away at the unprotected creature on the ground.

"I'll teach yer a lesson yer won't ferget . . ."

Suddenly the whip stopped in midswing. It went taut as Hisk pulled on the handle. He tugged at it but was yanked backwards. The young mouse had the end of the whip coiled around his paw.

Hisk's eyes bulged with temper as he shouted at the intruder, "Leggo my whip, mouse, or I'll gut yer!"

The weasel reached for the dagger at his waist, but he was not fast enough. The mouse hurled himself upon Hisk. Wrapping the whiplash round the Captain's neck, he heaved hard. Hisk thrashed furiously about in the dust, choking and slobbering as the lash tightened. Gurrad blew a hasty alarm on a bone whistle he carried slung about his neck.

In a trice the mouse was set upon by the nearest six guards. He disappeared beneath a jumble of ferrets, weasels and rats as they pounded him mercilessly, stamping upon his paws and breaking his hold on the whip. They continued relentlessly beating him with spearhandles, rods and whips until Badrang intervened.

"That's enough. Bring him to me!"

His paws pinioned by whips and a spear handle pulled hard across his throat, the young mouse was dragged struggling and kicking into the stoat Lord's presence.

Badrang drew his sword and pressed the point against the young one's heaving chest. Leaning forward, he hissed into the captive's face, "You know the penalty is death for attacking one of my horde. I could run you through with my sword right now and snuff out your life. What d'you say to that, mouse?"

The strong young mouse's eyes burned into the Tyrant's face like twin flames as he gritted out, "Scum! That sword is not yours, it belongs to me as it belonged to my father!"

13

Badrang withdrew the swordpoint. He sat back, shaking his head slowly in amazement at the boldness of the creature in front of him.

"Well well, you're not short of nerve, mouse. What's your name?"

The answer was loud and fearless.

"I am called Martin, son of Luke the Warrior!"

"See the roving river run
Over hill and dale
To a secret forest place,
O my heart, Noonvale.
Look for me at dawning
When the sun's reborn
In the silent beauty
Twixt the night and morn.
Wait till the lark ascends
And skies are blue.
There where the rainbow ends
I will meet you."

The mousemaid Rose sat quite still as the last tremulous notes of her song hovered on the evening air. From a vantage point in the rocks south of Marshank she looked out to sea. The water was tinted gold and scarlet from soft cloud layers, reflecting the far westering sun at her back. Below on the shore an ebbing tide gurgled and chuckled small secrets to itself as it lapped the pebbles.

"Hurr Miz Roser, you'm cumm an' get this yurr supper. Oi bain't a-cooken vittles to lay abowt an' git cold 'n' soggy. Bo urr no."

Rose's companion Grumm waved a heavy digging paw at her, and the mousemaid wandered over to join her mole friend at the low fire he had been cooking on. She sniffed appreciatively.

"Hmm, wild oatcakes and vegetable soup! Good old Grumm, you could make a banquet from nothing."

Grumm smiled, his dark velvety face crinkling around two bright button eyes. He waved the tiny ladle which he always carried thrust through his belt like a sword.

"Hurr, an' you udd charm'ee burds outener trees with yurr sweet talken, mizzy. Set'ee daown an' eat oop."

Rose accepted the deep scallop shell full of fragrant soup. Placing her oatcake on a flat rock across the fire to keep it warm, she shook her head as she sipped away.

"You're worse than an old mousewife, Grumm Trencher. I wager you'd rock me to sleep if I let you."

Grumm wagged the small ladle at her. "Hurr aye, you'm needen all yore sleep. Urrmagine wot yore ole dad'd say iffen oi brought 'ee 'ome tired out an' a-starved, hoo arr!"

The mousemaid took a hasty bite of oatcake, fanning her mouth. "Oo, 's hot! There'll be no sleep for us until we've found out whether or not Brome is held captive in that dreadful fortress."

Grumm wiped his ladle clean with some sedge grass. "May'ap ole Brome jus' a-wandered off 'n' got losed, may'ap 'ee bain't catchered in yon fortress."

Rose shook her head.

"You must understand, Grumm, the name Brome and the word trouble go together. He was always in trouble with Father at home—that's why he went off wandering. You weren't there at the time but they had a furious argument over Brome just taking off and roaming as he pleased. Father said it was no way for the son of a Chieftain to learn his responsibilities, but Brome wouldn't listen, he ran off alone. Well, we've tracked him this far, Grumm, and I'm certain that my brother has run straight into trouble again. That's why I'm sure he's been taken by Badrang's scouts. I hope that he hasn't been forced to tell them where Noonvale is. The whole tribe of Urran Voh would be in danger if Brome gave away our location to that filthy Tyrant."

Grumm refilled Rose's shell with vegetable soup.

"Doant'ee fret, mizzy. Ole Brome can keepen his'n mouth shutted toighter'n a mussel at low toide, ho urr!"

The mousemaid unwound the throwing sling from about her waist. "I hope you're right, Grumm. I'd hate to think of the things those vermin would do to a young mouse to get information."

The mole patted Rose's back gently with a heavy digging claw. "Doant'ee wurry, Roser. Us'll get ole Maister Brome out'n yon pest'ole iffen him be in thurr."

When they had finished eating they extinguished the fire and broke camp. A stiff breeze had sprung out of the east, bringing with it a light spatter of raindrops which threatened to get heavier as night set in.

Scrambling down the rocks, the two friends gained the shore, their paws making soft chinking noises as they trotted through the shingled tideline. Marshank stood grim and forbidding up ahead, a dark hump of misery in the moonless night.

2

The old squirrel Martin had saved peered through the cracks of the wooden slave compound at the lone figure tied between two posts on the walltop above the main gates. His son, a burly male named Felldoh, stood behind the elder. He gritted his teeth savagely.

"The scurvy toads, they'll pay for this someday!"

Barkjon, the old one, shook his head sadly. "Martin will have a bad time tonight if the weather gets worse."

Felldoh thumped a sturdy paw against the wooden compound fence. "It's the morning I'm more worried about, when the gannets and gulls and those other big hungry sea birds come searching for food and see him tied up there. They'll rip Martin to bits!"

A weasel guard called Rotnose banged his spearbutt on the fence alongside Barkjon's nose.

"Gerraway from there, you two, or you'll be next up there with the mouse. Double work for you tomorrow. Get some sleep while you can. Sweet dreams now, hawhawhaw!"

Floodtide returned, bringing with it a storm. The gale shrieked, driving heavy rain before it. On the walltop Martin bowed his head against the battering elements. It was all that he could do, tied as he was by four paws between two thick wooden posts. Rain plastered the single frayed garment he wore close to his body, and the wetness ran down his back, into his ears, across his eyes and over his nose into his mouth, battering his bowed head and numbing his whole body, which shook and quivered in the ceaseless gale. He hung there, like a rag doll in the wind.

Martin's mind went back to the caves on the northwest shore where he had been born. Luke the Warrior was his father. He had never known a mother; she had been killed in a searat raid when he was a tiny infant. Luke had raised him the best way he could, but Luke was a warrior and sworn to the destruction of searats and corsairs. He was unused to rearing babies.

Martin was only two seasons out of infancy when his father and some other warriors captured a searat galley after a hard pitched battle on the shoreline. Flushed with success and driven by the awful rage to take vengeance upon his wife's murderers, Luke the Warrior gathered a crew and decided to sail off in his prize vessel, to wage war on the searats. Martin remembered he was still very young, but fired with a determination to accompany his father. Luke, however, would not hear of it. He left Martin in the care of his wife's mother, Windred. The day he sailed Martin sat stonefaced outside the cave. Luke could not reason with him.

"Son, son, you would not last two moons out there on the high seas. I cannot risk your life pitting you in battle against the sea scum I am sworn to do war with. Listen to me, I know what is best for you!"

But Martin would not listen. "I want to sail on the ship and be a warrior like you!"

Luke spread his paws wide and sighed with frustration. "What am I going to do with you, Martin? You have my warrior spirit and your mother's determination. Listen, son, take my sword."

It was a fighting sword and well used. Luke pressed it into his son's paws. The young mouse gazed wide-eyed at the battle-scarred blade and gripped the handle tight as if he would never let go.

Luke smiled, recalling the time when his father had passed the sword on to him. Tapping a paw against the crosshilt, Luke said, "I can see it is in you to be a fighter, Martin. The first thing warriors must learn is discipline."

Martin felt as though the sword were speaking for him. "Tell me what to do and I will obey."

Relief surged through Luke as he commanded the would-be warrior. "You will stay and defend our cave against all comers, protect those weaker than yourself and honor our code. Always use the sword to stand for good and right, never do a thing you would be ashamed of, but never let your heart rule your mind."

He tapped the blade once more as its pitted edge glinted in the winter morning.

"And never ever let another creature take this sword from you, not as long as you live. When the time comes, pass it on to another, maybe your own son. You will know instinctively if he is a warrior. If not, hide the sword where only a true warrior who is brave of heart, would dare go to find it. Swear this to me Martin."

"I swear it, on my life!" The young mouse's grey eyes reflected the wintry sea as he spoke.

Coming back to reality, Martin lifted his head in the teeth of the gale. Was it a tear, or just rain running from his eyes as he pictured the small figure standing upon the pebbled strand alone, waving the sword in a warrior's salute as his father's ship was lost on the horizon in an afternoon of snow and icy winter spume.

Martin's head slumped onto his sodden chest as he recalled the day of his capture. Timballisto was a budding warrior, several seasons Martin's senior. He had been left in charge of the tribe by Luke. The young mouse resented his older friend's authority and often showed it by wandering far along the coast, away from the safe boundaries of the caves. It was on one such day that Martin took his father's sword, following the tideline north until the short winter afternoon began darkening. He was busy chopping away with the great blade at a driftwood log, reasoning that he could not be scolded for bringing back firewood to the cave fires.

Windred saw him from afar. She had been following his pawtracks since early noon; they stood out clearly in the smooth wet sand, marked with a straight furrow where the swordpoint trailed at Martin's side. She hurried forward scolding her grandson. "Martin! I've been out of my mind with worry. What have you been told about going off alone? D'you realize you're almost a league from the caves?"

Suddenly Windred stopped berating him. She was staring beyond Martin to where a band of villainous-looking creatures were running along the shore towards them. The old mouse threw off her shawl. "Martin, come to me. We must get away from here. Quickly!"

The young mouse turned and saw the corsairs. Dropping the firewood, he took up the sword in both paws. "Run Grandma!"

Windred would not have run anyway, but she was rooted to the spot with fear. A stoat headed the band. They stopped within two paces of their victims. The stoat grinned wickedly. "That's a big sword for a little mouse to be wielding. You'd better give it to me before you hurt yourself."

The sword was heavy and Martin's paws were tired, but he held it point forward, unwavering. "Leave us alone, stay back! My father told me never to let another creature take this sword from me!"

Now the corsairs began spreading out slowly, encircling Martin and Windred, licking knives and spearblades as they chuckled evilly at the old mouse and the small would-be warrior. The stoat took a pace forward, his voice deceptively friendly. "A wise beast your father. Did he ever tell you about those who could slay with a single spear thrust? Like this . . . or this!" As he spoke the

20

stoat brought up his spear and began jabbing expertly at Martin. The young mouse parried, fighting off the questing spearpoint amid the laughter of the cruel corsairs.

At a nod from the stoat a weasel ran forward from behind Martin. He dealt the young mouse a heavy blow with an oaken pikestaff, laying him out flat on the sand. Badrang picked up the sword. Stepping over Martin's senseless body, he winked at Windred. She was held tight between two searats, tied and gagged by her own shawl, eyes wide with terror. The stoat stared along the swordblade at her.

"Well Grandma, he's a bold brat, that one of yours. Hmm, nice sword. It should serve me well. Hisk, we've wasted enough time. Chain these two up and get 'em back to the slavelines."

Shackled to Windred, Martin was half-dragged, half-carried further north along the wintry shore into the gathering night.

It was in the short hours before dawn that Martin came awake, shivering and moaning as a fiery drum of relentless pain beat inside his skull. Whips cracked, he was pulled upright by other slaves as the chain began moving.

Then came the long march. . . . Two seasons, trekking under the rods and whips of slavedrivers, tied by the neck to a succession of wretched creatures, all captives together. He lost count of the days. They rolled interminably on into spring, summer then autumn, with Windred long dead from hunger, thirst and hardship under the lash.

Martin recalled his grief for the old mousewife, the closest he had ever come to knowing a mother: his stifled tears and the leaden weight of sadness at her loss, the feeling of loneliness and desolation without her. She had deserved far better a fate than the one she suffered. His body began trembling at the thought of the vermin who had caused all of this cruelty.

Badrang!

21

The laughing, sneering, commanding stoat, swaggering along wearing the sword he had taken from Martin.

A strength born of built-up rage coursed suddenly through the young mouse. He stood erect, tugging at his bonds, oblivious to the pounding storm as a mighty roar welled up from deep inside him.

"I am a warrior! Martin son of Luke! I will live, I will not give in and die up here! Do you hear me, Badrang? I will live to take back my father's sword and slay you one day! Badraaaaaaaannggg!"

Stormwater filled his mouth, rushing winds tore at his face.

"Martin son of Luke, can you hear me?" a voice called up to him from the shore outside the fortress.

He could not see the speaker but he heard the voice clearly above the gale.

"Yes, I hear you. What is your name?"

"There are two of us, my friend Grumm Trencher the mole and myself, Laterose, daughter of the Chieftain Urran Voh. We heard you calling out. Tell me, is there a prisoner in there called Brome, a young mouse? He is my brother."

Martin could feel the storm beating the senses from him. He rallied and shouted back. "I do not know of a mouse called Brome and I don't think I'll have much chance to. I am sentenced to die up here, Laterose."

The answer came back in as kindly a tone as the mousemaid could shout under the circumstances.

"Laterose is my full title. Please call me Rose. My friend and I will do anything possible to help you, though we cannot climb up—the walls are too sheer and high. What can we do? Is there a message you wish carried to another creature?"

Martin shook his head. "No message. I am alone. The guards told me that if I live through the night the big sea birds will finish me off in the morning. Is there any way . . . you can keep them . . . off me?"

Rose thought for a moment before answering.

"Maybe, yes. We are not warriors, but we can use our slings. Also I know a trick to drive sea birds away."

She waited, but there was no reply. Grumm stepped away from the wall, out on to the beach, shading his eyes against the downpour as he gazed up at the limp figure slumped between the posts.

"Yurr, ee'm lost 'is senses, fallen aconshuss, if'n you ask oi, pore creetur!"

Rose joined Grumm, and together they watched the unconscious form sway slackly as the elements assaulted it. The mousemaid chose a hard round pebble and fitted it to her sling.

"We must help him to live, we must!" Her lip quivered as she spoke. "Ooh that Badrang, the cruel cowardly, heartless vermin . . ."

Grumm chuckled softly. "Noice wurrds fer a mousey-maid, oi must say. Hurr hurr, him'n ull live sure 'nuff, iffen 'ee be arf as ill-tempurred as 'ee, mizzy."

3

Dawn came pearly grey, shot with shafts of peach and dusky pink as the sun broke the eastern horizon in the wake of the night storm. The sea was a dim shade of oily turquoise, with cream-crested waves in the middle distance. Badrang the Tyrant had his carved throne chair brought out on to the courtyard, where he could watch the fun. Gurrad the rat and Skalrag the fox stood along with two weasels called Lumpback and Stiffear, awaiting orders as the Tyrant stoat pointed to Martin's limp figure with his sword.

"He looks strong enough to have lived through a bit of wind and rain. Gurrad, go and wake the sleeping beauty. When he's conscious and wriggling about, the birds'll soon spot him."

Gurrad sniggered as he looked up at the circling sea birds that were beginning to mass above the fortress.

"Aye, Lord, that lot look in good appetite as usual, eh?"

Badrang nodded. "Never knew a gannet that wasn't. Ho there, Hisk! Don't send the slaves to the quarry yet, parade 'em out here where they can see the sentence being carried out. It'll show 'em what happens to anybeast who puts a paw wrong in my fortress."

Gurrad slapped Martin around the face with a wet piece of rag until the young mouse revived. He held a beaker of fresh water to the captive's lips, chuckling as the prisoner drank greedily.

"That's the stuff. Drink up now, mouse. Those sea birds'll soon be down for breakfast. Hehee, look at 'em, big uns, ain't they? Great pointed beaks they've got, good as a knife fer rippin' an' tearin'. They'll enjoy you . . ."

Martin managed to spit the last of the water full into Gurrad's face. The rat backed off, spluttering nastily.

"Tough, eh? Well, I 'ope they takes yer eyes first!"

Chancing a glance upwards, Martin could see a great gannet preparing to dive. Two other grey gulls were beginning to swoop low, and others rushed to join them in the descent for food. His paws were swollen by the wet ropes that held him tightly. He struggled wildly, shutting his eyes tight after Gurrad's cruel remark.

All eyes were on Martin now, the horrified slaves, the gloating horde of Badrang, the hungry sea birds. Plus two other pairs.

Rose and Grumm were crouched behind a stony outcrop on the beach, the young mousemaid watching very carefully as she placed a paw across her throat and took a deep breath. The birds wheeled and dived lower towards the struggling figure bound between the posts on the walltop. Grumm nudged his friend urgently.

"Aow, do 'asten an' 'urry, mizzy. They burds be a-goen t'peck Marthen to death. Aowurr, oi carn't lukk no moare!"

Grumm closed his eyes tight as the sea birds dived for the kill.

Badrang had forgotten to scan the seaward horizon that day, preoccupied as he was with Martin's death sentence. A sail appeared two points north on the eastern horizon. It was a great green single-masted craft, practically invisible against the sea because of its camouflaged coloring. Three banks of oars protruded to port and starboard, one atop the other, giving it the appearance of a monstrous insect crawling over the waves. It was Badrang's old partner in murder and treachery upon the high seas, a stoat like himself.

Cap'n Tramun Clogg of the great ship *Seascarab*!

Clogg was a villainous sight, an enormously fat stoat dressed in stained and tawdry silks, wearing a massive pair of carved wooden clogs. Every part of his fur wherever possible was plaited and braided—beard, eyebrows, moustache—all over his gargantuan body. Plaits and braids stuck out of his ragged sleeve frills, spilled through rents in his shirt, coat and pantaloons, even curled over the tops of the oversized clogs. He gnawed on a half-dead lobster as he slurped seaweed grog from a flagon, belching aloud and spitting shell fragments everywhere. Throwing back his tousled head he roared up at the lookout, a ferret in the crow's-nest.

"Boggs, any shape o' land out there yet, matey?"

The keen-eyed Boggs peered into the distance. "Naw, Cap'n, nary a glimmer o' . . . Wait . . . aye . . . land ahoy!"

The lobster tail fell from Tramun Clogg's open mouth, to disappear down his open shirt front.

"Haharr harr, I knowed it! Where away, Boggs y' ole bilgedog?"

"Two points south, Cap'n. Aye, an' there be a liddle lump a-stickin' up, either a cliff or some buildin'."

Clogg gurgled happily. Drawing a broad cutlass from his sash, he began honing it on the sole of his left clog.

"Bring 'er about two points, Growch. If Badrang ain't there I'll eat me clogs, on me oath I will. Gritter, tell the crew to put some vinegar into their oarstrokes; 'urry now, matey. With this wind in our sails an' a flowin' sea, we'll make landfall soon. Hohohoharrharr! Won't me ole messmate Badrang be pleased ter see 'is great-uncle Clogg agin after all this time!"

At the wheel Growch gave a villainous cackle.

"Pleased, yer say, Cap'n. I reckon Badrang'll pop 'is cork!"

Clogg flung the empty grog bottle over the side. "An' if he don't, I'll pop it for 'im, haharr!"

Like a great green bird of ill omen, the *Seascarab* came about and headed for Marshank as Tramun Clogg mused aloud to himself.

"Iffen I knows Badrang, 'e'll 'ave slaves aplenty, too many fer one beast to own. An ole matey like 'im won't begrudge enough fine slaves to row the *Seascarab*—'ell's teeth, I should say not. A pore lubber like me without a single slave to me vessel. Asides, tain't fittin' fer corsairs an' searats to row their own craft. So I'll just nip in nicely an' ask 'im 'andsome like to fit us out with row-beasts. Badrang'll give 'em to me, 'e's a nice cove. An' wot if 'e don't, why then I'll just slit 'is gizzard an' take 'em, I'll use 'is skull as me figurehead an' feed the rest of 'im to the fishes. Only fair, ain't it, Growch?"

Both pirates burst out laughing at the joke. Clogg liked a joke, but he was joking in deadly earnest this time. He hated Badrang.

The sea birds came diving in voraciously at Martin's unprotected body. They were within a hair's breadth of his head when a wild, ear-splitting screech, halfway between a whistle and a cry, rent the morning air. Immediately, the scavenging birds swooped away and zoomed high into the air, shrilling anxiously and wheeling about willy-nilly. Another loud screech followed, and the gulls and gannets milled about high above Martin, some of them bumping into each other in their apparent confusion.

Badrang gaped upwards in amazement. "What's the matter with 'em, why aren't they tearing him apart?"

A further screech followed, even louder and more angry-sounding than the former two. This time the sea birds sheared off sharply and dispersed.

The Tyrant stoat was furious. "What in the name of hellgates is going on?"

A ferret called Bluehide, who had lived in the far north, called out as he scratched his ears in puzzlement. "That's the huntin' cry of a great eagle. I've heard it afore!"

Gurrad shoved him scornfully. "Garn! There ain't no great eagles on this coast."

A small venturesome kittiwake who had just arrived on the scene took a swift dive at Martin. The screech rang out swift and harsh. The frightened kittiwake took off like a sky rocket.

Bluehide shrugged, eyeing Gurrad in a patronizing manner. "That's a great eagle's huntin' cry, I'd stake me oath on it!"

The rat raised his spearbutt threateningly. "Listen, addlebrain, I've said there ain't no gr—"

"Gurrad! Stow that gab and get over here!"

The rat broke off his argument with the ferret and scuttled across to Badrang's side. The Tyrant scowled as he glowered at the clear blue sky.

"Never mind what it is, there's something about that's scaring the sea birds witless. We'll have to tempt them down on to the mouse with a bait they can't resist. Bring a dead fish from the cookhouse."

Hurriedly the fish was brought to Badrang. He took his sword and cut the cord holding up the weasel Lumpback's ragged kilt. There was a snigger from the slaves as Lumpback stood grinning sheepishly with his only garment draped around his footpaws on the ground. Ignoring the weasel's plight, Badrang tossed the cord to Gurrad.

"Here, tie the fish to this and hang it round the mouse's neck. That'll bring hungry sea birds in to feed, eagle or no eagle."

From their hiding place on the shore, Rose scanned the sky. It was clear and free of sea birds.

"Thank goodness I won't have to do the eagle call again, Grumm. It was beginning to strain my throat."

"Hurr hurr," the mole chuckled. "Oi be glad too, mizzy, 'twere a vurry froightenen sound. Oi didden loik et one liddle bit, hurr no."

Grumm peeked over the rocky outcrop at Martin on the walltop. "Mizzy Roser, 'earken! Wot be they villuns a-doin' to Marthen?"

The mousemaid began twirling her loaded sling. "I don't know, but whatever it is we'll have to stop them!"

Gurrad was trying to get the cord noose that held the fish over Martin's head, but the young mouse was ducking and struggling wildly. The rat was losing his temper.

"Hold still, mouse, or I'll pin this fish t'yer with me spearpoint!"

Thwock!

Gurrad dropped the fish with an agonized yelp as the slingstone bounced off his paw.

Badrang did not see the stone. All he saw was Gurrad dropping the fish and hopping about sucking on his paw. The Tyrant stood up, knocking his thronechair backwards as he yelled at the unfortunate rat.

"Stop playing the fool an' get that fish round his neck before I come up there and batter some sense into you with it!"

As Gurrad bent to pick the fish up, Grumm fitted a sizeable rock into the spoon of his ladle and whipped it off in the direction of the rat's bent bottom.

Thwump!

It struck hard and true, knocking Gurrad from the walltop. He plummeted over and landed with a sickening thud in the courtyard below.

Badrang leapt forward, sword in paw, waving at the creatures around him.

"To the walltop, quick. Somebeast's hurling rocks!"

They piled up the broad wooden ladders on to the walltop.

Rotnose and Hisk were first up. They were immediately hit by flying stones. Hisk fell senseless, Rotnose crouched, massaging an aching breastbone. Badrang ducked another salvo as he went into a half-stoop, shouting at the others, "Where are the stones coming from, can you see?"

Skalrag stood upright, peering at the seemingly deserted shore. "Must be somebeast hidin' out there, Lord!"

Below, at the corner of the courtyard where the slaves were grouped, the big squirrel Felldoh decided to take part in the action. He ducked to the back of the crowd, picking up several large pebbles as he went. With energy born of anger, he chucked a large rough stone at the back of Skalrag's head. Many times Felldoh had bent under Skalrag's rod; now was the chance to repay the sadistic fox.

The flying rock did not strike Skalrag's skull, it narrowly missed, but took half of his left ear in the process, ripping it off as it whizzed by. Felldoh immediately flung two more stones, then keeping his paws at his sides gazed around in amazement as if some other creature were doing the throwing.

As Skalrag screeched in pain, Stiffear sprang up, pointing down into the courtyard as he shouted excitedly, "The stones are coming from inside our own fortress!"

Thwack!

A stone from the shoreside struck him square in the back.

Rotnose, still rubbing his chest, sneered at Stiffear, "Rubbish, they're coming from the shore, I tell yer. I was hit meself . . . . Eeeyowch!"

A stone from the courtyard stung his tail. Confusion reigned on the walltop. Badrang and his creatures did not know which side the missiles were coming from. The Tyrant lay flat and raised his head slightly. He could not see the shore clearly but he had an uninterrupted view of the sea. His stomach churned suddenly and he began to curse at the sight his sharp eyes rested on. One more quick look to ascertain that he was not wrong sent Badrang scrambling for the ladder, calling hoarsely as he went, "Cut that mouse down from there and bring him with you. Get down into the fortress, quick!"

"But, Sire, we think that there's somebeast behind those rocks slinging stones . . ."

Badrang shot a venomous glance at Rotnose as he hissed, "Do as I say, scumbrain. We've more to worry about than a few stones. Tramun Clogg's out there with the *Seascarab*, sailing on a direct course for us!"

Grumm was running out of good rocks to fit his ladle when Rose pointed to the wall.

"Look, they've had enough, they're cutting Martin loose and retreating into the fortress. Thank the seasons that we were able to help the poor mouse, eh, Grumm?"

The mole mopped his brow and sat with his back against the rocks of their hideout on the beach in the hot midmorning sunlight.

"Yurr, boi 'okey, us'ns serpintly gave they vurmints summat to think abowt. Oi gave 'em billyoh wi' moi ole ladler, hurr hurr!"

Rose could not help grinning at her faithful companion. "So you did, Grumm. That ladle comes in useful for other things than stirring soup with."

But Grumm was not listening. Facing seaward, he was pointing straight out at the *Seascarab*, which was drawing closer by the moment.

"Lookit, mizzy. Searatters an' vurmints, oi'll be bounden!"

A chill of fear ran through the mousemaid. Corsairs! They had seldom visited this coast, but the tales of horror and death that surrounded the raiders from the sea were legendary. Hastily they gathered their few belongings.

"Let's not hang about here, Grumm. Come on, we'll lie low in the marshes behind the fortress."

31

Cap'n Tramun Clogg was in high villainous humour. He cut an awkward jig, his clogs clattering noisily on the poopdeck.

"Haharrharr! I reckernizes that flag flyin' o'er yon place ashore. Ho lucky day, I knowed it, I could feel it in me clogs! There's me messmate of bygone seasons Badrang, built hisself a stone castle, pretty as you please. 'Ow many pore liddle slaves would yer say it took to work on a place like that, Crosstooth?"

A wicked-looking fox draped in purple bandannas scratched his chin. "Hmmm, I'd say lots, Cap'n."

"Lots an' crowds?"

"Aye, lots 'n' crowds."

"Which is most, Crosstooth, lots or crowds?"

"Why bless yer 'eart, Cap'n, crowds, that means lots an' lots!"

"Haharrharr, well said, matey. Break out the weapons while I lays plans for a reunion party with me ole messmate Badrang!"

Martin stood swaying on swollen footpaws, his arms still bound. Badrang sat upon his thronechair, eyes narrowed as he watched the reprieved prisoner.

"Hmm, like I said before, you're not short of nerve, Martin. Hearken to me now, I could use a creature like you."

From beneath hooded eyelids Martin watched the Tyrant as he spoke, the young mouse's gorge beginning to rise at the stoat's proposal.

"How would you like to be a Captain in my horde? The best of food, slaves to command as you please, I'll even give you a spear to carry if you swear loyalty to me as your master. Well, what've you got to say to that, young un?"

Martin made no reply. His paws were deadened by the tight bonds, but his rage was aroused and his jaws were strong. He launched himself in a flash upon Badrang, setting his teeth into the stoat's outstretched paw and biting it savagely to the bone.

The Tyrant roared and bellowed in agony as Martin was set upon by guards, his jaws prised apart with a dagger blade as rods and spearbutts beat furiously at him. The young mouse went down on the ground as Badrang sprinkled blood about, shaking his paw in anguish as he gritted from between clenched teeth, "You'll wish the gannets had got you by the time I'm finished with you, whelp. Oh, don't worry, you'll die, but not fast. Fraction by fraction until you scream to welcome death. Take him away and lock him up. I'll see to him after I'm rid of Clogg!"

Inside the courtyard, slightly to the left of the main gate, was a prison pit, dug deep into the ground with a heavy grating on top. The cover creaked as it was slid to one side. Martin was hurled in, still with both paws bound to his sides. He fell through the darkness and landed with a cushioned thump on something soft. There was a grunt and somebeast was helping him upright while another untied his bonds.

A gruff voice spoke. "Martin, well at least you're still alive. I'm Felldoh the squirrel."

The young mouse rubbed his paws, grimacing as the blood began circulating properly. The squirrel rubbed and patted him until he felt able to move easily again. Martin recognized him. He knew Felldoh as a kindred spirit, another born rebel who had fallen foul of the vermin regime's justice.

"Felldoh, what are you doing down here?"

"Awaiting the Tyrant's pleasure like you, Martin. That rotten toad Stiffear saw me flinging rocks at him while he was on the walltop. Still, you saved my old dad and I did what I could for you, matey."

Martin grasped the big squirrel's paw in the darkness. "You are a true friend, Felldoh. Thank you!"

They both sat on the hard-packed earth floor. There

was a movement to Martin's right, and as he tensed a small quiet voice echoed hollowly in the pit.

"What do you suppose Badrang's going to do with us?"

Martin peered into the dimness. "Who's there?"

Felldoh reached out and brought their paws together. "Martin, this young feller was here before I arrived. Meet Brome."

"So, Brome," said Martin

He was younger and smaller than Martin and Felldoh, and his voice sounded tiny and frightened. "I never did harm to anybeast. I was lost and blundering along the shore one night when the sentries on the wall saw me, and I was captured and thrown down here. Did they capture you, Martin? Will they keep us down here for ever?"

Patting his paw and ruffling his ears good-naturedly, Martin reassured the youngster. "You stick with us, Brome. We'll get you out of here. While I was staked out on the walltop, Felldoh was throwing rocks from inside and your sister Rose chucking them from outside. She's out there with a mole named Grumm. I owe them my life."

Brome grasped Martin's paw. "Rose and Grumm! Hahaha, good old Grumm, I knew they'd find me. With those two out there and you and Felldoh in here we'll escape easily. It'll be as simple as picking daisies!"

The joy and relief in the young one's voice was so evident that Martin felt a wave of sympathy for him. Nudging Felldoh in the darkness, Martin spoke with a confidence he did not feel.

"Aye, simple as picking daisies, eh, Felldoh."

The squirrel was a kindly beast, he threw his paws about both of them, playing along with Martin's bravado.

"Right, lads. Three warriors like us and extra help from outside? Hah, the only thing Badrang'll eat for

34

dinner will be our dust when we scoot out of here. Friends together!"

Shortly after that Brome fell asleep, cushioned between Martin and Felldoh. Their eyes now accustomed to the gloom, they sat staring at each other.

"Easy as picking daisies. Hmm, when was the last time you picked daisies, matey?"

"A long time ago, friend Felldoh. Some of them were pretty tough to pick as I remember. But not impossible."

"Aye, with a little outside help we might stand a chance."

Martin yawned and settled down beside Brome. "Sleep first. Being tied out on a walltop in a storm isn't the most restful place around here. We'll think of something later, friend. We can't disappoint this young un."

Felldoh sat listening to the soft snores of his companions. "Oh yes, let's think of something later," he chuckled lightly to himself. "How to sprout wings, and defeat Badrang and his horde with outside help from a mole and a mousemaid. By my brush, why didn't I think of those two good ideas before?"

4

The ship *Seascarab* rode at anchor in the bay as four longboats were beached above the tideline. The pirates had come ashore. Surrounded by his savage ragtag crew, Cap'n Tramun Clogg strode into Fortress Marshank. Badrang had the way lined with heavily armed soldiers. They gripped spears tightly, scowling at the ill assorted mob from the *Seascarab*.

With a great clatter of clogs Tramun hauled out his cutlass and roared playfully as he made a mock dash at Badrang's soldiers. They drew back in alarm and Clogg winked roguishly at them.

"Haharr, caught yer nappin' there, mateys. You've all gone soft playin' at bein' landlubbers. Ho there, Frogbit, Nipwort, an' you, Fleabane. Been a bit o' water passed under the keel since we sailed t'gether. Yore lookin' plump an' prosperous these days."

Swaggering up to the Tyrant's wooden longhut, Clogg booted the door. "Anyone 'ome t'receive a pore seadog who's down on his luck?"

The weasel captain Hisk swung the door open and announced in a dignified manner, "Enter, Cap'n, my master awaits your pleasure."

"Oh do 'e now, well ain't that pretty!" a searat called Oilback sniggered at Hisk.

Badrang knew he was playing a dangerous game, but slyness and treachery had always been the order of the day between himself and Clogg. The idea was for neither stoat to show he was afraid of the other and to keep up a pretence of being old friends. With this in mind Badrang rushed at his former partner, hugging him tightly as he dropped into corsair slang.

"Well well, burn me bilges if it ain't Cap'n Tramun Clogg. How are yer, ye ole wavedog?"

Tramun pounded the other's back, grinning widely. "Badrang, me messmate, stripe me but yore lookin' fit as a fish an' spry as a wasp. Oh, it is good for me ole eyes t'see ye agin, me 'earty. Look wot I've brought fer you!"

At a signal from Clogg two searats upended a cask upon the table. They smashed in the head and scooped out two beakers, which they presented to the stoats. Badrang brought the drink swiftly to his mouth, halting slyly as Clogg took a great gulp of his. It flowed down through the pirate stoat's chinplaits as he swigged noisily.

"Damson wine, matey. The best on earth—an' all fer me 'n' you!"

Badrang took a drink that was more of a sip than a gulp. "Prime stuff. You allus knew a good barrel o' drink, you rascal."

Clogg released Badrang and slumped down in the Tyrant's thronechair, resting his clogged footpaws noisily on the tabletop.

"Just like in the ole days, eh?"

Badrang seated himself on the edge of the table, smiling. "Aye, just like in the ole days, mate!"

"Ow long is it since we was last t'gether, d'you reckon?" Clogg took another swig, grinning and winking.

Badrang took a sip, pursing his lips. "Too long, I'd say, Tramun. It's good to see you agin."

They continued to play the game, this time with

Clogg's paw straying close to his cutlass, while Badrang toyed with the bone handle of a long skinning dagger.

"I recalls when we was last together, you left me stranded on a reef whilst you sailed off wid twoscore slaves, half o' which was mine by rights." Now the pirate's voice began to carry a menacing undertone.

Badrang's face was the picture of injured innocence. "Me sailed off 'n' left you? More the other way round, as I recall. There was a mighty storm an' we were blown off course. My vessel was wrecked an' the slaves lost, all of 'em. When you never turned up to 'elp me, I trekked off overland an' ended up in this place."

In a trice the time for merriment and reminiscence was over. Clogg hurled his beaker at the wall and stood up.

"Aye, an' lookit you now, Lord Badrang if yer please! Surrounded by a fine fortress an' a passel o' slaves, I'll wager. Well, I wants what's due ter me, I've come fer my share!"

Badrang leaped up, confronting his enemy eye to eye. "I worked too hard to get what I've made 'ere, Clogg. Yore share is nothin' an' that's what y'll get!"

"Do yer hear that lads?" The pirate stoat drew his blade. "Let's show this black-'earted swab that we ain't 'ere to beg. We've come to take a full complement of slaves to row the *Seascarab* from all three decks!"

With a wild roar, Clogg's crew unsheathed their weapons and stood ready for slaughter.

"Make a move an' yer Cap'n's a dead un!"

The Tyrant made his move like lightning. Kicking aside Clogg's blade, he grabbed the stoat's plaited beard. A dagger appeared in his other paw, dangerously close to Tramun's throat.

"This blade is poisoned. One nick is all it takes. Hisk!"

"The archers have surrounded these quarters, Lord," the weasel Captain called from the doorway. "They're standin' ready with poisoned shafts. None of this scum will leave alive."

Clogg held up a paw to his crew. "Wait, hold yer rush, lads. Put those carvers up."

He was still smiling, but Badrang could sense the animal rage behind Clogg's grinning features as the pirate addressed him.

"You win, matey, though I never thought you'd use a dirty trick like poisoned weapons against an ole shipmate. Put up yore blade. I'll go peaceful like, back to me ship."

Badrang stood at the main gates until every last corsair was out of his fortress. The Tyrant was satisfied he had outwitted his foe without bloodshed, which would have been considerable on both sides if a fight had broken out inside Marshank. The archers had their shafts trained on Clogg as he jabbed a warning paw at his enemy.

"That's twice you've crossed me, Badrang, but the third time I'll win. I'm goin', but ye can take an oath I'll be back, so don't rest easy, matey. One dark night I'll slip in when yore least expectin' it. Then I'll slit yer gullet, take the slaves an' burn this fancy place down round yore dead ears. That's a promise!"

Owing to the heightened tension and upset of the pirates' visit, it was not until late night that the prisoners were fed. Armed with a bowl of kitchen scraps and accompanied by Gurrad, a young male otter named Keyla stood dropping the leftovers through the grating to the prisoners below. Gurrad drew his cloak close against a chill breeze from the sea. He wanted to be back by the fire, eating roasted fish and drinking the damson wine that Clogg had left.

The rat shoved Keyla sharply. "C'mon you, stir your stumps. It's cold out 'ere!"

Keyla shrugged as he sat down on the grating, poking scraps between the bars one bit at a time.

"Cold, sir? I think it's quite warm out here. Still, you

do look a bit drawn and peakish. Maybe you're coming down with fever."

"Fever? I ain't got no fever." The rat shuddered and sniffed.

Gurrad was quite taken aback when the young otter stood up and tucked the cloak more snugly around him.

"You never know, sir. Those searats bring all kinds of illness ashore with them. Why don't you take yourself indoors by the fire and have a nice beaker of wine? I'll see to these idiots. Huh, they're only making things harder for us other slaves, behaving the way they do. Dim-witted fools. You run along now, sir. I'll take care of feeding these three."

Gurrad hesitated a moment then shivered as a fresh wind blew around him. That seemed to settle the issue.

"Listen, I'm getting inside where I'll be warmer. Don't be too long out here and report straight back to the compound guard when you're finished, d'you hear?"

Keyla threw the rat a smart salute. "Don't you worry, sir. I need my sleep, I won't be long. Better hurry now, your eyes look a bit cloudy to me."

Gurrad needed no further urging. He scurried off shivering and rubbing at his eyes, convinced he was sickening for fever.

Giggling quietly to himself, the otter pressed his face to the grating and called down, "Felldoh, are you all right?"

The squirrel stood upon Martin's shoulders and drew himself up so he was close to the bars.

"Keyla, my friend, listen carefully. Here's what I want you to do."

Rose and Grumm stood on the tideline, watching the silvery wake of *Seascarab* as the craft headed out, veering on a southerly tack into the open sea.

"Yurr Miz Rose, worr'm you surpose 'ee villyuns wanted?"

Rose tossed a pebble into the shallows. "I've no idea,

Grumm, but whatever it was they didn't seem too happy leaving here."

The two companions walked back to the fortress walls, to the spot beneath the main gates where Rose had conversed with Martin. The mousemaid looked up at the twin posts with rope ends blowing loosely from it in the night wind.

"I hope Martin is all right. Trust Badrang to think up something cruel like that, binding a poor creature up there in the middle of a storm—"

Grumm held up a paw for silence. "Shush naow, Roser. Do 'ee 'ear that? Somebeast a-singen'."

Keyla had a fine deep voice that carried well. Rose and Grumm listened to his song as it drifted over the walls to them.

"I know a mouse called Martin,
And a young un who's named Brome,
Captured by some vermin scouts
As he strayed from his home.
So if you're out there list'ning,
I'll pause awhile and wait,
For I've been singing half the night
On this side of the gate."

Rose almost wept for joy. She was answering in an instant, being both a good singer and balladeer. Grumm grunted softly as she hugged him tight with happiness, her clear voice ringing out plaintively on the night breeze.

"My name is Rose of Noonvale,
The tribe of Urran Voh,
My only brother is called Brome,
And Martin's name I know.
We're here so we can help them,
So please, friend, tell to me

41

What we can do to aid those two
And try to set them free!"

Immediately a hurried few lines rang out clear in reply.

"A vermin guard approaches.
Quick, get yourselves from sight.
I'll try to get back to you
This time tomorrow night!"

Heeding the warning, Rose and Grumm withdrew swiftly to the rocky outcrop where they had hidden earlier that day.

Fleabane and Rotnose the weasels came striding forward and grabbed Keyla roughly.

"What's all the singin' for, otter? You ain't got nothin' to sing about."

"Yeah, slaves don't sing. What were you singin' about?"

"Well, you see, Gurrad thought he had fever," Keyla explained, "so he went inside and left me to feed the prisoners. When I finished giving them their food I thought I'd better sing an old otter charm to keep the fortress free from sickness."

"Singin' charms, what a load of ole nonsense!" Fleabane sneered.

Rotnose was superstitious and terrified of sickness. "No it ain't. Come on, otter, let's hear you sing it."

Keyla obliged, making up the words as he went along.

"O spirit of the seasons
Who rules the land and sea,
From crabby claws and runny snouts,
Good spirit, keep us free.
From tummy ache, soretail and sniffs,
From grunge and whisker cramp,

42

From wobbly paws, and flurgy twinj,
O keep all in this camp."

"Hah! Grunge and wobbly paws, rubbish!" Fleabane
scoffed aloud. "And who's ever heard of flurgy twinj?"

Keyla looked aghast at the weasel. "You don't know
what flurgy twinj is?"

"No, and I don't care!"

Keyla leaned close to the two guards whispering confidentially, "I knew a fine big strong hedgehog long
ago, he laughed at flurgy twinj. Poor creature, he never
laughed again!"

The young otter looked so serious that the weasels
were taken aback.

"Take no notice of Fleabane, young un. He's a fool,"
Rotnose apologized in hushed tones. "You carry on
singin' yore charms, an' sing an extra one fer me."

The two guards carried on their patrol arguing among
themselves.

"Wobbly paws and grunge, I still don't believe it."

"Listen you, don't scoff at what yer don't know about.
Lookit that mark on yer ear—that could be the start of
grunge."

"Where? What mark?"

"There, that sort of yellow mark on yer left ear. Can't
yer see it?"

"Loafbrain, how c'n I see me own ear? Er, does it look
serious?"

"Well, it wasn't there at the start of the season. I think
we'd best learn the words of that charm. How does it
go?"

"From flurgy paws and grungy tummy,
Spirit keep us free.
Wobbly whiskers an' dah de dah . . ."

"Dah de dah yerself, boulder bottom. They're not the
right words!"

43

Keyla laughed aloud as he made his way back to the compound.

5

Badrang ordered a wallguard to be posted night and day against the return of Tramun Clogg. He harbored no doubts at all that the pirate would be back, doubly bent on revenge and conquest. Extra guards were put to watch the slaves when they were quarrying stone, fishing or tending crops to feed the horde.

Felldoh's father Barkjon had wheedled himself on to kitchen duty. He kept his old eyes and ears open, gathering all the information he could. In the slave compound at night he discussed it with others. Since Martin's open defiance of Badrang and Felldoh's rock throwing, a new mood was beginning to make itself felt among the captives. Keyla, Barkjon and a hedgehog named Hillgorse were a little bolder than the rest. They soon became the ringleaders of a rebellious little group that met each night around the compound fire. Barkjon was a squirrel with a wise old head, and everybeast listened when he talked.

"We must do all we can to help Felldoh and Martin escape, and the other little mouse Brome. If they can make it to freedom, I know that they will do all in their power to defeat Badrang and free us all. Felldoh and Martin are the only ones ever to defy the Tyrant, I am certain that if they were on the outside they would not leave us here to rot in captivity."

There were murmurs of agreement from the creatures that crowded round to listen at the meeting. A mouse called Purslane, who sat with her husband and babe, called out, "Tell us what to do, Barkjon. We're with you."

"Get them extra rations to keep up their strength," Keyla answered for the old squirrel. "Shellfish or shrimp if you're out with a fishing party, crops or fruit if you work in the fields. They need to be fit if they're to escape."

A female otter named Tullgrew spoke up. "What if you work in the quarry like I do? How can I help?"

"Hinder, hamper, work as slowly as you can," Hillgorse answered her. "If at all able, try to steal anything that can be used as a weapon—tools, sharp rock shards, anything. They may all be needed someday."

"Don't listen to them. You'll only land us all in trouble."

Barkjon stood up and gazed out over the slaves. "Is that you, Druwp?"

A surly-looking bankvole who was trying to hide behind others lifted his head. "Yes, it's me."

Tullgrew grabbed him and stood him upright. "Then don't hide at the back muttering, stand up and speak up face to face with others instead of slinking about."

"Go on, Druwp, have your say." Hillgorse nodded towards the bankvole.

It was clear whose side the bankvole was on when he spoke. "We're slaves, and it's better to be alive than killed trying to do foolish things. Badrang and his horde are too strong for us. If you start stealing fish and crops and tools we'll all be punished. I don't want to be suffering for the foolishness of others. Count me out of your plans!"

Purslane threw a piece of firewood at Druwp. "Shut your snivelling little trap. I've seen you hanging around the guards and carrying tales. You're a sneak, Druwp, a toady!"

Angry murmurs arose from the crowd. Barkjon held up a paw for order. When there was quiet he confronted the bankvole.

"Unfortunately, we cannot count you out of our plans, Druwp. You are one of us, therefore all we do affects you and anything you choose to do must affect us. Together we can be a stream, coursing its way powerful and silent. Even a small stream can wear away large rocks. But separate us and we become as single droplets of water, ready to be scattered by the flick of a paw. You are either on our side, or you are with Badrang and his horde."

Druwp lowered his eyes avoiding Barkjon's gaze. "I am alone, I side with nobeast. Leave me to live my own life as I see fit."

Barkjon silenced the angry murmurings of the slaves with a growl. "So be it, Druwp. No creature is forced to join us. You may stay alone. But let me warn you, bankvole, if one word of our business reaches Badrang and his creatures, I will hold you responsible. When that happens you will be a deadbeast. I promise this!"

Druwp slunk out of the crowd to a deserted corner of the compound. The silence that followed was eventually broken by Keyla.

"Oh well, if that's all for tonight I'll be on my way. Feeding time for the prisoners, you know."

Rose and Grumm lay behind the rocks, watching Fortress Marshank, helpless and unable to approach the gates because of the two sentries who stood on the walltop keeping a lookout for the return of Tramun Clogg.

The mousemaid shook her head despairingly. "With those two up there we won't be able to communicate with our friend. What can we do, Grumm?"

"Oi says we sit'n toight an' wait. You'm friend be a

cleverbeast, 'ee'll think o' summat, miz, you'm see, hurr aye."

Inside the fortress Keyla was racking his young brains for an idea. He poked scraps through the grating as he whispered to the prisoners below.

"They're guarding the walltop, mates. It's going to be difficult getting instructions to our friends out there. Any ideas?"

"Hey down there, what's all the whisperin' about? Are you talkin' to those prisoners? If ye are I'll lay me spearhandle across yer back!"

Keyla spread his paws wide appealingly. "Not me, sir. I haven't said a word. It's these poor wretches in the pit, they're callin' to me. They say that they've got the fever and they want to be let out."

Frogbit and Nipwort, the two rats who were on guard, looked at each other, taken aback by the news.

"Fever! I knew it, mate. Gurrad was shiverin' like a leaf last night. He sat by the fire drinkin' wine, an' this mornin' said 'e was stayin' in 'is bunk cos of the pains in 'is 'ead."

"Nah, that was just through guzzlin' too much wine. There ain't no fever in this fortress, mate."

"No? Well, what about ole Fleabane, got a great yeller mark on 'is ear. It was bleedin' this afternoon!"

"Huh, that's cos the fool's been scratchin' at it to make it go away. Nah, there ain't no fever 'ereabouts, take my word."

"That's exactly what I said, sir," Keyla called up to them. "But these three down here are convinced they've got fever or plague or something horrible. Come down and take a look at them, sir."

"What do we want lookin' at mouldy prisoners," Nipwort scoffed. "Our job is up 'ere lookin' out fer other things."

"Listen," Keyla whispered down to his friends, "they

48

can't stop sick creatures shouting out feverishly. If Rose is outside she'll hear you."

Below in the pit Martin grasped his friends' paws.

"Who has the loudest voice, mates?"

Brome swelled his little chest out. "Try me, listen to this . . ." Cupping his paws, Brome yelled aloud in a piercing howl, "Somebeast, anybeast, can you hear me? Help us, there's fever down here!"

Both Martin and Felldoh had to cover their ears. The youngster had lungs like bellows and a howl like an injured wolf.

"Help, help! We're dying of fever. What's the matter, can't you hear me?"

Nipwort clenched his paws and ground his teeth together. "Of course we can 'ear yer! Stop that yellin' or I'll come down there an' kick yer tail until it's blue!"

"Oh yes, sir," Brome howled back louder than ever. "Please, sir, kick us, beat us, but come down and see us. We're dying slowly of fever. The place is a plague hole. Come down and see for yourself!"

Frogbit shuddered. "Fat chance! I ain't goin' down there an' catchin' a sickness."

Nipwort was in complete agreement. "Nor me, mate. They c'n yell an' holler all they want. I'm not puttin' a paw anywhere near 'em."

Through her tears Rose sat back, giggling helplessly.

"Heeheehee! That's my little brother all right. Remember he used to scream and shout like that back home until Mama let him have his own way?"

"Yurr, oi amembers miz. Oi used t'plug moi ole ears oop wi' grass. If'n yon choild 'as fever wi' a voice loik that, oi be a taddypole!"

Rose held her throat, and throwing back her head she gave the eagle call.

Grumm winced and covered both ears. "Moi moi, wot

a fambily furr noisenin'. Maister Brome'll know furr sure us'ns kin 'ear 'im naow, miz."

The eagle screech rent the night air again. Brome clapped his hands joyfully. "That's my sister Rose all right. She can screech as good as any eagle."

Martin patted Brome heartily on the back. "Great work, young un. Rose can hear us! Right, get ready to send her the message."

From the walltop Nipwort shook his spear at Keyla. "You started all this, otter. Listen, they've even upset that eagle bird now. Get away from there, go on! Get back to the compound. You've caused enough mischief around here!"

Keyla knew his job was done. Martin and his friends could send their own messages to the outside. The young otter trotted off grinning happily as the two guards argued away on the wall.

"I'm not putting up with this row all night."

"Oh no, then go down there an' shut them up."

"Me? Huh, I'm stayin' right up 'ere, mate!"

"An' so am I, mate. We'll just 'ave to ignore the noise an' keep watch fer the *Seascarab*."

"Ignore the noise! Are you jokin'? Lissen to that!"

"Roseyrosey rosey, Grummgrumm grumm! Lissena-mee lissenamee!"

The eagle screech sounded again. Rose and Grumm were listening.

Nipwort and Frogbit plugged their ears with the screwed-up corners of their ragged cloaks and concentrated on watching the sea.

Brome sent the message in fine howling style.

"In the middle of the gate set your faces.
Oh, I'm dyin' of the fever!
Walk to the south about twenty paces.
It's a terrible thing this fever!

50

There are three of us in this awful pit.
The fever, the fever!
As deep as three mice and a bit.
I'm goin' to die of fever!
We need the claws of a good old chum.
The fever, the fever!
I know that you can do it, Grumm,
Don't let me die of fever!"

There was a moment's silence, then the call of the eagle screeched out three times. Rose had received the message.

A quiet peace fell over the star-traced seas, the shingled beach and the weary sentries on the walltop. The only sound was small waves gently lapping the land as the tide ebbed. Frogbit unplugged his ears. Nipwort followed his mate's example.

"Cwaw! Ain't it lovely an' quiet."

"Aye, I think the eagle bird frightened 'em inter silence."

"Silence, wot a lovely word."

"It'd sound better if you shut yer gob an' gave it a chance."

Rose had written it all down on a smooth rock with a piece of sea coal. She read the instructions carefully to Grumm.

"Face the center of the gates, walk twenty paces to the south. Brome says there's three of them in a pit that is as deep as three and a bit mice. So if we, or should I say you, dig down twice my height then straight tunnel from the twenty-pace mark, sooner or later you'll break into the pit at about head height. Can you do it, Grumm?"

The mole winked as he flexed his huge digging claws. "Can oi do et, miz? Can burds floiy in sky, can fishers swim in 'ee seas? Hurr hurr, 'twould be easier'n eatin' yore mama's li'l apple puddens!"

"If you rescue Brome, I'll see that my mama bakes you more apple puddings than you could shake a stick at, when we get back to Noonvale." The mousemaid hurled herself on Grumm and stroked his velvety back fur the wrong way.

"Ohoohoohurrhurr, mizzy. Doant you'm do that. Et tickles, hoohoohurrhurr!"

6

Skalrag the fox watched as Badrang tore at a roasted sea bird and drank deeply of the good damson wine that Clogg had brought him.

When the Tyrant stoat had eaten and drunk his fill he wiped his mouth daintily on a dockleaf and nodded at Skalrag.

"Make your report."

The fox swallowed visibly then spoke, moving from paw to paw as he did so. Badrang had that effect on most creatures. His swift mood changes were a byword among the horde.

"Lord, there are no signs of Clogg and his ship. The sentries are keeping a sharp eye out day and night. The prisoners in the hole have some sort of sickness, Lord. It may be fever. Bluehide and Lumpback are taking stock of the armory. Everything else is quiet and in order. There is nothing more to report."

Badrang poured himself a little more wine. "Fever, eh? That young mouse, Brome, he must've brought it in with him. Pity, I was going to have some fun with those three, make an example of 'em. Still, fever is a good enough lesson to the slaves. Throw the wrongdoers in the pit where they'll catch the fever. What a clever idea, slaves getting fever from slaves. They can't blame us for that, eh, Skalrag? Hahahaha!"

The fox laughed nervously along with his master. Badrang suddenly stopped laughing, leaving the other to carry on. Skalrag's thin giggle trailed away as the Tyrant's eyes hardened.

"I've just had another clever idea, Skalrag. If my fortress isn't finished by the end of summer, I might just throw a few of my Captains in the fever pit to rot. That'd liven their ideas up. What do you say?"

Skalrag could feel his paws beginning to shake uncontrollably. "A spl-splendid idea, Lord!"

Rose waited until the wallguard changed. There was a considerable interval when nobeast was on the walltop, and she took advantage of this to sneak up to the fortress. Standing facing the centre of the gate, she measured out twenty paces to the south. Marking the wall with a piece of charcoal, she dodged back to the cover of the rocks. Grumm was waiting for her. He nodded over to the X marked on the stones of the fortress wall.

"Be that et, Miz Roser?"

She nodded, watching him sizing the area up. Rose trusted Grumm to do the job swiftly and silently. In all the country there was no stronger digger than her friend.

The mole scratched the tip of his button nose. "Yurr, tain't easy, but tain't 'ard noither, miz. You'm see they rock o'er thurr?"

It was another rocky outcrop, similar to the one they were hiding behind. Rose let Grumm explain his plan.

"That thurr rock be on straightline wi' thoi marker. Oi'll start diggen frum thurr. Thatwise they vurmin guarders on wall woant see us'ns, an' you'm kin spread tunnel durt behoind 'ee rock."

The plan was perfect. It was but the work of a moment to slip from one rock to the other. Grumm took one last look at the mark on the wall, muttering calculations to

himself as he squinted at it. Then he h
digging paws to the earth and recite
charm.

"Luck to oi an' every mole,
As ever went to dig an 'ole.
Tunnel gudd for all oi'm wurth.
Mole be best when diggen urth."

Rose was amazed at his speed and strength. Grumm went straight down in a shower of pebbles and sand, widening as he went. The mousemaid sat and waited. Digging a flat oatcake from their pack, she munched it and sipped cold mint tea from a canteen.

Soon Grumm called out to her, "Do'ee jump daown yurr, mizzy. Urry naow!"

Without a backward glance, she leaped into the hole. Grumm caught her easily and set her steady. She looked up as he rumbled, "Bo urr, that be 'zactly two mousey lengths."

He was right, it was exactly the height of two mice.

"Yurr, stan' on moi 'ead an' climb owt naow, Roser. No sense in you'm agettin' all durty. Wot udd yore mama an' dad say if'n oi brought you'm back all mucked up. Hoo urr!"

The mousemaid hopped out, assisted by Grumm, and began strewing the rubble from the hole around as he dug steps in the side of it.

Blowing sand from his snout, Grumm eyed his work. "Nawthin' fancy, but 'ee'll do, hurr aye."

He went straight to tunnelling through the bottom side of the hole in a direct line, faster than any two moles in the whole of Noonvale.

Skalrag stood at the rear of Badrang's longhut, trying hard to stop his paws shaking after the interview with the Tyrant. A bankvole was idly pulling up weeds that

t the side of the building. The fox watched
while before calling to him.

wp, over here!"

e bankvole pretended not to hear but worked his
ay along until he was close to Skalrag. The fox looked
this way and that, making sure he was unobserved as
he spoke out of the corner of his mouth.

"Well, what's happening in the compound, matey?"

"I'm not your matey or anybeast's," Druwp answered
without looking up. "There's lots happening in the compound but it'll cost you food and wine to find out."

Skalrag looked at his paws. They had steadied some-
what. "I know that. You'll find a roast fish and some
wine here tonight, just under the corner there, where it
usually is. Now tell me what's happening."

Druwp's voice was low-keyed and surly. "I'm taking
a chance doing this. If they ever found out they'd kill
me for sure. So I'd like a proper whole roast fish, none
of your table scraps, and some of the dark damson wine
the corsairs brought when they paid a visit."

Skalrag's eyes widened. "How d'you know they
brought damson wine?"

Druwp sniffed. "You'd be surprised at what I know.
Well, do I get proper food?"

"Yes, yes, get on with it." Skalrag chewed impatiently
at a hangclaw.

"Right, listen close now. There's three ringleaders,
Hillgorse the old hedgehog, Barkjon the squirrel and
that young otter called Keyla. These three are urging all
the slaves to steal fish, crops and also tools from the
quarry, sharp stones, anything they can make into
weapons. There's a plan of some sort to free Martin,
Felldoh and another mouse from the prison pit. Keyla
has been doing something when he takes the food to the
prisoners each night."

Skalrag urged his informer on. "What's the plan?
What is Keyla doing? Why do they need weapons?"

Still keeping his eyes down, Druwp shrugged. "I don't

know how they plan to get them out of the pit and I'm not sure what Keyla's up to. But the general talk is that when they're free they'll be able to help from outside. Meanwhile the others are collecting weapons against the day when they get a chance to strike back at Badrang and all of you. That's all I know. I've got to go now."

Skalrag placed a footpaw swiftly on Druwp's neck, holding him still a moment. "You've done well, Druwp. I'll make sure the fish and wine are the best. But find out more. I need to know more. When will I see you again, my friend?"

The bankvole struggled loose of Skalrag's paw and hurried off.

"I'm not your friend. I'll be in touch."

In the gloom of the prison hole young Brome was getting very depressed after the initial euphoria of contact with the outside had faded. He began to speculate miserably.

"Suppose they get caught outside the fortress, where will we be then?"

Felldoh tried reasoning with him. "Don't be silly, Brome. Your sister and that mole aren't daft, they know what they're doing."

The youngster was silent awhile, then he started again. "They might have the directions wrong. Suppose Grumm tunnels the wrong way. He could have missed this place by a few lengths. Just think of it, poor old Grumm, digging and digging and getting nowhere while we sit down here twiddling our paws."

Martin gave Brome a light thump on the back. "Here now, what's all this gloom an' doom for, young feller? You've already told us that Grumm is the champion digger in all the country. Well, let me tell you, moles are amongst the most sensible beasts over or under land. If your friend Grumm is a champion digger, why, I'd trust him with my life anyday. So would you, eh, Felldoh!"

Before the squirrel had a chance to answer, a spear-blade clanged on the grating above. The three friends looked up. They could not see clearly but Skalrag's voice was unmistakable.

"They say you've all got the fever down there. How d'you feel? Sick, dizzy, sweating? Not very nice, is it?"

Felldoh laughed scornfully. "It doesn't hurt as much as the rock that I hit you with, mangenose!"

Skalrag banged the grating with his spear angrily. "I've half a mind to come down there and run you through with my spear . . ."

"But you won't, will you, because you're terrified of catching fever,"Felldoh's answer came back mockingly.

Skalrag thwacked his spear on the grating a few more times. "You're right, squirrel, I won't come down. But then nothing else will, and that means food or water. Hah! We don't feed useless mouths around here, nor do we play nursemaid to sick beasts. So you can all stay down there until you die and rot!"

The fox swaggered off, proud that he had won the argument.

Martin felt a tear from Brome's cheek as it damped his paw. He threw an arm about the youngster. "I don't know about rotting, but pretty soon he'll get a rotten surprise when he finds we're gone from here. Imagine the fox's face!"

Brome managed a sniff and a smile. "Haha, yes, and we'll be safe in Noonvale."

Martin began kicking the side of the pit wall. Felldoh caught on and joined him. Their footpaws thudded away at the packed earth wall.

Brome squinted at them in the darkness. "What are you doing?"

"Giving your mole friend a little help and guidance. He's probably very sensitive to underground noises. Take no notice of us, Brome. Tell us about Noonvale. Where do you live? What sort of a place is it? Are the creatures nice and is the food good? Go on!"

As they listened Martin noticed that Brome's heavy

mood of sadness disappeared when he talked of his home.

"Er, let me see, what sort of place is Noonvale? Well, it's a deep glade far in the forests, a secret place, you might say. At dawn the sunlight comes filtering like golden dust through the oaks and sycamores and elms. It is quiet; you can almost hear the sounds of peace. Light blue smoke drifts up from the cookhouse fires, mingling with the green leaves above. Soft mosses and dark green grass carpet its slopes, and there are flowers—columbines, foxgloves, bluebells, wood anemones and ground ivy. Ferns grow there too. Sometimes I would lie among them at dawn, catching dewdrops on my tongue . . ."

Felldoh blinked back a tear, surprised by the young one's eloquence. "Sounds like my kind of place, Brome. What about the creatures there?"

"Hmm, the creatures. Well, there's my sister Rose and me, our father is Urran Voh, Chieftain of Noonvale, and our mama's name is Aryah. We live with other creatures who have found Noonvale—moles, squirrels, hedgehogs, even some otters. My father rules the vale. He is always very kind, but sometimes he can be stern to naughty ones. You would like my mama, though. She is the best cook anywhere."

Martin almost forgot his aching paws as he thumped away at the wall. "Does she cook anything nice?"

"She cooks everything nice," Brome sighed longingly. "Mushroom and chestnut stew, wild onion and leek soup, spring vegetable pasties, nutbread, oatfarl, wheatcob, all piping hot from the ovens. She bakes blackberry and apple tarts, plum maple pudding, elderberry pie with yellow summercream, gooseberry preserve scones, hot with buttercup spread—"

Felldoh massaged his shrunken stomach as he wailed aloud. "Stop, stop! I can't stand it. All that beautiful food!"

"Mushroom and chestnut stew, plum maple pudding,

oh my aching teeth!" Martin wiped a paw across his dripping mouth.

Brome gave a loud chuckle as he mischievously continued tormenting his hungry friends. "My father helps the moles and the hedgehogs. They brew all our drinks—dandelion ale, strawberry cordial, chestnut brown beer—"

"Owoooh! Chestnut brown beer. Stop, you little fiend, stop!"

Martin and Felldoh beat their footpaws harder against the wall.

Grumm backed out of the hole, pushing a mound of earth before him. Rose cleared it away, helping the mole out into the late afternoon sun.

"You seem to be making good progress, Grumm."

Rattling his digging claws against the rock to clean off the loose sandy soil, the mole blinked his eyes against the sunlight.

"That oi be, miz, hurr aye. Oi be a-goin' the roight way too, bo urr. They beasts be a-bangen loik two drummers at a winter fayre, guidin oi straight to 'em. Hurr hurr, et woant be long naow, Roser. Afore midnoight, oi'd reckern."

Rose wriggled excitedly. "Midnight! Wonderful. It should be fairly easy to get clear of Marshank under cover of darkness. Oh, Grumm, you're a dear!"

The mole made his way back to the tunnel, murmuring to cover his embarrassment, "Oi bain't no deer, oi be a mole, an' doant 'ee fergit it, mizzy!"

7

A sliver of moon appeared, like a slice of lemon rind suspended in the soft star-strewn darkness. The tide was at full flood, without a wind to drive it. Small silver-tipped waves lapped shyly on the shore, gradually devouring the coastland up to the tideline. Little sound was heard, save for the muted splash of muffled oars and the hoarse muttered curses of Cap'n Tramun Clogg as he urged the four longboats through the dark waters.

"C'mon, bend yer backs, ye bottlenosed bandits. Yer might've broken yer mothers' 'earts but ye won't break mine. Pull, me bullies, pull!"

Clogg's ship was beached around a point south of the headland. The wily stoat was planning a surprise attack on Marshank. The corsairs rowed steadily as Clogg kept watch.

"Harr, there 'tis, me buckoes. Badrang's fine castle! May'aps it won't look so fine when I'm done with it. Oilback, Wetpaw, keep those ropes an' grapplin' 'ooks close by. Poison arrers, eh. I'll give that schemin' stoat a night to remember. 'Ere, but wot am I talkin' about? Deadbeasts don't 'ave no memory, an' that's what 'igh 'n' mighty Badrang'll be when I lays sword to 'im. Dead!"

The four boats pressed on through the night waters,

laden with hardened ruffians all armed to the teeth with bows, arrows, pikes, spears, daggers, slings and a variety of swords.

Lumpback and Stiffear were on the walltop keeping guard. The two weasels lounged against the timber posts. Lumpback was not in the best of moods. He prodded Stiffear with his spearbutt.

"Stop drummin' yer paws. It's gettin' on me nerves!"

Stiffear had been half asleep. He grabbed his spear, bristling. "I'm not drummin' me paws, slobberchops. Look, they're still!"

"Watch who you're callin' slobberchops, you. Something's drummin'. Can't yer 'ear it, like a sorta soft tappin noise?"

"No I can't, an' if you prod me once more with that spear I'll shove it up yer snout. Huh, drummin' noises. It's prob'ly yore tiny brain drummin' round in yer thick skull!"

They jabbed their spears at each other and snarled a bit before going back to watching the sea.

"I can 'ear it, drummin' away," Lumpback started muttering again, "only softlike, but I know I can 'ear it. Stiffy, see that rock out there on the shore, that one yonder—I could swear I saw a pile of sand bein' chucked up in the air above it!"

"First drummin', now it's piles o'sand!" Stiffear blew a long sigh of impatience. "Wot's the matter with you, toadbrains? Did you eat some bad fish for yer dinner?"

Lumpback pointed with his spear. "Hah, there! I saw it again, like sand bein' tossed up in the air, right above that rock, see!"

Stiffear stared hard at Lumpback, shaking his head pityingly. "That's the crabs 'avin' a dance. They do it every few nights y'know, kickin' the sand up with their liddle claws an' jiggin' away like billyo."

"Don't talk rubbish!" Lumpback curled his lip in a sneer.

Stiffear lost his temper then. "Yore the one talkin' rubbish, y'fool! Next thing, I suppose you'll be seein' the shore swarmin' with corsairs. . . . Garrgh!" He fell forward with a long barbed arrow protruding from his neck.

Lumpback screamed as the dark shapes hurried towards the fortress walls.

"Attack! Attaaaaaack!"

Rose had seen the corsairs first. She was about to empty more rubble away when the soft thud of paws on sand reached her ears. Turning towards the sea, the mousemaid could see the four boats on the tideline and a mob of dark shapes scurrying across the shore towards Marshank. She jumped down into the shaft Grumm had dug and held her breath. Fortunately, nobeast saw her. They dashed past swiftly, intent on reaching the fortress.

Anxiously she crouched at the tunnel entrance, murmuring under her breath, "Grumm, where are you? Oh, hurry, Grumm, please!"

Brome had fallen asleep. He lay between Martin and Felldoh as they slapped their feet wearily against the prison pit wall. Exhaustion was overcoming them both, and they grunted with exertion as they tried to continue.

"Can't keep this up any more, Felldoh. How about you?" Martin gasped.

The squirrel nodded droopingly. "Me too, mate, the young un could be right. Maybe his mole friend has tunnelled in the wrong direction."

Suddenly Martin's frustration boiled over. With a wild effort he kicked the wall fiercely, shouting between each thud, "We're not going to die down here!"

Without warning both his footpaws shot through the side of the wall and a muffled cry rang out from the hole.

"Bo urr, zurrs. 'Old 'ard, tis oi, Grumm!"

Badrang leaped from his bed as Gurrad roused him with a panicked squeak.

"Lord, it's Clogg an' his corsairs. They're attackin'!"

Throwing on a chainmail vest and grabbing his sword, the Tyrant pushed his frightened henchrat to one side.

"Of course he is, addlebrain. I wouldn't expect him to do anything else. Come on. Are the horde positioned on the walls?"

Gurrad scurried along at Badrang's side. "Aye, Lord, they were up as soon as the guard shouted a warning."

"Good. I'll be at the main gate. Send Skalrag to me right away!"

Moments later Skalrag came hurrying down from the walltop. "Sire, they're pressing hard, but we're holding 'em off!"

"Where's Clogg's ship? On the tideline or in the bay?" Badrang yelled to the fox above the clash of battlesound.

"There's no sign of it, sire. They came in longboats."

Badrang pondered a short moment then rapped out orders. "He'll have come in from the south—he sailed off that way. The ship is probably beached or anchored round the other side of the headland. Right, listen hard now, Skalrag. Take ten good archers, get oil, tinder and flints, find Clogg's vessel and burn it to ashes with fire arrows. Leave over the back wall while the thick of the fighting's at the front. Go, and don't fail me!"

As Skalrag hurried to do his master's bidding, the Tyrant dashed up the ladder to the walltop and joined the mêlée.

Arrows whistled through the night from both sides. Clogg was trying to keep up heavy volleys of shafts and slingstones to make the defenders keep their heads down. Badrang seemed to be everywhere at once, hacking at grapnel ropes, hurling boulders and roaring orders.

"Don't let them grapplers get ahold, slash the ropes! Push that siege ladder over! Hisk, get to the north corner, use the big spears and long pikes to stab downward! You there, take four more and get down into the courtyard. Reinforce the gates with anything—rocks, timber, sand—anything you can lay paws on!"

Cap'n Tramun Clogg howled aloud at his archers and slingthrowers as he awaited the upside-down longboat that was being trundled over the beach towards him.

"Give 'em blood an' brokenbones, ye black-livered flotsam! Growch, keep those arrows a-flyin' an' make every one count! Haharr, Badrang, I'll soon be wearin' yer guts fer garters! Bring that longboat t'me, 'earties. We'll knock on the Tyrant's door, haharrharr!"

The longboat's keel was plated with a heavy sheath of copper that culminated in a lump at its prow. Upside down, it made a battering ram. Twenty or more vermin stood underneath the boat, using it as an umbrella against missiles from the walltop. Tramun Clogg joined them, heading the operation, roaring orders gleefully.

"Straight ahead as she goes, buckoes. Pound that ole door to splinters, mates. Charge!"

Paws grasped the undersides of the craft tightly as they raced madly across the shore. Arrows, spears and rocks bounced vainly off the plated keel, unable to stop the corsairs' battering ram striking Marshank's gates with tremendous force.

Whump!

Most of the ram crew fell flat under the impact as thick copper plate met door timber with a splintering crash. Paws a-tingle from the reverberation, they hoisted the boat aloft under Clogg's triumphant commands.

"Hoho, cullies. Back 'er off an' let's do it again! Gruzzle, Dedjaw, Floater! Up front 'ere with me. Arf a dozen whacks like that'n an' we can use yonder gates fer toothpicks at our victory feast! Nothin' can stop wavebeasts such as us mates. Chaaaaaarge!"

Gurrad slashed at a climbing rope with his cutlass. Feeling the walltop shudder slightly as the ram struck once more, he looked anxiously towards Badrang. The Tyrant had a stack of light javelins at his side, and he was throwing them with deadly accuracy, snarling with satisfaction each time he was rewarded with the screams of another searat impaled by his good aim. Pausing momentarily, he grabbed a passing ferret.

"Tailwart, get down below and see that the gates are well shored up with rock and rubble. Clogg can batter our doors until his whiskers turn grey. If there's enough packing behind 'em he'll never break through."

The battle raged on into the night, its infernal din of roaring clangour overriding the hiss and swell of the restless sea.

Brome was last to enter the escape tunnel. Grumm hauled the young mouse in alongside him.

"Gudd to see you'm, maister. You be looken fitter'n a bumblybee."

Martin and Felldoh pounded the mole's furry back joyfully. "Well done, friend. Brome was right, you are a champion digger!"

Grumm wrinkled his nose modestly. "No more'n moi job, zurrs. You uns get along naow. Oi'll bide yurr awhoil an' patch up yon 'ole so's nobeast be a-knowen 'ow him'n excaped. Hurr hurr, 'twill give they Bardang vurmint sumthen to puzzle o'er, a hempty pit wi' no marks o' breakout, hurr hurr."

The three friends crawled on all fours through the darkness, Felldoh's tail touching the tunnel top and brushing down a light drift of sand. Closing their eyes, they pushed forward in the eerie underground silence, their bodies quivering with the anticipation of freedom. It was the battlenoise and a soft breeze tickling his whiskers that told Felldoh they had made it. He sneezed and rubbed fine sand from his eyes as Rose helped him out.

"Up you come, treejumper. Is Grumm with you?"

The squirrel rolled to one side as Martin pulled himself from the tunnel. Together they hauled young Brome out as Martin answered, "He'll be along shortly when he's blocked off the hole. Phwah! I've swallowed so much sand I'll be spitting it out all season."

"Here, wash it out with some cold mint tea."

Martin rubbed dust from his eyes and stared at the mousemaid as he accepted the canteen of liquid. He was thunderstruck.

"You must be Martin."

He stared silently into the most gentle hazel eyes that ever reflected starlight, lost for words as a quiet smile spread over the mousemaid's serene features.

"Drink up, Martin. Your friend and my brother are waiting their turn."

He took a quick mouthful, suddenly finding his voice as he did. "Yurn b'rosty nose!"

"I beg your pardon?" Her laughter was like a summer breeze among bluebells.

Martin took another gulp and cleared his throat. "Sorry. You must be Rose."

Felldoh grinned as he grabbed the canteen from his friend's faltering paws. "Aye, she is. Remember me? I'm Felldoh, and this other creature is Brome. Your name's Martin and the beast whose head you're standin' on is our rescuer Grumm."

Martin hastily shifted his footpaw, mumbling an apology as the mole levered himself from the tunnel.

"Thankee, maister. Hurr, et be gurt 'n' noisy out 'ere wi' they vurmin a-killen each other o'er yonder."

Suddenly Martin became aware of the battlenoise around Marshank. It shook him out of his daze and he began thinking clearly.

"Oh er, right! Well, I think our best bet is to put as much distance between ourselves and that lot right away!"

Felldoh bristled slightly. "I can't leave until my father is free. I'm staying."

Martin gripped his friend's paw. "We won't be a bit

of help to anybeast if we get killed or captured in the midst of a battle. Listen, Felldoh, I'm with you. One day we'll free all the slaves from Badrang's clutches, but right now we're only five, too few to stand against the Tyrant's horde. I say we should go to Noonvale. Brome and Rose's father is a Chieftain, and surely he will tell his tribe to help us. Then when we are strong in numbers we can return and defeat Badrang and all his vermin, wipe them from the face of the land and free our friends. What do you say?"

Brome shook his head. "My father Urran Voh is a creature who goes his own way. He will never leave Noonvale. As for our tribe, well, they generally do what he tells them to."

Rose spoke up. "Aye, brother, our father is as stubborn as you—that's why the two of you always quarrel. But maybe I can persuade Mother. She'd ask him to help you. I know she would."

Martin held the squirrel's paw tighter. "What do you say, Felldoh? Shall we give it a try?"

There was a moment's silence, then Felldoh nodded. "I'm with you. If we can raise an army at Noonvale then one day I'll return to dance on Badrang's grave!"

Martin's eyes shone at the thought of it. "And I'll be dancing with you, friend, holding the sword that once belonged to my father!"

Rose, Brome and Grumm clasped their paws with Martin and Felldoh over the escape hole.

"We'll do it, friends together!"

8

Cap'n Tramun Clogg was beginning to feel discouraged. No matter how hard and long he beat at Marshank's gates with his battering ram, they seemed to hold up. Gruzzle, Dedjaw, Floater and the rest were seated on the shore beneath the upturned boat, blowing for breath as they massaged weary paws. Clogg struck the side of the boat with his cutlass.

"Wot's the matter, yer lily-livered seascum? Weary already? Come on now, 'earties, up on yer paws an' give it one more go. She's splinterin', I tell yer. Why, a couple more bangs an' we'll be through inter the fortress!"

Gruzzle sucked noisily at a skinned paw. "Ahh, Cap'n, I thought you said one more go arf an hour back, an' we're still chargin' those gates like madbeasts."

Clogg cocked a fierce eye at the complaining sea rat. "Yore grizzlin', Gruzzle, always grizzlin'. Now up off those hunkers, mate, an' charge that gate, afore I charges you wid this frogsticker!" He waved his cutlass threateningly.

There was a knocking on the outside of the boat.

"Cap'n, it's Wetpaw. Come quick an' take a look out 'ere!"

The boat was lifted and Clogg poked his head from underneath. "Lookit wot, mate?"

The ferret pointed to reddy-orange glow illuminating the sky beyond the headland. It took a moment for realization to sink in, then the pirate stoat let out an agonized wail and began tearing at his braided beard, the clumsy wooden clogs clicking together as he performed an anguished jig on the shore.

"Whaaaagh! The slime-coated villain's burnin' me ship! Yarrggh! Me luvverly *Seascarab*, pride o' me 'eart! Badrang, yer rotten foul-nosed worm, stinkin' screw-tailed stoat, warp-eyed snotty-snouted shark!"

The corsair crew looked on in dismay as their Cap'n gave full vent to his spleen. Hurling himself at the gates, he hacked with his cutlass, kicked with his clogs, even gnawed savagely at the woodwork with his teeth as he yelled between mouthfuls of splinters, "I'll rip yer liver 'n' lights out an' feed 'em to the crabs. I'll cut off'n yer 'ead an' throw it in yer face. I'll string up yer tripes fer riggin'. I'll pickle yer tail in burnin' brine. I'll . . . I'll. . . . Yaaahaaagh!"

Skalrag and his archers stood paw-deep in the sea, the water scarlet and gold with reflections from the blazing vessel. They blinked as ashcloth from the sail drifted sootily by on the breeze. The *Seascarab* was settling down in flames on the shallow bay bed, and timbers crackled as blazing pitch bubbled from seams. Two rats who had been left on watch were draped limply in death over the gunwales, blazing arrows extinguishing themselves in their backs. With its great green sail burned away, the mast stood like a fiery beacon against the star-studded night. It cracked and broke, falling in an avalanche of sparks. The vessel heeled over, listing at a crazy angle as sea water met flames with a loud steaming hiss.

Skalrag turned to his archers, satisfied. "There's one ship that won't put out to sea again. Form up and follow me. We'll take care of those longboats before we head back to Marshank."

The wily fox did not want to attract attention from the battle area by burning the longboats.

"Put up those bows, use your swords an' knives to hole these boats. That'll leave Clogg trapped on the shore."

Unaware that the longboats were being destroyed, Martin and his companions were heading for them, figuring to take one and sail further up the coast, where they would leave the boat and travel to Noonvale for help.

Felldoh looked to the fiery glow beyond the headland. "We'd better hurry. Those searats will be coming for the longboats to see if they can save their ship."

Martin glanced back towards the fortress as he remarked to his friend, "Good guess, Felldoh. There's a whole bunch of them coming this way!"

The dark shapes of yelling corsairs could be seen leaving the fray and making for the longboats. Martin grasped Brome's paw.

"Let's put a move on, otherwise they'll catch up with us."

Grumm had been looking ahead towards the boats. "Hurr, lookit, thurr be other vurmin by they boats an' they see us'ns!" he groaned in dismay.

Felldoh gritted his teeth. "Foebeasts behind an' before us, Martin. Either way is trouble."

Martin sized the situation up quickly. "We can't turn back now. There's less of 'em in front of us. Keep going. We'll have to chance rushing them. Rose, take Grumm and Brome, pick out a boat and get going. Felldoh and I will hold them off. Please don't argue, just do as I say. Right, Felldoh?"

The big squirrel nodded. "Right! I recognize that half-eared rogue at the boats—it's Skalrag. There's about ten with him. Let's get at it, Martin!"

The young mouse and the squirrel dashed towards Skalrag's group, yelling at the top of their voices.

"Freedom! Chaaaaaaaarge!"

Skalrag was not sure whether the swiftly advancing pair were armed, though he knew by their warlike cries that they intended doing battle. The fox hesitated a moment, unsure whether to meet them sword in paw or go for his bow. He lost the initiative, barely having time to shout a warning to his archers before Martin and Felldoh were on him. The squirrel grabbed Skalrag's sword paw, struggling to get hold of the blade as Martin dealt the nearest rat a flying kick with both footpaws.

"Help me, help!" Skalrag was screaming.

Now some of Clogg's creatures spotted the activity by the longboats. They unsheathed their weapons and dashed forward to protect their boats. Two rats went down under the hefty digging claws of Grumm and a hearty wallop from a chunk of driftwood held by Rose. Brome began shoving the smallest of the boats out into the surf, and Grumm and Rose lent their weight to his efforts. Martin was holding on to one rat who was trying to stop the boat, while he held the head of another under the water. Felldoh had a stranglehold on Skalrag, whose sword belt had snapped; both sword and belt were lost somewhere in the shallows. The corsairs came charging in, yelling, surf splashing beneath their paws.

Rose leaned over the stern of the small boat, pulling Brome in while Grumm found the oars. She began shouting. "Martin! Felldoh! Over here, quickly!"

Thinking swiftly, Martin stunned a sea rat with a heavy blow. Grabbing a half-throttled Skalrag from Felldoh, he thrust the fox at the corsairs.

"Here, mates. One of Badrang's lot, tryin' to steal our boats!"

With a concerted howl of rage the corsairs threw themselves upon Skalrag and another rat Felldoh pushed towards them.

Martin nudged his friend, whispering urgently. "Quick, into the boat!"

Half wading, half swimming through the night-dark waters, they made for the boat. Grumm and Brome held oars over the stern to them.

"Burr, 'asten, zurrs!"

As they grabbed the oars and began climbing aboard, the corsairs suddenly realized what was going on.

"Those ain't searats. Stop 'em!" the ferret called Boggs yelled hoarsely.

Martin scrambled into the boat, but Felldoh was having a hard time with his huge bushy tail weighed down by sea water. The rat called Growch floundered forward and seized the squirrel's footpaws. From the boat Martin managed to grab Felldoh by his other two paws, then another searat latched on to Felldoh's tail and a tug of war began. Felldoh was stretched between water and boat, helpless, his mouth filled with salt water.

Rose leaned over the stern, wielding an oar.

Thonk! Boff!

She stunned the rats with two direct hits. Martin heaved mightily and Felldoh came tumbling into the boat.

While some of the corsairs held Skalrag and his platoon prisoner, the rest jumped into the boats and began rowing after the escapers.

"Row!" Martin cried out to his friends. "Paddle with your paws! Anything! Hurry. They're coming after us!"

Grumm sat in the stern, not moving. Rose looked at him curiously.

"Come on, Grumm. Paddle, don't just sit there."

The mole shrugged unhappily. "Oi carn't move, mizzy. Iffen oi do, us'll sink. Oi be setten roight on a gurt 'ole in 'ee boat!"

The mole sat, completely soaked, blocking the hole as best he could, with water swilling around the bottom of the boat.

Brome started to laugh. Felldoh eyed him disapprovingly.

"I can't see much to laugh about, young un. It's not a very funny situation we're in."

Brome held his sides as he tried to paddle and stop laughing at the same time. "Whooheehee! I'm sorry, Felldoh, can't help it, heeheehee! Oh dearie me! Look at those creatures, hahahahahaha!"

The two boats loaded with corsairs that were following were only going one way. Down!

Rose joined in with Brome's laughter. "Of course, that's what Badrang's creatures were doing, holing the boats after they'd set fire to the big ship. Lucky old us, we picked the one with the smallest hole in it!"

The corsairs' faces were a picture of abject misery as they baled furiously, while the boats filled up and sank beneath them. They floated about, treading water and watching the small craft, low in the water but going strong, head straight out to sea. A joyous shout rang out across the choppy night waves as the little boat pulled away.

"Freeeeeeeeeeeeeee!"

9

Dawn brought with it a lull in the battle at Fortress Marshank. The weather was humid, and a heavy grey sky hung like a pall with greenish purple tinges out on the horizon. Badrang stood with Gurrad on the walltop, his battle-weary horde ranged along the ramparts, dull-eyed as they ate breakfast and catnapped at their positions. The Tyrant stoat noted with grim satisfaction that he had successfully defended Marshank against the corsair invasion. But Clogg was a resourceful enemy. What would his next move be?

Oily-looking plumes of smoke rose into the still air from the cooking fires of the corsairs on the shore. The pirates were in surly mood. Not only had they failed to breach the gates of the fortress, but they had also suffered the indignity of having their ship gutted by fire and sunk. Cap'n Tramun Clogg and several of his messmates were holding an interrogation session behind a semicircular rocky outcrop close to the tideline.

The unfortunate Skalrag and six of his remaining archers were the prisoners they were questioning. They huddled together on the beach, cruelly bound paw and muzzle with tough dried kelp strands. Skalrag stifled a terrified whimper as he stared wide-eyed at the ruthless faces of the searats and the vicious twinkle in the eyes of Clogg. The pirate stoat drew his cutlass, grinning evilly as he licked the blade and squinted along it towards the quaking fox.

"Harr, tell me, Skalrag, what would you do to anybeast who set fire to yore ship an' scuttled 'er?"

Skalrag's muzzle was tightly bound. The most he could manage was a strangled sob. Clogg swung the cutlass at the petrified fox's head. It clipped several whiskers and neatly severed the gag. Skalrag fainted clean away in a heap. The corsairs laughed uproariously as they doused him with sea water to bring him round.

Tramun Clogg put the point of his cutlass to Skalrag's nosetip. "I wouldn't chop yer 'ead off, bucko. Ho no, that'd be too quick fer the likes o' you. Avast, mates. Tell this scum wot we do t' ship burners an' scuttlers."

The corsairs tickled Skalrag with their knifepoints as they told him.

"String 'im upside down in a crab pool!"

"Roast 'im o'er a slow fire!"

"Chop off 'is paws an' make 'im eat 'em!"

"Use 'im fer a batterin' ram agin the fortress gates!"

"Oh no, please, Cap'n," Skalrag wailed in despair. "Don't let them do it. I was only carrying out Badrang's orders!"

Clogg sat by the fox and stroked his head soothingly. "There there now, matey. Dry yore eyes an' don't blubber no more. Ole Tramun Clogg's got an 'eart soft as swansdown. I won't let nobeast kill yer. But 'earken now, y' must swear on yer oath that you'll do exactly as I tell yer."

Skalrag nodded vigorously. "I will, Cap'n, I will. I swear on my oath as a fox!"

Tramun chuckled as he patted the fox's cheek tenderly. "Of course yer will, matey, cos if yer don't, the things my crew threatened to do to yer would be as nothin' to wot I'd do when I caught up with ye. Lissen now, 'ere's wot you'll do . . ."

"What about them?" Skalrag nodded towards his six bound comrades.

Tramun winked broadly. "Oh don't fret yore 'eart over that lot. Worms like that'd be too much trouble as galley slaves. They'll be fishbait afore nightfall, mate."

Skalrag's former archers gave a muted moan of anguish.

The slave compound was a circular palisade of upright logs driven into the ground and bound together by ropes. It had a single gate, which was generally kept locked. Inside, the occupants shifted as best as they could for themselves. Most slept on their sack mattresses against the walls, some underneath a rough wooden awning that shaded part of the structure. At night the slaves were allowed a fire in the center of the dirt floor.

Keyla and the rest of the slaves had been on barricade duty all night, piling rubble and rocks against the gates to reinforce them against the battering ram. Now they sat locked inside the slave compound, relieved of quarry and field labors while Marshank was under siege.

Old Barkjon shook his head. "It's a bad business. If Badrang wins, we'll still be slaves here. However, if the victory goes to the corsairs, we'll all end up as galley slaves after we've been forced to refloat their vessel or build a new ship. Slavery is bad enough, but the life of a galley slave is worse than death."

Amid the troubled muttering that followed, Keyla came forward.

"That's the bad news, now here's some of the good. Before we were herded back in here at dawn, I checked the prison pit. There was nobeast inside. Martin, Felldoh and Brome have escaped—they're free!"

Barkjon's chin quivered a little as he patted Keyla's paw. "That is good news indeed. My son Felldoh a free creature! He'll bring help to us, you'll see!"

"Aye and Martin too," Hillgorse the old hedgehog

chimed in. "He's a tough one, that young mouse. He'll see that we get help of some sort!"

The slaves nodded agreement, one or two of them even emitting low cheers. Barkjon silenced them with a wave of his paw.

"Keyla, was there something else you wanted to say?"

The young otter held a piece of sacking. It clinked as he strode about speaking in a low clear voice.

"All very good, but what are we doing to help ourselves? It's no use just sitting here on our tails making fine speeches and waiting for others to do something. Look!"

He flung the sacking open and weapons clattered to the ground. "Three knives, a spearhead and four slings. I collected them from dead vermin while we were working through the battle last night. There's a start to our armory."

Purslane, a mother mouse, stepped forward carrying her infant. She took an axehead and a broken swordblade from inside the little one's shawl and added them to Keyla's weapons.

"I managed to get these. It's not much but it's a start."

Others started to come forward and add their contributions.

"This dagger's got no handle, but it's sharp."

"Here's the top from a long pike. It only needs a pole."

"I got a whip and these two arrows. The bow was too big to carry."

"Pouchful of slingstones, a sling and this iron hook."

A hedgehog, little more than a baby, tottered out and threw his offering on the small pile of armaments. "Dagga an' stones to fro'!"

The otter called Tullgrew began gathering them up. "Well done. We'd best hide these until the right time comes along. I'll bury them in the earth underneath my pallet."

Hillgorse nodded approvingly. "Good work. Remember now, stick together, help each other, steal anything

78

you can from Badrang's creatures. Each day, my friends, we will become stronger, more determined. Only our bodies are held in slavery. Our minds and hearts are free."

The meeting ended, Tullgrew began burying the weapons. Druwp the bankvole pretended to be sleeping, but he was noting through half-closed eyes the spot where Tullgrew was digging.

Slavebeasts snuffled and moaned in their slumbers. The fire burned low in the crowded compound, and stars in the soft dark sky looked down on the misery of the wretched creatures below as they slept, all save two.

Keyla was still watching Druwp!

Dawn light found the small boat had been carried far out by the ebbing tide. It bobbed about on the heaving grey waves like a leaf in a storm. Felldoh, Martin and Brome baled with paws and oarblades, trying to splash the water over the sides. They were fighting a losing battle. Rose stood in the stern, straining her eyes for a sight of land. All she could see were mountainous grey-green waves wherever she looked. Grumm sat miserably, blocking the leak with his bottom, baling with his little ladle as the boat settled ever lower in the water.

"Burr, oi can't swim. Et be a shame t' finish up drownded."

Something struck the side of the boat, causing the timbers to creak. Brome looked up from his baling.

"I hope that was a rock or something floating by. I'd hate to think it was a big fish!"

Rose peered down into the water. Her eyes went wide with shock. She looked up, pretending to scan the horizon.

Her brother shook his head. "C'mon, Rosie, you can't fool me. I saw you gaping into the water. What's down there?

"It's a big fish!" Rose's voice was little more than a whisper.

They stopped baling. Felldoh chuckled halfheartedly, "Big enough for us to catch and eat?"

Rose shook her head. "The other way round, friend. It's big enough to catch and eat us!"

There was another thump against the boat's side. Grumm sat tight, staring uncomfortably at the sky.

"Burr, oi 'ates t' think o'moi pore bottom a-poken through 'ee bowt wi' a gurt fisher swimmen under oi."

The fish struck again!

This time it fractured the planking, and sea water squirted in as the boat settled lower.

Martin grabbed an oar. "This will make a good float, Felldoh. You and Brome hang on to that other oar. I'll take this one with Rose and Grumm. If we get separated, we'll meet up at Noonvale. Look out, here we go!"

The boat filled up, sea water rushing in over the sides as it dropped from beneath them, plummeting into the depths below. In an instant they were all in the sea, struggling and kicking out as they held on to the oars. Submerging his head, Martin gazed down into the depths. He could dimly make out the gigantic shape of some deep-sea fish as it chased the sinking craft into the greeny depths. As he pulled his head from the waters, Rose was shouting. "Brome, Felldoh, over here. Can you reach us?"

The young mouse and the squirrel were being swept away on the crest of a big roller, while Martin's oar was being pushed under, weighted as it was by three creatures. Instantly, Martin released his hold on the oar. It bobbed up and began travelling away from him on the waves, and he struck out after it. Rose paddled madly, turning the oar so it would drift nearer to Martin.

Grumm helped as much as he could, calling out, "Marthen, swim o'er 'ere. See iffen you'm can catch a hold o' moi paw!"

Painfully Martin came fractionally nearer his friends on the oar. Rose kicked back with all her might to hold the oar from being swept off, and Grumm stretched himself full length in the water.

The sun began breaking through the windswept grey cloud masses, bringing with it a heavy summer rain slashing and hammering on to the face of the deeps. Half blinded and spitting sea water, Martin felt his outstretched paw come in contact with Grumm's footpaw. He clung on furiously for dear life as Rose cried out, "Hang there, Martin. Just tread water. It'll relieve the weight on this paddle. When I'm tired I'll change places with you."

Rose kicked out with the waves, sending the oar skimming along through the rain-washed sea.

Felldoh had his mouth open to the sky, trying to drink in some rainwater. Brome had heaved himself up on the oar. Anxiously he scanned the sunny stormswept wastes.

"There's no sign of 'em. The waves are too high!"

Before Felldoh had a chance to reply, the water beneath them heaved and they were both lifted high into the air. The big fish had hauled the sinking boat around like an empty peapod. It had found something to play with! Its huge body buffeted and banged the boat about.

Felldoh was still holding on to the oar as the fish temporarily lost interest in the boat and charged at the oar. The squirrel saw the wide mouth gaping through the water. Rows of pointed white teeth and a cavernous pink interior whooshed through the sea towards him. Felldoh let go of the oar and submerged. He felt a thump on his back as the giant creature seized the oar and made off with it, frolicking and leaping, sometimes half its own length above the surface. Suddenly it dived and was gone.

The hull of the upturned boat struck his head as Brome leaned over and seized his ears. "Gotcha, matey!"

Scrambling and kicking, Felldoh managed to haul

himself on to the upturned keel, where Brome was clinging with all paws.

"Whew! That was a close call. Still, fair exchange is
no robbery. The fish can have the oar, we'll keep the
boat."

Felldoh wiped dashing rain from his eyes. "Let's hope
that monster doesn't feel playful again and come back
for the boat after he's chewed our oar up. Hang on to
my tail and steady me, young un. I'm going to take a
look around for the others."

With Brome clinging to his tail, Felldoh stood gingerly
and surveyed the stormy scene. Sunlight shafted down
through the cloud masses, which were showing areas of
bright blue sky between them. The wind whipped the
wavetops into white foam, sending massive rollers
combing across the main.

"Any sign of 'em?"

Felldoh shaded his eyes from the rain with a paw.

"Not a glimpse, but there's a dark splotch on the
horizon that must mean land. It must be floodtide—
we're headed straight for it."

Brome was not sure whether it was rain or tears in
his eyes. "Thank the seasons for that! I wouldn't become
a seafarer at any price. Leave the water to the fishes, I
say."

The morning wore on, but the rain showed no signs
of abating.

Grumm clung to the oar, half asleep, with Rose hanging
on to his footpaw. Martin paddled doggedly on, pushing
the oar in front of him, his body numbed from the cold
of the sea and the driving rain. The sun was now coloring the sea in glorious tints. Rose stared at it through
salt-rimmed eyes, lost in its beauty for a moment until
Martin's voice cut into her reverie.

"The sun sets in the west, doesn't it?"

Rose nodded. "Hmm, suppose it does."

Martin's voice became suddenly hoarse with excitement. "This is the Eastern sea. If it were morning the sun would rise on its horizon. Don't you see what that means, Rose?"

"I'm too tired to work it out, Martin. Tell me what it means."

"It means that we have to face inland to see the sun in the afternoon. So if we can see the sun in front of us now, we are travelling towards land!"

Rose came fully awake, hauling herself up on Grumm's back she gave a loud yell.

"Land!"

It was still distant, but it was definitely land. Dark cliffs showed against the sky. She patted her mole friend's wet back heartily.

"Land, Grumm! It's land ahead!"

"Oi woant berleev et until these yurr diggen claws c'n scrape it, mizzy, an' then iffen et be so, thiz yurr beast woant never even be caught drinken water agin, never moind a-swimmen in et."

Martin found renewed strength and kicked out harder towards firm ground.

10

Hisk the weasel Captain watched the bankvole rummaging about near Badrang's longhouse. Sneaking silently up, he pressed a dagger against the unsuspecting creature's back.

"Be very still or you're a deadbeast!"

Druwp did not move, nor did he show any surprise. "My name is Druwp. Kill me and you'll answer to Skalrag. I'm his spy."

Hisk moved the dagger point up to Druwp's neck. "You're lying. I think I'll kill you anyway."

"Do as you please, Captain," Druwp shrugged. "But I have valuable information."

"Like what, for instance?" Hisk curled his lip contemptuously.

"Like the three prisoners in your pit, for instance. They're not there any more. They've escaped."

Hisk spun Druwp around to face him. "You're lying. Nobeast could escape the prison pit!"

Druwp let a sly smile cross his lips. "Then go and see for yourself. If I'm lying, you can always kill me later. I'm not going anywhere."

Hisk grabbed Druwp by the neckfur and held the knife to his throat. "Then I'll go and see for myself. If you're lying, I'll come back and kill you. Skalrag won't save you—or didn't you know, he's been missing since last night."

Badrang was on the walltop when Hisk sidled up and whispered in the Tyrant's ear, "The three beasts we had in the prison pit are gone."

Badrang narrowed his eyes. "Gone? What d'you mean? They've died or been killed?"

"No, Sire, they've escaped."

"Rubbish, nobeast escapes my prison pit."

"That's what I thought, Sire, but they're gone sure enough. I went down and checked myself. The strange thing is that there's no sign of escape. The grating was locked tight and the pit was secure."

"How did you find out they were gone?"

"A bankvole slave, name of Druwp, told me. Said he was Skalrag's spy."

Badrang toyed with a lethal-looking dagger, tapping it against his teeth. "Hmm, he may be useful to us. Have him brought to my longhouse tomorrow. Make sure none of the other slaves know."

A cry rang up from the shore. "Badrang, ole messmate! Sing out, 'ave you 'ad enough?"

"Is that you, Clogg, me 'earty?" The Tyrant smiled thinly as he slipped back into the old corsair language. "I'm the one should be askin' you that question. I've burned yer ship, stoved in yer boats an' left you with nought but the sea behind yer and me wid me fortress an' me horde in front of yer. What d'ye say t' that?"

Cap'n Clogg's irrepressible laughter rang out of the darkness. "Haharr harr! But yer a few beasts short. My bullies slew a good number o' yours, an' I've got yer ole messmate Skalrag, trussed up like a fowl ready fer the pot. Oh, and some of yer darlin' liddle slaves 'ave escaped. Did ye know that?"

Badrang tapped the dagger against his teeth before he replied. "Out wid it, Tramun. Wot d'ye want?"

"A truce an' a parley wid me ole one-time shipmate."

"Oho, there's a change of tune for yer. Why should I parley wid the likes of you, yer great plaited seaswab?"

"Cos iffen yer don't, I'll lay long siege to yer great palace. It don't cost nothin' to camp right 'ere on yer doorstep an' fish yer waters, an' plunder yer fields. Me an' my buckoes ain't goin' noplace. I could keep a war goin' until yore dim in the eye, long in the seasons an' white in the beard. Then you won't get no fancy empire built, an' sooner or later yer horde'll starve. So be a good cove an' parley wid me."

Badrang considered the offer for a moment. "Give me until mornin' to think about it, Tramun. Meanwhiles, 'ow about you returnin' Skalrag as a sign o' good faith?"

"Haharrharrharr! You allus was a canny one, matey. So be it, then. Open yer gates an' we'll let the fox go."

Now it was Badrang's turn to chuckle. "The gates stays shut an' locked. You ain't goin' to get 'em open with a batterin' ram or a fox. I'll 'ave some o' my beasts let down a basket on a rope, and we'll hoist Skalrag in wid that."

"Hoho, ain't you the suspicious one, an' me comin' 'ere in all good faith. Righto mate, we'll play yer liddle game. Boggs, Growch! Loose the fox an' point 'im 'ome-wards. Good night to ye, Badrang, an' may the sunny seasons hover round yer bunk."

Badrang sheathed his dagger. "An' good night to you, Tramun. May the gentle breezes allus fill yer sails wid the scent of southern roses."

An hour later, Badrang had Skalrag on the torture rack extracting information from him.

Brome and Felldoh got on all fours and kissed the damp sands several times. It was sweet to be on land, whether damp or dry.

The squirrel took stock of their position. "I know exactly where we are, Brome. You see all this charcoal on the tideline?"

Brome's paws crunched on the stuff as he bent in the darkness and picked up a piece.

"Hmm, it's burnt wood, half waterlogged. Wonder where it's from?"

Felldoh pointed out into the bay. "Right there, mate, where the corsair ship burned and sank. Over yon hills lies Fortress Marshank, so we'd best go quietly."

Brome grasped Felldoh's paw firmly. "Where you go I go, mate. By the way, where are we going?"

"To Noonvale, eventually. But first we must look for our friends. We'll find somewhere to hide up for a bit and dry out. Then we'll see if we can lay our paws on some food. We can't do a thing until it's light, except rest and eat."

They walked south across the beach, towards the cliffs. Brome chattered incessantly.

"Rest and eat, that sounds like a good idea. I'll bet an acorn to an eggshell that's exactly what Rose and Martin are doing right now, lying back and feeding their faces. Grumm'll be doing the cooking. Next to my mama, he's the best cook in Noonvale, once he starts stirring stew or soup with that little ladle he always carries. Mmmm! It smells so good. Why, I'll even bet that he's found so —"

"Hush, Brome. What's that sound?"

The squirrel had clamped a swift paw across his garrulous young friend's mouth. Both creatures stood stock still, listening. The sound carried on the night breeze. Instruments were playing and somebeast was singing. Brome pointed to a faint glow emanating from a crevice in the cliff face. When they were closer, the friends both bellied down and crawled the rest of the way cautiously.

It was a type of lean-to tent, erected between a two-wheeled wagon and some rocks. A fire glimmered, throwing the creatures inside into grotesque silhouetted shadows against the canvas. Brome and Felldoh lay in the darkness listening to the song.

"Oh, we're the Rambling Rosehip Players,
And we please both old and young.
O'er field serene and forest green
Our praises have been sung.
We're the Rambling Rosehip Players,
And we'll take on any part,
Bring a tear to your eye to make you cry
Or joy to the saddest heart.
Though the road be tough and the patch run rough
And weather be cold or grey,
With a smile and a song we'll travel along
On our Rambling Rosehip way. Hey!"

A heavy voice boomed out as the song finished "No, no! Ballaw, you're supposed to catch Celandine as the last line is sung. You did it far too early and she wasn't there to take the fan from Gauchee. It's not good enough. Let's try it again from the beginning. One, two, Ooooh, we're the Ram ... Ballaw! Will you stop eating that pastie and take up your position. Here, give me that confounded thing. You've had quite enough!"

A half-eaten mushroom pastie was flung from the lean-to and struck Felldoh squarely between his ears. The pastie was followed by a hare, who dived on it, jumping on Felldoh's head in the process.

"Bad form that, chuckin' a chap's supper about, Rowan. Hey there! There's a bally squirrel here, tryin' to use me pastie as a hat!"

Confusion followed. Brome leaped on the hare, trying to wrest him off Felldoh. The squirrel was hanging gamely on to the hare's whiskers, trying to avoid the long flailing legs. Mice, a mole and two squirrels came pouring out of the lean-to, tripping and falling into the confusion of paws, legs, ears and tails. Pandemonium reigned as the jumble of creatures squeaked, grunted and howled. Felldoh was a seasoned fighter. Scrambling from under the others, he climbed to the top of the heap, about to set his teeth into the tail of whoever was headlocking Brome.

"Here, what's all this about? Come out of it this instant!" Felldoh was swung aloft by a massive paw to find himself staring into the stern dark eyes of a big old female badger. She growled fiercely at him.

"Clamp those lips and put those teeth out of sight, otherwise I'll do a bit of biting—and I've got bigger teeth than you!"

With her other paw, the badger cuffed out, sending creatures rolling this way and that. Catching sight of Brome, she hoisted him high off the ground in her other paw and shook him.

"Behave yourself, you little wretch! What's your names, both of you, and what're you doing hanging around our camp?"

Felldoh reached between his ears. Disentangling a bit of pastie, he tasted it and nodded approvingly. "Hmm, mushroom pastie. Wait, don't tell me, it's been fried with spring onion gravy. Very nice!"

The hare picked up the remains of the pastie from the ground. Wiping it off, he ate it, speaking through mouthfuls.

"If y' wanted some of our tucker, old lad, you should knock on the wagon an' ask politely, wot? 'Stead of sneakin' round."

Brome waggled his paws indignantly from his position in the air. "We weren't sneaking around, we saw your firelight and heard you singing so we came over to investigate. Oh, by the way, I'm Brome, only son of Urran Voh, and this is Felldoh, late of Marshank. Hello!"

The badger set them gently down as the hare made a very elegant leg. "Pleased t' meetcher, I'm sure. Allow me to introduce us. We, sirs, are the Rambling Rosehip Players. I am Ballaw De Quincewold, actor and tragedian. My large friend here is Rowanoak. She is our cart puller, props mistress and principal baritoness. The two young squirrelmaids there are Trefoil and Celandine, soubrettes, sopranos and acrobats. The mole Buckler is our juvenile lead, comedian and catcher. The two mousemaids, Gauchee and Kastern, are balancers, chorus and general company cooks. There you have it, m' friends. Er, would you like supper?"

Brome pulled at his slack belt. "Indeed we would, sir. My backbone was just talking to my stomach about food. They tend to stick together when I'm hungry."

The hare nodded admiringly, his floppy ears waving to and fro. "Well said, young feller. A creature of infinite jest, wot?"

Inside the lean-to it was snug and warm after the stiff night breeze on the shore. The Rambling Rosehip company were kindness itself to Felldoh and Brome. They were given cloths to dry off their sea-damped fur as they sat round the fire sipping carrot and celery broth from scallop shells. Rowanoak brought out two tunics similar to the ones the rest of the Rosehips wore, quartered gold and crimson with a green border and black tie belt.

"Here, you'd best put these on, though I'll have to let yours out a touch when I have time, Felldoh. You're quite a sturdy sort for a squirrel."

Celandine stroked Felldoh's strong bushy tail. "Hmm, I'll say you are!"

Felldoh coughed nervously and accepted a hot mushroom pastie from Buckler. The friendly mole passed Brome a sizeable wedge of pie.

"Yurr, maister. 'Unny an' blackb'rry. Speck you loik summat sweet."

The young mouse took a bite and rolled his eyes. "Mmm, do I ever. Sweet things are good for the voice, you know."

Gauchee was nibbling an apple and a carrot together. "Are they? I never knew that. I only eat apple 'n' carrot myself. Do you sing much, Brome?"

Without warning, Brome let forth a swift yodel with

his piercing tenor voice. "Tralalalalalalarrr! Do I indeed! Try and stop me, Gauchee."

Ballaw picked up a small harecordion and tuned it. "Good f' you, young feller. D'you know the Bobble O riddle song?"

Brome winked. "You play it and I'll sing it."

Ballaw played the introduction and Brome began singing, with Rowanoak providing a fine baritone harmony line. It was so catchy that the entire company, even Felldoh, clapped their paws in time with the lively melody.

"Bobble O Bobble O Bobble O,
If you know, tell me where I do grow.
High above the lowly earth,
And yet I flourish for all I'm worth.
Bobble O Bobble O Bobble O,
Tell me now if you think you know.
I hang between the earth and sky,
Green or brown as the seasons pass by
As around me all the birds do fly,
and just before winter away go I.
Bobble O Bobble O Bobble O-ohhhh
Tell me true, I'd like you to try!"

There was long applause and Brome had his back patted so heartily it began to ache.

"Excellent, top hole, young un!"

"You'm gorra foin voice, zurr Broom!"

"Oh, it was the best I've ever heard. You never missed a beat!"

"Well done. I wish we had a tenor who could sing half as good!"

Felldoh scratched his head. "What was it?"

Brome took a bite of his pie. "What was what?"

"The thing in the riddle song, green, brown, growing in the sky and then flying away before winter with the birds. What was it?"

Ballaw nodded towards Brome. "That's for the singer to tell, old lad."

Brome winked at Felldoh. "What else could it be but a leaf?"

Rowanoak sat down between the two friends. "Now, tell me about yourselves. Where are you from and how did you come to this place?"

Outside, the wind whistled across the bleak Northeast Sea. The rain had stopped and a quarter-moon showed between the scudding night cloud formations, throwing down a moving pattern of dark and silver across the shore. Snug in the crevice of the lowering cliffs the company crouched in their makeshift tent. Inside the lean-to, Felldoh and Brome sat around the fire, eating and drinking as they related their story to the new-found friends they had made, the Rambling Rosehip Players.

11

When the rain stopped, Martin felt his footpaws touching solid ground beneath the water. He stood upright with the sea lapping his neck, shaking Rose and Grumm, who had both fallen asleep.

"Land. We've made it. Help me push this oar ashore."

Hardly feeling the wood of the paddle, their bodies numbed from constant immersion in cold sea water, the three friends crawled out onto a sandy beach situated at the foot of high dark cliff formations. They sat on the sand, shivering and hungry, their teeth chattering and paws trembling uncontrollably.

Through salt-bleared eyes Grumm peered up at the cliffs. "Wunner wot be up thurr?"

Martin rose stiffly, massaging his limbs. "Some small cave where we can shelter for the night, I hope. Do you two want to rest here while I take a look?"

Rose and Grumm staggered on to their paws.

"I don't like it here. Grumm and I will go with you."

"Burr aye, 'tis creepy rounden yurr!"

The rocks were dark and slippery from the rain. Martin went in front, with Rose bringing up the rear. They kept Grumm in the middle as he was not a very good climber. Moles seldom are. Holding the paddle between them, they strove upwards, scrabbling and sometimes sliding back in the darkness. After what seemed an eternity of grappling with the wet cliff face, they rested on a narrow ledge. The three friends sat catching their second wind, listening to the tide far below as it surged and hissed along the night-cloaked shore.

Martin peered upwards. "I think if we climb a little further there is a much broader ledge above us. There's bound to be some sort of cave or crevice where we can shelter."

"Carn't oi stay yurr," Grumm sighed wearily. "Moi pesky ole paws be gone a-sleeping on oi."

Rose rubbed her molefriend's paws vigorously. "Poor Grumm. Champion diggers can't be champion climbers too. Not far to go now and you can have a good sleep. I'll get breakfast tomorrow so you can have a little extra lie-in."

This offer perked Grumm up no end. "Burr. Thankee koindly, Miz Roser. You'm a guddbeast!"

Martin gave an involuntary shiver. "There's something about this place I don't like. Still, this is where we landed up, and beggars can't be choosers. Come on."

All three had their paws on the rim of the ledge after a short hard climb when the nets came hurling down and enveloped them. Tough, close-woven meshes of kelp, weighted down all around with stones. The friends were swept from the rock face and held dangling, their paws, tails and heads entangled in the snaring nets. Tiny dark shapes, masses of them, jibbered and pranced on the broad ledge as they hauled their catch swiftly upwards. It was over in a flash. Martin, Rose and Grumm were landed like fishes and swiftly clubbed into unconsciousness.

Swimming up through dark mists, Martin's head lanced with pain as he opened his eyes, in bright sunlight. A stick prodded him sharply in the back.

"Biggamouse wake up! Muggamug! Plennygood catchim!"

The young mouse opened his eyes fully and saw he was boxed inside a stout wooden cage. Tiny mouselike creatures with long wiggling snouts surrounded the cage. They danced up and down with excitement. One more venturesome than the rest darted forward and jabbed Martin's paw with a sharpened stick.

"Gotcha gotcha, Biggamouse! Higgig! Notso big-ganow!"

The young mouse reacted speedily. With a swipe he snapped the stick, baring his teeth savagely as he gripped the wooden bars.

"Gerroutofit, you jibbering little idiots, and leave me alone!"

He shouted so loudly that the tiny creatures scattered like chaff before the wind, clapping paws over their ears.

Martin glared through the cage at them, growling fiercely, "Keep your distance, or I'll eat you all!"

He clashed his teeth several times, sending fresh pain waves through his throbbing head. Rubbing a sizeable bump on the back of his skull, Martin looked around and took stock of his position.

His cage was in the entrance to a large cave. On the opposite wall he could see two other wooden cages, in which the senseless forms of Rose and Grumm lay. More of the tiny creatures passed, giving him a wide berth. They were carrying several fish which had been lashed to driftwood poles—smelts, shannies and butterfish they had brought up from the shore.

Behind them, carrying nets and fishing gear, came a hedgehog. His footpaws had been bound to a heavy log that he was forced to tow in his wake. Martin shook the cage bars, calling to him.

"Hey! What is this place and who are all these little wretches?"

The hedgehog gave Martin a quick smile and a friendly wink. "I'm Pallum. Be still. I'll get back to you."

He was urged on by more little creatures following up the rear.

"Urryurry, pinpiggy. Mouthashut!"

As they passed into the recesses of the cave, Grumm stirred. "Burr oo! Moi pore ole 'ead, et be bumpen an' a-bangen orfully."

The sound of the mole's voice seemed to waken Rose. Immediately she was up on her paws, and despite her aching head she battered and tugged at the bars of her cage.

"Let me out of here this instant, d'you hear. Let me out!"

Grumm held paws over his ears. "Hurr, doant ee make such a gurt noise, mizzy. You'm 'urtin' moi brains."

Martin was relieved his friend had suffered no permanent damage. "Grumm's right, Rose. Best lie still. How do you feel?"

The mousemaid managed a wan smile. "Apart from being caged up with an ache in my head and a bump like a thrush's egg, plus a raging thirst and an empty stomach, I feel fine. How are you this morning?"

Martin grinned wryly. "Actually, I feel pretty silly. Wait until you see the beasts who did this to us."

As if on cue, several of the tiny creatures materialized out of the dimness at the rear of the cave.

Grumm nodded. "Pigmy shrews. Oi moight 'ave knowed!"

"Pigmy shrews?" Martin echoed the name questioningly.

The hedgehog came lumbering up to them, surrounded by pigmy shrews. They chattered ceaselessly in their odd dialect, some of them sitting impudently on the hedgehog's towing log, their ride adding to the burden he dragged along. It did not seem to bother him unduly. He smiled in a foolish, disarming way.

"Hello there. It's me, Pallum. Listen, never look angry in front of pigmy shrews. Smile all the time. It confuses them."

Martin pasted a large grin on his face as he introduced himself and his friends. The shrews were never still, hopping, jumping, dancing and gabbling on in an unintelligible manner. The one who had jabbed Martin with a stick began to do it once more. The young mouse dodged this way and that to avoid the sharp wood, grinning furiously as he spoke from between clenched teeth.

"Pallum, let me tell you something, friend. In a moment I'm going to grab that stick and stuff it up that little wretch's long squiggly excuse for a nose!"

Pallum shook his head smilingly. "It'd be the worst day's work you ever did, Martin. These are babies—squidjees is their proper title. The tiny scum poking you with the stick is the worst brat of all. That's Dinjer, one and only son and heir to Amballa, Queen of the pigmy shrews. She'd have you killed for sure if you laid paw on her little darling. Wait a moment, I think I can stop him."

Turning to the offender, Pallum addressed him in pigmy shrew language. "Higgig, Dinjer, goodagood, you pokeymore biggamouse!"

Dinjer stopped instantly and began trying vainly to belabor Pallum's spiky hide with the stick.

"Pinpiggy shuttamouth! Notell Dinjer whattadoo!"

Pallum chuckled as the infant flailed unsuccessfully at his spikes. "Contrary little snips. Best way to stop 'em is to encourage them. They'll always do the opposite to what you want, specially this one."

Rose wiped a paw across her parched lips. "Pallum, is there any chance of us getting some food and water?"

A tiny drum sounded from within the cave. Pallum held up a paw. "That'll be the Queen, Amballa. When you speak to her, bow your head and call her Ballamum. Be very respectful. She's vindictive and all powerful round here. Don't mention the word higgig—that means you are laughing, and she might think you were laughing at her. Please do as I say and leave the rest to me."

97

Amballa was a plump little figure. She wore golden pantaloons and a cloak of light blue. On her head was a coronet studded with bright shell pieces and small polished beach pebbles. A seagull feather stuck up at the back of it. Had she not been such an important personage the three friends would have burst out laughing at the comical sight she made.

Drawing herself up to the peak of her minuscule height, she pointed a tiny sword at Martin.

"Biggamouse, you! What namesay?"

"O Ballamum, I am Martin." The young mouse bowed his head, speaking respectfully. "That other mouse is called Rose and the mole is Grumm. We mean no harm to you or your tribe of pigmy shrews."

Amballa leaped forward in a rage, jabbing through the bars with her sword so that Martin was forced to jump backwards.

"Biggamouse biggamouth! What shrew pigmy? No shrew pigmy here 'bout!"

Pallum towed his log forward, interceding on Martin's behalf. "Mightygreat Ballamum, sillymouse knownot tribename Highbeast, still sleepymuddle from banga-bang on headplace."

Martin caught on to Pallum's message and rubbed his head, muttering. "Phwaw! Sleepymuddle, sleepy-muddle!"

Amballa squinted suspiciously for a moment before she appeared satisfied, then she broke into laughter.

"Higgig higgigig! Highbeast givvayou plenty banga-bang, yougo sleepasleep suddenquick. Higgig higgigig!"

Martin nodded ruefully. "Highbeast mighty warriors, bangabang plentyhurt."

Pallum winked approvingly at Martin before tackling Amballa on behalf of her captives.

"O Ballamum, nogive these sillybeasts mouthfood or gluggadrink. Theynot get obblewood an' caretake Squid-jees. Ballamum killemdead!"

The Queen made as if to kick Pallum, but did not

because of his spikes. She drew herself up and proclaimed regally, "Ballamum saythis! Nofeed lazymouths, workaneat. Bring obblewoods. Sillybeasts makegood Squidjeenurses. Higgig higgigig!"

The pigmy shrew tribe laughed with her as they jigged and cavorted about the cave.

Pallum looked astonished at the Queen. "Great Ballamum, wisest Highbeast, howyou thinkathis?"

Amballa curled her lip disdainfully.

"Thatcos menot pinpiggy, me Ballamum ofall Highbeast!"

Later that afternoon the three friends sat eating nutstudded shrewbread and drinking dandelion cordial. Like Pallum, their footpaws had been skilfully bound to hefty logs which they had to drag round as they walked. Martin kicked at his.

"Obblewood, a wooden hobble, not only that but we've got to play nursemaid to those tiny Squidjee hooligans. I think I would have preferred death!"

Rose giggled. "Oh come on, Martin. You love them really, especially little Dinjer."

At the mention of the villainous infant, Martin clenched his paws. "Oh yes, I love him so much I could hug him, right around his foul little neck, tighter and tighter!"

Grumm finished his meal hurriedly. "Look owt, yurr cooms 'ee little vurmin an' 'is crew."

Headed by Dinjer, a crowd of Squidjees descended on the captives. They spilled the cordial and thrust aside the shrewbread.

Dinjer prodded Martin with his stick impatiently. "Upnow, biggamouse. Wego pullaride on obblewoods!"

Martin and Grumm spent the remainder of the afternoon towing gangs of Squidjees around. The tiny beasts sat on the wooden hobbles, singing and laughing uproariously as they urged their transports on to greater speeds.

Rose had been detailed with Pallum into cleaning up the little ones' sleeping area and making beds.

Martin and his friends picked up much of the pigmy shrews' language during the course of the day. It was relatively simple when they realized that the Highbeast tribe spoke by running words together in pairs, sometimes in threes. Toward evening, Martin and Grumm supervised Squidjee suppertime. The mole wiped wild oat porridge from between his ears where a bowl had been upturned.

"Burr, they'm Squinjers serpintly be woild liddle villyuns. Iffen oi 'ad moi ladle to paw, why oi'd tan a few tails, oi tell you'm!"

The Squidjees, who could not understand a single word of mole talk, chuckled madly as they squirted strawberry cordial from their mouths at the mole.

Martin sighed, the fixed smile on his face beginning to hurt. "They've got the table manners of a wolfpack. Great seasons! Look at the way they waste food and mess it about."

Pallum and Rose appeared, smiling dutifully. "Comecome, sleepytime, Squidjeebabes. Sleepytime!"

This was the signal for a mass escape. The infant pigmy shrews fled, squealing, to hide, wanting the captives to chase them.

"Higgigig, catchus, chaseymouse!"

Pallum knew all the hiding places from long experience. As they gathered the little ones up for bed, Martin noticed Amballa and several of the other pigmy shrews watching them carefully lest they became roughpawed or spoke harshly to the babes. Squidjees were almost revered in the Highbeast tribe.

The tiny beasts ran wild over the newly made beds, flinging the covers about and trampling pillows.

"What do we have to do to make these rogues sleep, Pallum?" Martin groaned.

"Singasong."

Instantly the Squidjees flung themselves flat on their

beds, straightening the covers about them and plumping pillows as they called out. "Singasong, wewanna singasong!"

Pallum immediately began singing.

"Go to sleep, you filthy bunch.
I'd love to lay you all out with a punch.
How'd you win a mother's heart
With a squiggly trunk like an eel's back part?
Is that awful smell the reason?
You haven't been washed all season.
So go to sleep in your scruffy beds.
May nightmares enter your beastly heads,
And when sunlight heralds the new daybreak
May you wake with tummy ache."

Strangely, the Squidjees were half asleep. Smiling and yawning they mumbled. "Verynice, verynice. Singamore."

Stifling a chuckle, Grumm took over with his deep soothing bass.

"You'm a dreadful 'orrible crew
An' oi wuddent give to you
Supper nor dinner, brekfis' nor tea,
Oi'd spank the dayloights out of 'ee.
An' oi'd make 'ee wash ten toimes each day.
'Til you'm bad manners wurr scrubbed away."

Tiny snores announced that the Squidjees were all asleep.

Rose mopped her brow with relief. "Whew! Thank the seasons the little monsters are finished for the day. Small wonder their mothers don't look after them."

Pallum pointed to some spare mattresses in the corner. "All right, you can stop smiling now and get some rest. Lie there and relax. I'll go and get some supper for us.

I think I saw a big mixed fruit pudding with cream and some new cider."

Grumm flopped down thankfully, swiftly followed by Martin and Rose. Their wooden hobbles clacked together noisily and Rose winced as she held up a paw.

"Sshh! Not so much noise. You might waken the monsters."

"Burr, oi'd throw moiself offen 'ee clifftop iffen they waked."

"From slavery to slavery in one easy pawstep, where will it end?" Martin sighed loud and long.

Rose shook his paw comfortingly. "In Noonvale someday. We won't be here all our lives with a warrior like you about, Martin. Being a nursemaid is not in your stars. I wonder what became of Brome and Felldoh. They'll have drifted in to land, no doubt. That Felldoh is a good tough squirrel. I know he'll look after my brother. I hope they're safe and well."

Martin could hardly keep his eyes open as he watched Pallum approach bearing a heavily laden tray.

"Wherever Felldoh and Brome landed up, they couldn't possibly be worse off than us. Nursemaids to those tiny rogues. Huh!"

12

An alliance had been made between Badrang the Tyrant and Cap'n Tramun Clogg. Still not trusting each other, the two villainous stoats affixed their signatures to a sprawling birch-bark parchment, Badrang writing his name in a curly flourishing script, whilst Clogg laboriously scrawled an X and a crude sketch of a wooden clog, his mark. It was witnessed by Gurrad the rat for Marshank and Boggs the ferret for the corsairs. Tramun repeated the terms as he and the Tyrant took a joint beaker of best parsley wine.

"Harr, so, as I sees it you're goin' to call off yer troops an' lend me some slaves to refurbish an' refloat my ship. Meself on the other paw, won't attack, 'arass or demand slaves from you. I'm to unnerstand that the slaves you lend me is still yores an' 'ave to be returned. Right?"

Badrang sipped his wine and nodded, tapping the parchment. "Aye, agreed, and don't forget all this. At such times as you have a seaworthy craft to sail off in, I keep half of your crew as hostages. When, or if, you return having taken more slaves, then they get divided equally between us and you get your hostages returned to give you a full crew."

Clogg stroked his plaited whiskers, narrowing one eye. "Fairly said, partner, fairly said. An' I can feed me crew from yer supplies an' billet them 'ere in yer fancy fort, though I'm never to tell other corsairs or searats as I may come across on the 'igh seas the location of this 'ere place."

Badrang nodded, refilling Clogg's beaker. "Right! But don't forget, Tramun, after the first cargo of slaves is split between us you guarantee to sell any further slaves from other voyages only to me. I'll give you the best of weapons, trade goods and supplies."

Clogg slopped wine as he threw back his head and drained the beaker, then draped a paw around Badrang's shoulders. "Haharr, just like in the good ole days, eh, matey!"

The Tyrant reciprocated by throwing his paw about Clogg's neck. "Aye, as y' say, just like in the good ole days, Tramun. But this time there'll be no underpaw dealings, traitors nor spybeasts."

"Spybeasts? I ain't never used spybeasts, matey." The pirate stoat adopted a look of injured innocence.

"There, there." Badrang patted Clogg's neck affectionately. "I know you haven't. There's nothing worse than a spybeast. Why, if I thought there was one in my fortress I'd tie him to the gates and let my archers use him for target practice. Look, just like that fox over yonder."

He turned Clogg's neck with his paw so that the corsair was looking at the inside of Marshank's main gates. The carcass of Skalrag hung there, stuck with so many arrows it was like a pincushion.

Even though he was seething inwardly, Clogg grinned from ear to ear. "Foxes was allus traitors. I never liked that one."

Badrang tightened his grip on Clogg's neck momentarily then released him. The Tyrant matched the corsair grin for grin.

"Neither did I, matey, neither did I!"

Early morning sun bathed the shore beyond the headland, promising a high hot day. Rowanoak harnessed herself between the shafts of the Rosehips' gaily painted cart and they moved further along the shoreline, away from the close proximity of Marshank. Felldoh and Brome enjoyed the company of the Rambling Rosehip creatures greatly; they had been accepted immediately as friends and possible members.

By midmorning they had set up their camp on the clifftops, where they had an excellent view of the area without revealing their presence. The hare Ballaw De Quincewold and Rowanoak were in close conference while the rest unpacked and prepared lunch. Brome helped Gauchee and Kastern to prepare a leek and bean soup, sniggering with the two mice as they watched the pretty squirrel Celandine trying to flirt shamelessly with a much embarrassed Felldoh as he unloaded the cart, blushing to his tailtip at her simpering compliments.

"Oh Mister Felldoh, you're so strong! You lifted that trunk as if it were no more than a feather. I'll bet you must be the most powerful squirrel in the whole country!"

Felldoh was completely lost for words. He turned away from the cart and started breaking some driftwood up for the fire.

Celandine dabbed at her brow with a dainty lace square. "Oh my, oh my. I'd be all season just trying to break one teensy piece of that wood with an axe, and look at you, sir, snapping it in those great paws of yours like it was dead grass!"

Trefoil the other squirrelmaid unceremoniously bundled a pile of tunics at Celandine. "Here, missy, get your paws wet washing those through and leave that poor fellow alone before he turns into a beetroot!"

The temptress flounced off in a huff, laden with dirty washing. Trefoil began snapping wood alongside Felldoh.

"Take no notice of her, friend. I've seen her fluttering her eyelashes at dragonflies."

Buckler the mole was erecting the awning as a sunshade. "Burr aye, she'm a gurt flutterer, that un," he chuckled. "Oi losed moi 'eart to 'er long seasons agone. Hurr, but she'm a foin arctress too!"

The food was good and simple, hot soup followed by wheatflour pancakes spread with wild honey. The company lounged beneath the awning, eating and drinking cool mint and buttercup cordial from an old stone jar.

Rowanoak shook her great head.

"What in the name of trees and turnips made us ramble this far up the land, I'll never know. We had good times in the south, friendly creatures to entertain, nice places to stop awhile . . ."

Ballaw the hare made a pancake disappear with alarming speed. "True, true, but what's a chap got up here in this bally neck o' the woods? Fortresses, tyrants an' corsairs. Bit thick, isn't it, wot? About the only decent thing was meeting you two jolly lads."

The rest of the company murmured agreement.

Rowanoak stared patiently at the hare. Ballaw carried on guzzling cordial, unaware that he had interrupted her flow. "If you're quite finished, Mister De Quince-wold?" she continued.

Ballaw dispatched another pancake, daintily licking honey from his paws. "Not finished dealin' with these pancakes, Rowan me old oak, but don't let me stop you talkin'. You eat less when y' talk. Hawhaw!"

The badger eyed him frostily before continuing. "Thank you! Now what I have to say concerns our new friends Felldoh and Brome. Here is what I propose. We're up here anyway, for better or worse, so we may as well do something useful. It goes without saying that we will keep our eyes peeled for any sign of their companions, Brome's sister, Martin and the mole Grumm. But meanwhile, as Felldoh has told us, his father Barkjon is a slave in that dreadful fortress. It makes my blood boil when I think of a creature being enslaved, robbed of freedom, beaten, starved and forced to labor for some jumped-up villain. What do you think?"

There was an instant chorus of agreement with Rowanoak.

"Shame, poor old Barkjon!"

"It's a flamin' liberty, wot?"

"Yurr, nobeaster should be slave to anuther!"

"Oh, I can't imagine it, we've always been free!"

"It's disgraceful. That horrid stoat!"

Rowanoak let them carry on working up their indignation before carrying on with her speech. When they had done she continued.

"When Ballaw and I formed the Rambling Rosehip Players we took on only talented creatures we knew we could rely on. I personally have never been disappointed in any of you, that is why today we are all gather—"

"Oh, stop takin' a bally seavoyage to get round a cockleshell, old gel. We all want to rescue Felldoh's old pater, don't we?"

"Aye!" The response was loud and wholehearted.

"Good show. Then let's stop jawbangin' an' get to it, wot?"

Rowanoak passed Ballaw the pancakes and honey. She was smiling. "Thank you, Bal, you old rascal. Now we need a strategy, and you know the best way that a travelling company can scout the land?"

Buckler held up a sticky digging claw. "Yurss, marm, Us'ns goo thurr an put on 'ee show!"

"What?" Felldoh spluttered on his drink. "Now just hold fast a moment friends. It's very kind of you to offer to rescue my dear old dad. But we've an appointment with Martin in Noonvale. Our plan is to raise an army and free *all* the slaves. And anyway you'd last as long as a leaf on a bonfire at Marshank."

Kastern the mousemaid chuckled. "Listen, squirrel, if you'd been half the places we've been and done a quarter of the things we've done, you'd know better."

"Chaha! I'd say y' would, old lad. Gauchee, remember

we put on the courtin' of the frog an' the caterpillar for all those fierce toads in the south swamps?"

"Do I ever!" The mousemaid nibbled her carrot, shaking with mirth. "With you playing the villainous toad uncle. I thought those toads were so enraged they were going to toss us in the swamp!"

Celandine giggled. "And they would have, too. Good job they let Celandine butterfly tie them all up with the magic rope that would make them all handsome. Heeheeheehee!"

The whole company fell about laughing as Kastern pointed at Rowanoak. "That was when Badger Bountiful hoisted them all up into a tree and told them they too would turn into beautiful butterflies and fly away. Hahahahahaha!"

"Hoohoohoo! You should've seen their bally faces when we ate all their feast and went off, leavin' 'em all hanging' from a tree waitin' to turn into butterflies. Hawhawhaw!"

When the laughter had subsided, Rowanoak winked at Felldoh and Brome, "No need to worry about us. We know what we're doing."

Felldoh grasped the badger's paw. "I don't know how to thank you."

Trefoil was rummaging in the cart. "Oh, don't thank us. We won't be doing it all on our own—you two will be taking part in the show."

Brome leapt up in alarm. "But they'd recognize us right off!"

Kastern placed a huge frog mask over the young mouse's head. "There, your own mama wouldn't recognize you now."

Rowanoak clapped her hefty paws together. "Righto, clear the food away. We've got a show to rehearse. Felldoh, you look strong enough to be a good catcher . . ."

Celandine fluttered her eyelashes. "Ooh, he could catch me anytime of the season!"

Rowanoak gave her a glare then ignored her. "Brome, sorry you can't sing on this job. Your voice is too recognizable. However, you would make rather a good frog maiden."

"Me, a frog maiden?"

"Why certainly, old lad. An' I'll be your wicked uncle toad. Hoho, me proud beauty, you shall never marry that caterpillar!"

Felldoh shook his head in bewilderment as Buckler stuck a large red ball on the tip of his nose. "It sounds just crazy enough to work!"

13

It was still early morning and already Martin was feeling tired. He and his friends had been roused several times that night by the familiar Squidjee cry, gluggadrink. It seemed that every baby pigmy shrew woke at least twice nightly wanting a drink.

Rose hauled her log away from the noisy breakfast table. She was spattered with food and drink.

"Good morning, Martin. You'll never guess what's planned for the morning after breakfast is through."

Martin shook his head. "Don't tell me, I don't want to know."

Rose told him anyway, stifling a smile as she did. "We're taking all the Squidjees down to the beach for a paddle in the rock pools. Evidently the whole tribe goes down there every day to check on their fishing nets. If it's good weather like today, the little fiends are brought along to amuse themselves."

"Oh how nice. It will be fun!" Martin put on his fixed smile.

Grumm and Pallum had their paws full wiping off sticky baby whiskers. "Cumm yurr, you'm—'orrible liddle toad. Thoi whisker'n be full o' oatmeal."

The Squidjees dodged about chanting ceaselessly. "Wannago shoreshore! Wannago shoreshore!"

Descent to the shore from the high cliffs was not as difficult as it first looked. There was a hidden stairway, cunningly carved into the rock by the pigmy shrews. Martin and his companions had to make the trip several times. Watched by Amballa and her ever vigilant shrews, the four friends had to carry each Squidjee piggyback fashion down to the sand. When all the shrews were attending their nets, the Queen turned to Pallum.

"Squidjees playnow, youwatch plennygood!"

She shook her sword at them in warning before seating herself comfortably where she could keep an eye on everything.

The Queen's infant son Dinjer was trouble on wheels. The other Squidjees were relatively calm and happy, burying Grumm up to his neck in the sand. Martin, Rose and Pallum were building a sandcastle for some others. Pallum pointed to Grumm.

"That was what I always hated, when they decided to bury me. Grumm seems to be enjoying it."

The mole pulled loose a digging paw and waved to them. "Burr aye, 'tis noice 'n' cool on an 'ot morn loik this'n."

"Stillagrumm, staystill!"

Several Squidjees started draping wet seaweed on the mole's head.

Martin looked about for Dinjer. Rose spotted him.

"There he is, the little blaggard. Look, climbing!"

Dinjer had strayed from the rest and taken a notion to scale the cliff face. The section he chose was slippery and steep, with sharp crags sticking out above it. Martin's patience snapped. He leaped up, pointing at the miscreant.

"Get down from there, you stupid little beast, or you'll fall!"

The Queen heard him. Angrily she threw a rock, catching Martin sharply on his unprotected back.

"Biggamouse biggamouth! Notalk Ballamum son like-that, badtalk. Ballamum killslay biggamouse!"

Martin was about to make some reply when there was a loud screech. "Yeeeaaakkk!"

A great gannet had swooped down and snatched Dinjer from the rocks. The infant pigmy shrew was carried high into the air, held by his tail and the hem of his loose robe in the lethal amber beak of the predator. He wriggled and squealed like a midget piglet. Immediately all activity on the shore ceased as Amballa's wails rent the air.

"Waaah waaah! Dinjergone himdead likefather, likefather!"

"I remember that when I was younger," Pallum whispered to Rose. "Dinjer's father was taken by a big gannet like that one. Poor little mite, he's as good as dead now."

Amballa had slid down from her seat on the rocks. She covered her eyes and wept inconsolably. "Nomore Dinjerbabe! Himgone, deadnow!"

Martin grabbed her by the paws, pulling her upright. "Notdead, Ballamum, Dinjer notdead. Biggamouse savehim!"

Seizing the Queen's sword, which was no more than a dagger in his paw, Martin bowled the nearest two pigmy shrews over and snatched their fishing net. Dashing off along the shore after the gannet, he called back to his friends. "Get more nets and follow me. Hurry!"

The gannet soared upwards, wheeled, and dropped down on to a high ledge in an isolated part of the cliffs. Dinjer was stunned by the landing. The infant lay limp between the big bird's well-clawed and webbed feet. There was a large untidy nest on the ledge, with two scrawny half-feathered gannet chicks in it. On seeing their mother they set up a cackle.

As he ran, Martin watched the bird descend and alight on the high ledge. Without pausing, he ran to the cliff face directly below it. Pausing only to grip the swordblade in his teeth, he hurled the fishing net upwards. The meshes caught on the rocks. Giving a quick tug to check its firmness, Martin began climbing, pulling himself up paw over paw on the tough kelp net. When he reached where the net had caught, he disentangled it, whirling it around his head he hurled it aloft, catching another rocky crag. Again he began hauling himself up over the meshes.

Below on the beach, the whole of the Highbeast pigmy shrew tribe had gathered. They watched as Martin continued his ascent. Rose began spreading the other nets on the sand, lashing four of them together. The pigmy shrews were getting in her way, ignoring her as they trampled the nets and gazed up. Rose, Pallum and Grumm bulled into them, pushing them backwards.

"Get out of the way. Can't you see we're trying to help him?"

One of the Highbeasts kicked out at Rose. "Cheekamouse! Notalka me likethat."

Amballa bit him savagely on the neck and knocked him down. "Gettaway quicknow like mousesay, allayou!"

A piercing cry came from Dinjer as he woke and saw his predicament. "Eeeee! Helpme helpmeeeeee!"

Martin heard the cry and redoubled his efforts, throwing the net upwards and scrambling over it. He chanced a quick look up—only about three more lengths to go.

Dinjer's tear-stained face appeared over the rim of the ledge. "Eeeeeee helpadinjer eeeeeee!"

He was dragged back by the formidable beak of the gannet. The huge bird tossed him against the side of the nest. Dinjer curled up tight as the two hungry chicks tried to crane their floppy necks over the edge of the nest to get at him.

Below on the shore, Amballa hid her face in horror of what might happen to her little son. Rose put a comforting paw around the Queen's shoulders.

"Nocry, Ballamum. Biggamouse Martin is mighty warrior. He will get your Dinjer back, yousee, yousee!"

Amballa seemed to understand Rose. She clung to the mousemaid as she anxiously watched the high ledge.

Breathing raggedly with exertion, Martin pulled himself up on to the ledge, hauling the net up after him.

Dinjer saw him and jumped up, yelling. "Biggamouse Martinmouse, savemeeeee!"

The gannet turned its bright dangerous eyes on Martin as he took the sword from his mouth.

"Dinjer, nomake nonoise, bestill, still!"

The gannet took a stalking stride towards Martin, lowering its lethal yellow beak. The young mouse swung with the little sword. It clacked harmlessly off the great bird's beak, but caused the gannet to stop where it was. Now Martin shook the net out and swished it at the bird's feet. It took a step back. Behind him he could hear Dinjer sobbing with terror. Working his way across the ledge, jabbing with the sword and sweeping with the net, Martin gradually got himself into a position where he was between the gannet and its nest.

Sensing danger to its chicks, the gannet began spreading its wings, lowering its neck and opening its beak wide as it hissed at the intruder. Martin knew there was not much time, it was getting ready to attack. He would have to act quickly. Throwing back his head, he shouted aloud into the gannet's face, hoping that he could be heard below on the beach.

"Stretch the nets! Hold them up, lots of you. Be ready!"

Rose heard him. She had thought of giving her eagle call, but if Martin or Dinjer were in the nest they would be crushed under the gannet, which would naturally sit on its nest to defend the chicks against anything. Grasping a corner of the net, Rose held it high, yelling aloud, "Holdup net. Stretch it tight. Now!"

The Highbeast tribe stood uncertainly for a moment, until a harsh order from Amballa their Queen sent them scurrying to the edges of the net, with Rose, Pallum, Grumm and Amballa at each corner.

The Queen snapped out directions. "Holda netup, upup! Stretcher tightnow!"

The net was ready, up and tightly stretched.

Martin reached back with his footpaw, keeping a wary eye on the gannet as he kicked Dinjer lightly.

"Movenow, Dinjer. Get over to the edge . . ."

Dinjer began crawling on all fours. The gannet, sensing it was being robbed of its prey, tried to pass Martin to get at Dinjer. Martin jabbed with the sword. This time he nipped the bird in its open mouth. It retaliated with lightning swiftness, pecking him sharply in the side. Martin drew his breath in short at the pain. He clamped his paw over the spot, feeling warm damp blood.

Dinjer was now at the edge of the cliff, peering over at the dizzy drop down to the shore.

"Jump, Dinjer, jump!" Martin hissed at him.

"Eeee nojump nojump, Dinjer 'fraid!"

There was nothing else for it. Martin turned swiftly and gave the baby pigmy shrew a hefty kick on the bottom that sent him flying outwards over the edge.

"Yeeeeeeeeeeeehhhkkkk!"

Whump!

Dinjer bounced up and down in the center of the net. Saved!

The gannet gave a shrill squawk and attacked Martin. Leaping to one side, he whirled the net and threw it straight over the bird's head. The kelp fishing net enveloped the gannet's head and one wing, and draped on the ground, trapping one of its webbed feet. Martin fell to one side, dragging at the net. The bird's head came awkwardly askew and it tried to pull its leg free. Martin kicked out at its other leg, sending the gannet crashing on its side, loosely trapped in the net.

The young mouse leapt up, his chest heaving. The net would not hold the big sea bird for long and he did not wish to kill it. The two chicks were squawking raucously in the nest. Turning to the fallen mother bird, Martin loosed off the net. Then he ran for the edge shouting aloud, "One for the net coming doooooooo-own!"

He leaped into the blue summer morning, up and out. Momentarily he was robbed of breath as the wind whistled past his ears. Spread-eagled, with all limbs flailing, he dropped like a stone, plummeting down into the net.

Whumff!

A mighty cheer rose up from everybeast on the shore.

Rose, Pallum and Grumm hurried to help Martin from the net. The mousemaid tore a strip from her smock.

"You're hurt. Let me see. Oh, thank goodness, it's not serious!"

Martin let her bandage his side. Amballa came over, smiling through her tears. Martin offered her sword back but she refused.

"Martinmouse warriormouse, greatbrave, savemy Dinjerbabe. Ballamum saythis. Warrawant? Anything foryou!"

Pallum nudged Martin as he whispered, "She's just offered you anything you want for saving Dinjer. I've never heard the Queen do a thing like that before."

A silence fell over the assembled Highbeasts. Martin lifted the sword and with two swift strokes freed Rose of her hobbling log. Striding purposefully over to Pallum and Grumm, he slashed through the kelps that bound them to the logs. Pallum could not remember being without the great log impeding his footpaws. He held the broken kelp ends and wept silently.

Martin faced the Queen of the pigmy shrews eye to eye. "We want free!"

The silence on the shore intensified as Amballa drew herself up regally, her fierce little eyes burning into Martin's. "Ballamum saythis. Yougo allfree!"

The ranks of the Highbeast tribe parted to let the four friends pass through. They walked in silence, holding the slashed kelp ends lest they tripped.

Suddenly Dinjer ran out in front of Martin, swinging a stick. He struck the young mouse, hard as he could. Martin winced as he took the blow full across the face. Dinjer was in a foul temper, striking and screaming as his tantrum grew.

"Biggamouse kickamee. Killslay biggamouse. He kickamee Dinjer!"

Instantly Amballa was between the two. She grabbed Dinjer, snapped the stick and threw it away, then seizing her son by his tail she began spanking him hard with her free paw.

"Martinmouse rightsay you stupid . . . little . . . beast!"

The loud cheers of the pigmy shrews, coupled with Dinjer's anguished wails, cut through the sunlit morning as the four friends strolled free along the beach, away from pigmy shrews and captivity.

Grumm smiled fondly. "Burr, tha' sound be loik music to moi ears!"

14

While Cap'n Tramun Clogg took a party around the headland to see what he could salvage of his ship, Badrang attended to other matters. Druwp the bankvole stood before the Tyrant in his longhouse. Badrang had his aides, Gurrad and Hisk, bring food for the spy. Roast sea bird, baked fish, new bread and a flagon of damson wine were placed in front of Druwp, but the treacherous creature had suddenly lost his appetite. He eyed the long thin whipping rods held by Gurrad and Hisk, completely overawed in the presence of the mighty Badrang. The bankvole had told them all he knew, but Badrang was not satisfied. Danger radiated from the stoat's eyes. He was in an unpredictable mood.

"Let me get this straight, Druwp. You knew that the prisoners were going to escape from the prison pit, but you don't know how they did it. You know the ringleaders of the slave resistance and you know they have buried weapons, but you don't know what their plans are. Don't play me for a fool, bankvole. Give me some good hard information that I can act upon."

Druwp swallowed hard, his mouth dry as a bone. "I know exactly where the weapons are buried, Sire."

Badrang smiled at Hisk and Gurrad. Coming swiftly

out of his chair, he patted Druwp's back, feeling the spy flinch beneath his touch.

"Good, good. That's what I want to hear. Tell me exactly where they are."

"Lord, they are inside the slave compound, buried in the earth beneath the sleeping pallet of an otter called Tullgrew. I watched her digging the hole. She did not know I saw her."

Badrang turned to his aides. "Come on, let's go and take a look. You have done well, Druwp. From now on you will be my eyes and ears in the ranks of the slaves. Sit down, eat, drink and be easy."

When Badrang and his cronies had left the longhouse Druwp felt his confidence returning, his appetite too. Seating himself at the table, he poured a large beaker of wine and tore off a leg from the roast sea bird. The bread smelled good and fresh as he stuffed it hungrily into his mouth. Quaffing damson wine and setting his teeth into the hot meat, Druwp allowed himself a rare smile. Let the others be helpful and noble to each other. He was in the business of self-preservation.

The slaves had lain idle since the hostilities with Clogg, but they knew it would not last. Badrang would soon have them toiling under the lash. The afternoon was warm and lazy with hardly a breeze. They made the most of it, lying about in the sun.

A mouse called Yarrow wandered over to the palisade and peered through a gap. "Barkjon! Badrang is comin' this way with Gurrad an' Hisk."

The old squirrel was instantly at his side. "Yes, I see them. I wonder what they want?"

Badrang stood in the center of the compound, a knowing smile hovering round his lips. The slaves shuffled nervously as Hisk and Gurrad wandered amongst them, flicking the long thin rods. The Tyrant's voice was soft, almost friendly, as he addressed his captives.

"Well, you've had a nice easy few days, but it'll be back to work in the morning. Stand by your beds while we take a head count."

They hurried to obey, giving Hisk and Gurrad's rods a wide berth. An eerie silence settled over the whole place as the two Captains walked around the nervous creatures standing by their pitiful sacks of straw which served as beds. Gurrad took one side, Hisk the other, tapping their canes against each animal's chest as they counted.

Hillgorse the old hedgehog stood in front of a very young mouse called Hoopoe. As Gurrad's cane snaked out to touch the youngster, Hillgorse batted it aside with his paw. He spoke out, his voice bold and enquiring. "What's all this about? What do you want of us?"

"Hillgorse, is that your name?" The Tyrant's voice was still deceptively friendly.

"That's what they call me."

"Hmm, I thought so. Let me see now, which one of you is Barkjon?"

Felldoh's father took a pace forward. "I am Barkjon."

Badrang's eyes roved this way and that. "Keyla, is there a young otter named Keyla?"

"Aye, that's me!" Keyla held up a paw.

Badrang stared at the otter a moment. "Good, good. You can tell me which one is Tullgrew. Another otter, like yourself."

Keyla exchanged glances with Barkjon and Hillgorse before replying. "Tullgrew? There's no Tullgrew here."

Badrang's voice hardened. "Lie to me and you'll die, all three of you. Who is Tullgrew?"

The otter could not see her friends endangered. She held up her paw. "My name is Tullgrew."

Badrang strode across to her and kicked the sack of bedding grass. "Move that and start digging."

Slowly Tullgrew did as she was bid. The noon sun beat down on the compound. A small cloud of dust arose where the otter toiled away, digging the sandy clayish ground with both paws. Barkjon looked across to Hillgorse. Their eyes were sad with resignation.

Tullgrew dug until she was standing in a pit half her own height. Sweat ran down into her eyes, hiding the look of puzzlement in them.

Badrang sensed something was amiss. "Gurrad, Hisk! Throw that otter out of the hole and take over!"

The two Captains scrambled to obey. Putting their rods aside, they heaved Tullgrew out of the excavation and began digging fast and hard under the Tyrant's hot angry eyes. All their questing paws found was earth and more earth.

They were almost at head height when Badrang snapped at them, "Get out of it, fools. Can't you see there's nothing there?"

As they pulled themselves out, Gurrad, the shorter of the two, slipped and fell back into the hole. There was an audible snigger among the slaves. Badrang whirled round to face them. "We'll see how long you laugh doing double workloads tomorrow!"

Hisk helped the rat out and they padded warily behind the Tyrant as he swept out of the compound, his cloak billowing darkly against the noonday brightness.

Tullgrew spread her dusty paws wide. "What happened to the weapons? They weren't there."

"By the seasons! I wonder where they went." Keyla's face was the picture of innocence.

Barkjon waggled a paw under the otter's nose. "You know, you young rascal!"

Keyla smiled mischievously. "Aye, I know, but Druwp doesn't. He watched Tullgrew bury them, and I watched him. When he fell asleep, I gently pulled Tullgrew and her bedding to one side. She was asleep too, weary after all that digging. So I just dug the weapons up and found a new hiding place for them."

Tullgrew shook her head in amazement. "But where did you put them, Keyla?"

"Hah! Right in the center of the compound, there, where Badrang was standing when he first came in. Hee hee hee!"

Druwp was sitting among the remnants of his feast sipping the last of the wine when the longhouse door opened with a bang. Badrang entered, flanked by Gurrad and Hisk. Wine spilled as the flagon went flying against the wall. Druwp's chair was pulled from under him, and in a trice he was flat on his back with the Tyrant's footclaws against his quivering throat.

"You made a fool of me, Druwp." The stoat's voice grated with a rage he could hardly contain. "I don't like being made to look a fool. I should kill you, but I won't. You will continue spying for me. However, first you must learn a hard lesson!"

A sob rose in Druwp's throat as Badrang called to his Captains, "Bring me those rods, then guard the door so he can't run!"

The hot still summer evening was bringing the day to a close. Tramun Clogg's crew sat out on the shore grouped around cooking fires. The Cap'n would not allow them to be billeted in Badrang's "fancy fort", where they could be surrounded by the Tyrant's horde while sleeping— better the open shore close to the tideline.

Clogg had inspected the hulk of his ship at low water. There was a chance the hull could be towed ashore and saved to rebuild upon. The corsair's clothing steamed as it dried on him by the fire. He gnawed on a toasted mackerel and swigged noisily at a jug of old seaweed ale.

He did not notice the strangely clad hare who was sitting beside him in the twilight until the creature spoke.

"I say, old lad, any chance of a nip at that seaweed ale? I'm very partial to a drop of the old beachwater."

The unflappable Clogg hugged his jug close as he

eyed the odd beast indignantly. "Git yer own ale, rabbit. 'Ere, you ain't one o' my crew?"

The hare nudged him cheekily and winked. "Should bally well hope not. Flippin' rabble, wot, wot?"

Tramun turned to the nearest searat. "Ahoy, Growch. Who is this cove? One o' Badrang's?"

Growch squinted at the hare. "Can't recall seein 'im at the fortress, Cap'n. Shall I run 'im through for ye?" He drew a long rusty dagger.

Ballaw, for it was he, suddenly shot his paw out at the fire. "I say, look!"

A huge column of green flame rose wreathed with yellow smoke.

The corsairs fell back from the fire. A chunk of fish fell from Clogg's open mouth to disappear down the front of his steaming shirt.

"Stripe me, a magic rabbit. 'Ow d'yer do that, matey?"

"Can't tell you, old top. Me throat's too parched for words."

Clogg passed the jug of seaweed ale. "Then wet yer whistle wid this 'ere."

Ballaw scrubbed the rim of the jug with his paw then emptied it with one long gulp. The searats were totally amazed.

"Waste o' good ale, that was. Like pourin' it down a well!"

Ballaw leapt up straight and gave a piercing howl. "Owooooo!"

He fell flat on his back and lay quite still.

"Haharr, I knowed it," Clogg chuckled. "'E's gone an' done hisself in from 'oggin' all that ale too quick. That'n's a dead rabbit, mates!"

"No he ain't, Cap'n. Look, the rabbit's comin' to life!"

Ballaw's long legs kicked out and upward, once, twice, thrice. He began moaning, holding one paw to his throat while he stuffed the other down his mouth.

Clogg squinted closely at the stricken hare. "Wot's 'e doin' now, Crosstooth?"

"Looks like summat is stuck in 'is gullet, Cap'n. Oh, look out!"

The corsairs gasped in amazement as Ballaw began pulling a long ribbon from his mouth. It opened out wide and frilly. Out and out it came as the hare pulled faster, paw over paw, changing colors as it issued from his mouth—red, blue, pink, brown, green, purple, culminating in a vivid yellow with large black letters written upon it.

Ballaw sat up and read it aloud. " 'Cap'n Tramun Clogg' —why that must be your goodself, sir!"

Clogg scratched his plaited beard fiercely. "Aye, that's me name. 'Ow'd you know?"

Ballaw leaned close to Clogg's ear. "It'd shock you what us magic rabbits know, my good fellow. Here!" He presented Clogg with a rosy apple that he appeared to pull from the pirate stoat's ear.

Tramun clacked his clogs together with delight. He was immensely taken with his new-found friend.

"Gruzzle, Boggs, fetch wine an' vittles fer our magic rabbit 'ere. C'mon, matey, tell us yer name."

Ballaw bowed courteously. "Tibbar!"

"Tibbar, wot sorta name's that?"

"Why, it's simply rabbit spelled backwards, me old buckadoodle."

"Haharrharrharr! Yore a good un, Tibbar. Do more magic fer us."

Ballaw adopted a droopingly sad face. His ears flopped downwards. "Alas and alack, old mateyfriend, I must go. But would you like to see some more magic creatures? We could put on a show of legerdemain, a tale of unrequited love and skulduggery that would astound you!"

"Aye that we would, Tibbar matey." Clogg nodded eagerly. "When'll ye bring yer friends?"

"Tomorrow eve just after sunset, into the courtyard of yonder fortress, if I have your promise that none shall harm us."

The Cap'n held a grubby paw to his stomach, which he valued far more than his heart. "Promise? You 'ave me oath as a corsair, matey. You an' yer mates is to be treated like queens an' kings made o' butterfly wings, and I'll slit the gizzard of anybeast that looks the wrong way at ye!"

"Until tomorrow night then, sweet Cloggo!"

Ballaw flung his paw out at the fire. There was a puff of heavy purple smoke, a blinding white flame, and he was gone.

The corsairs stood in a hushed group around the fire, rubbing their eyes after the flaring white brightness.

Gruzzle shook his head sadly. "The magic rabbit's gone, shipped out in a flash. D'you think 'e'll turn up again like 'e said 'e would, Cap'n?"

Clogg fished about in his shirt until he found the chunk of mackerel. He nodded as he chewed on it. "Bless yer 'eart, Gruzzle, o' course 'e will. Tibbar's me matey. D'you 'ear wot 'e called me? Sweet Cloggo. Ain't that 'andsome!"

Ballaw trotted back into camp humming snatches of a tune he was composing. Rowanoak's voice greeted him.

"Lookout, everybeast, it's Tibbar the magic rabbit, fresh from his corsair debut."

"Magic rabbit yourself, you old stripehound." Ballaw helped himself to a large wild cherry flan. "Well, chaps an' chapesses, the jolly old wheeze worked. We open tomorrow night in the main courtyard of Fortress Marshballyank. Leave it to De Quincewold, eh wot?"

"Ballaw, you deserve three hearty cheers!" Felldoh shook his head admiringly.

The theatrical hare's ears stood up indignantly. "Stow the applause. I'd sooner have three hearty suppers and some decent cordial to wash away the taste of that corsair's seaweed ale. Dreadful swill! That Cap'n Clogg's chaps aren't goin' to last long drinkin' that stuff. Dearie me no, they'll end up warped or rotted. Take m' word."

Under a quarter-moon on clifftops still warm from the day's sun the Rambling Rosehip Players rehearsed for the following night's performance. Felldoh and Brome learned the business quickly. They had to.

15

More than a day's journey south on those same clifftops, Martin and his friends camped for the night. Unable to risk a fire in strange and possibly hostile territory, they sprawled wearily at the edge of a small scrubby woodland that grew up almost to the cliff edge.

Grumm massaged his ample stomach as it gurgled plaintively. "Hurr 'scuse oi, moi tummy's a-thinken moi mouth 'as fergotted 'ow to eat."

Rose propped herself up on two paws. "What I wouldn't give for a plain ordinary oatmeal scone spread with honey right now."

The scone hit Rose on the head, landing on the ground beneath her nose. She sat up, looking at it with astonishment.

"Where in the name of apples and acorns did that come from?"

Grumm picked it up and took a bite. "Burr, 'tis still warm an' spreaded wi' 'unny too!"

"Hoi! Can I have one too?" Pallum called out cheekily into the darkness.

No sooner had he spoken than a scone thudded on the ground by him. The hedgehog chuckled with delight, not questioning where the food came from. Pallum was a simple soul, practical too.

"Go on, Martin. Have a go. Ask for one!"

The young mouse was standing alert and upright, Amballa's small sword in his paw. He peered into the darkness murmuring, "Yes, I'd like a scone with honey. Wouldn't mind something to drink too. Strawberry cordial would be nice."

The scone struck his footpaw. He did not see which direction it came from. As he bent to get it a voice called out of the woods, "You'm can 'ave the scone, moi dears, but oi bain't thrown moi gudd beakers abowt an' spillen drinks 'ither 'n' yon. Hoo arr no!"

Grumm leaped up waving his ladle, which he had retrieved from the pigmy shrews. "Oi'd be knowen that speak. 'Tis a moler loik oi!"

A mole came plodding out of the darkness. She was dressed in an oversized mob cap and a huge flowery pinafore.

"Hurr, oi bain't nawthen loik you'm, maister. Oi be just loik oi, Polleekin."

She sat on the grass beside them, wiping her paws on the flowered apron and conversing as if they had always been there.

"Moi 'eart, 'twas an 'ot summer day t' day, et surely wurr. Oi was gatheren oop 'ee scones after coolen 'em off in 'ee shade, when oi yurrs sumbeast a-longen furr scones, so oi throwed him'n summ."

Rose laughed her merry tinkling laugh. "Oh you're so kind, Polleekin. Thank you!"

The mole stood up, dusting herself off busily. "Oi aspeck yore well 'ungered an' thursty too. Young uns allus are, partickly travellers. Coom on then, 'ome wi' oi."

They introduced themselves and told Polleekin their story as she led them to her dwelling in the wood.

Grumm looked up at it, hardly able to believe his eyes. "Moi seasons! A moler liven oop inna tree. Hurr!"

Polleekin did actually live up in a tree. It was an old

dead oak that had fallen at a crazy angle against a tall rocky outcrop. The trunk was practically a stairway. They followed her up to a large comfortable room built between three thick boughs. It was floored with driftwood and cordage and roofed with the same material, tightly chinked with moss, earth and leaf packing to keep out wind and weather. The walls were formed by the foliage of the surrounding trees, skillfully woven together. They sat on a low mossy branch broad enough to be a bed, listening to Polleekin chatter as she prepared their supper.

"Hurr, oi be all alone in 'ee wurld naow. Fam'ly growed, troibe gone, so oi do as oi loiks wid moiself, liven in 'ee tree, fearen nobeast an' given welcumm to most, hurr aye."

The supper when it came was little less than spectacular. Strawberry cordial, dandelion and burdock beer and hot mint tea. From a small stone charcoal-fed oven the homely mole produced a stew of carrot, turnip, peas and leeks, a large cottage loaf and a button mushroom turnover garnished with parsley. From her larder came a dark heavy fruitcake with maplecream topping and an assortment of wildberry tartlets. She bustled about, laying them on the floor.

"Get thoi jaws round that liddle lot. Oi allus keeps vittles in plenty yurr, you'd be apprised at 'ee visitors oi gets, moi dears."

Conversation and talk went out of the leaf-screened windows as they applied themselves to the business of serious eating. Polleekin watched them, rocking back and forth on a springy bough and tapping her old digging claws together. Only when they had slowed down to the picking stage did she venture to speak.

"They creeturs you'm be a-looken for bain't passed thisaways."

Rose sighed as she poured herself some of the fragrant mint tea. "I hope they're safe and well, Polleekin."

The mole closed her eyes, nodding slowly. "Ho,

they'm safe enuff an' awroight furr 'ee moment, mizzy, never fret."

Pallum stared at her curiously. "How do you know?"

Still nodding and smiling, with closed eyes the mole spoke. "Oi knows lots o' things but oi doant know why oi knows 'em. Places, faces, 'appenings an' all manner o' things runs in an' out o' moi ole 'ead, loik beefolks in an' out o' ee hoives."

Martin stared fixedly at the wise old mole, his food forgotten. "Yes, I had a feeling when we first met that you were not ordinary."

Polleekin shrugged, opening one eye to look at Martin. "Oi carn't 'elp it, maister. You'm be a wurrier beast loiken thoi daddy afore you'm. That liddle knoife bain't 'is sword. You'm got a longways t' go afore yon sword cooms back to 'ee. Doant maken you'm less'n a wurrier, tho'. Oi seen gurt brave wurriers in moi long seasons, but none like you'm, Marthen."

The mole went into a doze then. She talked no more. When they were finished eating they lay back on the broad comfortable bough and were soon asleep. Moonlight filtered through the leaves on to the faces of the four friends as they slumbered. Polleekin moved silently, touching each of their faces tenderly. She shook her head and wiped her eyes on the flowery apron.

"Pore young uns, so much 'arpiness an' sadness afore 'ee, iffen on'y you'm knowed. Oi be glad moi seasons are near run an' oi doant 'ave to carry otherbeasts' loives around in moi ole 'ead for long naow."

Martin opened his eyes to the song of small birds with dawn sun filtering green and gold through the leafy walls of the tree house. Rising silently, he climbed down to the woodland floor. There was a cool spring rising out of the rocks, bubbling its way into a small pool. The young mouse swilled his face and paws, shaking away the droplets and drying off with a pawful of grass. Polleekin bustled past with a small rush basket.

"Mawnin', zurr Marthen. Lookee, liddle mushyrooms, celery, lettuce an' early 'azel nutters, green uns, some dandelion an' crabapples."

Pallum appeared, looking into the basket and nodding hungrily. "Mmm, they look lovely and fresh."

The old molewife slapped his paw away as he reached for a young button mushroom. "Gurr, you'm young roguer. 'Old still till oi make thoi breffist."

Grumm and Rose took a hurried wash at the spring. Shaking themselves dry, they scrambled swiftly back up to the tree house for breakfast. Polleekin could work wonders with vegetables, and she did. They feasted on mushroom and celery soup garnished with young dandelion petals, followed by the scones she had baked the day before, now well soaked through with honey. Rose poured crabapple cider for them as the old mole began outlining her luncheon menu.

"Oi'll bake a gurt cake wi' woild plum 'n' damson from moi last autumn larder. Hurr, an' meadowcream aplenty to go wid et."

"Rurr, oi'm drefful sorry, marm but us'ns be gone afore long." Grumm's voice was heavy with regret.

Polleekin wiped hefty digging claws on her apron. "Aye, so you'm shall, tho' oi dearly wisht 'ee would stay yurr wid oi awhoil, p'raps two day or more."

Rose sat next to the old molewife, patting her back. "I wish we could stay for ever, Polleekin, but we must get to searching for my brother Brome and our friend Felldoh. That is, if they still live."

Polleekin sighed. "Oi told you'm larst noight, mizzy. They two be aloive an' well. Doant ask me 'ow oi knows, 'cos oi cuddent tell 'ee, but take moi word, oi knows it fer sure. You'm three creeturs be best travellen straight fer Noonvale. Stay 'way from 'ee vurmin fort. Bad fortune awaits 'ee thurr iffen you'm return."

Martin leaned forward. "What sort of bad fortune, Polleekin?"

The old one closed her eyes, rocking back and forth. "Nay, zurr Marthen, 'tis not for oi t' say, lessen oi be a-tellen lies an' moi ole mem'ry be playen tricks loike it do sometimes."

The friends did not pursue the question further, though Rose had a request to make of Polleekin.

"You told us to travel to Noonvale. I for one think it a good idea. But I'm afraid I haven't the foggiest idea where it is from here. We're completely lost. Can you help us?"

The mole opened her eyes. Moving slowly about, she began rummaging through her larders and stores.

"Oi'm no good at markin' an' maken wroiten, mizzy. Yurr, take this an' mark as oi say whoile oi make up thoi supplies."

Rose took the proffered barkcloth and charcoal stick. With great care the mousemaid wrote everything down, sometimes making Polleekin repeat things two or three times until she was satisfied. The old mole-wife gave out her instructions almost grudgingly as she went about the business of making up four packs of provisions.

Pallum watched her, shaking his head and smiling fondly. "What a wunnerful ole molewife. I bet even Squidjees would be nice to her. My 'eart and stummick is longin' to stay longer in this place with Polleekin, but we've got to go. Still, I'll make myself a promise by my spikes that I'll return 'ere someday an' taste her cookin' again."

Midmorning sunlight lanced through the gently swaying foliage as Polleekin wandered silently off to replenish her larders. The four friends sat studying the message she had dictated to Rose. Grumm smiled sheepishly. "Hurr, oi'm drefful iggerant at wurdin', Miz Roser. Kin you'm read it to oi?"

Rose read the message slowly.

"Follow your frontshadow, do not stop
Till you reach the one with dead three top.
See the twin paths, beware of one
Sweet as the spreading atop of a scone.
Camp close by night, watch out by day
For the three-eyed one who bars the way.
More you will not learn until
Meeting the warden of Marshwood Hill."

Martin scratched his chin thoughtfully. "I wish Polleekin would have explained it a little clearer."

Rose shrugged. "She doesn't want us to go. The poor
old creature loves to have company. However, knowing
that we must carry on and find Noonvale, she did the
best she could with her rhyme. Let's take it a bit at a
time as we go. *Follow your frontshadow, do not stop.* What
in the name of seasons is a frontshadow?"

Pallum shouldered his pack. "I think it's when the
sun is at our back, and the shadow we throw is in front
of us. Come on, let's make a start. Now let me see." He
looked up at the sun, calculating which way it would
travel. "This way, straight into the woodland. In two
hours the sun will be at our backs."

Grumm picked up his pack reluctantly. "But whurr's
Miz Polleekin?"

Rose pointed into the scrubby thickness surrounding
them. "Somewhere in there, having a quiet sulk, I
shouldn't wonder. Ah well, I don't blame her. I feel
pretty bad about leaving here myself, but we must go.
I'll sing her a farewell. She'll hear it, I'm sure."

The friends set off into the warm midday. Martin kept
his eyes on the country ahead, listening admiringly to
Rose's beautiful singing voice.

"Goodbye, my friend, and thank you, thank you,
    thank you,
It makes me sad to leave you upon this summer day.

Don't shed a tear or cry now. Goodbye now, goodbye
   now.
I'm sure I'll see you somehow, if I pass by this way,
For the seasons don't foretell
Who must stay or say farewell,
And I must find out what lies beyond this place.
But I know deep in my heart
We are never far apart
While I have a mem'ry of your smiling face.
Goodbye, my friend, and thank you, thank you,
   thank you,
Your kindness guides me ever as I go on my way."

Grumm sniffed, wiping away huge rolling tears as
they pressed into the leafy fastness. "Hurr, fair breaks
moi 'eart, you'm reckern she 'eard 'ee song, Pallum?"

Martin pointed swiftly to a patch of rustling ferns.
They caught a glimpse of flowered apron disappearing.
"Don't fret, Grumm. She heard Rose's song. Look!"

Four slices of plum and damson cake spread thick
with meadowcream, affixed to the drooping branch of a
hawthorn, hung bobbing in their path like strange fruit.

Grumm picked one. Sitting down on the ground, he
began eating, smiling through the tears that coursed
openly down his homely face. "Moi 'eart but she'm a
wunnerful creetur. Oi'd be fair proud t' be a choild of
that thurr moler."

BOOK TWO

Actors and Searchers

16

Evening shadows lengthened as the hot day drew to a close. The shore lay warm and dusty beneath the last rays of daylight. Fortress Marshank's gates were thrown open wide. Torches and seacoal fires illuminated the courtyard as the corsair crew mingled with the Tyrant's horde. An alfresco supper had been laid for the two leaders and their aides. A temporary jollity prevailed in the light of the promised entertainment, though Badrang and Clogg still regarded each other suspiciously.

The Tyrant stoat nibbled a leg of roast gull, sipping daintily from a beaker of greengage cordial as he smiled patronizingly at the corsair Cap'n. Tramun Clogg sniffed at a pickled mackerel. With a defiant grimace he dunked it thoroughly in Badrang's cordial bowl and wolfed it down in one mouthful. Choking and coughing, he grabbed a half-empty puncheon of kelp beer, tilting it to his mouth and drinking deeply as it splashed widespread down his braids on to the tabletop. With a loud belch and a villainous grin, he slammed the puncheon back on the table.

"Harr, that's better! Ho lookit, 'ere comes me mate Tibbar an' 'is pals!"

Badrang eyed the approaching troupe scathingly.

"Hmm, so this is the entertainment we've been waiting for?"

Clogg half drew his cutlass, thrusting his face close to Badrang. "Aye, so 'tis, an' they're friends of me good matey Tibbar, so don't you fergit it."

Badrang turned his head, avoiding Clogg's fish-laden breath. He had dropped his corsair accent now that he held the upper paw. "Forget it? How could I? You've done nothing but gabble on about it all day."

Clogg was offended by the Tyrant's manner. He squinted fiercely at him. "That weren't gabblin', matey, 'twere a warnin'. Don't mess with those creatures, an' get any thoughts o' slave-takin' outta yer 'ead, Badrang. It's double bad luck to any who tries to 'arm me magic friends, see!"

Brome felt himself freeze beneath the huge frog mask that enveloped his head. The sight of Badrang and Marshank caused panic in his mind.

Rowanoak pushed him gently from behind. "Hurry along now, young froggy. Hop to it!"

Remembering that he was invisible beneath his disguise gave Brome the confidence he needed. Giving a loud croak, he hopskipped into the center of the courtyard and began setting up the scenery from the cart with the other Rosehip troupers. Felldoh was concealed beneath a big comical fox outfit. The tongue wobbled and the eyes rolled every time he moved his head. Beneath the mask, Felldoh peered wildly around, seeing each familiar hated face: Badrang, Gurrad, Hisk. But no sign of his father Barkjon.

Ballaw was in his element. The show, mixed with the ever present danger of appearing before enemies, made his heart beat fast with excitement. Dressed in the flowing costume of Tibbar the magic rabbit, he cartwheeled boldly up to the leaders' table and tweaked Clogg's plaited beard.

"Cloggo, me old crab carcass, me jolly old wavedog companion, top o' the evenin' to you, wot wot?"

Tramun laughed uncontrollably, highly amused at his new friend's antics. Ballaw produced two spoons from Clogg's beard and began clacking them rhythmically together by bouncing both spoons off the corsair stoat's vast stomach.

"When's a stoat not a stoat?
When he wears clogs an' a velvet coat!
When's a stoat an old seadog?
When he's whiskery friskery attery biskery Cap'n
    Tramun Clogg!"

"Whoa hoho harrharrharr! Ain't 'e a caution, ha-harrharr!" Clogg thumped Badrang heartily upon the back. The Tyrant managed to put his beaker down before cordial spilled on his polished breastplate. He glared at Clogg before turning to Ballaw.

"So you're the magic rabbit. Well, let's see some magic."

Ballaw took Badrang's beaker and emptied it at a single gulp. Before the Tyrant could protest, he refilled the beaker from a nearby flagon and tossed the contents of it into Badrang's face. The Tyrant gave a gasp of surprise and threw up his paws, only to find that the beaker showered him not with drink but with dead leaves. Clogg fell off his chair laughing.

"See, I told yer, that's me ole matey Tibbar the magic rabbit! Haharrhohoho! Make more magic, Tibbar."

Ballaw bowed elegantly as he leaped down from the table. "Lord Badrang, what d'you wish, old chap—a play, or more magic?"

Badrang refilled his empty beaker, checking to see that it was greengage cordial, and not dead leaves. "I'll go along with friend Clogg here. Make more magic." Ballaw extended his paw dramatically.

"Bring forth the deadly dagger of death!"

Gauchee and Kastern came forward, bearing between them a red silk cushion. On it lay a long dagger which glittered wickedly in the firelight. Rowanoak chanted in the background,

"From the deepest darkest dungeons,
'Neath the mountains of the moon,
Comes the dreadful dagger of death,
To bring a creature to sad doom!"

Rowanoak then came forward, dragging Celandine. The squirrelmaid threw a paw to her brow, protesting theatrically,

"No no, no no! Not I, Not I.
One so young and pretty as me
Is far too fair to die!"

Ballaw took the dagger. Producing an apple from an astounded searat's ear, he sliced it in quarters with the glittering blade, smiling wickedly as he called to the assembled vermin,

"See how sharp an' murderous is me blade.
Who would like to see me kill the maid?"

Immediately, there was a silence. Celandine looked so tearfully beautiful nobeast made a sound to condemn her. Except Badrang.

"Run her through, rabbit, and be done with it!"

Celandine shrieked and strove to get away as Rowanoak held her tightly, helpless before Ballaw. The hare held the dagger high.

"Badrang, your name is feared throughout the land.
My Lord, I kill this maid at your command!"

He struck at Celandine. She screamed.

"Aaaaiiiieeeeeee!"

The blade appeared to bury itself full length in the squirrelmaid's body, though it had collapsed secretly back into the dagger's handle. Celandine took the handle in both paws as Ballaw let it go. She looked as though she were trying to pull it out of her, though she was really pressing it in. Ballaw turned, his face a mask of horror, paws quivering as he held them to his face.

"Alas no more I'll laugh or sing.
I've murdered her, the pretty little thing!"

Celandine staggered about, moaning pitifully.

"Nor more I'll see the dawning o'er the trees,
Nor see the golden sunlight in the sky,
The seasons change, the birds, the flow'rs, the bees.
Alack a day, poor me who has to die!"

Buckler stood close to her, banging on a small drum as he muttered out of the side of his mouth, "Coom on, miz, daunt 'ee make a banquet o' it. 'Urry oup an' die!"

With a final heartrending sob, Celandine flopped gracefully into Rowanoak's paws and died, still clutching the dagger to her.

As Rowanoak bore the squirrelmaid's limp form around, some of the corsairs began muttering.

"Shame, she were a pretty liddle beast."

"Aye, mate. That rabbit might be magic, but 'e's fair 'eartless!"

Cap'n Clogg took a huge draught of kelp beer. "Harr, Tibbar, matey. What'd you want ter croak 'er for? The show's spoiled now. You gone an' ruined a good night's entertainment!"

Ballaw twirled his magic rabbit cloak. "There, my good friends, speaks a stoat with a heart o' gold; me old companion Cloggo. Just for you, I'll bring her back to life."

Rowanoak laid Celandine on the ground. Ballaw knelt over her, chanting.

"Here lies a young maid who's been killed.
With my own paw I thrust the knife.
Without a drop of her blood spilled.
See, I bring her back to life.
Hocus pocus dumbeldum dreary, wackalup one two
    three four five,
Gawrum pawrum cockalorum, maid rise up and
    come alive!"

He took hold of the dagger and made a great show of pulling it out of Celandine, heaving and grunting until at last it stood free and shining as he waved it in the air.

The young squirrelmaid sat up, rubbed her eyes and smiled prettily as she stretched. "Where am I? I must have fallen asleep!"

There was great cheering and applause for the marvellous trick. Ballaw swiftly collapsed the dagger back into its handle, stowed it beneath his cloak and brought forth an identical one. This, however, was no trick dagger. The hare stuck it in the tabletop between Clogg and Badrang for their inspection.

Tramun tested the weapon, slamming its point down hard into the table several times. "Tibbar, matey, yore the magickest rabbit I ever clapped eyes on!"

Badrang never bothered testing the knife. He sat back, chin on paw. "Very good, rabbit. Can you do any more tricks?"

Ballaw pointed at Felldoh in his ridiculous outfit.

"More tricks, you say? Attend me here,
My magic is no trick.
Yon fox, I'll make him disappear,
With a wave of my magic stick!"

Rowanoak whispered in Felldoh's ear, "Now is the

chance to free your father. Try to remember what you were told. You won't get a second opportunity. Good luck."

The badger donned a massive black cloak as Buckler and Trefoil unloaded a box from the cart. Ballaw clapped Felldoh on the shoulder, haranguing him loudly as the stage was set.

"Now then, young fellah, you cunning fox,
How'd you like to disappear?
Just place yourself inside yon box,
And like a flash you're out of here!"

Felldoh backed off, his head flopping comically as he pleaded,

"What? Vanish me, sir Tibbar, no,
To what strange place would I then go?
Under the sea, or maybe up there,
To regions of the nether air.
I pray you, sir, please let me be.
Magic Tibbar, don't vanish me!"

Ballaw turned to the crowd. They were laughing at the comical fox's plight. Assisted by the rest of the company, he got a chant going that was soon picked up by everybeast.

"Where's the best place for the fox?
Locked up tight inside the box!"

The entire company leaped upon Felldoh and dragged him yelling to the box. There was utter confusion as they thrust him in and he sprang out again. In, out, in, out he went, with the delighted hordes of vermin leaping about chanting louder and louder,

"Where's the best place for the fox?
Locked up tight inside the box!"

Ballaw ran to the fire shouting madly, "In! In! Get him in, I say!"

He extended both paws to the fire.

Whoosh!

A great smoky gouting column of flame lit up the night. Red, green and brightest blue. There was a yell of alarm as creatures fell back, rubbing at their eyes in the blinding light.

Felldoh concealed himself beneath Rowanoak's huge black cloak. She moved swiftly away to the edge of the firelight and shook the brave squirrel free from the enveloping garment. Felldoh rolled deep into the shadows, flattening himself against the wall as he made his way to the slave compound. Buckler beat furiously on his small drum, secretly kicking away at the box so that it moved and shook. Trefoil stood at his side, her lips scarcely moving as she called out in a loud imploring tone,

"O pity, gentle creatures, lack a day.
Don't leave a poor fox here all locked away!"

Clogg nudged Badrang roughly. "Hoho that's settled the fox's 'ash. Tibbar's got 'im stowed tight in that there box!"

Kastern and Celandine paraded round, holding up a variety of big old-fashioned locks complete with keys and many lengths of tough seakelp rope.

"Who will lock the fox up tight?"
"Who will bind the box up right?"

There was no shortage of volunteers. Searats and corsairs mingled with members of the Tyrant's horde as they crowded round the box. Some proudly showed

144

their skills in rope knotting, while others secured the locks through the box's metal eyelets.

Ballaw strutted round the secured box, nodding with satisfaction.

"Lashed stoutly by good seafaring beasts,
By honest soldiers locked firm,
No creature could possibly get out of there.
Not even the smallest worm."

Badrang plucked the long dagger from where it stood quivering in the table. He strode across to the box, his lip curling as he addressed Ballaw.

"Has the fox disappeared from inside the box now?"

Ballaw's long ears twitched. He held up a cautionary paw. "Wait, Sire. Let me weave the spell."

He circled the box, gesturing and leaping.

"Now you vanish, unfortunate one.
A wave of my wand and you are gone.
Others may search and seek in vain,
But you will never be seen again!"

By sleight of paw, Ballaw produced a hazel twig. He tapped the box sharply, once, twice, thrice, calling out,

"Ongum bongum wollagum woe,
Vanish, disappear, dematerialize. Go!"

Turning to Badrang, he panted in mock exhaustion and bowed. "He is gone, m'lord. The box is empty. Shall I show you?"

The Tyrant smiled evilly, shaking his head. "No. Leave the box secured. But if the fox is really gone, I'm sure you won't mind me doing this!"

Darting forward, Badrang slammed the dagger down with furious energy straight through the box lid, up to its hilt. There was a horrified gasp from the onlookers, followed by a mad roar from Cap'n Tramun Clogg as he charged out, cutlass upraised.

"Murderer! I warned ye, Badrang, none of these magic beasts was to be harmed. You treacherous scum!"

Ballaw acted swiftly. Tripping Clogg, he grabbed the cutlass and ran the box through with it, using both paws. Turning, he helped the pirate stoat up and dusted him off.

"Nay nay, Cap'n. If I say the fox is vanished, then you can be sure he's gone. Hi there, you, Gurrad! D'you fancy throwin' your spear at the box? Anybeast, come on, have a go!"

There was silence for a moment, then Gurrad threw his spear. The heavy weapon crashed through the box, protruding from the other side. It was like a signal. Immediately, daggers, spears, arrows and even swords flew through the air. In seconds the box resembled a pincushion. When the missiles had stopped, Ballaw gave the box a mighty kick with his long hindpaws. It fell apart, showing everybeast that the fox had really vanished.

The hare spread his paws wide, grinning. "You see, when Tibbar the magic rabbit performs magic, it is real!"

Amid the hearty applause that followed, Druwp's voice squealed out from the direction of the stockade.

"The slaves are escaping. Help, come quick, they're escaping!"

17

The four friends had trekked through the scrub woodlands all afternoon, their shadows lengthening in front of them heralding the onset of evening. It had been a still, hot day, and the going was slow in the heat. Rose wiped her brow as she caught up with Pallum. Martin had been clearing ahead with his shrew sword.

"Phew, it'll get a little cooler as night falls, but then we'll lose our frontshadows in the dark."

They waited as Grumm caught up with them. The mole blinked as he wiped the moist tip of his nose. "Hurr, be cooler unnerground, us'ns a-goen t' make camp soon, Marthen?"

"Good idea, Grumm. We deserve a rest. Where d'you suggest we camp?"

"Burr, oi dunno. Wot say 'ee, Miz Roser?"

The mousemaid stood on tip-paw looking around. "Straight ahead, I'd say. It looks less scrubby and the trees are taller, like a proper forest. Let's camp by that old dead oak."

A slow smile spread across Pallum's face. "Do you mean that old dead oak with the three tops . . . ?"

Rose clapped her paws together as she recited the lines. *"Follow your frontshadow, do not stop, till you reach*

147

the one with dead three top. Hahah, that's it, an old dead three-topped oak. Come on!"

They lay in a mossy hollow at the base of the long dead forest giant, eating supper and looking up at the night sky. Above the woody canopy countless stars bejewelled the dark velvet expanse, and a silent fiery-tailed comet flashed across the peaceful scene. Rose picked at a small carrot and turnip farl as she passed the canteen of mint and lavender cordial to Martin.

"Well, we found the dead three top easy enough. Tomorrow we'll look for the twin paths. Oh, I do hope Brome and Felldoh are all right. I'd hate to think of us lying here eating if they needed our help."

Martin took a sip from the canteen. "Trust Polleekin's words, Rose. There's nothing else we can do. Brome is young, but Felldoh will look after him—he's a warrior."

The mousemaid looked at the short shrew sword sticking in the ground close to Martin's paw where he could reach it quickly.

"What's it like, being a warrior?"

"I don't know really," Martin shrugged. "I won't consider myself a warrior until the day I take my father's sword back from Badrang."

Rose tossed a piece of her bread. It bounced off Martin's nose. "Silly, of course you're a warrior. Even Polleekin saw that. I know you're a warrior because you protect others. Look at the way you've helped me and Grumm, and Pallum. And the way you dealt with that big seabird. Nobeast but a warrior could have done that."

Gentle snoring noises came from the mole and the hedgehog.

Martin chuckled. "No good asking them, they're sound asleep like I should be. Us warriors need lots of sleep, you know. Good night, Rose."

Long after Martin had gone to sleep, Rose lay awake thinking of her home in Noonvale.

"Noonvale." She said the name in a whisper to the star-strewn night.

To her it meant peace, happiness and security, filled as it was with family and friends. Noonvale, the secret place of the ancient northeastern forest. The young mousemaid closed her eyes and fell into a deep slumber, far from home. Noonvale.

Dawn arrived soft as a feather on air. Martin opened one eye and watched two ants trundling off with the tiny piece of bread that Rose had thrown at him. He lay still, thinking of Noonvale. He had talked with Rose the previous day. As they walked, she told him about her home, with Grumm adding the occasional comment.

The more Martin heard of the place the more he liked it. Maybe someday he could live there, with Rose and her family and Grumm and Pallum . . .

"Coom on, zurr Marthen. You'm a-goen t' loi thurr all season?" Grumm prodded Martin with his little ladle. "Naow, wot'll 'ee 'ave fer breffist. Oi c'n make zoop."

Rose sat up, rubbing her eyes. "No soup, Grumm. We'll eat from the packs."

Martin stood and stretched. "Aye, best not light a fire in strange country."

Grumm wandered off, muttering to himself. "Burr, no foire. Oi do loiks moi zoop of a mornen, leastways oi'm not a-goen wi'out fresh water. Oi'll go an' seek summ out."

Rose smiled as she dug apple turnovers out of her pack. "He's a proper old grump some mornings. Should've been called Grump instead of Grumm. Here, have one of these turnovers. He'll be back soon with fresh water. That's another thing he insists on most mornings. Even in winter, he'll sit out sucking icicles in the snow."

Pallum, Martin and Rose broke their fast with apple turnovers, some candied hazel and chestnuts and the remains of the cordial from the canteen. They sat enjoying the quiet woodland as the sun warmed the morning. Pallum kept some food out for Grumm as he repacked their provisions.

Rose stood up, looking around anxiously. "Where has that mole got to? He only went for water. I'll give him a shout . . ."

"No, don't raise your voice, Rose. If Grumm can hear it then so can others. Come on, we'll take a quiet walk and look for him."

Martin could see that Rose was concerned for her friend. She kept shaking her head and murmuring under her breath, "He's never usually gone this long. Grumm, silly beast, where are you?"

They were not far into the tall trees when Martin stopped. Pointing ahead, he leaned close and whispered, "*See the twin paths, beware of one Sweet as the spreading atop of a scone.* There they are, Rose. The twin paths. Look."

Two definite paths twisted and curved away through the tall treetrunks, one to the left, the other to the right.

"Maybe Grumm's gone down one, but which one?" Rose's voice sounded small in the huge silent forest.

"Neither, I 'ope. They both look pretty fearful. Maybe I best stay 'ere and wait in case Grumm shows up. You two can explore the paths. I'd only get in the way."

Rose could see that the hedgehog was afraid. She patted his prickles carefully. "Good idea, Pallum. Come on, Martin."

They ventured a short way along the path that ran to the right. It wound and curved but seemed safe enough. Martin shook his head. "Let's try the left path."

Creeping stealthily forward, they explored the left path. It seemed more tangled and overgrown than the other and oppressively hot. Again Martin halted. He made a gesture towards his ear, indicating that Rose should listen. The mousemaid heard it right away. It was a thick, heavy humming, like nothing she had ever heard. Straining her ears, she caught a low, frightened whimper.

"That's Grumm!"

"Aye, and it's coming from round that bend. You stay here, Rose." Martin drew his small sword.

"I'm coming with you. I couldn't stay here, Martin." Rose caught on to his paw.

"All right, but stay behind me and try not to make any noise."

They inched forward carefully. The humming grew heavier until it seemed to be part of the very air they breathed. There was an overpoweringly sweet smell everywhere. Martin brushed aside a wild dogrose and they rounded the bend.

It was a very strange scene that met their eyes.

Bees! There were literally millions of the insects. They swarmed on shrubs, bushes, trees and all over the ground. A fallen elm blocked the path completely, and gigantic hives stood everywhere along it—old hives, new hives, half-built hives and old broken ones. Honeycomb could be seen exposed in parts, thick, golden and wax-seamed. Amber nectar dripped to the ground and onto the heavy fungus that grew around the fallen tree. With his back almost touching the trunk sat Grumm, the small ladle held against his nose so that he could breathe. Rose stared wide-eyed. It was hard to distinguish Grumm from the bees that swarmed on him. They were all over his furry body, from footpaws to eartips, covering him completely and buzzing dangerously. Grumm had his eyes tight shut. Every once in while he would make a small frightened sound around the ladle that protected his nostrils.

"Sit still, Grumm," Rose said in a husky whisper. "Don't cry, there's a good mole. Martin and I are here now."

"Hurrmm, Miz Roser." Grumm's voice sounded muffled as he talked around the ladle. "They'm trapped oi daown yurr. Ooch! They stingen oi, not all at oncet, moind, just when they feels loik 'avin' some fun with oi. Ooch!"

Rose kept her voice low. "I'm sorry you're being stung, Grumm, but sit still and we'll have you out of there soon."

Martin spoke out of the side of his mouth. "Rose, they've got us trapped now. There's as many behind us as there are in front, and they're blocking our way out. Ow! I've been stung on the footpaw and they're beginning to swarm on me. You can't fight bees with a sword. Owch!"

Rose looked at Martin then down at herself. "That's strange, not a single bee has landed on me. Look!" She held her paw forth. Not a single insect tried to land on it.

Martin blinked in surprise. "How d'you do it . . . ? Owch!"

Realization dawned on Rose suddenly. "Martin, Grumm, don't speak, don't say a single word. I've noticed that every time you speak you get stung. Now, the bees aren't stinging me, so it must be because they like the sound of my voice. I've got an idea. Listen, I'm going to start singing. If they like my voice when I speak, they're sure to like it if I sing gently. As soon as you feel that it's safe, then take my paws and we'll walk out of here, or at least give it a try. Well, here goes. Let me sing a bit first."

Martin and Grumm remained still, like two statues covered by masses of slowly moving bees. Rose began her song.

"You will find me at Noonvale on the side of a hill
When the summer is peaceful and high,
There where streamlets meander the valley is still,
'Neath the blue of a calm cloudless sky . . . "

Right away Martin noticed a difference in the behavior

of the bees. The buzzing diminished to a low back-ground hum and the insects that were crawling over him ceased their activities.

"It's working," he whispered urgently to Rose. "Keep singing. I'm going to take your paw. Grumm, can you hear me? Reach out for Rose's paw when she sings."

Rose continued, her voice like warm breeze on a soft night.

"Look for me at dawning when the earth is asleep.
Till each dewdrop is kissed by the day,
'Neath the rowan and alder a vigil I'll keep,
Every moment that you are away . . ."

Rose stretched her paws forth. Feeling Martin and Grumm take them, she turned and began walking back down the path with a slow, measured pace. Martin and Grumm trod carefully alongside the mousemaid. She continued singing, and as they went the bees began dropping off and buzzing lazily back to their hives.

"The old earth gently turns as the seasons change slowly.
All the flowers and leaves born to wane.
Hear my song o'er the lea, like the wind soft and lowly.
Oh, please come back to Noonvale again."

Pallum was waiting anxiously at the entrance to the path. At the sight of his friends returning he did a small dance of joy, coupled with anxiety at the lumps and bumps raised by the bee stings.

"Haha! There you are, thank the seasons! Oh, look at you, Grumm, all covered in swellin's. What happened?"

The mole smiled at his worried friend. "Bo urr, that be anuther story, Pallum. Move asoide so us'ns can set daown an' rest us'ns' weary bodies, hurr?"

The three travellers slumped against a spreading sycamore. Martin shook his head in amazement, burying his short sword point down in the loam. "Thank you, Rose. That was marvellous. Who needs a sword to defend us? That's the second time you've won a victory with your voice—first as a sea eagle, then as a singer. You know, the strange thing is that I hardly noticed the bees. All I could hear was your song. I could have listened to it for ever!"

Pallum made poultices of dockleaves, nightshade and mud. "Sit still now while I put these on your stings to cool them. Best thing in the world for stings. How's that?"

"Ooh, you don't know how good that feels," Martin sighed gratefully as the fire died from the stings under Pallum's ministrations. "All we need now is another song from Rose."

Grumm spat away a bee sting that he had nipped out with his teeth. "Ho yurss, Miz Roser be the noicest songer in all Noonvale. 'Er daddy an' oi watched many a time whoil she singen 'ee burds outen 'ee trees."

Rose was all a-fluster. She jumped up and shouldered her pack. "It was only an old Noonvale song. Every young creature there can sing it as well as me. Come on you two, or are you going to sit there all morning?"

The mousemaid set off down the path at a lively pace, with Martin and Grumm bringing up the rear as Pallum pulled stings from them.

"That's it, right there in the middle of my back. Ooh, that's better. Get that one on the side of Grumm's neck."

"Oochooch! Go easy, zurr 'edgepig. You'm wurser than 'ee liddle peskers as put yon stingers thurr!"

They made good progress that day, though the woodland grew high and gloomy as they traversed it. It was noontide, yet the sun could hardly be glimpsed through the high interwoven foliage canopy. Dim green light filtering down gave the path an eerie quality of unreality. Halting by a little brook, the four friends made a late lunch of applescones washed down with the cold sparkling water. When they had finished, Grumm and Pallum sat dabbling their footpaws in the brook, grunting and making small noises of happiness as the babbling water gurgled over their paws. Martin and Rose sat behind them, nudging each other and stifling silent giggles as they watched the pair enjoy their paddle.

"I see you. Beware!"

Quick as a flash, Martin leaped up, drawing his sword at the sound of a booming voice in the half-lit forest. He held up a paw, cautioning his friends to silence. They waited a moment, then the voice echoed out a second time.

"Go back, small ones. Leave my path!"

"Who are you?" Martin shouted then, surprised at how the forest echoed and magnified his voice.

"I am the Mirdop." The spectral sound rumbled about the treetrunks. "I see all. None can pass me. Go back!"

"We mean no harm," Martin replied, keeping his voice friendly as possible. "We are only travellers trying to reach Noonvale!" Leaning aside he whispered quickly to Rose. "Keep him talking. I'll try and find out where he is!"

"Be still, all of you!" the voice rang out, hollow and angry. "For I am Mirdop, born in a storm at the night of winter's moon! I see all! I slay all!"

Placing her paws firmly together, Rose did a magnificent harsh grating voice which rang and echoed wildly.

"And I am Martin the Warrior. I have slain more than the hairs on your hide! I have defeated Amballa and Badrang. Let us pass!"

There was more silence, then the voice called threateningly, "One warrior is nought to a Mirdop. I will eat him up!"

Rose resorted to her own natural voice as she answered, "There is more than one warrior here, there are four! I am Rose, the deadliest slayer in Noonvale. I eat Mirdops for breakfast. What say you, Pallum the Mighty?"

Pallum swelled until his stickles separated and shrieked out, "Yahoooo! I am Pallum the Mighty. I carry a thousand swords! I too eat Mirdops, though generally as snacks! Stay clear of me and watch out for my friend Grumm the Growler!"

"What is a Grumm the Growler?" the mysterious Mirdop voice answered them. This time Rose thought she caught a note of hesitation in it.

The mole shuffled forward, brandishing his ladle. "Oi be Grumm the Growler, a gurt moighty beast! Oi makes zoop out o' Mirpods an' sangwiches from they tails, ho urr!"

"I care not who you be." The Mirdop's voice sounded definitely unsure now. "Go back or die. Nobeast passes the Mirdop!"

"Hurr, then they be allus a furst toime!"

"Stand aside or we'll go right over you!"

"Mirdop or no Mirdop, we're coming!"

"Stay back, keep away." The Mirdop voice sounded strained and frantic now. "I've fought foxes, battered badgers, whipped weasels, strangled stoats . . . Owooooaaahhheeeh!"

"Over here, friends. Hurry!" Martin's voice rang out loud and clear.

From somewhere up in front of them came a crashing and the most dreadful earsplitting screams and yells.

Rose grabbed a fallen branch and shook it fiercely. "The Mirdop must have got Martin. Come on. Chaaaaarge!"

The three travellers rushed forward along the path to where the horrible noises rose to a deafening intensity.

18

Tullgrew and Keyla threw themselves upon Felldoh, hugging and patting the brave squirrel.

"Haha! Good to see your battered old face again, mate!"

"Aye, yore a sight for sore eyes all right friend!"

Felldoh winked at them cheerily.

Helped by Tullgrew and Keyla, Felldoh battered aside two logs from the compound wall. It was difficult to keep the joyous slaves silent and orderly. Barkjon and Hillgorse hurried them through, encouraging and advising quietly.

"You get through, marm. I'll pass you the young un."

"Haha! We're free, Barkjon. Free as the air!"

"Not quite. Keep your voice down and hurry please."

"Hillgorse, can I take my bag of shells? They'll make good cups and platters. I've collected them for three seasons."

"Leave them, we may have to run for it. You'd only be slowed down lugging that lot along."

Felldoh and Keyla had taken the two logs from the palisade, laying them against the back of the fortress main wall to form an easy way to the top. They lifted and pushed the slaves up to where Tullgrew waited with a stout kelp rope. One at a time she swung them out over the top.

"Now I'm going to lower you down. Let go of the rope and jump as soon as you can. There's bedding mattresses down there to break your fall. Hurry now, we need the rope for the others."

In the midst of the bustle, Barkjon found time to grasp his son's paw. "Felldoh, I knew you wouldn't let us down. Where's Martin?"

The squirrel hugged his father quickly. "That's a story for another day. Come on, let's free these slaves, old bushtail!"

For the first time in many a long day Barkjon grinned happily. "Old bushtail yourself, whippersnapper. I'll wager you don't go over that wall faster than I do!"

It was as they were laughing together that Druwp shouted, "The slaves are escaping, help, come quick, they're escaping!"

Badrang kicked over the banquet table. Hauling out the sword that had once belonged to Martin, he laid about him with the flat of the blade.

"Get to the compound, quick! I knew something like this would happen. Come on, stir your stumps, you addlebrained scum. Move!"

The Tyrant's horde stumbled over each other, grabbing weapons as they rushed to do their master's command. Badrang dashed about like a madbeast, using the flat of his blade as a rod, smacking heads and paws with numbing force.

"Hurry, run! Are you deaf or stupid? Move, you mudworms!"

Tramun Clogg sat on the overturned table, still drinking and eating, a sly smile hovering on his greasy lips.

"Ho dearie me, the liddle slaves are all runnin' off. 'Ere, Gruzzle, d'you reckon it's 'cos they don't like it 'ere?"

The Tyrant cast a murderous glance at the corsair stoat. "This is all your fault, Clogg—you and your magic rabbit with his performing friends. They've got something to do with this, I'm certain of it! Well, aren't you going to help?"

Clogg slopped kelp beer down his whiskers as he drank. "They're yore slaves mate, you see to 'em. I'm only a pore 'onest wavebeast who's down on 'is luck."

Quivering with rage, Badrang pointed his sword at the corsair. "Don't worry, I will. But you look to those magic friends of yours and hold them here until I get back. I'm holding you personally responsible for them!"

The Tyrant dashed off after his horde.

Ballaw glanced uneasily at Rowanoak. "D'you hear that, old gel, looks like we're in for a spot of bother, wot? Plan number two I'd say, eh!"

Brome tugged at Buckler's tunic. "What's plan number two?"

"Hurr 'tis pretty simple, maister. When you'm be in trouble an' they audience doant loik 'ee no more, then us'ns run fer it loik billyoh!"

Rowanoak began singing softly to the Rambling Rosehip Players.

"I think we'll call it a day,
Back to the cart I say.
It's exit left without any pay.
We'd be better off far away!"

The company began sidling unobtrusively towards their cart.

Clogg staggered upright. Throwing his drink down, he began tugging to free the cutlass from his waist sash.

"Ahoy, Tibbar. 'Old 'ard there. Where d'you think yore off to?"

Completely unruffled, Ballaw made an elegant bow.

"Love to stay, old Cloggo old stoat, but you know how 'tis. We need our jolly old beauty sleep."

Tramun tipped the wink to Boggs, Crosstooth and Gruzzle. In a trice they had the pirate crew surrounding the players.

Clogg licked the blade of his cutlass and closed one eye. "An' all the time I thought you was me mateys. It ain't friendly like runnin' off so soon. 'Ow's about you doin' one more bit o' magic fer ole Tramun?"

Ballaw gave the stoat a large toothy grin and a wink. "Why certainly, me old wave walloper. One more piece of magic, just for you, comin' up right away. How'd you like to see me vanish the entire troupe, cart an' all, presto, just like that!"

"Vanish the 'ole crew of ye?"

"That's what I said, old sport."

"An' the cart too, an' all of this whilst yore surrounded?"

"That's the ticket, Cap'n!"

"Haharr, 'tis impossible. But you carry on, matey!"

Ballaw collected several hefty pieces of firewood and distributed them to the troupe. Meanwhile, Rowanoak harnessed herself to the cart shafts. The hare indicated by sweeping dramatic gestures that they all climb up on to the cart. When they had, he joined them.

"Laydeez an' gennelbeasts, watch closely! As you see, we are all holding a large magic wand each. That is, with the exception of my good friend the magic badger there. Now watch closely please, as my old uncle Flobbears used to say. The speed of the paw always deceives the eye, an' more often than not blackens it. Are you ready? One, three, two four, whatever. Chaaaaarge!"

The huge female badger threw all her weight and speed against the shafts, sending the cart forward like a runaway boulder on a mountainside. It smashed through the surrounding corsairs, sending them scattering like ninepins as the troupe flailed and thwacked away at searat heads with their large magic wands.

Clogg was taken aback momentarily, then he was up and pursuing the cart as it headed for the open gate of Marshank.

"Stop' em. It's a trick!"

Ballaw caught Gruzzle a hefty blow, sending him ears over tail. "Of course it's a trick, old lad. I told you it was!"

Tullgrew gave a shout of alarm from the walltop as she saw the horde pounding towards the compound. "Lookout, Felldoh. They're coming!"

Only half of the slaves were over the wall. Felldoh looked around in desperation as Hillgorse and Barkjon came running to him. The horde were now pelting around the outside of the compound towards them.

Barkjon groaned aloud. "There's too many and we have no weapons!"

Felldoh gritted his teeth. "At least half of us got away. Wait, this might hold 'em off a bit!" Grabbing a chunk of rock, he called up to Tullgrew, "Throw that rope down!"

Catching the rope, Felldoh secured the rock to one end of it and began swinging it as he advanced on the horde. It took out several of them before they hurriedly backed off. The chunk of rock circled and whirred in a deadly blur as Felldoh roared, "Come on. Who's next, you stinking bunch of cowards! Come on!"

"Get him, you dolts! Rush him!" Badrang howled with rage as he pushed his creatures forward.

Grabbing a spear from a weasel called Rotnose, Badrang hurled it. Still swinging the rock, Felldoh leaped to one side. The spear missed him but took Barkjon through his shoulder. Immediately, Hillgorse pulled the spear from his friend. The hedgehog was powerfully built despite his age. Wielding the spear with a strength born of desperation, he launched himself at the horde of foebeasts, plunging and stabbing wildly. In the narrow space between stockade and wall they were driven back

161

by the spear and the swinging rock. Hillgorse stuck the spear in the ground by Felldoh.

"Give me the rope, young un. Take the spear and get your father away from here, he's been wounded. Do as I say, quickly!"

Felldoh grabbed the spear as he felt the rope taken from his paws by Hillgorse. Tullgrew had climbed halfway down the two log steps on the wall, and between them they hauled the semiconscious Barkjon upwards. Two arrows found Hillgorse as others clattered and bounced off the walls around Tullgrew and Felldoh, who had succeeded in gaining the walltop with the limp form of Barkjon held between them.

Bravely Hillgorse swung the rock, his strength failing as he shouted at the walltop, "Get away from here, Felldoh. Save your father and the others!"

Another arrow struck Hillgorse, and the rope slipped from his paws. The old hedgehog's eyes were misting over as he gave a final roar and hurled his spiky body into the ranks of the enemy.

Felldoh tried to scramble back down to Hillgorse, but Tullgrew hung on, pulling him back. "We must escape. He gave his life so we could be free!"

Felldoh bit his lip until blood showed. He took one last look at the scene below. Badrang and his horde were beginning to mount the logs and scale the wall, and the slaves who had not managed to escape were forcing their way back into the compound through the gap they had made. Felldoh still had the spear in his paw when he noticed who the last of the slaves was and shouted his name.

"Druwp!"

The treacherous bankvole did not turn. He knew who was calling him. He tried to squeeze through the gap back into the stockade but found his way blocked by the slaves inside.

"Out of my way or I'll report you!"

Those were the last words that Druwp spoke. Felldoh

threw the spear, harder than he had ever thrown anything. It found its mark between the traitor's shoulder blades.

"Jump!"

Holding Barkjon between them, Felldoh and Tullgrew leaped from the walltop into the night. It was a good drop, but the straw-packed mattresses broke their fall. The others were waiting for them. They looked this way and that, unsure which would be the best direction to take in the darkness. Suddenly a nearby rumbling caused them to crouch down in the wall shadows, and a voice rang out.

"What ho, is that the disappearin' fox?"

Felldoh gave a sigh of relief. "Ballaw! I see you managed to escape safely."

"Rather! Though at the moment there's a posse of pirates hot on our paws. I say, have you got ladies an' young uns there?"

"Aye, and a wounded father, and any moment now Badrang'll be coming over that wall with his horde."

"Calls for a bit of quick thinkin', wot? Righto! Get the babes, mothers an' wounded into the cart. Everybeast fit to run get pushin', but wait until I give the word . . . Wait for it . . ."

The sound of Clogg's crew rounding the outside of the back wall blended with the shouts of Badrang and his horde, who had now reached the walltop. Ballaw kicked the last of the straw mattresses away into the night and joined his friends at the cart.

"Head south smartly now. Look alive, you chaps. Go!"

The wheels of the small wagon nearly left the ground as it shot forward, propelled by every able-bodied creature. In moments it had clattered off into the darkness.

Badrang pushed Hisk and Gurrad off the walltop. Grabbing others, he began shoving them off into space.

"Jump, you lily-livered toads. The slaves did it easily enough. Come on, you there, Nipwort, Fleabane. Jump!"

Bodies went flying from the walltop. Horde soldiers shut their eyes and leaped, preferring the drop to Badrang's towering anger.

The removal of the cushioning straw sacks made the landing hard for those who did not land on the heads of Cap'n Tramun Clogg and several of his crew members.

Ballaw had judged his timing right. Confusion reigned in the darkness as the corsair crew and the Tyrant's horde fought each other tooth and claw in the night.

19

A monster stood on the path in front of Rose. It had the body of a fox, the talons of an owl and a huge snakelike head with three big goggling eyes surmounted above rows of fearsome teeth. Dashing madly along to where the dreadful screams were issuing from, the mousemaid tried to stop at the sight of the horrendous apparition. Grumm and Pallum cannoned into her back, sending her staggering straight into the arms of the nightmare beast. She screamed aloud in terror as she blundered into its embrace.

Then it collapsed on the path in a dusty heap. Straw, grass, bark, dead ferns and feathers swirled everywhere.

Rose sneezed, spitting out a mouthful of downy fur as Pallum and Grumm came gingerly forward to help her up.

"Burr, wot be et?"

"Huh, Mirdop, it's nothing but a great big doll hanging from the trees by bits of creeper!"

Rose dusted herself down, looking around wildly. "Where's Martin?"

The horrendous screams had stopped. To one side of the path Martin sat upon a great hollow log, chuckling quietly. "Bravo, Rose. You've just slain your first Mirdop!"

The mousemaid looked flustered. "But how . . . and you . . . those screams . . . ?"

"Come over here and I'll show you."

Martin bent beside the hollow log and called aloud, "Go back, for I am the Mirdop and I will slay you!"

The sound thundered and reverberated around the forest, magnified by the hollow ash log.

Grumm uncovered his ears when the noise faded.

"But oo wurr a-doen all 'ee shouten?"

Martin took them around the other side of the big log to where four rabbits, obviously mother, father and two young, were lying slumped.

"Oh dear, you haven't killed them, Martin?" Rose gasped.

The young mouse shook his head and smiled. "Of course not. I couldn't harm creatures like these. I sneaked up and saw what they were doing, so I thought I'd take a leaf out of your book, Rose."

The mousemaid looked mystified, then Martin explained. "Remember, the warrior who uses the voice instead of the sword? Well, I crept up behind them and started yelling as loud and horrible as I could. Of course, being new at this sort of thing, I suppose I underestimated the power of my cries. The rabbits seemed to freeze then fainted right away!"

Rose hurried to the side of the two babes. She stroked them tenderly until they began whimpering and moving. "Poor little things. You great bully, Martin. Fancy doing an awful thing like that!"

Grumm and Pallum had to hide their faces to stop bursting out laughing at the sight of Martin, paws outstretched in bewilderment.

"I didn't hurt them. What was I supposed to do, set about them with my sword, or ask them nicely to please stop terrorizing travellers? You're the one who went and destroyed their Mirdop. Bully yourself!"

Rose fussed about, wetting the older rabbits' mouths with water until they revived. Instantly they drew back in horror.

"Aagh! Go away, you savage creatures. Which one is Grumm the Growler, and who is Pallum the Mighty and Rose the Slayer?"

Grumm tugged his snout respectfully at the female rabbit.

"Hurr 'tis oi, marm. But oi doant mean 'ee no 'arm."

Martin took a slightly stronger line with them. "Er, just a moment, please. I think it's we should be asking the questions. What d'you mean by shouting threats and trying to intimidate travellers on this path?"

The father rabbit held a shaky paw to his brow. "Please, not so loud, we're really delicate creatures, you know. Allow me to introduce us. I'm Fescue, this is my wife Mildwort and these are the twins Burnet and Buttercup. Mirdop's the family name, hence the, er, figure we have to keep away intruders."

"Oh yes, it was Fescue's great Grandpa who built it," his wife interrupted. "One never knows what horrid types of beast want to wander abroad on our path. Please don't harm us, we were only protecting ourselves."

Rose sat by Mildwort Mirdop and spoke soothingly. "We wouldn't dream of harming a nice little family like yours. I'm sorry we frightened you, but we were rather scared ourselves with all that threatening and roaring you were doing."

Fescue laughed nervously. "Er yes, haha, rather good, wasn't it? By the way, have you had tea yet?"

Grumm's stomach made a small gurgle as he rubbed it. "Us'ns be allus ready furr vittles, zurr. Do you'm 'ave zoop?"

Mildwort stared down her snub nose at the mole. "Hardly. Soup is not good for one at this time of day. Follow me, please."

They followed the Mirdop family down into their burrow. It was large, comfortable and spotless. Behind their backs, Pallum made a snooty gesture with paw to nose, and Grumm nodded in agreement.

Tea was a very formal affair in the Mirdop burrow. First the guests were given lavender-scented soap, warm water and soft barktowels to wash and dry their paws. The two young rabbits were sent back several times until their parents were satisfied that their paws were cleaned properly, then they all sat down at a small table.

Mildwort Mirdop brought a large pot of steaming mint tea with honey to go in it, a platter of wafer-thin cucumber sandwiches and seven tiny oat scones, each lightly spread with raspberry preserve. She seated herself, and in the silence that followed murmured quietly to her husband; "The grace before tea, dear."

Fescue coughed gently to clear his throat. They all stared down at the spotless tablecloth while he repeated the grace.

"For all we receive for tea,
Thanks to the seasons be.
Partake we sparingly
Of this good meal."

As they each chose a cucumber sandwich, Mildwort scolded Burnet. "Sandwiches first, scones later. Put it back please."

Baby Burnet scowled slightly. "Scones are my fav'rite."

Fescue tweaked his ear lightly. "Baby bunnies should be seen and not heard, Burnet. Don't talk back to your mother. How many times must we tell you!"

The meal was eaten rather quickly in polite frosty silence. Grumm made a sucking noise as he drained his teacup and sat back. "Hurr, they'm noice scones, marm. Oi'm partial to a noice scone."

Mildwort sniffed. "So are we, Mr. Grumm. There are more in the cupboard for tomorrow."

Fescue smiled nervously as he nodded agreement.

"Indeed there are, dear. No sense in overstuffing with food. Er, you say you are bound for Noonvale. I've no idea where the place is. We've always lived by our path, never moved away. I'm afraid I can't give you any directions, but I'm sure that from here you'll have to cross the west marshes. My advice to you is watch out for lizards. Nasty things—cannibals, I might add!"

Baby Burnet nodded and agreed with his father. "Cabbinals!"

"Burnet!" Fescue looked severely at him. "Do not interrupt your elders and betters. You are excused from the table. You too, Buttercup. Don't stray far from the burrow and try to keep clean. Bedtime soon."

Like two silent shadows, the little ones got down from their chairs, bobbed a curtsy and a bow to the guests and left the burrow with their mother's voice ringing in their ears.

"Walk, don't run. How many times must I tell you!"

As she cleared away the tea things from under the noses of the still hungry travellers, she said in a strained voice. "You are welcome to stay the night in our burrow."

Rose kicked Grumm beneath the table as he searched for crumbs. "How nice of you, Mrs. Mirdop, but we wouldn't dream of imposing upon your good nature. Besides, we have a long journey ahead of us and we must go while there is still daylight. Er, you mentioned cannibal lizards, Mr. Mirdop?"

Fescue Mirdop helped his wife to fold the tablecloth. "Oh yes, so I did. Right, here's what you must do. At the edge of the forest the marshes begin. Find the place called Marshwood Hill. If the lizards trouble you, then strike the gong you will see hanging from a hornbeam tree. The Warden will take care of you. He's such a nice creature, isn't he, dear?"

Mildwort Mirdop nodded vigorously. "Oh yes, the Warden of Marshwood Hill, a very, very nice creature!"

They took their leave of the Mirdops, thanking them for a pleasant stay. Mr. and Mrs. Mirdop waved before retreating back down their burrow. Grumm rummaged through their ration packs until he found some candied acorns and chestnuts. The two baby Mirdops were playing in front of the burrow, and he gave them a pawful each of the nuts.

"Yurr, babbies, eat'm oop noice'n messy loik. They'm guid'n sweet."

Further along the path, Martin and Rose fell about laughing as Pallum imitated the hungry Grumm at tea, taking both the parts of the mole and Mrs. Mildwort Mirdop.

"Burr, oi'm pow'ful 'ungry, give oi a scone, missus!"

"No no, you nasty rough mole, one is quite sufficient!"

"Hurr, then give oi summ zoop, marm."

"Soup? Lack a season, the ruffian will eat us out of house and burrow. Go away and be off with you, you gluttonous beast!"

Grumm drew his ladle and shook it at Pallum. "One moor wurd out of 'ee an' oi'll raise a bump on you'm spikers!"

Late that evening they reached the forest edge. Standing on a small rise, they looked down on the great West Marshes spreading as far as the eye could see. Grasshoppers chirruped in the short hillgrass and myriad swarms of flies and midges were everywhere.

Rose shooed a cloud away with a dead fern. "Whew! I'm not sleeping the night out here. Let's go back and camp in the fringe of the trees. We can face this lot in the morning."

They slumped down wearily beneath a sycamore and a beech. A slithering nearby caused Martin to jump up. Two long slowworms snaked away hissing noisily, disturbed from their rest. The creatures made no move to attack, but Martin stood with short sword drawn watching them slither down the side of the rise toward the marshes. Pallum began collecting dry firewood and digging a shallow pit.

"It's all right, they're only slowworms. Evil-looking reptiles, they do lots of hissing but they can't really harm you. Right, Grumm, what'll it be? Cucumber sandwiches or one scone apiece?"

The mole was busy digging out some mushrooms he had found. He looked up, shaking soil from his snout energetically. "Zoop, we'm 'aven zoop! Aye, an' oi'll make a pudden too, wi' some apple an' blackberries growen over yonder."

Night fell warm and mild, with the small fire burning red as they sat around it, well fed and satisfied with their day's progress.

"Tut tut, Mr. Grumm the Growler," Rose teased Grumm. "If I were you I'd put half that pudding away for the morrow. You've eaten far too much already and it's way past your bedtime!"

The mole looked up from a ladleful of pudding and snorted, "Oi should've left you'm be'oind wi' they Mirkdops, mizzy. Teach you'm some manners, hurr!"

They watched a full moon move silently from behind pillowy night-cloud formations, it hung in the sky like a still, new-polished silver coin.

The two slowworms had returned. With them was a band of lizards twoscore strong. Their tongues slid silently in and out, filmy eyes blinking constantly against the dry warmth of the night. The two slowworms indicated where the sleeping travellers lay by thrusting their heads forward and hissing. The lizard leader, a great red-frilled reptile, nodded his head slowly as he watched the glow from the red embers of the fire dying lower. Soon the fire would be cold and the four travellers deep in sleep. The lizards waited patiently, watching their leader, waiting for him to move.

20

It was fully dawn when the escaped slaves and the Rambling Rosehip Players made their way back to the hide-out on the southern cliffs. Puffing and panting, they threw themselves down on the grass and lay in the cool morning breeze. Gauchee came later than the rest. She had been watching their backtrack, covering the cart marks and keeping a wary eye peeled for pursuers. The mouse sat with her back to the cart.

"Nobeast following us, they must still be busy fighting among each other."

Ballaw flopped his long ears thoughtfully from side to side. "Maybe so, but they'll try and find us. I can't imagine old Badthingy lettin' half his slaves an' us off that lightly. We'd be best postin' a guard. I'll take first watch, me an' this jolly-lookin' young mousey feller here. What's your name, sir?"

"They call me Juniper."

"Righto, Juno, me old nipper, you an' me are first guard."

Rowanoak blew tenderly on her paws. "Ooh, that's better! This dashing about all night doesn't suit me any more. Not as young as I used to be. Kastern, what are you up to this morning?"

"Well, there's lot of new mouths to feed," the sensible

172

young mousemaid explained, "so I'm going to organize a forage party, see what we can find to swell our larder out a bit. I'll take some of our new companions when they've had a rest and a bite of breakfast."

Rowanoak liked to keep her paw on the pulse of activities in camp. She sat down and began massaging her footpaws.

"Hmm, good idea. Who's on cooking duties this morning?"

Trefoil wiped wheat flour from her paws on a dock-leaf. "It looks like it's me again. I did it yesterday too. That Celandine was supposed to take her turn today, but she's probably off fluttering her pretty eyelashes at the new arrivals and enchanting them all."

"Oh, is she. Well, I'm not having any of that!" Rowanoak stood up decisively. "There are no shirkers in this troupe, everybeast pulls their weight. Where is she? Celandine! Celandine, it's no use hiding, missy. I want a word with you, m'lady!"

Rowanoak searched the camp several times before she began to get worried. Nobeast had seen the pretty squirrelmaid.

Ballaw left sentry duty a moment to call an assembly. "Attention please. Has anyone seen Celandine?"

Barkjon held a healing poultice of herbs to his injured shoulder. The wound was not as serious as it had appeared the previous night. Felldoh held his father's head upright as Brome fed him soup from a scallop shell.

"Drink up, sir. This is made from green nettles and I don't know what, supposed to help recovery."

The old squirrel licked his lips as he finished the soup. "It tastes very nice. What's going on over there, some sort of meeting?"

"It's a young squirrelmaid, one of the company, she's missing."

Barkjon sat up a bit, resting his back against his son's

paws. With his eyes half-closed he nodded slowly. "I remember now. Was she an extremely pretty creature?"

Brome put aside the empty shell. "Oh yes, d'you recall her?"

"Indeed I do. Though I was only half conscious, I remember seeing her face over the back of the cart as she pushed. I thought she was the nicest-looking squirrel I had ever seen. I must have dozed off awhile, because when I woke she wasn't there any more. Perhaps she tripped and fell."

"Aye." Brome nodded, recalling the wild dash from Marshank. "We were going so fast that nobeast would have noticed. She's either lost or captured by now."

Felldoh laid his father down carefully. "If she's lost I'll find her."

Barkjon struggled to get up. "But what if she's captured, son?"

"Then I'll free her, or die trying!" Felldoh's strong face radiated anger and hatred. He strode off, leaving Brome and Barkjon gazing after him.

The old squirrel shook his head. "Let him go, Brome. There is a great rage in my son against all that Marshank stands for. You were only there a short while, he has spent most of his life as a slave. I know how he feels."

Soon the news was all over the camp that Celandine was either lost or captured. Ballaw posted Buckler on guard with Juniper. He conferred with Rowanoak awhile, then they both went to talk with Felldoh.

The squirrel was sitting by the fire. At his side lay a pile of short heavy driftwood lances. He was hardening their points to needle sharpness by burning and rubbing them on a rock. Felldoh was intent on his work and he did not even bother to look up as the hare and badger approached.

"What ho, treejumper. Looks like you're armin' yourself up to start a one beast war there, wot?"

Felldoh continued sharpening the short lances as he

replied, "Whatever it takes, I've got scores to settle at Marshank."

Rowanoak squatted alongside him. "Need any help, Felldoh?"

He pulled another lance from the fire and began grinding it to a point on the rock. "It's not your fight. I got your troupe into this, and it's time I did a bit myself without endangering others."

Rowanoak nodded understandingly, realizing Felldoh was in no mood to be argued with. She watched him awhile before picking up one of the lances and weighing it in her paw. "How far can you throw one of these things?"

Felldoh took the lance and stood up. "Far enough. My muscles are stronger than most after seasons working in Badrang's rock quarry." He threw the lance from the clifftop. It sailed out over the beach a fair distance before burying itself point first in the sand.

"Not bad at all." Rowanoak winked at the hare. "Ballaw and I can throw a short lance twice that distance."

"I'd like to see you try!" Felldoh laughed humorlessly.

Ballaw sought around until he came up with a piece of driftwood not quite as long as the lances Felldoh was making. Taking a knife, he cut a deep notch across one end of the wood, then hefted it and made several throwing motions. A few more adjustments to the wood with his knife and Ballaw nodded with satisfaction.

"That's about right, old chap. Pass me a javelin—any one'll do."

Felldoh selected one of the short heavy javelins and gave it to Ballaw. The hare laid the javelin flat along his piece of wood, point forward and the other end resting against the notch he had cut. With the weapon lying flat on the wood against the notch, he drew back his arm, took a short hopskip and flung out, holding on to the wood. The javelin soared away, passing Felldoh's

175

weapon on the beach, travelling onward and finally splashing down into the water on the tideline, almost out of sight. Felldoh gasped as Ballaw gave him the piece of wood.

"Here, old lad, you have it. Simple device, eh wot? Makes your throwing arm twice its length and gives you double the distance."

Felldoh looked at the javelin launcher as Ballaw continued, "We've won many a supper at tribe gatherings in the south with one of those. There was always some big brawny beast wagered he could throw a javelin farther than me or Rowanoak."

The badger offered her paw to Felldoh. "Now do you want our help?"

Felldoh grasped the big paw, his eyes alight with resolve. "Let's go and see if they've got Celandine at Marshank!"

Accusations flew thick and fast at Marshank, Clogg and Badrang blaming the whole thing on one another in the wake of the confusion at the rear wall. While the remainder of the slaves were under heavy guard, the other corsairs and horde members gathered in the courtyard to witness the argument raging between their leaders. It was a fine show of rage, spleen and insults.

"Hah, Lord 'igh an' mighty Badrang, is it? Can't 'old on to arf a passel of defenceless slavebeasts. Yore a lobstertail!"

"I'd sooner be anything but a complete idiot who lets the enemy into Marshank and has the gall to call them friends. You always did keep your brains in your clogs, Tramun, you buffoon!"

"Buffoon yerself. Ye blown up pollywoggle! There was me an' the crew nearly catchin' those creatures, an' wot did you do? Jumped off the wall on to our 'eads, you jellyfish!"

"Jellyfish? You're the one who started all this mess, addlebrain!"

"Oh, is that so? Then who set fire to my ship and who let the slaves escape? You've brought bad luck on both of us, fiddlebrain!"

"Shut your mouth, you pigtailed poltroon, or I'll shut it for you!"

"Haharr, now yore flyin' yer true colours, jugnose. I'm not stoppin' round 'ere to bandy words with the like o' you, I'm off to do somethin' useful. Gruzzle, Boggs, form the crew up fully armed."

"Hold hard there, woodenpaws. Where d'you think you're off to?"

"Well, clean out yer mucky lugs an' lissen whilst I tell yer. Those slaves that escaped last night is now free beasts, you got no jurisdiction over 'em anymore, Badrang yore Lordship. So, if any beast were to recapture 'em, then they'd belong to the finder, an' that'll be me if yer please. Come on, lads. Away, boat's crew!"

Badrang watched Clogg and his crew march off through Marshank's front gates.

"Shall we form the horde up and stop 'em, Lord?" Gurrad whispered anxiously to the Tyrant.

Badrang gave the rat a withering glance. "Stop them, what for? Let me do the thinking, Gurrad. If Clogg recaptures the slaves, where's he going to take them, what's he going to feed them on, where's he going to keep them penned up?"

Gurrad looked puzzled, "I don't know, Lord. Where?"

Badrang tapped a paw against his skull. "That's why you're a hordebeast and I'm a leader, Gurrad. What else can Clogg do but bring them back here. When he does, I'll take them from him. So, what could be simpler than allowing Cap'n Tramun Clogg to be our slave chaser."

Gurrad sniggered gleefully, rubbing his paws together. "You're a clever one, Sire. A real clever one!"

Badrang buffed his claws on his fir and inspected them. "I could buy and sell an oaf like Clogg anyday. He'll soon find that out to his cost."

Celandine was lost. When she tripped and fell while running through the night with the cart, the young squirrelmaid had cracked her head and passed out on the spot. Dawn had broken a full hour before she came to. Celandine's first reaction was to sit and cry, and she did so. Sobbing and wailing broken-heartedly, she lay on the clifftop, kicking her footpaws and nursing a bruised lump, just below her ear near her jawline. At regular intervals she would stop and sniff, calling out the names of Ballaw, Rowanoak, Buckler and Felldoh. Hearing no reply, the pretty squirrelmaid would throw herself back full-throated into a bout of copious bellowing and weeping. Why did no one come? There was always somebeast round to dance attention when tears flowed down her beautiful face. It took quite a long time for Celandine to realize that she was totally alone, so she set about doing what she did best, preening herself and attending to her looks. She brushed, licked, dusted and primped, holding her head coyly on one side so that the curve of her bushy tail hid the unsightly bump she had suffered. Then she sat again and bemoaned her fate aloud to the bright morning air.

"Owwww! Why doesn't somebeast come for me? My head's aching and I must look a dreadful sight. Owww! I'm hungry and thirsty and dusty and dirty and now I'm lost. Owoooh!"

The weasel Floater had been scouting ahead. He made his way back to where Clogg was leading the crew.

"No tracks of the carts, Cap'n. They finish over yonder. Musta been somebeast coverin' the trail."

Clogg looked at the ground, chewing one of his beard plaits. "Covered, ye say? Bad fortune fer us, matey. Lookit, 'ere comes ole Crosstooth. May'ap 'e 'as some news."

The fox pointed at a tangent to where the cart tracks had finished. "Found a set of pawprints goin' thataway, Cap'n, but 'tis only one beast."

Clogg spat the plait out and scratched his nose. "One beast is better than none I allus says mate, lead on!"

They had not gone far when the sounds of Celandine's lamentations reached their ears. Tramun Clogg signalled for silence. Bellying down, the corsairs breasted a low hill. They peered over at the weeping squirrelmaid.

Gruzzle shook his head sympathetically. "Ain't she pretty, Cap'n. It's enough t' break yer 'eart!"

Clogg chewed at a dandelion still attached to its stem. "Aye, 'tis sad, matey, an' even sadder when I thinks of the way I'm goin' to make that liddle beauty wail when I tickles some information out o' her with me cutlass point."

Celandine was still crying and talking aloud to herself.

"Oh, why don't any of the troupe come and find me? Owww! Oh dear, I mustn't weep so much or I'll look all ugly and puffy."

"Ho, that ye will, me liddle weepin' willow. Come on now, dry yore eyes an' give ole uncle Clogg a big smile!"

Celandine looked up in terror. Standing not ten paces from her was the corsair stoat and his villainous crew. She choked out a small frightened whimper as Clogg drew his cutlass and advanced on her, grinning wickedly.

21

Martin and his friends were captured so quickly it made their heads whirl. One moment they were sleeping peacefully, and in a twinkling they were dragged up on to their footpaws. Tough vine ropes secured their paws tight with nooses that locked around their necks. The dark slithering shapes of lizards were everywhere, slinking around the treetrunks and writhing over each other, making no other sound than a sibilant hiss.

With his paws pinioned to the sides of his head by the vine that encircled his neck, Martin struggled to get loose and reach his short sword, shouting to Rose and the others.

"Rose! Are you all . . . gaaaargh!"

The big red-frilled lizard pulled savagely on the vine, choking Martin into silence. The young mouse tugged either side of his neck, striving to loosen the vine so he could breathe properly. Then they were off at a headlong run, pulled along cruelly with countless lizards flanking them and shoving from behind. Splashing through marshwater, cludging through mud, crashing through nettles, they rushed through the night.

Rose sobbed for breath. Tripping on a root, she fell flat in some ferns. The speeding reptiles did not stop or even slow, they continued their mad stampede, dragging her along thumping and bumping across the soggy earth. How she fought her way back upright Rose never knew, but she was certain she would have been dragged to her death had she not done so.

Grumm's short legs battered the earth as he was dragged and swept along in the midst of the lizard throng. Somewhere close he could hear Pallum's ragged gasps as his friend fought for air on the end of a strangling vine noose.

Battering through evil-smelling liquid and bubbling marsh gases, they pelted onward, mud flying everywhere as lizard tails waved and scaly legs leaped high in the reptile stampede. Martin lost all count of time or distance until, like his three friends, he passed out from lack of air and was dragged along by the neck.

Morning in the marshes was overcast with wraithing grey mist tinged with yellow sulphurous wisps. The four bodies that lay tied to stakes were practically unrecognizable as a mole, a hedgehog and two mice. They were completely covered in thick caking mud and clay from the wild run.

Martin stirred and coughed. His throat hurt abominably.

"Martin, are you all right?"

It was Pallum. The hedgehog resembled a round ball of clay.

"Pallum. I'm alive at least. How are you?"

"Be much better when my old neck stops hurtin'. I've been awake an hour or more, but I lay still. Didn't want to attract attention from those creepy lizards—they're all round us."

Martin strained his neck slightly. The vine was still looped around it, though now his paws were free. Lizards were everywhere, just sitting and staring at them. He noticed the large red-frilled leader had the short sword lying on the ground in front of him.

Martin crawled across to Rose. Loosening the vine on

her neck, he patted her muddied cheeks, calling her name. "Rose, Rose!"

A jumble of lizards dived on him, pulling the noose tight as they dragged him away from Rose. Martin fought back as best as he could, shouting through the scaly bodies that enveloped him, "I was only trying to let her breathe, you scaly villains. Let me go. We weren't trying to escape!"

The big red-frilled lizard stalked slowly across. He kicked the others off Martin and dragged the young mouse back to his stake. Hissing softly, he gave the vine a final sharp tug, indicating that Martin should stay in that spot. Flicking his serpentine tongue, he turned and slid gracefully back to his former position.

Pallum looked across at Martin and shrugged. "Don't say much, do they? We'd best sit tight and wait for Rose and Grumm to come around."

Both Rose and her mole friend revived some short time later. They sat massaging sore necks, easing the tight vines off to enable easier breathing. The big red-frill gave the vines a tug when he thought they had messed enough with them. He hissed softly and sat watching the four captives.

After a while, they got to know the rules. They were allowed to talk, but only in quiet tones. If they talked loudly, or pulled at the nooses, the lizards would yank hard, tightening the vines, and hiss soft warnings at them.

Grumm picked burrs and mud from his face. "They'm sloimy vurmints, aroight. Soilent, tho'. Nary a word do they'm lizzyards be a-speaken."

"Hush now, Grumm," Martin muttered quietly and urgently. "They're coming over here!"

Silently a group of lizards came to each of the prisoners and deposited by them four large gourds of water. The reptiles retreated and sat watching.

Rose tilted one of the gourds and sipped, then she

drank deep gratefully. "It's water, good clean and fresh. I never knew it could taste so nice."

They drank their fill, dashed some in their faces to wash away the dirt and grime, then sat waiting. Next to come was a great wooden pan fashioned from a section of lime trunk. The red-frilled leader indicated that it be placed in the centre of the area between the four stakes, where the captives could reach it. Again the reptiles retired to watch.

The vessel was filled with a warm cream-coloured mixture. Pallum ventured a dip into it with his paw. He licked at the stuff and shrugged.

"Food. Tastes like some kind of porridge. Not much flavor in it, though. Hmmm, yes. I think it tastes a bit like mushroom."

They all tried some and agreed it was palatable enough, but had hardly any taste.

Grumm shovelled a pawful into his mouth. "Hurr, tain't zoop or nothink noice, but et ain't bad, burr no."

Rose had taken several mouthfuls. She splashed a little water on her paws to cleanse them. "Huh, it's not very good either. I've had enough of that tasteless mush, thank you."

The red-frill stalked sinuously over to her. He tugged the vine sharply, indicating that she should carry on eating.

Rose sighed and looked across at Martin. "Old frilly neck won't be happy until we've eaten all our dinner up like good little creatures. I suppose I'd better try some more."

Martin licked his paw and dug in again. "Mushroom porridge. It's deadly boring."

"Huh hu huh!" Pallum chuckled as he spoke through a mouthful. "D'you think they're trying to fatten us up a bit?"

Suddenly they stopped eating. The horror of what the hedgehog had just said dawned on them.

"What was it Mr. Mirdop said," Rose whispered in a hushed voice. "Cannibal lizards!"

Twice that day more bowls of porridge and gourds of water were brought to them. If they showed signs of refusing to eat, the big red-frill would tug on the vines until they began choking.

Grumm groaned as he noticed several of the reptiles scraping ashes from a long pit at the edge of the lizard settlement. Others began laying charcoal and dry wood in it.

Martin seethed silently. If only he could break away and reach his short sword, but it was impossible—they were watched by scores of gaping lizards who seemed to have little else to do but sit and look at them. The young mouse lay back, his mind racing furiously against the insurmountable problem.

A dipper appeared on a low branch nearby. The little bird nodded its head from side to side, ruffling its handsome browny red plumage and preening at its fawn-colored breast. It made a twittering noise and Rose looked at it strangely.

"Martin, that bird is talking to us."

Noting that the lizards were still watching, Martin kept his voice to a quiet conversational level. "Can you understand it, Rose?"

"I think so. It's said the same thing twice now. *Ganna aitcha ganna aitcha.* I'm pretty sure it's saying, *Going to eat you, going to eat you*, meaning the lizards are going to eat us."

"You're right, Rose." Martin trembled with excitement, trying hard to keep his voice under control. "The lizards must not be able to understand it or they'd have chased it off by now. See if you can get it to carry a message to the Warden of Marshwood Hill."

"Ganna alpiz, ganna alpiz?" Rose made a strange noise halfway between a whistle and a chatter.

The little dipper nodded, pecking at the branch. "Alpichoo alpichoo!"

Pallum had been listening. "What did it say?"

"I tried to ask it for help." Rose explained. *"Ganna alpiz,* sounds a bit like *going to help us.* It replied, *Alpichoo,* which sounds like *help you!*"

Grumm came in on the conversation. "Ho urr, but 'ow you'm goin' t' say Warden o' Marshywood 'ill?"

Rose pondered a moment. "Right, how does this sound?" She made a lilting sound. "Whoa hoo din alpiz! Whoa hoo din alpiz!"

The dipper puffed out his tiny chest and flew off trilling, "Whoa hoo din! Whoa hoo din!"

Martin sat up slowly. "Well, he's gone now. I take it that *whoa hoo din* meant *warden,* Rose?"

"It was the closest I could get. *Whoa hoo din alpiz. Warden help us.* Let's hope the dipper understood. Oh no, they're bringing more porridge."

Silent lizards replaced the empty bowl with a fresh one of the sickly warm mushroom porridge and full water gourds were brought.

Rose held her stomach and pulled a face. "Yukk! I can't eat any more of this filthy rubbish!"

The red-frill came striding over. Martin could tell that he was going to tug Rose's neck vine tight. The young mouse's warrior spirit boiled over at the thought of the reptile tormenting Rose. As the red-frill stalked past him, Martin let out a yell and smashed the water gourd over its head. In a flash they were grappling. Martin's neck vine strained tight as he pushed the red-frill's head straight into the porridge, leaning his full weight to keep it there as he tried to drown the reptile.

"Here, frilly. Try some of your own medicine!"

Before Rose, Pallum or Grumm could help, a mob of lizards were upon Martin, smothering him with their pulsing bodies as they freed their leader. Four of them untied Martin's neck vine from its stake. The red frill hissed balefully at him, tongue flickering in and out constantly. Helpless and weighted down by numbers, the young mouse was dragged off towards the firepit. Two lizards put flint to tinder and leaped back as a curl of smoke arose. Other lizards flung themselves on Rose, Pallum and Grumm as the mousemaid screamed at the top of her voice,

"Leave him alone, you filthy crawlers. Put that fire out!"

22

Sometimes in a pinch frivolous young squirrelmaids can turn out far more resourceful than they themselves would have known. So it was with Celandine. As a Rambling Rosehip Player, she had acted the part of the brave and beautiful heroine many times. Now was her chance to give a star performance.

Cap'n Tramun Clogg advanced on her, leering and winking roguishly. "Haharr, don't be afeared o' me, pretty little bird. Soon you'll be singin' just fer me!"

Celandine backed off, throwing up her paws in horror. "Begone, you great ugly toad. Put not a paw near me!"

Clogg, who had always imagined himself as a handsome buccaneering beast, halted indignantly. "Ugly toad? You hardnosed liddle snip, come 'ere, I say!"

"Never. I would rather die!"

"Hoho, missy, that kin be arranged. Now be still or you'll make it worse on yoreself . . ."

Clogg leaped at her, clutching with his free paw. Celandine stumbled back, half tripping. She grabbed a pawful of the sandy soil and flung it straight into the corsair's face. Regaining her balance, she dashed off.

Clogg dropped his cutlass and sat down hard, pawing at his eyes, which were jammed full of loose, gritty dust.

"Get after that bold baggage an' catch 'er," he howled

at his crew. "Lively now! I'll 'ave 'er ears fer dinner an' 'er liver 'n' tripes tore out!"

Only Gruzzle stayed back to look after Clogg. The rest set off at a run after Celandine, laughing and cheering. They knew a single squirrelmaid could not get far with an entire crew of corsairs hard on her paws.

Celandine ran as she had never run before, wishing that she had not added all the frills and furbelows to her Rambling Rosehip tunic. They impeded her and often caused her to stumble. Behind her she could hear the whoops and guffaws of her pursuers as they drew closer. The squirrelmaid's breath came in ragged sobs. She was unused to running any great distance. Cap'n Clogg had made it plain that he meant her harm, and there was no telling what might happen to her if she fell into the claws of searats and corsairs. Death would be inevitable. Not knowing where she was running to, Celandine forced her flagging limbs onward.

Three searats, Gritter, Crableg and Bluddnose, took the lead, outstripping the rest of Clogg's crew easily. They were good runners, lean and fit.

A sand dune rose up in front of Celandine, and there was no way round it. She panted fitfully, going down on all fours as she attempted to scramble up the hill. Crableg put on an extra spurt and dived forward. He managed to catch the squirrelmaid's back footpaw. Wriggling swiftly on to her back, Celandine kicked out. She caught him hard on the snout, causing Crableg to release her. The searat was so close he could have reached out and touched her.

"You ain't goin' to be pretty no more, squirrel!" he snarled as he wiped a stream of blood from his snout on to the back of his paw.

Whipping a curved dagger from his waist sash, he brandished it. Suddenly a wooden lance seemed to grow out of his chest. Crableg looked down at it and fell dead with a foolish expression of surprise on his face. The slaying happened so quickly that Gritter and Bluddnose had not seen it. They arrived panting at the dune to find their messmate lying dead, with the short wooden lance protruding from him like a ship's mast. There was no other creature in sight except the squirrelmaid, her eyes wide with horror.

Gritter drew his sword and walked uphill towards her. "You killed Crableg wi' that piece o' wood, you liddle serpint!"

As he raised the sword, another javelin came whistling through the air and transfixed him through the throat.

Bluddnose had drawn his sword, but his nerves failed him. With a small wail of fright he flung the weapon away and took to his heels, back towards the main group, who were now in sight.

Celandine sat shocked, looking at the two dead searats in front of her.

"Celandine, climb the hill, get up here quickly!" a hoarse, urgent voice called from the hilltop.

She sat staring at the carcasses of Crableg and Gritter, unable to comprehend what had happened.

"Move yourself, missy," Ballaw's voice rang out theatrically. "Come on, up here or you'll miss your cue!"

Automatically, Celandine picked herself up and scrambled dumbly to the hilltop. Rowanoak's huge paws swept her over the hill and out of sight. The badger clamped a paw over the squirrelmaid's mouth, and Ballaw and Felldoh fixed fresh javelins on to their throwers.

Crosstooth the fox had always liked Crableg's curved dagger. He took it from the searat's lifeless paw and tucked it into his belt as he nudged Gritter's body with his spearshaft.

"Y'mean to tell us that the pretty liddle squirrel did this?"

Bluddnose was shaking uncontrollably. "Well, there was nobeast else 'ereabouts. She musta did it!"

189

The ferret Boggs curled his lip scornfully. "Did ye see the squirrel kill 'em?"

Bluddnose sat down on the duneside, head in paws. "No, I never. One moment they was large as life, next thing they're both dead. She must've done it. Can't yer see, she's vanished. I knew we should never 'ave messed with magic beasts!"

A weasel called Floater swapped his own chipped and rusted sword for the better blade that Gritter had once owned, and scoffed aloud, "Vanished me tail! We seen 'er go over this 'ere dune. See, there's the beauty's paw-tracks. I'm goin' up there an' get 'er meself."

Clogg stumped to join the rest, with Gruzzle at his side, still trying to clear the corners of his Cap'n's eyes with a none too clean silk kerchief. Tramun shoved him away and patted Floater's back.

"Aye, there's the laddo. Up the 'ill ye go, Floater. Sing out if you sees anythin' up there."

As they stood watching the weasel scale the dune, Clogg muttered in his beard to himself. "Nay, it weren't no snip of a squirrelymaid did fer two tough rogues like Crableg an' ole Gritter. The beast that did this could sling a lance good an' proper."

Shielding his eyes, Clogg squinted up at the weasel, who had made it to the top of the hill.

"Ahoy, Floater. Any signs o' life up there?"

The weasel waved his paws wildly, shouting aloud, "Cap'n, it's threeeeeeeeeeee!"

Floater came tumbling awkwardly back down the dune, flopping this way and that, hampered in his fall by the short lance through the center of his back. The body halted its sliding descent right in front of the Cap'n's big wooden clogs.

"Three o' me best fightin' beasts slain. Harr, the mur-derin' scoundrels, 'ooever they are. Right, buckoes, arm yerselves an' take the 'ill. Chaaarge!"

Clogg stood back, whirling his cutlass as he urged them on. The charge was not a notable success. Nobeast wanted to reach the top first, and there was a deal of hanging back and accidental stumbling before Clogg realized what was going on. The pirate stoat did a small dance of anger, clogs clicking sharply.

"You bottlenosed bloaters, get up that 'ill right now, d'ye hear me. That's an order from yer Cap'n. Go on, chaaaaarge!"

They stood awkwardly about a third of the way up the dune, still unwilling to storm the hilltop. Clogg unsheathed his cutlass and began bustling his way up, knocking crew members left and right as he did.

"Out o' me way, yer mack'rel-faced, milk-swiggin', muck'eads. Yore nothin' but a pack o' ring-tailed cowards!"

As they turned to look sheepishly at him, a searat called Wulpp screamed when a short javelin zinged out of nowhere and slammed right through his footpaw. The charge immediately deteriorated into an undignified rush down the hill.

Clogg followed in their rear, berating them soundly. "One liddle spear an' yore all runnin' about like beetles in a bucket. Ho shame! I never thought I'd see the day a crew o' mine would dash off without even seein' the enemy!"

When they were a reasonable distance from the big dune, the corsairs stopped and sat down on a grassy sward. Tramun came clattering up, with Wulpp limping slowly several lengths behind. The corsair Cap'n slumped down and began emptying sand from his clogs.

"Gruzzle, I'm fair disappointed in you, matey, an' you, Dedjaw, an' you, Boggs. Mateys, what are ye all afeared of, a few ole sharpened wooden sticks?"

Whang!

A needle-pointed lance arced out of the blue summer sky, narrowly missing Tramun Clogg as it pinned his coat skirt to the ground. The corsair Cap'n leaped up as if he had been beestung, ripping his coat from the quivering lance in the process.

"Tidal waves an' typhoons! There must be a monster be'ind yon 'ill. Nobeast could hurl a lance that far!"

The rout continued, with Clogg in the lead as they scurried back to the safety of Marshank.

Behind the sand dune, Felldoh lay watching over the rim at the retreating corsairs.

Ballaw blew a long sigh of relief as he put down his javelins and thrower. "Good job they never charged the bally top an' stormed us. There was enough of the blighters."

Rowanoak dusted sand from herself. "There certainly was. Imagine if they'd got past us, our camp is only over the next hill, south and east on the clifftops."

Celandine suddenly bounced back as if nothing had happened. Primping the lace hems of her tunic, she remarked airily, "Oh yes, I had an idea it was, that's why I headed over this way!"

Ballaw rolled his eyes upward in mock despair. "You dreadful little fibber, miss! You were coming this way because a band of ruffians were chasing you."

"O them!" Celandine tossed her tail huffily. "I knew they wouldn't get me!"

Felldoh turned around from the dune rim. "But how did you know?"

Celandine clasped both his paws, fluttering her eyelids wildly. "Because I knew in my heart that my brave Felldoh would come to my rescue, and you did."

Rowanoak smiled and shook her huge head. "Come on, brave Felldoh, let's get this ruthless charmer back to camp!"

Felldoh felt his face burning as Celandine hung on his paws, praising him outrageously.

"You're so strong, so courageous, and so accurate with your sharp little sticks. Ooh look, I pricked my paw on one!"

When they had gone, Brome emerged from hiding. He

had followed Felldoh with the intention of joining him, until the badger and the hare decided to help his friend. Brome had stayed out of sight, knowing that Ballaw and Rowanoak would have sent him packing, back to camp. So he secreted himself in a clump of tor grass and watched them rescuing Celandine. Brome had grown a lot bolder since his escape from Marshank. He admired Felldoh and wanted to be like him, but he was treated as a young one in the camp. Brome climbed the dune and peered down on the three dead corsairs, imagining himself launching lances alongside Felldoh and simmering with resentment at being left out.

He slid down the dune on his bottom and sat looking at the three lifeless figures. After a while the young mouse ventured to pick up the sword which lay near Gritter. He swung it in the air, trying a few fancy strokes, an idea forming in his head as he did. There were still a good number of slaves to be freed from Marshank. Imagine the looks on the faces of Felldoh, Ballaw and Rowanoak if he, Brome, came marching back with a score or so of slaves that he had rescued.

The more Brome swung the sword the more he liked the idea. He would do it!

Arming himself with the sword and a dagger from Floater's belt, he dressed himself up in an assortment of corsair gear which he took from the three bodies. Smudging up his face with a few pawfuls of dust, Brome pulled the brim of Crableg's floppy hat down at a rakish angle and set off for Fortress Marshank. Swaggering along like a villainous searat, he practised the brogue.

"Haharr, I'm Bucktail, as good a matey that ever sailed the seas an' plundered landlubbers. Haharr an' hoho!"

23

As Grumm, Pallum and Rose tugged at their neck vines they screamed and shouted insults and threats, despite the menacing presence of the lizards who surrounded them. Martin did not waste breath on words. He fought savagely tooth and paw as the reptiles dragged him bodily towards the fire pit. The red-frilled leader stood impassively by, tongue flickering, throat pulsing, silent as the rest of his tribe. Martin drew blood from several of the beasts, kicking, butting, biting and gouging whenever he could force a movement among the swarming lizards whose bodies swamped and stifled his every attempt. The fire took off and began crackling, pale wisps of smoke rising to blend with the fetid air as hungry golden red flames danced and flickered in the cooking pit.

A piercing off-key cry rang through the marshlands. Immediately all activity among the lizards stopped. The noise rent the still air a second time. It was not a pleasant sound, something akin to the screech of a gate with rusty hinges, coupled with a loud gurgling ululation. The red-frilled leader's head shook from side to side, eyes flickering and filming as he hissed what appeared to be some type of warning or command. The rest of the reptiles went into swift, silent action. Hustling Martin and his three friends together, they hauled the neck vines tight, securing them firmly to the stakes so that the four captives were forced to lie with their faces in the dirt. Ferns, leafy boughs, rushes, shrubs and all manner of vegetation were piled hurriedly on the prisoners until they were lost to view. Several lizards perched on top of the pile, stretching themselves out as if napping. Beneath the oppressive heap, Martin and his companions fought desperately for breath.

A fully grown male grey heron stalked majestically into the lizard encampment, towering high over the heads of the reptiles as they stood still like statues. The Warden of Marshwood Hill was an immense bird. He glared down at the lizards from his enormous height, dark-pupilled, pale gold eyes watching them from over a savage yellow pair of beak spikes. Throwing back the snakelike column of his powerful neck, he gave throat to a chilling shriek, the twin black feathers on his skull back vibrating.

The dipper zoomed down from the branches of a gnarled wych-elm at the edge of the clearing. It landed among the lizards perched on top of the vegetation and did an excited hopskip dance. The grey heron moved fearlessly and fast, long black sticklike legs pounding the ground as it spread awesome silk grey wings and charged the heap. The lizards scuttled over each other in their attempts to get out of its way, but they were flung high into the air as the heron scattered the foliage, demolishing the entire pile with wings, beak and claw webbed feet.

Martin, Rose, Grumm and Pallum lay exposed on the ground, writhing feebly as they pulled at the taut neck vines. The Warden's dangerous amber beak clacked perilously close to their heads as he severed the vines with careless ease. He watched them for a moment until Martin's eyes opened. Leaning close, he spoke to the young mouse in a precise clipped manner.

"Lie still, stay there. Do not interfere, lizards! Got to deal with them!"

The Warden strode a measured pace around the camp. There was complete silence. He glared at the reptiles. The lizards stood motionless, tongues in, eyes filmed over as if completely cowed by the mad intensity of the heron's stare. Martin watched, fascinated. The whole affair was carried out in complete silence. The heron would point to the captives with its beak then glare at the lizards. They remained motionless. Regardless of whether or not he trod on heads, bodies or tails, the Warden stalked about the camp, finally halting in front of the red-frilled leader. With a slow contemptuous movement of one leg, the heron flicked the red-frill over on to its back. It was obviously a challenge that the lizard leader had to accept. Wriggling upright, the red-frill hissed and circled to attack.

Lying between Pallum and Martin, Rose watched in horror as the grey heron's beak flashed down. "Oh, how horrible!"

Martin covered her eyes with his paw. "Don't look, Rose. I think I can guess what he's going to do next!"

Grumm turned his face aside. "Burr oo, dearie oi! Never could oi be that 'ungry!"

Pallum nodded in agreement as the Warden turned on another lizard. "Guaw! I never seen nothing like that. It's disgusting!"

Martin shrugged. "Maybe you've forgotten, but those lizards were going to eat us. The big bird is dealing out his justice to them."

The killer's beak flashed down several more times until the Warden of Marshwood Hill had taken his fill. He swallowed and gulped, then threw back his head and gave a sharp cry. It was a signal that the lizards were dismissed. They scattered into the marshes in seconds, leaving the camp deserted except for the four friends and the grey heron. Wiping his beak methodically on a grassy tussock, he strode across to them.

"I am Warden of Marshwood Hill. These are my marshes, and I am the only law. Lizards are lawbreakers, toads and snakes also. I do what must be done!"

Martin bowed formally. "I am Martin, this is Rose, Pallum and Grumm. We wish to thank you for saving our lives. We are travelling through your marshes on our way to Noonvale. I was hoping you could help us with some directions."

The little dipper had landed next to Rose. She was stroking its head. The Warden preened his huge downy breast awhile as if considering what Martin had said.

"I know no Noonvale, but I have heard its name spoken. I will guide you through my marshes. Obey my laws, or I kill you. Lawbreakers must be killed. Gather your things, and follow me."

Martin picked up his sword, Grumm found his ladle, Rose and the dipper found the packs—they were untouched, the lizards had not bothered with them.

"Can you put out fire?" The Warden pointed his beak at Pallum. "I do not like fire."

The hedgehog was about to reply when Grumm ambled over.

"Oi c'n put they'm foire out, zurr Wardun, ho urr."

The mole positioned himself by the fire pit and set to work with his remarkable digging claws. Shooting damp marsh earth backwards, he dug furiously. In a short time the fire pit was reduced to a smouldering mass, covered in the earth that Grumm had spread on it.

The Warden nodded abruptly. "I could not do that. You are a useful creature."

Grumm tipped a paw to his snout. "Thankee, zurr, tho' you'm 'as thoi own uses, oi 'spect, keepin' 'ee law in these yurr swamps."

But the Warden was not listening, he was stalking off out of the camp, calling back to them, "Come, follow me. I will guide you through my marshes to the mountain. I must stay here, I am the law."

As they trekked over what appeared to be a slender trail through the wetlands, Grumm whispered to Pallum, "Yurr, they burd doant say much, do 'ee."

Pallum could not resist doing a comical impression of the Warden. Strutting stiff-legged, he glared at Grumm and spoke sharply. "I am the law. These are my marshes. I am the law!"

Both the hedgehog and the mole burst into subdued chuckles.

The Warden turned and glared at them. "Make fun of the law, and I deal with you. I am the law!"

Pallum and Grumm froze for a moment then they saluted vigorously. "Yes, sir. Understood, sir!"

"You'm 'ee law, zurr. Ho urr, gudd, foine!"

Martin walked along with Rose. He nodded at the little bird hopping by her side. "I see you've got a new friend, Rose. What's his name?"

The mousemaid stroked the little creature's downy head. "Dipper, that's what he is and that's what I'll call him. Martin, did you hear what the Warden said—he'd guide us to the mountain. I wonder where that is."

"Me too. I suppose the only way we'll find out is by following him. He seems to know the country well enough."

"Oh yes, and d'you know why that is?"

Martin smiled knowingly. Leaning close he whispered into Rose's ear so that the Warden could not hear.

"Because he is the law!"

The marshes were dreary, foggy and misty, drab and treacherous. The travellers followed the grey heron step for step, being careful not to deviate from the tortuously narrow trail. Either side of them, moss-hung branches stuck up like spectral limbs from the green-dark ooze that exuded occasional bubbles and wisps of swamp gas. The only sign that evening was approaching was that the atmosphere grew decidedly gloomier. The Warden halted at a juncture where two paths crossed to form a wooded islet. They sat down in the damp grass as the grey heron looked about.

"Camp here tonight, travel tomorrow."

Grumm took out his ladle and set about snapping dead twigs. "Hurr, thank gudness fur that. C'mon, Pallum, lend ee thoi paw yurr."

The piercing eyes of the Warden stopped them in their tracks. "What do you do?"

"Make zoop, zurr." Grumm waved his ladle about, chuckling. "Fer zoop you'm need a foire. You'm loik moi zoop."

"I do not know zoop. Make no fire. I am the law. I do not like fire!"

Somewhere nearby a frog croaked in the marsh. The Warden followed the direction of the sound with his savage eyes. He swallowed hungrily. "Stay here, do not move. Frogs are about. They are lawbreakers. I am the law, I will deal with them!"

He stalked off into the darkening mists. When he was out of sight, Pallum gave a short, humorless laugh. "Looks to me like the law wants its supper."

Rose was unpacking rations. "What a dreadful idea!" she shuddered.

Martin helped her prepare their meal. "Maybe so, but without the Warden of Marshwood Hill we'd have been lizard lunch today. The bird is a necessary evil, believe me."

Rose laid out two fruit flans, some hazelnut scones and the last canteen of mint and lavender cordial. The food was a bit battered and squashed but still very tasty. Rose laughed as they watched the dipper pecking furiously at a scone.

"Oh look, Martin, Dipper's really enjoying himself. I'll bet he's never tasted anything as nice."

The tiny bird sprayed them with crumbs as he attempted to communicate his pleasure to his new-found friends.

"Goodiz, goodiz!"

After supper, the dipper whistled and chirped happily. When he had finished they applauded him. Martin lay back, sipping at the tangy cordial.

"Wish I could sing like that. I've got the worst singing voice in the world. Come on, Rose, sing something to cheer us up in this gloomy marsh."

The mousemaid obliged willingly, her wondrous clear voice ringing melodiously into the deep marshland night.

"O happy is as happy does,
Misery never useful was,
And I am happy now because
I'm with the ones I love.
Sing fol lol loh a lairy lay,
Let the sun shine bright all day,
So I'll go happy on my way
With the good ones that I love.
O fie on you, O great disgrace,
Look at that sad unhappy face,
I'll not walk with you, not one pace,
You're not the one I love.
Sing dumble dum and derry dee,
You'll have to smile to come with me,
Till happiness doth let you see
You're the one that I love!"

The dipper chirped appreciatively as they applauded. Grumm shook his head admiringly. "Oi loikes that un, Miz Roser. Allus makes oi feel loike darncen!"

Rose gave the mole a playful shove. "Well come on, old Grummchops, it's ages since I saw you dance!" Grumm stuck his digging claws in his ears, rolling from side to side with embarrassment. "Ho no, oi'm no gurt shakes at 'ee darncen. You'm papa allus used to larff when oi darnced."

"Well, papa's not here now, so you'll dance—or we'll tell the Warden that you've been making fun of him!"

200

Rose picked up Grumm's ladle and shook it at him in mock anger.

"Ho no, you'm wudden do a thing loik that."

"Oh yes she would!" Martin and Pallum chorused together.

Grumm stood up, shuffling his paws. "Hurr, s'pose oi better sing 'n' darnce then. You'm awful crool beasts."

Rose could see that the mole wanted to sing and dance. "Come on, Grummyface, do your party piece, the one about your old grandfather. I like that one."

Mole dancing is a curious spectacle and is invariably accompanied by singing. Grumm held up his digging claws and did a small hopskip.

"Naow Granfer were a pow'ful mole.
Scratch a tunnel dig an 'ole,
The moightiest eater, so oi'm tole,
In all of all 'ee wuddlands.
You'm should've seen him eaten cake.
Granmum said, fer gudness sake,
Oi'll start 'ee oven up to bake
An' twelveteen cakes oi'll make.
If Granfer ate wun, him ate two,
Ho dearie me, oi'm tellen you,
Him ate those twelveteen cakes roight throo,
Then went asleep till zummer.
An' when 'ee zummer sun did break,
My ole granfer came awake,
The gudd ole beast drinked all 'ee lake
An' left 'ee fishes sobbin'.
Him'n story as oi've toald to you,
Oi swears as every wurd be troo,
Iffen you'm think oi tole fibs to you,
Then go an' arsk 'ee fishes!"

Rose, Pallum and Martin were falling about laughing as Grumm took a bow. He was puffing from the exertion of song and dance combined.

The Warden appeared as if from nowhere. He stared hard at Grumm and shook his head once. "Good at putting out fire, not at singing. Mouse Rose is the best singer. I know this. Sleep now! Dipper, you go back to your family nest!"

Sometime before dawn Martin stirred. Vague muffled sounds had gradually wakened him. He lay awhile taking stock of their hostile surroundings. The muffled sounds continued. Rolling over slowly, he checked the sleeping forms of Rose, Grumm and Pallum. They were deep in slumber, breathing peacefully. Martin's eyes strayed over to where the grey heron was lying. It was hard to tell in the darkness, but he sensed that something was not right. He peered long at the bird, his paw straying to the short sword stuck in the ground near his head. The Warden appeared to be rolling about in his sleep, making muffled noises.

Slowly Martin rose until he was crouching. Placing his paws carefully among the damp grass tussocks, he edged over. Something slimy slapped him in the face as he reached the moving figure of the Warden. There were dark shapes all over the great bird, and it was moving more slowly and weakly. As his eyes became accustomed to the darkness, Martin saw that creatures he could not make out were strangling the grey heron, winding about its neck while others secured its legs and wings.

So that was what the muffled noises were. They must have been attacking the Warden for some time because the big bird's struggles were very weak. Martin threw himself into the fray with a shout that wakened his three friends instantly.

"Yaaaaah, Maaaaartin!"

24

It was getting towards evening and shadows were beginning to lengthen on the shoreline as Brome climbed down from the cliffs. Ahead of him he could see Wulpp, the searat who had taken Felldoh's javelin through his footpaw, limping along by himself. Suddenly Brome had an idea that might gain him entrance into Marshank. He padded silently up until he was almost level with Wulpp.

"Hi there, mate. You the beast they left be'ind?"

Wulpp sat down on the sand, wincing as he nursed his paw. "Aye that's me. What's yer name, matey?"

Brome sat down by him and began ripping a strip from his shirt. "Harr, I'm Bucktail. Cap'n sent me back for ye. I was walkin' along the clifftops when I saw you down 'ere. 'Old still while I binds that paw up fer ye, messmate."

Wulpp gritted his teeth as Brome worked. "Aagh, it 'urts bad, Bucktail. Wot d'ye think, will it give me a limp for the rest o' me life?"

"More'n likely, bucko." Brome nodded as he tied the improvised bandage off neatly. "You was lucky it didn't catch you 'igher, or you'da been a goner. Come on, mate, up on yer paws. I'll give yer a lift back to the fortress."

Hopping on one paw, the injured searat threw an arm

about Brome's shoulders and leaned on him as they made their way slowly back. "Bucktail, eh. Well my name's Wulpp, an' I won't fergit yer fer the 'elp you've give me this day, messmate."

They entered the fortress as darkness fell. Nobeast paid much attention to them both. The main center of attraction was the continuing feud between the two leaders. Clogg sat on the courtyard stones, surrounded by his crew as he tore ravenously at hard bread and dried fish, guzzling seaweed ale from an oversized tankard. Badrang stood on the porch of his longhouse, haranguing the corsair.

"Now let me get this right, one creature, a single squirrelmaid at that, killed three of your great hairy waverobbers and wounded another. Well, lack a season and lose a day!"

Clogg hurled a hard crust at Badrang. It fell short. "Harr go an' boil yer 'ead, stoatears. You was safe enough inside o' yer fancy fortress surrounded by yer lubbernosed 'orde!"

Badrang leaned over the porch rail, his voice mocking. "And what, pray, was the dreaded Cap'n Tramun Clogg doing while this dreadful slaughter took place? Hiding from the squirrelmaid?"

Clogg's nose glinted purple with rage as he spat out dried fish. "It weren't no squirrelymaid did the killin', it was those excaped slaves o' yourn throwin' javelins, an' by the way they could throw I'd 'ate t' be in yer shirt if they attacks 'ere!"

The Tyrant spread his paws appealingly to the listeners. "Why should they come back here after escaping? Strikes me they'd want to put as much distance between themselves and Marshank as possible. By the way, how's your ship refloating coming along?"

A slow smile spread across Clogg's villainous face. "Much the same as yer stone quarryin' an' field croppin', me ole messmate. 'Ave yer done much empire buildin' today, haharrharr?"

Stung by the taunt that had rebounded on him, Badrang pointed his sword at the corsair. "I'll remind you that you're eating my food, Clogg, and your worthless mob of seascum are filling their bellies at my expense too. But all that's going to change. From now on if you want to eat our supplies at Marshank you'll have to earn your food like any of my creatures!"

Clogg hurled the tankard. It smashed on the ground in front of Badrang as the corsair bellowed defiantly, "We ain't yer creatures, me an' my crew is seabeasts, rovers an' freebooters. We're 'onourin' you by takin' our meals 'ere 'cos you owe us that much, you boat-burnin' barnacle. We'd 'ave sailed off from this fort long since but for yer treachery!"

Brome threw a paw about Wulpp, steering him towards the walls of the slave compound. "C'mon, mate, let's find someplace for you to sit easy. We can't stand around listenin' to those two stoats jawin' each other to death while yer paw's injured bad."

They sat with their backs against the wooden fence. "Harr, 'tis rest you need, Wulpp." Brome spoke loudly on purpose. "A good deep sleep'd do you a power o' good, matey. Sleep, the best healer of all!"

Wulpp did not argue. He was weary and his footpaw throbbed relentlessly. Closing his eyes, he lay back.

"Right you are, Bucktail. I feel like I could sleep fer a season!"

Keyla had been listening to the two creatures on the other side of the fence. Curiosity overcame the young otter, and he was not long in climbing the timbers to peer over the top at the pair.

Brome made sure that Wulpp's eyes were closed and they were not being observed, then he swept the floppy hat from his head and grinned cheekily up at Keyla.

Holding up a warning paw, he pointed at Wulpp, stroking the searat's head gently and crooning in a soft voice, "Sleep, matey. You need a long deep sleep, long an' deep."

Keyla understood. He gave a broad wink and disappeared.

Brome continued speaking soothingly to the half-asleep Wulpp. "Sleep, matey, that's all you need, sleepy sleep sleep . . ."

Wulpp's eyelids flickered. He glanced at Brome and smiled lazily. "Bucktail, me ole matey, you looks like some kind o' mouse without yore hat on . . ."

Assisted by a mouse named Yarrow, Keyla popped up over the compound top. Between them they held a big improvised sandbag.

Whump!

Wulpp's head was a target they could not miss. The heavy object landed forcefully, knocking the searat out like a light.

"He's got enough on his mind to keep him asleep a good while," the irrepressible Keyla giggled. "Brome, what are you doing back here, friend?"

The young mouse clamped his floppy hat back on. "I've come to get you and the rest away from here, Keyla, though I thought you'd have escaped with the last lot."

The young otter shook his head. "I could have, but there's old ones and some babes here that weren't quick enough to get away. I couldn't hop it and leave them just because I was young and fast, now could I?"

Brome propped Wulpp's head on the sandbag as if it were a pillow. "You're a good otter, Keyla. Listen, here's the plan. We'll get them all out between us, tonight."

Gurrad watched as Badrang poured poison into a flagon of blackberry grog.

"Great seasons, Sire, there's enough in there to lay an army out!"

206

Badrang shook the small vial to make sure the last drops went in. "Clogg could never resist a drop of blackberry grog. It'll be his last drop, laced with wolfbane and hemlock. There's not a creature born who could drink that and live to tell the tale." He pulled Gurrad close, his voice a sinister hiss. "Listen now, rat. Here's what you must do!"

The rat called Oilback threw his knife. It zipped through the air to bury itself deep in the driftwood spar set up on the beach. Cap'n Tramun Clogg grunted as he tugged the quivering blade free and returned it to its owner.

"Good throw, matey. I likes to see a beast who's skilled at slingin' a frogsticker. Do it agin, Oilback."

The searat twirled his knife expertly, closed one eye, sighted and threw hard. This time the blade went a third of its length into the timber. Clogg clapped his back heartily.

"Haharr, yore a murderer born, Oilback. Now cock a lug, matey, an' listen to a liddle plan that I've arranged fer that stingy grubswipin' former partner o' mine . . ."

The moon appeared over Marshank, casting pale light and deep shadow over the fortress where three separate schemes were being laid, two for death and one for freedom.

Brome hastily rearranged his corsair gear. There was little difference in the ill-assorted rags worn by Clogg's pirates and those of Badrang's soldiers and in no time Brome looked every inch the hordebeast. Keyla did the same, improvising with Wulpp's tawdry rags.

Minutes later, two ruthless hordebeasts marched straight past the guards and into the slave compound.

"Stay at the rear and help any stragglers," Brome signalled to Yarrow. "Righto, listen friends, all you have to do is follow Keyla and me. If anybeast stops or challenges us, don't you say a word, leave the talking to me.

Stay in the shadows as much as possible, don't hurry too much and above all, be silent!"

They set off towards the main courtyard with Brome and Keyla leading the group.

Badrang corked the flagon, shaking it well before he gave it to Gurrad.

"See if they're asleep, don't chance it otherwise. If everything is all right, then sneak up close to Clogg. He's usually sleeping near to the largest campfire. Place the flagon in his paw, or as close as you can get to it. That stupid plaited buffoon doesn't care what he drinks. When he wakes in the morning the flagon will be the nearest thing to him. He'll pop the cork and guzzle it right off. I know him of old. Go now. I'm trusting you to do the job right, Gurrad."

Swathed in a dark cloak, the rat left the longhouse.

Standing in the shadows at the side of the longhouse was another cloaked figure. Oilback held his knife by the blade, ready to throw. The doorway area was illuminated in a patch of moonlight. His paw trembled a little from the tension of waiting and the enormity of his task. It was not just any common crewbeast that got to kill Lord Badrang, the Tyrant of Marshank. No, it was he, Oilback, the best knife-thrower in all Cap'n Clogg's crew.

He heard the creak of the door as it opened. Tightening his grip on the blade, he closed one eye and took aim. A cloaked figure stole out, shutting the door carefully behind it. Oilback grunted with exertion as he hurled his weapon.

It was a good throw. The cloaked figure collapsed silently off the porch. Oilback hurried forward. Retrieving his knife from Gurrad's throat, he wiped the blade, giving a low snarl of dismay when he saw the dead features of the creature he had slain. It was not Badrang!

His footpaw struck something—a flagon of wine. Never being one to pass up a free gift, he rammed it into his tunic and turned to run away. It was at that exact moment Brome was passing with the slaves. Oilback ran slapbang into Brome.

There was a moment's silence as they confronted each other, then Brome said in a quiet but commanding tone, "What are you doing around here?"

Oilback answered hesitantly, thinking fast as he did. "Er, oh, I'm, er, gettin' rid of this dirty spy for Lord Badrang. He's one o' those corsairs. I caught 'im 'angin' about 'ere!"

Brome nodded. "Good!"

He was about to turn away when Oilback became suspicious. "Just a moment, mate. What are you doin' wid that bunch?"

Keyla stepped in boldly. "If it's any of your business, we're puttin' them in the prison pit. Lord Badrang doesn't want this lot escapin' like the others. He wants 'em down the pit where he can keep an eye on 'em!"

The corsair was slightly taken aback by Keyla's aggressive stance. "Oh, er, right. Well I'll bid ye good night."

Unfortunately they were both travelling in the same direction. Keyla and Brome were forced to walk along with Oilback, who was heading for the main gate, which lay in the same direction as the prison pit. They walked in silence with the slaves following.

Oilback glanced at the thirty creatures. "Yore gonna have a job on yer paws gettin' all them down that pit. They'll be standin' on each other's 'eads."

"Do em good!" Brome sniffed officiously. "We're not here to argue, we carry out our Leader's orders an' don't ask too many questions."

The searat nodded agreement. "Aye, that's all the likes of us can do, eh, mate!"

Though the gates of Marshank were open to the corsairs camped on the shore, there was still a sentry posted on top of the wall. It was the ferret Bluehide. He saw the slaves being led to the pit and called down, "What in the name of frogfeathers are you doin' down there?"

Oilback winked at Keyla and shouted back arrogantly, "What does it look like we're doin', takin' a swim?"

Bluehide shook his spear. "Leave that gratin' alone. All those beasts can't fit down there. Besides, there was three escaped from that pit!"

Brome sighed wearily. Placing paws on hips, he called out in an insulting manner, "It's none of your business how many slaves Lord Badrang wants us to put in the pit. And another thing, those three wouldn't have escaped if the sentry that night had been keepin' an eye on this grating. They broke out by movin' it."

Bluehide fixed his eyes on the grating, leaning his elbows on the walltop. "Well, they won't escape from there tonight while I'm watchin'."

"You weren't put up there to watch gratings, slop-head." Keyla called out in a stern voice. "It's your job to keep a close eye on those corsairs on the shore!"

Now Bluehide was completely confused. Keyla chuckled as he slapped Oilback heartily across the shoulders. "Ha ha ha! That showed him, eh, matey?"

Oilback continued on his way, laughing falsely as he answered. "Ho ho ho! It certainly did, mate. I'll just take a look out there meself. You can't trust corsairs y' know!"

Keyla and Brome waited until Bluehide had his back to them on the wall top, then shifted the heavy grating to one side.

"Whew, that was a close thing!" the young mouse murmured under his breath.

Outside in the shadow of the wall, Oilback wiped sweat from his nose, muttering silently to himself. "Whew, that was a close thing!"

He uncorked the flagon and took a deep drink to calm his nerves.

* * *

210

Brome and Keyla ushered the freed slaves into the pit and then climbed in after them, pulling the grating shut over them once they were in.

An old mousewife called Geum started to complain aloud. "It's stuffy down here. I'm stuck like a pea in a pod. Why did we have to come into this dirty place?"

Brome was thumping the walls to find the opening. "Hush, Mother, this is the way we're going to escape. Keep your voice down."

But Geum was not about to be quiet. "The main gate was open. Why didn't we just go out that way? And don't call me mother, cheekyface. I'm not your mother!"

Keyla clamped a paw across her mouth. "Silence, you old scold! Brome knows what he's doing. We wouldn't stand a lame sea bird's chance of walking through Clogg's crew to freedom. This way we'll come up between some rocks beyond their camp. Have you found the opening yet, Brome?"

A shower of loose earth and some pieces of driftwood fell on to the heads of Keyla and Geum.

"Hahah! Here it is," Brome cried excitedly. "For a moment I wasn't sure I could find it. Good old Grumm, he did a great job disguising his tunnel. I'll go first. Keyla, you and Yarrow help the others in and bring up the rear. We'll have to move fast, there's not many hours left until dawn. The last thing we want is to be caught out on the open shore."

It took a considerable time to get all the slaves into the tunnel. They pushed up against each other in the darkness, infants began whimpering and Geum started to complain again.

"Ugh! It's dark and stuffy down here. I don't like it!"

Yarrow shoved her further along from behind. "None of us are exactly joyful about being down here, old one. Just keep going, and put a latch on your lip. You're upsetting the little ones."

Geum's dignity was offended. "Stop pushing me, you

young rip, and mind how you speak to your elders. Oh dear, there's sand falling on the back of my head."

Brome crawled as fast as he was able to. Hearing Geum's last statement added to his haste. He knew the tunnel was only a makeshift affair and could collapse at any moment, particularly now, with the added disturbance of thirty-odd creatures blundering their way through it. Suddenly, just when he thought he was at the end of the tunnel, Brome found he could crawl no farther. The young mouse let out a groan into the thick air.

The tunnel had caved in at the exit end. They were trapped!

25

Rose was wakened by Martin's cry and the great feathered bulk of the grey heron rolling over her. Something brushed by her. She felt slithering scales and kicked out at them.

Martin was locked in the coils of some reptilian creature, what it was he did not know. It felt like a snake, but it had more than one head and tail. Stabbing viciously with his short sword, he was rewarded by the sound of anguished hissing as the coils fell away from him. Nearby Grumm swung out with his ladle and caught something hard on the skull. It went limp. Pallum hung on grimly to a third sinuous shape as Rose battered it with a supply pack. Martin felt another reptile at his back. Swinging sharply, he slashed crosswise and stabbed down twice. The creature was instantly slain.

Rose was still hitting with the pack as she cried out in the darkness, "Fire, Grumm. Make fire!"

The mole fumbled for flint and tinder as Martin found Rose and Pallum in the darkness. Afraid to use his sword in such close proximity to them, he dropped it and went headlong at the creature they had been trying to tackle. Butting, punching and kicking like a mad beast, Martin rendered the thing senseless.

There were no more opponents to fight. They stood

still while sparks flew and Grumm could be heard blowing on the tinder. Suddenly there was a small flame. The mole fed it with dry grass and twigs. In the ensuing firelight they viewed the attackers and the attacked. It was the two slowworms they had first seen on entering the marshes. They were both dead, slain by Martin, and lying stunned close by was an enormous grass snake and a young adder.

Grumm shuddered violently. "Surrpints!"

Pallum scrambled over to the limp figure of the Warden. "I think they've killed him!"

Rose was at his side instantly. "Let me take a look."

As she inspected the big bird, Martin called Pallum and Grumm to help him. Between the three of them they heaved the bodies of the four reptiles into the deep ooze of the marsh.

"Over here! This bird is alive!"

Rose was massaging the Warden's long neck. His eyelids fluttered feebly as she rubbed skillfully. One of the heron's eyes opened momentarily. "I am the laaaaaww!" it managed to croak.

The mousemaid put a paw to its beak. "Yes I know. Be still now, those snakes nearly strangled you. Grumm, put some water on to heat and see if you can find some soft moss and herbs to make a poultice."

As dawn broke over the little camp, Rose sat nursing her patient. The Warden was a fierce bird, quick to recover and hard to keep still. She had bound his neck with a warm soothing poultice of moss and herbs, checking the rest of him to assure herself that the young adder had not struck him.

"You'll be all right, the adder didn't bite you. Warden, please lie still. Your neck was badly squeezed. Try not to move it."

The grey heron tried to rise but fell back croaking hoarsely, "Snakes are lawbreakers. I will punish them. I am the law!"

214

Grumm looked up from the soup he was making. "Doant you'm never be soilent, burd? Close thoi gurt beak. Hurr!"

As they were held up by the Warden's injuries, breakfast was a leisurely affair. Pallum roasted some vegetables, leek, pennycress, and shallots. Grumm made excellent wild celery and herb soup then experimented on some barley scones. The Warden became so fierce when Pallum tried to feed him soup that the hedgehog hid behind Grumm. "I don't think he likes your soup."

Grumm shook his ladle at the heron. "Doant be natural, creetur not loikin' moi zoop. He'm never grow big 'n' strong loik oi."

"I am Warden of Marshwood Hill. Warden does not eat zoop!"

"Oh, goo an' boil thoi 'ead, gurt burdbag!"

Rose was surprised at the Warden's powers of recovery. Barely halfway through the morning he was up and walking as he conversed with Martin. The young mouse told him the story of what had taken place in the night. The big bird glared savagely at him.

"I thank you. Martin is mouse warrior, but you must learn!"

"Learn what?"

"Learn to kill all lawbreakers. Two snakes not dead!"

"But I threw them in the swamp."

"Next time kill first, then they will never break the law again!"

The Warden was inflexible when dealing with lawbreakers.

By noon they were back on the path again, travelling behind the Warden. Rose was mentioning to Martin that the mists were beginning to clear and sunlight was now plainly visible filtering through, when Pallum called, "Ahead, look up!"

There was the mountain. Rising above the mists into the summer day, it towered in solitary splendor, the lower slopes clad in verdant pine, rising to shrub and wild lupin, which gave way to naked dun-hued rock all the way to its majestic peak.

Grumm shielded his eyes with a digging claw, peering up. "Well, dig moi tunnel! Us'ns got t' cloimb yon gurt 'ill?"

The Warden halted, fixing them with his fierce eye. "You can see the mountain?"

Rose nodded her head, awed at the sight. "We surely can. Have we got to climb over it?"

The heron stood on one leg. "No, only halfway. Do you see the cave?"

The four friends searched the rocky mass, straining their eyes. Martin looked at Rose and shrugged before turning to the Warden. "We cannot see a cave, but if you say it is there then we believe you. Halfway up, you said."

The Warden nodded. "Yes, halfway up. It is a tunnel through the mountain. Now I must leave you. These are my marshes. I am the law here. I stay."

With an awkward hopskip he took to the air, wings beating until he caught a thermal. Swooping over them, the bird called out, "You saved my life. I will not forget this. You are not lawbreakers. Maybe I will be able to help you someday. I go now. Goodbye!"

As he swooped away, Rose cried aloud, "Thank you for your help. Besides the cave, is there anything else we should look out for when we climb the mountain?"

Wheeling in a half-turn, the heron called a final message, "Ask Boldred, the mountain is not mine. These are my marshes and I alone am the laaaaaa-aawwwwwwww!"

With that, the Warden of Marshwood Hill was gone, soaring above his domain of treacherous ooze and reptilian subjects.

In the late afternoon they came out of the marshlands. Crossing a stretch of dry scrub country, the four travellers stopped at the fringe of pines in the mountainous foothills. It was green and shady where Martin decided they would camp.

"We'll rest here until the morning before attempting to climb the mountain. A good meal and a long sleep is what we need."

Grumm shook the food packs out, his homely face a picture of dismay as he took stock of their supplies. "Burr, 'ardly any vittles left!"

Two wizened apples, a few pawfuls of wheat flour, one or two candied nuts and three raspberry scones were all that remained of Polleekin's good food. The mole shook their final canteen. "Lack a day, on'y arf full o' mint cordial!"

Rose chuckled as she prodded her friend's tubby little stomach. "Oh dearie me, Grumm Trencher, are you going to let us all starve and waste away to leaf shadows?"

Grumm polished his ladle vigorously with dry grass. "You'm a snip, Miz Roser, no mistake about that! Roight, oi'm taken charge yurr an' now. Pallum, surch furr veggibles, zurr Marthen, an' you'm, Miz Roser, lukk for water an' gather wudd. Oi'll see wot can be 'unted oop. Listen now, oi wants you'm all back yurr afore sunset. Be that clear?"

Pallum, Martin and Rose giggled as they whispered among themselves. Grumm waved the ladle at them. "Oi said, be that clear?"

They turned to him with serious faces, trying hard not to laugh as they stood stiffly to attention saluting.

"To hear is to obey, Lord Grumm!"

"We will not come back empty-pawed, O Mighty One!"

"We are yours to command, for you are the law!"

They dashed off laughing, leaving Grumm polishing his ladle. "Oi doant see nuthin' funny. Vittles be serious, ho urr!"

Twilight found the four friends seated around a cozy little fire. Their foraging had proved extremely fruitful: apples, early wild plums and some green acorns, parsley, dandelion, wild oats and a piece of honeycomb, which Pallum had found floating in a small rivulet of ice-cold mountain water. There were also a few mushrooms and some watercress which had been growing by the rivulet. Grumm borrowed Martin's sword and used the blade to peel and chop. The others took their ease, laying back under a small spreading pine to watch him.

"Hurr, mushrooms 'n' cress goes with parsley 'n' danneeline," the mole explained as he prepared supper. "Chop up they green acorns too. 'Twill make gudd zoop, a'most thick as stew." He paused to rap Rose's paw with the ladle as she tried to steal a wild plum. "Gurroff, mizzy! Oi needs they, to put wi' last o' flour an' woild oaters an' hunny. Chop 'ee apples vurry liddle. Pass oi yon flat stone, oi needs it furr moi asperimend."

Martin looked at Rose as he passed Grumm the flat thin rock. "Asperimend? What does he mean?"

"He means experiment. Grumm is always experimenting with food. He's very good, his experiments can turn out tasty."

The soup when it came was savory, and they blew on it as they sipped it from their scallop shells. Grumm had patted his mixture of wild plum, flour, oats, honey and apples into small round cakes that he cooked on the flat rock over the fire. The sweet smell wreathed round the camp as he turned off the first batch to cool in the grass. Taking one gingerly, he broke it, giving half to Rose. "Wot you'm think o' that, mizzy?"

The mousemaid juggled it in her paws, blowing on it as she took several quick nibbles. "Oh, Grumm, it tastes wonderful. So sweet and sticky!"

The mole wrinkled his snout in a satisfied manner. "Hurr, oi knew 't would. Oi'll make a couple o' batches an' we'll pack they'm furr rations. Oi 'opes oi c'n amember moi asperimend when we reaches 'ome to Noonvale."

Grumm gave them a cake apiece to eat after their soup. He was packing the rest of them away when a cracking of branches coupled with screams and wild laughter sounded close by. Before Martin could retrieve his sword from Grumm, a dozen or more young squirrels bounded into the camp, screeching, scrabbling and fighting. One of the creatures tripped and stumbled over Rose. He snapped at her and pushed her roughly as he struggled to rise. Martin was across to him in a twinkling. He dealt the squirrel a hefty blow and sent him sprawling again. Now the camp seemed to be full of wild-looking squirrels. They wore sashes of gaily colored barkcloth and had bird feathers fastened to their tails. Disregarding the four travellers, they fought and screeched all round them, ignoring the upset and discomfort they were causing. One creature grabbed hold of Grumm, using him as a shield to escape from another, who was trying, apparently, to steal the feathers from his tail.

Martin had stood enough. He did not want to kill any of them as they had not directly attacked him or his friends, but he was determined that they should be taught a lesson. Seizing Grumm's ladle, he dashed at the two who were whirling the mole about as one tried to catch the other.

Whopp! Thock!

Martin dealt out two stunning blows which sat the wild pair down flat on their tails. He brandished the ladle and roared, "Stop this! D'you hear me? Stoppit this instant!"

The squirrels halted, panting heavily and grinning at each other.

Martin shook the ladle, his voice stern and loud.

"You hooligans, what d'you mean by dashing in and wrecking our camp like this, eh? Have you no manners at all? You're like a mob of wild beasts!"

219

One squirrel grabbed a feather from the tail of another and hopped nimbly on to a low pine branch. "Hah! 'Snot your land, it's ours. We're the Gawtrybe, we do what we like. So there!" He stuck his tongue out impudently at Martin.

Pallum was quick. Leaping up, he caught the branch and twanged it, catapulting the squirrel onto the ground. The other squirrels thought this was hilarious and started doing it to each other, one leaping on a low branch as the other twanged it off.

Rose was furious. Placing her paws on her hips, she yelled at them, "Do you want me to call the Warden of Marshwood Hill?"

They stopped momentarily again, then started laughing as one of their number began imitating the grey heron's sticklike walk and doing a passable impression of the bird.

"I am the law, I slay all lawbreakers! Heeheehee, Warden can't touch us, he only rules the marshland, never comes up here!"

Rose drew herself up to her full height. "Then I'll tell Boldred!"

All activity ceased. They looked around nervously, then one of them pulled an impudent face. "Yah, you can't, 'cos she's not here, look!" Jumping up and down, he chanted, "Boldred, Boldred, boulder-head old Boldred!" Spreading his paws wide, he smirked cheekily, "See, she's not here!"

With a series of wild whoops the squirrels sprang off into the trees, leaving the camp at peace once more. Martin stood listening to them as they shrieked and shouted off into the gathering night.

"The Gawtrybe, eh. I don't like that crowd one little bit. We'd best post a sentry tonight. I'll take first watch. Grumm, will you take second? You can use my sword."

The mole brandished his trusty ladle fearlessly. "Burr, this be all oi'll need furr they rarscally beasters!"

Rose placed damp wood on the fire to burn slowly

through the night. She sat with her back against a pine and settled to rest. "Martin, did you notice how they stopped when I mentioned Boldred? I know they joked and clowned a bit, but they're obviously scared of her. I wonder who Boldred is and where we can find her."

Martin shouldered the small sword, his keen eyes questing around the night-cloaked woodland. "Your guess is as good as mine, Rose. I don't think we've seen the last of the Gawtrybe, though."

However, the night passed uneventfully for the four travellers, the wooded foothills remaining calm and peaceful. The following morning was presided over by a hot blue cloudless sky, promising even greater heat as the day progressed. They breakfasted sparingly on cold water and some of Grumm's invention cakes before setting off to scale the mountain.

Three hours after dawn, they left the forest, entering a country of sloping shale scree carpeted with shrub, fern and lupin. As they toiled upwards in the oppressive breezeless warmth, Martin gritted his teeth. Jibes and insults were coming at them from all around, though they saw no squirrels.

"Heehee, I'll tell the Warden on you!"

"Bad-mannered hooligans, campwreckers!"

"Heehee, still no sign of Boldred!"

"Please, Boldred, save us from the Gawtrybe, heehee!"

Pallum clapped a paw to his ear. "Yowch! They're chucking pebbles at me!"

A small stone clacked off Martin's swordblade. He kept his eyes straight ahead, speaking in a voice strained by temper. "Ignore them, the stupid vermin!"

"Ignore them, the stupid vermin, heeheehee!" a voice echoed back at him.

The young mouse was about to pick up a pebble and hurl it back in the direction of the voice when Rose halted. She muttered urgently to him out of the side of her mouth, "Look up ahead!"

The way was blocked by about fifty Gawtrybe squirrels. One, larger than the rest and obviously some kind of chieftain, stood forward. He scuffed the ground with his paw and pouted like a naughty infant as he spoke. "This is Gawtrybe land. You've got to pay to pass through."

Martin eyed him levelly. "We have only some food for ourselves, nothing of any value. I am Martin the Warrior, this is Rose, Pallum and Grumm. Let us pass. We will be off your land by nightfall."

The squirrel leader did a mincing little dance, holding his paws together imploringly as he mocked, "Let us pass, please. Let us pass!"

Martin noticed that more squirrels had come up behind them, cutting off any chance of retreat. The leader squirrel had more feathers in his tailbrush than any of the others. He arched the bushy tail skillfully towards Martin.

"I am called Wakk, leader of the Gawtrybe. Give me your sword and I'll let you pass."

The young mouse's eyes were cold as he answered, "Nobeast takes this sword from me!"

Wakk puffed out his chest and made his tail stand straight. "Then I will fight you for it!"

Martin curled his lip derisively. "Oh, you'll fight, my friend, backed up by all your bunch, I suppose."

Wakk did not sneer or joke. He held up both paws to show he was not armed. "No no, we two will fight together, just me and you. None of my bunch will interfere. Give your sword to the mousemaid, and let's see how good you are without a weapon."

Instantly, the squirrels formed a large ring. As Martin passed the sword to Rose he had his back turned to Wakk.

"Look out, Martin!" Pallum shouted.

He thrust the sword into Rose's paws and whirled around to see Wakk hurtling through the air at him, teeth bared and claws outspread.

26

Trapped!

The word ran back like wildfire along the creatures packed into the escape tunnel, and panic took over in the dark airless place.

"We're all going to die down here. Help!"

"Ooh, I knew we should never have tried to escape!"

"I can't breathe. Let me out of here!"

"At least we were alive in the stockade!"

"It's that Brome's fault, the stupid young fool!"

Something within Keyla snapped. Suddenly the young otter was crushing and pushing, lashing out as he climbed over heads, squeezing and scraping past other creatures, bashing out with all paws and his rudderlike tail as he battled towards Brome at the blocked exit.

"Gerrout of my way! I never came down here to suffocate an' die. Let me by, you stupid snivellin' moaners!"

Bulling and pushing, kicking and shoving, the resourceful otter strove on through the packed airless tunnel until he felt Brome's corsair rags in his paws. "Brome, what's the matter. Why can't we get out?"

His face touching Keyla's, Brome yelled in the darkness, "We were nearly out, I'm sure of it, but the exit's caved in!"

The otter pushed him backwards into the press of wailing slaves. "Get out of my way and give me space. I'll get us out of here!" With a surge of strength born of desperation, Keyla threw himself at the blockage, all four paws going like windmills. Despite the screams and cries of outrage from behind, he tore, bit, gouged, kicked, dug and flailed at the sandy earth as it sprayed around him in gouts and showers. His shouts could be heard throughout the tunnel as he flung his body forward.

"Eeyaahhh! What d'you want? Somebeast to dig? I'll show you how Keyla digs! Like this! And this! Wahoooooooooooo!" The otter's nose fountained blood as it struck a large rock. Keyla wrapped his whole body around it and yanked, grunting and squeezing past the rock, he savaged the loose earth, scraping, biting and thudding until his head burst through into the hole on the shore between the rocks. Wriggling out, Keyla spat earth, and wiped his mouth out with a paw. Chuckling quietly, he shook with delight.

"Haha, just shows what you can do when you feel like it!"

Brome leapt from the tunnel, casting aside his disguise and hugging Keyla tightly at the same time. "Keyla, you rogue, you did it, you got us free!"

Then it was Brome's turn to act sensibly. As he helped the first slaves out of the hole he issued instructions to Keyla.

"We were trapped down there quite a while. Time was lost, and it's not long until dawn. I'm going to run to the camp and get Felldoh with some others to help. I'll bring them back as quickly as I can. You must follow my pawprints, and move everybeast along as fast as you possibly can. Once the fortress is roused, Badrang will have his horde out after our blood!"

Dawn was crimsoning the grey from the sky as the ebb tide lapped gently on the shore. It was Bluehide's favorite time of day. He had catnapped most of the night through his sentry watch on the walltop of Marshank. Now he stretched gratefully in anticipation of breakfast and a sleep until noon. Shortly his relief arrived, another ferret called Stumptooth.

Bluehide passed the sentry spear over happily. "It's goin' t' be a scorcher of a day, mate. You'll sweat up 'ere."

Stumptooth took the proffered spear and leaned heavily on it. "Aye, yer right there, Blue'ide. Tain't fair, is it, me stannin' up 'ere on guard all day while those bone-idle slaves lie round the compound scratchin' theirselves."

"Hoho, don't you fret yer 'ead about the slaves, Stumpy." Bluehide began climbing down a wall ladder. "They're all down the prison pit. 'Alf of 'em will be dead afore the day's through!"

Stumptooth was pushing past Bluehide on the ladder. "Slaves in the prison pit? I never seen any an' I looks down there every mornin' when I passes!"

Bluehide landed on Stumptooth's head. They bumbled down the ladder to fall in a heap at the bottom. Scrambling on all fours, they both raced to the pit. Bluehide's jaw went slack in dismay.

"But, but, they was there last night," he began explaining. "I saw 'em go down with me own eyes. It was two of our horde put 'em down there . . ."

Stumptooth was not listening. He was dashing for the longhouse, screaming, "Escape! Escape! The slaves 'ave escaped!"

Badrang came thundering out, tripped over Gurrad's body, picked himself swiftly up and kicked the carcass bad-temperedly. "Slaves escaped? How many? Where?"

"From the prison pit, Lord!"

"Prison pit, who put 'em down there?"

"I don't know, Sire. Blue'ide was on duty las—"

But Badrang was not listening, he was dashing about the courtyard yelling, "Hisk! Fleabane! Get the horde together. Now!"

Half-asleep weasels, ferrets and rats stumbled out, pulling their clothes on as they trailed weapons behind them. Badrang was in a towering fury. He lashed out with the flat of his sword.

"You half-baked, slobberfaced slugs! Move! There still might be time to catch those slaves. Stir your stumps, you useless blatherbrained beasts. Filling your stomachs and resting your heads is about all you lot are good for!"

Hisk and Fleabane scuttled about, echoing their master's threats and insults, not quite sure of what they were supposed to do.

The Tyrant returned to Gurrad's carcass. Obviously Clogg had forestalled the assassination attempt. He would get rid of the body before Clogg saw it and started gloating. Grabbing a passing rat, Badrang snarled, "You, Nipwort, bring that thing and follow me."

Nipwort struggled along behind Badrang, dragging the limp figure as he tried to keep up.

With a frenzied burst of energy, the Tyrant stoat dragged the grating from the pit. Lying flat, he thrust his head in and could not fail to see the escape hole. "Here, Nipwort. Leave the body there and climb into this pit. See that hole in the side of the wall? Get yourself in there and see how far it goes. Report back to me when you find out where the exit is."

Before going to attend his horde, Badrang watched the unhappy Nipwort climb into the escape tunnel. When the rat was lost to view, Badrang pushed Gurrad's body into the pit and replaced the grating with a swift heave.

Tramun Clogg had been up and about before Badrang that day, anxious to know the result of his murderous plan. When Gruzzle and Boggs reported the finding of Oilback's body, Clogg knew the scheme had failed. Hastily they disposed of the poisoned rat, tossing him into the sea. Clogg had his crew stand by fully armed lest

Badrang should come seeking revenge for the attempt on his life.

Crosstooth the fox took a swift glance toward Marshank's open gates. "Stand by, Cap'n. 'Ere comes Badrang with trouble aplenty!"

Tramun stood prepared as the Tyrant and his horde pounded out across the shore. However, his keen ears caught the drift of what Hisk and Fleabane were shouting.

"Double quick, you lot. Come on there, Lord Badrang wants every last one o' those slaves back!"

"Aye, if you don't catch those escapers you'll find yourselves doing their work. So move!"

Clogg sheathed his cutlass, chewing thoughtfully on a beard plait as an idea formed in his sly fertile mind. "Ho buckoes, put up yer weapons an' foller me!"

With a look of concern on his villainous face, the corsair ran towards Badrang, calling out aloud, "Ahoy, matey. Wot's the trouble?"

The Tyrant stoat halted, glaring suspiciously at Clogg. "Didn't you know? The rest of the slaves escaped during the night!"

Horror and indignation stamped themselves on the corsair's features. "Why, the rotten bunch o' scallawags! I'll never get me new ship built now. Badrang, matey, let's call a truce between us until we catch 'em. Which way d'you reckon they went?"

Badrang could not waste time bandying words with his old adversary. He realized he would need all the help he could get to recapture the slaves. "They've probably headed south and to the cliffs. That's the way we're going."

Clogg stroked the braids on his chin thoughtfully. "Aharr, maybe that's wot they wants you to think, mate. Maybe they went north to fool ye. I'll take my crew that way."

Before Badrang could reply, Clogg had hauled out his cutlass and was running north along the shore with his corsairs. "Come on, you flotsam. If ye ever want to feel a deck neath yer paws agin, you'll 'ave to find them scummy slaves!"

Badrang led his horde off to the south at a lively run.

Nipwort emerged from the escape tunnel. Dusting himself down, he climbed on to the rocky outcrop to get his bearings. The tracks were clear. Shading his eyes against the morning sun, Nipwort scanned the shoreline. He saw the unmistakable form of a group in the distance. They were hurrying towards the cliffs. Turning round, the rat could see Badrang and the horde running in his general direction. Jumping up and down, he waved frantically.

"Over here, Lord! I can see them!"

Ballaw, Rowanoak, Buckler and Felldoh, in company with ten or more of the most able-bodied free slaves, jogged along the clifftop behind Brome. Felldoh looked grim as he muttered to the hare, "What a reckless little fool Brome is. He could have been captured at Marshank or smothered in that tunnel!"

Ballaw hefted his lance lightly. "Matter of opinion, old lad. If you fail you're a bally fool, if you win you're a jolly hero!"

Rowanoak puffed along behind them, towing the cart. "Ballaw's right. I'd say if he pulls this off he's a reckless hero; who would have thought it, young Brome!"

Brome stopped. Pointing down to the shore he yelled proudly, "There they are!"

Felldoh's eyes roved further afield. "Aye, and look who's following on the double!"

Rowanoak gave a great groan of dismay. "There's far too many of them for us. Our only hope is to get those poor creatures on to the clifftop up here before the horde gets to them. Come on, let's give it a try!"

Stout vine ropes were anchored to rocks and thrown over the steep cliff slope. Ballaw roared to the slaves, projecting his voice magnificently, "I say, you chaps. Over here!"

Felldoh and some others shinned hurriedly down the ropes on to the shore, and ran to help the stragglers. Buckler threw his paws about an old mousewife, glancing back at the pursuers. "They be comen on apace. Oi doant think us'ns ull make et!"

Badrang's paws slapped hard on the strand as he put on a great burst of speed, calling to his horde, "Come on, we've got 'em!"

Old Geum grasped the rope. Gazing upwards, she pursed her lips. "I'll never be able to haul myself up there. What d'you think I am, a young squirrel?"

"I don't know about a young squirrel, Mother, but you'll be a dead mouse if you hang about here!"

Felldoh threw Geum across his shoulder with a single heave and began hauling himself up the rope.

Buckler and six others launched a salvo of short javelins directly at the horde. Four of Badrang's creatures fell. The rest parted ranks, spreading themselves to avoid being hit. All of the escapers were now on the ropes, scrambling up the steep cliff face, fear of their pursuers and the scent of freedom lending speed to their paws. Felldoh had delivered Geum and hopped back down without using the ropes. Now he was on his way back up with two small young ones clinging to his tail. Buckler and the others were backed up hard to the cliffside as the horde advanced on them. Two had been brought down by spears from Badrang's creatures. Rowanoak looked worriedly down as she called to them, "Get on the ropes! Come up here!"

Brome and those on the clifftop began hurling javelins and slingstones to cover their friends' retreat.

Badrang dashed forward as Buckler began scrambling up the rope. He picked up a fallen javelin and hurled it.

The mole cried out in agony as it took him through the shoulder.

"Hold tight, Buckler, hold tight!" Rowanoak bellowed furiously as she seized the rope in both paws and heaved mightily.

Badrang leaped for the rope but found himself grasping dust. Despite the fact that there were six others climbing the rope above Buckler, the strength of Rowanoak's tremendous pulls made the whole thing fairly fly up. She dashed backwards, muscles straining, as she towed the taut vine rope behind her. It hummed and sang under the tension, sending creatures who were clinging to it flying along the clifftop on their stomachs.

Ballaw pulled the javelin from Buckler's shoulder. "How are you doin', old scout?"

The mole winced then smiled. "Take more'n a likkle ole spear to slay oi!"

"Ballaw, they're climbing the other ropes!"

Brome's shouts brought Ballaw to the cliff edge. Badrang was standing on the shore, directing his creatures upwards. "Get on those ropes, the rest of you start climbing. Come on, we can swarm them. They're too few to stop us! Move, you dolts, get climbing."

Felldoh pulled the last slave over the clifftop. Below him he could see ferrets, rats and weasels scaling the remaining four ropes, while the rest were climbing up, spurred on by Badrang.

Rowanoak joined Felldoh and stood watching. "Let them get a bit closer to us then I'll move."

"Move what?" Felldoh looked at the badger quizzically.

"Those four large boulders the ropes are tied to, of course!"

Ballaw waggled his ears expressively. "Should give the rotters somethin' to think about, wot! Let's do it now before they get any further. I'll get all the gang to lend a paw. Right, gather round, chaps, and I'll explain the drill."

Badrang was about to mount one of the ropes himself when he heard the ominous rumble from above. Leaping clear he shouted up, "Off! Get off the ropes! Back down, everybeast, quick!"

Some of the horde were almost at the top. They hesitated, looking at the long drop to the shore. Others clung to the cliff face, not knowing what to do.

Rowanoak threw her great bulk against the first boulder. It rolled quite freely. Ballaw and Felldoh had a thick branch under the next one. They levered down and the boulder began moving. Brome and some others charged the third boulder with the cart, setting it on the move as the stout little vehicle bumped it forward. Amid the screams and yells of panic as the first boulder came rumbling over the edge, Rowanoak dashed to the fourth and final one. She bulled into it with a deep growl. A ferret's head appeared over the clifftop as the boulder rolled forward. He gave a wail of dismay and flung himself into space.

The devastation caused by the four boulders was considerable. They tore huge chunks out of the cliff face as they bounced downwards, and several creatures tangled in the ropes attached to the boulders were given a fast, harsh sleigh ride on their backs down the steep slope. The less fortunate were crushed in the path of the great stones or caught by them as they bounced and thudded towards the shore.

Badrang had pulled a score of archers back. They knelt on the beach, directing a volley of shafts upwards. Cries from the clifftop told the Tyrant that his strategy was being rewarded.

As Rowanoak harnessed herself into the cart shafts, an arrow buried itself in the wood by her paw. "Time we weren't here, Felldoh. Can you and Ballaw get the slow and wounded in the cart double quick, please."

It was but the work of a moment. The cart trundled off at a fast lick, propelled by Rowanoak and every able-bodied creature.

"Cease fire, hold those bowstrings!"

Bluehide was the last to hear. He could not stop his arrow twanging off over the clifftop, nor could he avoid the swift kick from Badrang that sent him sprawling.

"What's the matter, cloth ears? Can't you tell that there's nobeast up there any more!" The Tyrant sighed heavily and sat on one of the boulders. "Hisk, Fleabane, count 'em up. How many did we lose?"

"Fifteen in all, Sire. About that many injured too."

"We got eight of theirs, though, and some more up on top must have been slain by arrows."

"Eight of theirs," Badrang snorted. "You mean eight of ours—they were my slaves. The only one of theirs was the mole. I got him, though I never got him good enough to finish him off."

The horde members sat about in silence, awaiting their leader's mood, which could range from indifference to foul bad temper.

Badrang watched them licking their wounds and retrieving their weapons. Then he summoned Hisk. "Take ten, make sure you've got a couple of good trackers. I want you to find where they've gone. When you do, report back to me at Marshank. Don't try to fight or even show yourselves, just come straight back to me with the information. Have you got that?"

Hisk saluted with his spear. "Yes, Lord. I will do exactly as you say!"

"Good. When they are least expecting it, we will come in full force and ambush them. They are not soldiers or warriors, merely escaped slaves and some ragtag actors who have been lucky so far."

Cap'n Tramun Clogg sat back in Badrang's chair, enjoying the comfort of the longhouse. He drank damson wine and picked his teeth with the bones of a herring he had eaten. His clogs clacked noisily as he swung his legs on to the tabletop and gave Crosstooth a huge wink.

"Brains, that's wot y'need to outsail yer enemies, brains!"

The fox shook his head admiringly. "An' you've certainly got 'em, Cap'n. You fooled ole Badrang!"

Clogg's huge stomach shook with merriment. "I'll 'elp ye to find the slaves, sez I. You go that way an' I'll go this way. Aye, an' this is the way I goes, straight round the back o' the fortress, over the wall with me bold crew, an' captures Marshank for meself. Haharrharharr. Is the gate locked, matey?"

Crosstooth poured himself a beaker of wine. "Locked, barred an' bolted tight, Cap'n. The crew is on the walls, well fed an' armed to the fangs!"

Clogg lost the fishbone in his stomach plaits and forgot it. "All waitin' for pore uncle Badrang to come visitin' with his tail atwixt 'is legs an' a flea in 'is ear. Hahaharr!"

27

Wakka, Chieftain of the Gawtrybe, was a savage fighter. Swift too, though not as swift as Martin the Warrior. The young mouse saw the squirrel hurtling through the air at him and danced nimbly to one side. Wakka hit the ground on all fours. Whirling fast, he was up and into Martin, setting his claws tight into Martin's sides, his sharp teeth seeking his opponent's throat as the bushy tail pushed itself stiflingly over the mouse's face. Martin bit into the tail hard, throwing himself backwards and shooting all four paws straight up. Wakka gave a shriek of pain and sailed over Martin's head, straight into a bunch of squirrels. Martin was up immediately. Joining both paws tight like a club, he swung out, knowing what the squirrels would do. They heaved their leader bodily back at the young mouse, hoping to crush him.

Whopp!

Martin's tight-joined paws cannoned straight into Wakka's nose. The squirrel sat down, licking away blood and seeing stars. His head cleared and he rushed Martin. This time he feinted slightly. As Martin leapt aside, Wakka went the same way and caught him. Locking his legs round the mouse's waist, the squirrel Chieftain clung like a limpet, scratching wildly at Martin's face. The young mouse winced as the foebeast's claws scored his cheeks deeply, trying to find his eyes. Martin threw himself forward, hitting the ground with Wakka beneath him. The breath was knocked from the squirrel in one gasp. Punishing him with another hard double pawblow to the nose, Martin was first up. With both paws held tight to his damaged nose, Wakka staggered up. Martin grabbed him, spun him around and leapt on to the squirrel's shoulders. Clamping his footpaws round Wakka's neck, Martin grasped both the squirrel's ears as tight as he could and pulled upwards.

The squirrel screamed in agony, jumping from side to side and trying to dislodge his tormentor, but Martin hung grimly on, jaw muscles rigid as he pulled the ears tighter and locked his legs harder. Wakka bucked and leaped all around the ring formed by his bunch as Martin rode him, pulling savagely until the tendons stood out on his paws. Half strangled and with his ears near pulled out by the roots, Wakka went down like a stone, dust rising around as both creatures hit the earth. Martin jumped free. Placing his footpaw on Wakka's head, he ground down hard, forcing the squirrel's injured nose into the dirt. The Chieftain of the Gawtrybe struggled feebly, sobbing for breath as Martin's paw stamped down harder.

The young mouse was breathing hard as he rasped out the question, "Have you had enough, squirrel? Because if you haven't, we can carry on until the death!"

"Gnurff! Gnurff!"

Rose ran out. Grasping Martin's paw, she cried piteously, "He's had enough. Don't kill him, Martin!"

The sound of Rose's voice brought Martin back to reality. Veils of red mist fell from his eyes and the Warrior's desire to kill left him. He allowed her to lead him back to his friends, and Grumm set about bathing his deep-scored face.

The Gawtrybe had gone unusually silent. They broke the circle, leaving their beaten Chieftain deserted in the dust. The squirrels dispersed into the ferns and lupins, where they immediately began howling with laughter and playing again, some of them sitting on others' shoulders and pulling their ears as Martin had done to Wakka.

Pallum shook his head gravely. "Listen to that. What a bunch of savages!"

Rose applied strips of dockleaf to Martin's wounded face. "There, that's the best I can do for now. Let's get away from this place. I hate it, and those horrible wild squirrels too!"

The tall lupins and ferns provided some coolness against the heat of the day as they made their way to the mountain slope. It was Pallum who spotted the cave, high up above them on the dusty dun-coloured mountain face it stood, like a single eye on some great beast.

Martin shook his head. "I doubt if we'll reach it by nightfall."

Rose was all concern for him. "Never mind if we don't, we can camp on the mountainside until morning and reach it tomorrow. There's no great rush, Martin. Take it slower. You must be tired after battling that big squirrel."

Martin touched his stinging cheeks. "Don't worry about me, Rose. I can walk as fast as anybeast."

The mousemaid put on a stern face. Stumping ahead, she imitated the Warden's stick-like gait as she mimicked the grey heron. "I say you will walk slower. I am the law!"

They fell about laughing and sat in the ferns while Grumm unpacked some of his invention cakes and a drink of water for each of them. Martin accidentally dozed off as Pallum was singing a little ditty.

"Oh, the hedgehog is a fine old beast,
All covered o'er with needles,
Not smooth, oh no, like some I know,
Eels an' fish an' beetles.

Some creatures calls us hedgepigs,
An' others says hedgedogs,
But I do know that frogs is frogs,
An' hedgehogs is hedge hogs!"

Rose held a paw to her lips. "Hush now, let him sleep awhile. He'll feel better for it."

It was getting towards late afternoon when Martin was wakened by the sound of Gawtrybe squirrels hooting and hallooing close by. He rubbed his eyes and noted the position of the sun in the sky.

"Oh no, have I been dozing the day away? We'll never make it to the cave tonight now!"

Rose gave him water to drink and redressed his face wounds. "Come on then, grumpy. Perhaps you'll be happier on the move."

Shadows were lengthening as they emerged from the ferns on to the scree and rocks of the actual mountain face. Again they found their way barred by large numbers of the Gawtrybe.

Pallum's bristles rose aggressively. "Not you lot again. What d'you want now?"

In the absence of their deposed Chieftain, they seemed to have several leaders.

"Wanna play!" one squirrel called out.

Rose eyed them frostily. "Well, we're not stopping you. Play as much as you like!"

"Heehee!" another squirrel sniggered. "No, we want you t' play!"

Martin drew his sword and took a pace towards them. "And supposing we don't want to play?"

"Heeheeheehee! Then the Gawtrybe kill you!"

It was then that Martin noticed many of the squirrels were holding axes made from a piece of shale tied in the notch of a heavy stick. He held up a paw. "Wait while I ask my friends."

The four travellers went into a huddle as Martin explained. "We'd last as long as a butterfly in a snowstorm trying to fight our way past that mob. I think we're going to have to play whatever stupid game they've thought up."

He could see that Rose was afraid, but she nodded. "Whatever you say, Martin. We're with you."

"Burr aye, iffen 'tis 'ee only way outen yurr, then so be et."

"You lead on, Martin. We trust you."

Martin smiled and patted Pallum carefully. Turning to face the waiting Gawtrybe, he addressed them.

"All right, we'll play your game. What do we have to do?"

"Heehee, you run and we chase you."

"That sounds like fun. Which way do we run?"

"Up the mountain, heehee!"

"Good, that was the way we were travelling, up the mountain. What happens next?"

"When we catch you ... Heehee ... We throw you off!"

Hatred for the Gawtrybe coursed through Martin's veins. He gripped his sword tighter but continued to smile as he spoke. "I don't think we're going to like this game. My friends and I could be killed."

Mass laughter greeted Martin's statement, many voices calling out from the bunch in imitation of him.

"We could be killed. Heehee!"

"What a nasty game. Heehee!"

Martin waited until the noise had subsided.

"Fair enough, we'll play," he continued in a reasonable voice. "But the Gawtrybe are squirrels, very strong, fleet of paw, very very fast!"

Cheers arose from the squirrels. They obviously enjoyed flattery.

Martin grinned cheerily, waving his paws for silence. "We are slow and weary. The game would not be much fun if you did not give us a start. Then it would be a really good game!"

Some of the squirrels started to chant. "Really good game, really good game, really good game!"

Martin pointed to a high ledge protruding some distance above them. "Let us climb to that ledge before you start chasing us. When we reach the ledge, I will shout *Gawtrybe*. That is your signal."

The squirrels changed their chant. "Gawtrybe! Gawtrybe! Gawtrybe!"

"Yes! Yes! Yes!" Martin yelled aloud.

They took up his cry. "Yes! Yes! Yes!"

Rose was trembling slightly as the horde of wild squirrels leaped and danced in front of them, waving their stone axes and chanting fanatically. Grumm gazed up at the high ledge through the digging paws that were covering his eyes.

"Hoo urr, oi bain't a beast oo loiks 'igh places, hurr no, zurr."

Holding his sword at the ready, Martin took Rose's paw. "Pallum, Grumm, stay close and tread carefully. Come on. If we can make it up to that cave, I think we'll have a good chance of holding them off."

Martin led the way. It was a tense situation. Howling squirrels waved axes in their faces, grinning unpleasantly. Martin bared his teeth and growled if any tried to paw them or come too close. Step by step the four friends made their way through the mad throng, Martin brandishing his sword, Grumm wagging his ladle warningly, Pallum extending his spikes and Rose swinging a foodpack in a businesslike manner. It seemed like hours, though it was only moments before they were clear.

Walking with deliberate slowness Martin spoke quietly to Pallum, who was bringing up the rear. "Pallum, take

239

a slow glance behind and see if they've made any move to follow us yet. Do it casually."

As Pallum turned his head, the Gawtrybe stopped chanting.

"They're standing stock still, the whole crowd of them, not making a move or a sound, just watching us!" Pallum's voice carried in it the tinge of fear.

Rose could feel countless pairs of wild eyes focused on them. The fur on her nape rose stiffly. "I've a feeling I'm not going to like this game, Martin."

The young mouse held her paw tighter. "Blank it from your mind, Rose. Think of Noonvale."

Reaching the first ledges, they helped one another up, ready to run should the Gawtrybe show any sign of pursuit. Sandy rock crumbled beneath their paws and slivering pieces of shale slid away down the mountainside. Two more small ledges to go. Martin dug his sword into a crack to aid his progress, leaning over the ledge and helping Rose to haul Grumm up. Pallum pushed the mole from behind.

Grumm scrabbled his way on to the ledge, not daring to look down at the crowd far below, still standing silent and waiting. "Oi doant moind unnergrounds but oi bain't too fond of oop yurr!"

Pallum nearly tripped and fell backwards on the final ledge. He was windmilling his paws as he teetered perilously at its rim. Acting quickly, Rose swung the foodpack. The hedgehog caught the shoulderstrap, and she hauled him back to the safety of the ledge. Now the Gawtrybe were beginning to chant and dance again, eager to be on the chase. The four friends stood on the ledge which Martin had nominated, watching them. Martin took the pack from Rose and shouldered it.

"Are we ready?"

They nodded. Pallum spat on his paws and rubbed them together. "Right, Martin. Give them the signal!"

The young mouse stared down at the dancing hordes below. "Look at them, mad, cruel beasts, playing games with the lives of other creatures. I wouldn't waste my breath shouting signals to the scum. Let them guess whether or not the game has begun!"

The four friends took off as fast as they could, up the mountainside to the cave high above.

It took several seconds for the dancing, yelling mob to realize they had been cheated, Martin had not shouted the signal for them to start chasing. With a concerted howl of rage, the masses of squirrels dashed for the mountain, waving their axes. From the heights the four friends paused to glance down. Martin had been right: Gawtrybe squirrels were strong and fleet of paw. They were climbing at an amazing rate, every one agile and swift.

The game for the lives of the travellers had really begun!

BOOK THREE

The Battle of Marshank

28

Brome and Keyla, together with Felldoh and the Rambling Rosehip Players, were the heroes of the hour. The thirty or so slaves who had escaped from Marshank with their aid cheered wildly, towing them round and round the camp on their cart. Being actors, the Rosehip company enjoyed applause in any form.

Ballaw took outrageously leggy bows, clapping his ears together comically. "Thank you dear creatures, thank you one and all!"

Rowanoak smiled benevolently, waving a huge paw. "Oh, you shouldn't really, it was nothing!"

Buckler, with one paw bound up against his injured shoulder in a sling, bobbed his furry head up and down. "Thankee, thankee. Oi'll be roight as rain in a few days!"

The rest of the company took their adulation gracefully, with the exception of Celandine, who fluttered her eyelashes constantly and blew outrageously sloppy kisses. "Wasn't I, marvellous, dears? I'd like to thank the rest of the troupe and all the other little creatures who helped me!"

Brome was up on the cart with the rest, but Felldoh was unused to such admiration. He wandered off alone from the camp, enjoying the warm evening as he savored the heady feeling of freedom.

Back at camp, the liberated slaves were marvelling at the ample larder kept by the troupe. A mouse called Purslane led her husband, Groot, and their baby, Fuffle, through an inventory of the contents.

"Look, Groot, dried fruits and maplecream. How many seasons since we tasted maplecream, I can't remember. Oh my! Will you smell these violet crystals and candied mintleaves!"

Groot opened a box, shaking his head fondly. "Nuts preserved in honey, chestnuts, beechnuts and acorns! D'you recall when you used to do them in late autumn, dear?"

Purslane brushed away a tear as she laughed. "Do I? You were the one who kept eating the nuts and licking the honey ladle. You were like a great babe. Fuffle, put those nuts down, they don't belong to us!"

The baby Fuffle gurgled around a mouthful of nuts. "Tasters nishe Fuffle likesum!"

Purslane was prising the nuts loose from his little paws when Rowanoak, who had deserted the victory parade, swept Fuffle up in a huge paw. She smiled fondly. "You eat as many as you like, little un. What is ours is yours."

Purslane and her husband thanked the badger profusely, but Rowanoak would hear none of it.

"Now that's enough of that, good creatures. Purslane, did I hear Groot saying that you could preserve nuts?"

Purslane gazed at the huge larder and its contents, longingly. "Preserve nuts? I could cook, bake, stew, make soups, salads, flans, cakes, tarts, trifles . . ."

Rowanoak held up a paw. "Trifles! That's one thing the Rosehip Players can't do, make a decent trifle. My dear, you don't know how many seasons I have dreamed of trifle. But listen, don't stand there telling me how good a cook you are. Why not get cracking and make a victory feast? I imagine there are others from Marshank who'd love to try their kitchen skills again."

Purslane, Geum, Ferndew and a hedgehog goodwife called Burrwen washed their paws and went to work. Night fell over the Rosehips' camp. The fires blazed merrily and old songs were brought forth to sing, as everybeast helped with the preparation of a great liberation meal. The young mouse Hoopoe, wearing a ridiculous hat woven from sedge grass, led the singing, conducting with a long onion shoot.

"Hey, give me cake and bring me ale,
And pudding ripe with plums,
Some cider, dear, so cool and clear,
To swill round teeth and gums,
Some round and golden mellow cheese,
And light brown nutbread, if you please,
With honey made by happy bees,
And I will be contented.
O fie the creature with long face
Who nibbles small and can't keep pace
With tartlets filled full berryfruit
And yellow meadowcream to boot,
Or soup with pepper and hotroot,
And burdock ale to quench it.
Oh, eat up, neighbour, drink up, friend,
May good fortune have no end.
Success to all that you intend,
And leave the pots till morning!"

The feast was one to remember, particularly since the freed slaves had young ones who had never attended a banquet, or even seen some of the dishes, let alone tasted them.

Old Geum sniffed as she passed Rowanoak a farl of hot barley bread filled with brown onion gravy and mashed turnip. "Just look at that little un, dipping strawberry tart into his soup. It's not right!"

The baby Fuffle was seated on Rowanoak's lap, enjoying himself immensely. The badger chuckled as she stroked his ears. "If it tastes nice to him and he likes it, then where's the harm? You eat up, you little rogue."

The two mice Yarrow and Hoopoe had purple lips and noses from drinking blackberry cordial, and yellow meadowcream tipped their ears, from where they had both been eating the same pudding out of a basin without using spoons or paws.

Celandine wiped her mouth daintily on a flimsy kerchief. "Oh goodness me, I don't think I can manage another bite!"

Ballaw eyed her plate, heaped high with summer salad and cheese. "I was just saying to Kastern and Gauchee the other day that you're lookin' a touch plump these days, m' gel, wot!"

The vain pretty squirrel pushed herself away from the food. "Am I really? Tell the truth, Ballaw. I'd hate to be plump!"

Ballaw pulled her plate across and emptied it reflectively, speaking between bites. "Well, er, chomp chomp, a touch more exercise, bit of firewood choppin', munch munch, and you'll be back to your former lovely slim self, m' dear, grumpff grumpff. I wouldn't worry too much."

Gauchee and Kastern sat gazing sadly at a beautiful damson flan topped with crisp thin pastry covered in whiterose cream and decorated with candied mintleaves and nuts. They were poised over it, holding a wooden spoon apiece, sighing regretfully,

"Golly gosh, it does look lovely. Far too nice to eat!"

"Hmm, I agree with you. It'd be a shame to spoil it, really!"

"But some other creature will if we don't."

"True, true. I know, let's do it gently!"

Brome sat next to Buckler, sharing a beetroot and mushroom pastie, an enormous thing, swimming in leek gravy. "Burr, oi c'n feel et doen moi shoulder a power o' gudd!"

"Huh, there's nothing wrong with your other

248

shoulder, it's doing the work of two. Stop shovin' me out of the way, you great hungry beast!"

Trefoil had an apple baked in honey. Each time she looked away, a piece of it went missing.

Rowanoak winked at the baby Fuffle as he licked honey from his paws. "Good, eh, mate!" Fuffle winked back with both eyes. "Good for Fuffle!"

Old Barkjon accepted a platter of summer fruits from Geum. He picked at them as he gazed at the other revellers. "I don't see my son. Have you served him with food, Geum?"

"He was hanging around at the edge of the camp before dark," the gossipy old mousewife sniffed. "Never sat down to eat with the rest. I suppose we're not good enough for him!"

Brome left his pastie to Buckler and spoke up in defense of his friend. "Don't you speak about Felldoh like that, old one. If it weren't for him and Keyla, you'd still be a slave!"

Geum bustled off in a huff. Barkjon smiled at the young mouse. "Well said, Brome. You are a true friend to my son. Have you seen him?"

Brome gathered up some food—a wedge of plumcake, a hunk of brown nut cheese, a small fresh-baked wheat farl and a jug. "I haven't seen him, sir, but I know where he'll be: doing a lone patrol and keeping watch for foebeasts while we sit here filling our bellies. I'll go and find him with this food. He must be hungry wandering the cliffs by himself."

Felldoh laid his javelins and thrower down. He sat with his back to a rock at the cliff's edge, staring out at the calm sea and the star-strewn sky. Though he was savoring freedom, the sturdy young squirrel was fighting down a rage that burned deep inside, against the seasons he and his father had spent in captivity. Hatred of Badrang and all the Tyrant stood for gnawed at him. The sound of somebeast close by drew his paws swiftly to the weapons on the ground.

"Felldoh, is that you, mate?"

The squirrel sighed as he relaxed his hold on the javelins. "Brome, what are you doing out here?"

The young mouse sat beside him and laid out the food. "Brought you a bite of supper. Are you hungry?"

Felldoh accepted the food gratefully. "Well young Brome," he said thoughtfully, "that was a reckless, foolish thing you did, but no one can deny that you showed great courage. No one can deny that."

"Redcurrant and roseleaf cordial. I hope you like it."

Felldoh balanced the jug on his elbow. "Like it? Does a fish like water!"

They sat together watching the sea and the night sky. Brome sighed and voiced aloud the thought that tormented him constantly, whenever he looked out over the deep waters of the main. "I often look at the sea these days and wonder if Martin, Grumm and my sister made it to land. I'd hate to think of them lying somewhere out there underneath the waves."

"What a silly notion!" Felldoh chuckled as he punched Brome's paw lightly. "Huh, they probably made it to land while we were still floundering about thinking of the idea. Listen, mate, if your sister and Grumm are with Martin, they're safe as a deep-rooted oak. That mouse has more warrior spirit in his left ear than most creatures I've ever come across. Why, I wouldn't be surprised to see them come marching across these cliffs right now, with the Noonvale army behind them!"

Brome looked out along the cliffs as if taking Felldoh at his word. Suddenly he pointed north. "Look, there is somebeast coming. About a dozen of 'em, I'd say!"

The two weasel trackers, Bugpaw and Flink, knelt to scan the ground in the moonlight. Hisk watched them impatiently. "What's the matter with you two? Surely the two wheel tracks of a loaded cart are clear enough to follow?"

Bugpaw looked up at the Captain. "The cart has been along here more'n once, Hisk. We're lookin' for the freshest set of tracks."

Flink traced the rutted outlines with his paw. "Buggy's right, an' it's double 'ard in the night. We could be follerin' our own tails. Why don't yer knock off an' rest up, it'd be a lot easier trackin' in daylight, Hisk."

There was a concerted murmur of agreement from the others.

The weasel Captain took a pace back and brought his spear up. "What's all this, a mutiny? Dig the dirt out yer ears an' listen to me. I'm Lord Badrang's Captain. If you disobey me you're disobeyin' him. The orders is to follow the cart tracks an' find out where they goes, an' that's what I intend doin'. Right, does anybeast want to argue it out with Lord Badrang when we get back to Marshank?"

There was a shuffling of paws and some sullen muttering.

"All right, Hisk, you've made yer point," a voice from the group called out. "Let's gerron with it."

Hisk gave a humourless laugh. "I'm glad you see it my way. Oh, and by the way, only Lord Badrang calls me Hisk. It's Captain Hisk to you lot. Remember that!"

Felldoh picked up his javelins. "They're Badrang's creatures. I can't hear what they're saying, but anybeast with half an eye could see that they're tracking the cart, trying to find out where our camp is. Here, take this javelin and follow me, Brome. Keep low and stay quiet."

The two companions headed back south along the clifftop, in the direction of the camp, scurrying on all fours as Felldoh followed the imprint of the cart tracks. Judging that he had gone far enough, Felldoh halted. "Do as I do, Brome. Cover the tracks until I tell you to stop."

Brome did not question his friend. He realized the urgency of the situation. Scuffing and brushing with their paws, they obliterated the twin ruts of the wheel-marks from the loose sandy earth.

Felldoh took a quick look around. "Good, that should do. Now take one of these javelins, and hurry!"

Dashing back to the spot where the cart tracks ended, Felldoh set the blunt end of a lance in the ground and began a swerving furrow towards a low hill in an inland direction. Realization of the plan dawned on Brome. They were going to lead the trackers off on a false trail. Scoring the ground with his lance end, he caught up with Felldoh. Away the pair went over the low hill, leaving in their wake two grooves.

Bugpaw halted and stood upright. "Look 'ere, clear as daylight an' fresh as a daisy. These are good tracks. Looks like they took on extra weight."

Flink sniffed the ground and nodded. "That's right, Captain Hisk. I can't smell badger anywheres near these ruts, and I can sniff badger a mile off. That means the big badger must've hurt its paw and had to ride up on the cart. The tracks are slightly deeper. Look!"

Hisk puffed out his narrow chest, satisfied he was back in control. "Good work, you two. Keep it up. Come on, let's go!"

The tracks led west, over the low hill and out across some furze land, through a patch of damp sandy flats and into an expanse of reedgrass. Hisk and his soldiers followed diligently, the weasel Captain issuing whispered orders as they dogtrotted across the patchy moon-lit landscape.

"Don't forget, silence at all times. When we find the camp we make a note of its position and head right back to Marshank. Lord Badrang'll take care of the rest."

* * *

Brome and Felldoh dragged the javelins behind them as they scurried into a heavily bulrushed area. The squirrel's paw squelched deep. He stopped, checking Brome as he did. "Halt, swampland! Let's hide over there, where the rushes are thickest. Here, take some more javelins. I'll cut you a throwing stick while we're waiting on Badrang's vermin. Hisk is their leader. Leave him to me—I've got scores to settle with that scumnosed blaggard. He bent many a rod over my back!"

Hisk shook his spear triumphantly. "The marshlands. that's where they're hiding. No wonder they thought they were safe. Who'd follow anybeast into marshes? Well, their secret hiding place isn't a secret any more. Keep your eyes peeled for a campfire among these bulrushes."

As he was talking, the trackers bypassed him and went ahead. Eager to complete their mission, they raced along with the tracks clear in the soft heavy ground. Flink pawed at a broken rush, noting the way grass had been trampled. " 'S funny, the ground's pretty soft here. They must have found a firm path to get a loaded cart into marshland, eh, Buggy?"

"Waah! 'Elp, I'm sinkin'. 'Elp me, mates!"

Hisk hurried forward. "Shuttup, loudmouth, d'you want them to know we're here!"

Flink stared at the dark patch of smoothness beyond the rushes. "It's Buggy. He's gone!"

Hisk grabbed Flink and shook him. "I told you to keep your voice down, idiot! Now, what d'you mean Bugpaw's gone?"

"S – s – sw – swamp!" Flink's teeeth chattered with fright. As he was speaking, both he and the Captain had started to sink. Hisk pushed Flink away from him as the tracker grabbed wildly at his spear. Flink fell over backwards and the ooze gripped him and engulfed him. The weasel Captain pulled one footpaw free. Stabbing his spear deep into the firmer ground, he hurriedly

253

hauled himself out. The others bumped into each other as they fought in the darkness to distance themselves from the swamp edge.

A rat called Fraggun stood on tip paw, peering into the patch where Bugpaw and Flink had been a moment before. "Where did they goooooo . . . oh!"

The javelin had filled his mouth, flashing out of nowhere like dark lightning.

Brome had never seen a creature killed at close quarters before. One moment the rat had been alive and shouting. Then in a flash he was slain. The young mouse was no killer. He stared in horror at Felldoh, who had just thrown the javelin. The squirrel's face showed little emotion as he fitted another javelin on to his throwing stick and whipped his arm back. Sighting on a shape in the darkness, he flung the missile and was rewarded by a gurgling scream. "Got him!"

The javelins and throwing stick dropped from Brome's paws. "You killed them!"

Felldoh slid another javelin along his throwing stick. "Aye, young un. It's called war! You'd best give me those javelins if you can't use 'em. Stay here and rattle these rushes, but keep your head well down. I'll be back soon."

With a grim light in his eyes, Felldoh crawled off.

Hisk threw his spear at the clump of bulrushes. "Over there, see the rushes moving, that's where they are!"

Spears and arrows flew in the direction he had indicated.

Brome was a brave and reckless young mouse, but the idea of slaying another living creature appalled him. Now other beasts were trying to kill him. Suddenly he knew the meaning of fear. He lay flat, doing as Felldoh had told him, tugging at the rushes so they rattled. Fragments of bulrush showered down on him as missiles crashed by overhead. His paws were shaking so much with fright that the long stems rattled furiously. What had started out as an adventure had turned into the stark reality of life and death.

Felldoh worked his way around to the other side of his foes. Silent as a shadow, the powerful squirrel used a single javelin as a stabbing implement, taking out a ferret and another rat. Felldoh had a javelin sighted on Hisk when a rat stepped in the way and took it through his side. The rat let out an earsplitting scream as he went down. Hisk turned, catching a glimpse of his enemy as the squirrel dodged off into the cover of the rushes.

"It's a squirrel, one of the slaves. After him!"

They crashed off into the marshes after him. Hisk took a swift head count as they went. A tremor of shock ran through him. Only five left, counting himself! He had taken ten soldiers and two trackers when he left Badrang. The squirrel had slain five, plus the two trackers who had been lost in the swamp. Enraged, Hisk picked up the spear of the rat who had fallen to Felldoh's last throw and followed the others.

Brome stopped shaking the reeds and lay still, wondering if Badrang's soldiers had caught Felldoh. The young mouse was frightened at being left all alone in the hostile marshland, but determined he should do something to rescue his friend. Gritting his teeth, he grasped his throwing stick firmly. He had no javelins, but at least he could use the stick as a weapon. There was a rustle in the vegetation nearby. Brome froze as a paw fell on his shoulder.

"Come on, mate. Time to get out of here!"

"Felldoh! Where did you come from?" The young mouse's voice sounded squeaky in the night silence.

The strong squirrel pulled him upright, explaining as he led the way to firmer ground, "I got about half of 'em, maybe more. Missed that scummy Hisk, though.

I've been leading them a pretty dance around the edges of this quagmire. They'll be lucky to find their way back to Marshank, let alone locate our camp."

They followed the false cart tracks back to the low hill and were soon in sight of the camp. Brome had to dog-trot to keep up with his friend's strong pace. "Felldoh, back there, I was, I mean . . ."

The squirrel winked and patted him kindly. "You don't have to explain anything to me. You're my matey. You were very brave tonight, young un. Not every creature can slay or take life. Don't worry about it. I've seen the time when I was like you. Wish I still was."

Brome shook his head. "You wish you were like me?"

Felldoh threw a paw about the young mouse's shoulder. "Indeed I do. It's slavery that has made me this way. I'd slaughter every one of Badrang's horde if I had my way. Then I'd be sure that every honest creature was safe from the threat of slavery, bending to the will and whim of a tyrant, cold in winter, hungry in summer, watching old friends dying around you from hardship. Hoping and longing for freedom through all those lost and wasted seasons of my life. You've never known that, Brome. Only a few days' captivity with Martin and me in the pit. I wish that I'd had a happy life in Noonvale like you, never knowing the burning hate that drives you on to slay enemies."

The camp was still. Fires had guttered low and creatures were sleeping peacefully. As they entered the camp, only Ballaw and the baby Fuffle were still awake, both munching steadily at the remains of the feast.

"What ho, you two." The hare waved a half-eaten pastie at them. "Come an' help us mop this lot up, wot?"

They sat down and tucked in gratefully, drinking deep from a bowl of cider with blossom petals floating on it.

Felldoh glanced at Fuffle over the rim of the bowl. "That little snip should've been snoring long ago."

Ballaw chuckled as he demolished the rest of his

pastie. "I know he should. Amazin' little blighter really. Bit like me, I s'pose. Can't rest while there's still tucker about. Ain't that right, me old Fuffle?"

The infant mouse halted his attack on a carrot and parsley turnover long enough to reply, "Fuffle like foo'. Plenny foo' make y' big!"

It was still several hours to dawn when Badrang and the horde halted within sight of Marshank. They rested, waiting until Fleabane and Findo, who were the advance scouts, returned. The two weasels came panting along the shore to where Badrang sat, and made their report.

"Clogg's taken over the fortress, Sire!"

"Aye, Lord. We could hear the noises of his crew, singin' and feastin'. Sounded like they was 'avin' a fine time."

Badrang stared impassively at the fort in the distance. "I might have known something like this would happen. Has Clogg posted wall sentries?"

"Two, Sire. Both over the front gates."

"No others that you noticed?"

"None but the two, Lord. We circled the place to make sure."

The Tyrant stoat stood upright slowly. "Follow me. I'll gut anybeast who makes a sound. Clogg has got to learn that he is only an idiot corsair. I am Badrang, master of all this coast. He'll soon find that out!"

29

"Give me a bunk up, Martin. I'm a bit short in the paw for this."

Martin shoved his sword flat under Pallum's footpaws and heaved. The hedgehog scrambled swiftly on to a higher ledge. Bringing up the rear, Martin hoisted himself alongside Pallum, halting a moment to note the progress of the Gawtrybe. The squirrels were catching up quickly, far too quickly for Martin's liking. He looked up to where the cave loomed like a black eye socket on the mountain in the night. Rose and Grumm were in the lead, assisting each other as they scrambled up the brown rocks which still radiated heat from the day's sun.

"Hurry, Martin," the mousemaid called down urgently. "With a bit of luck we might make it to the cave."

Grumm peered down at the crowds of nimble, screeching figures advancing upwards like the waves of a spring tide.

"Us'ns needen more'n a bit o' luck, mizzy. Need a gurt 'eap!"

"Don't stop, keep going," Martin yelled up to them. "Take Pallum with you! I'll act as rearguard. At least I'll stand a bit of a chance being above them with a sword in my paw. Go on, Rose. Do as I say!"

The mousemaid sat down firmly on an outcrop, her footpaws dangling over the landscape far below. "Oh no, if you don't start climbing I'm stopping here. Either we go together or not at all, Martin!"

Now the squirrels' wild faces could be picked out in the darkness, illuminated in silvery moonlight as they chattered and shrieked.

"Good game, good game!"

"Catch em an' throw 'em off, throw 'em off!"

Martin put up his blade and began climbing fast. "All right, I'm coming. Keep moving!"

Grumm slid back on the scree. Only the outcrop that Rose had been seated on saved him. Martin arrived behind him with Pallum, and together they shoved Grumm upwards. The mole was trying hard not to show his fear of high places, though every so often he clamped a digging paw across his eyes, moaning softly, "Oi carn't lukk up nor daown. Et makes oi vurry sick, oo urr!"

Rose reached down to grasp his paw. "Please, Grumm, keep climbing. It's not far to the cave now!"

Martin found a loose rock and hurled it down at the leading squirrels; they skipped aside with superb agility.

"Heehee, good game. We'll catch you, mousey!"

His paws aching from the strain, Martin pulled himself onward and upward, grunting with exertion as he shoved Pallum ahead. Suddenly Martin felt his footpaw being grabbed. One squirrel, faster than the rest, had sprinted up and caught him.

"Heeheehee, gotcha!"

With furious energy, he kicked back with his free footpaw.

"Yeeeeeeeeee!" With a drawn-out howl of despair, the squirrel hurtled out into empty space and was lost in the night. Shaking himself, Martin clambered on with the shouts of the Gawtrybe ringing in his ears.

"Heehee, sillybeast fell. Yeeeeeeeeeee!"

Martin could hear the swift nimble patter of their paws on the rocks behind him. Glancing up, he saw that

Rose had made it to the cave mouth. She pushed Grumm inside and reached her paws down to help Pallum, who was blowing and panting as he strove to gain the opening. The Gawtrybe were within a paw's-length when Martin arrived at the cave. Pushing Rose inside he stood in the entrance and drew his sword. Chest heaving, limbs trembling, Martin still managed a short laugh of triumph.

"Hahah! Come on, you thick-headed rabble. You can only come two at a time, and I'm more than a match for any two of you!"

Inside, the cave was like a huge rock-faced tunnel. The first thing Rose saw were two great luminous orbs. She jumped back in fright.

"Who's there?" The voice was awesome, harsh and thundering. It echoed around the rock walls.

Rose shrank back in terror. "Please, we're only harmless travellers hiding in here from the squirrels. They're trying to kill us!"

An enormous short-eared owl waddled out of the gloom. Rose cringed as it lifted a heavy taloned claw. It smiled, lowering its tone to a kindly whisper. "Don't be feared, mousemaid. We must act with all haste. Tell your friends to heed me not when I put on my great voice. Come."

The Gawtrybe leaped and chattered on the narrow escarpment at the cave mouth. Martin bared his teeth, slashing the air menacingly with his small sword. "I am Martin the Warrior. Anybeast who is fool enough, come and meet death!"

The squirrels screeched and leaped, pushing one another forward, but for the moment it seemed that none were too keen to encounter the foemouse who stood defending the rocky entrance. However, Martin knew that it was only a matter of time before the frenzied squirrels were pushed to attack him. Still facing his

260

enemies, he tried to communicate with Pallum in a low murmur.

"Hurry, get rocks to throw, sticks to beat them off, anything. They're getting ready for a charge. I'll be overwhelmed!"

A mighty bark-brown wing enveloped Martin, sweeping him lightly aside. The short-eared owl filled the cave mouth, its legs thick as yew branches tipped with lethal talons.

A wail of fear arose from the Gawtrybe. They fell flat wherever they stood, pressing their faces down on the mountainside.

"Eeeeee! Skyqueen! Eeeeee!"

The massive feathered head swivelled back and forth, huge golden pupils distending as its glittering black irises reflected the moon at their centres. Hunching over, it glared murderously at the quaking squirrels. "Boldred sees all! I was many leagues from here, yet I winged high and watched you torment these travellers. Brainless ones who live for pleasure without any thought of others, did you not think I would return?"

A moan arose from the prostrate squirrels. The great owl repeated her question, raising her voice to a maniacal shriek. "Answer me, did you not think Boldred would return?"

The mob remained silent.

"Where is your Chieftain?" Boldred screeched at them.

She turned a squirrel over with a swift flick of her beak. Its terrified tear-stained face stared pleadingly at her as it pointed in Martin's direction. "The mouse defeated him, Skyqueen. Eeeeee!"

Boldred gave a short coughing noise as if reassessing the situation. "This I already knew. Do I not know all? Answer me truly, why were the Gawtrybe persecuting these travellers?'"

The squirrel Boldred had elected spokesbeast hung his head, like a naughty young one caught with his paw in the cream. "Skyqueen, it was a game, we were only playing."

With a speed that the eye could scarce follow, the short-eared owl pinned the nearest six squirrels by their tails with her flashing talons, calling out over their cries, "Shall I play my game?" She spread her wings and rose from the ground, lifting all six with ease as the outspread pinions beat slowly in the night. "Speak! Shall I play my game . . . Or will you obey me?"

Rose clutched Martin's paw. "Is she going to kill them? Oh, I can't watch!"

"Don't fret, Rose," the young mouse whispered reassuringly to her. "The owl knows what she's doing. Leave it to her.'"

The Gawtrybe cowered on the rocks sobbing piteously, "Do not slay us, Skyqueen. Mercy. Eeeeee!'"

She dropped the six on to the heads of the others. Landing, she resumed her stance, accentuating her words with clacks of the dangerous hooked beak.

"You are dull, witless beasts with short memories, but I will not slay you this time. Next time I will, every one of you! Heed my warning! As punishment you will all stay on the ledge below here until sunset on the morrow. You will neither eat, drink, move or talk. Go now!"

Without a sound the entire Gawtrybe vacated the space in front of the cave entrance, dropping to the lower ledges where they sat in utter silence. Boldred flew out, hovering low over their heads. "Remember and obey, or Boldred will return!"

The four friends stood back as the owl landed in the cave mouth. She gestured them to keep quiet, indicating that they should move further into the tunnel, out of Gawtrybe earshot.

Boldred went ahead awhile, before ushering them into a cunningly concealed side chamber. They entered, surprised to see that it was illuminated by a shaft of moonlight which came from somewhere up near the cave's craggy ceiling. A friendly-looking full-grown male, perched alongside a small fluffy owlet, nodded to them.

Boldred waddled up on to a moss covered ledge and blew a loud sigh. "That Gawtrybe! Lack a day, they must think everybeast as stupid as themselves. D'you know what they said, Horty?"

The big male chuckled. "Don't tell me, they were only playing a game."

"Game indeed," Boldred snorted. "The scatter-brained little savages!"

She turned to the travellers. "Forgive me, but those squirrels do try my patience. This is my husband Hortwingle—call him Horty, he hates his full title—and this is our daughter Emalet. As you already know, I am the famous Boldred. Now, who do we have the honor of meeting?"

Martin, Pallum, Rose and Grumm introduced themselves. Boldred looked at Martin, nodding her head. "Martin, eh. You've got the look of a warrior. It's a good job you defeated the Gawtrybe Chieftain or they would have slain you all on the spot. Using the excuse of a game, of course."

Martin felt the scratches on his face. "Some game!"

Boldred nodded in agreement before turning to Horty. "I sat the entire mob of them on the lower ledges, no food or drink or talking until sunset tomorrow. That might teach them a lesson."

Horty stroked the downy back of Emalet. "You don't really believe that, do you? By tomorrow noon they'll have forgotten and wandered down to play in the foothills."

Martin inspected the cave. It was a comfortable jumble of family living with brushes, pens, inks, vegetable dyes and charcoal sticks scattered everywhere among large strips of bark parchment.

Grumm produced food and drink from their pack. As they ate, Boldred explained. "We are mapmakers and historians, that is why we don't have a lot of time to control the squirrels. One of us stays here with Emalet, while the other flies off to explore, and hunt for food too. As you see, we are short-eared owls, and as such are daytime hunters. Normally we would be sleeping now, but the cries of the rabble wakened us."

Rose bowed politely. "We're extremely lucky they did. Thank you."

Horty cocked his head at Boldred, and they both nodded. He turned to Rose. "Are you Rose, daughter of Urran Voh and Aryah?"

"Yes. Do you know my mother and father?"

"Oh yes. You'd be surprised just how much we both know, though it must be many long seasons since we were at Noonvale. You wouldn't remember us, you were only a tiny babe then. Always singing, as I recall."

Grumm scratched his head then held up a paw. "Oi amembers you'm zurr, an' you'm, marm, tho' oi wurr on'y a liddle tyke two seasons elder'n Miz Roser. You uns wurr oft in Noonvale, that be whurr us'ns be travellen to."

Boldred smiled with pleasure. "Yes. What a beautiful place! We were mapping the area at the time. I'd dearly love to go back there. Horty, would you take care of Emalet while I accompany our friends back there? It would make their journey a lot less perilous if I were to guide them."

Her kindly husband chuckled as he watched Emalet playing around his talons. "I don't mind at all, I'm a real homebird at heart. We get on well together, don't we, my little eggchick."

Emalet, who never made any sound, looked adoringly up at her father and snuggled under his wing.

The atmosphere in the owls' cave was so safe and homely that the four friends slept deeply for the remainder of the night.

Martin woke next morning and lay watching Rose

feeding one of Grumm's sweet flat invention cakes to Emalet. The owl chick waited respectfully for each fragment then wolfed it down with gusto, enjoying the sticky sweetness greatly.

Horty bustled in, chuckling as usual. "Those squirrels are still sitting silent and tight, Boldred. You must have given them a really stern lecture last night. Hey, come on, you sleepyheads, it's two hours past dawn!"

As they breakfasted, the owls conversed.

"Pity we couldn't coax old Warden up here. He'd straighten a few Gawtrybe tails, I'll wager."

"Wouldn't he just. There'd only be tails left by now. Warden would have eaten the lot of them. Can you imagine? I am the law, you are lawbreakers. Glump! There goes another one!"

"Hahaha, I suppose you're right. Maybe Polleekin could keep them in order. What d'you think?"

"Maybe she could. Polleekin would probably feed them so much they'd be staggering around, too fat to get in any mischief."

Martin looked up from his food. "You know Polleekin?"

Boldred preened her feathers. "We know her, in fact we know lots of creatures that you do. I didn't want to interrupt the tale you told us of your escape and journey last night or I would have mentioned some. Warden, those prissy Mirdop rabbits, Polleekin, Queen Amballa and her tribe—"

"And Badrang?" Pallum interrupted.

Horty shook his big feathered head. "We don't know that one, nor do we want to. He is evil, a blight upon the good land. It is certain death to know such creatures!"

Boldred spread her wings, indicating that she was eager to travel. "Come on now, we can't wait around gossiping all season about who we know and don't want to know. Just take it for granted that we know many, both sides of the mountain. Right, young Rose, let's see what we can do about getting you back to your home."

From either side the tunnel looked as if it was only a cave on the mountainside, but it ran clear through the rock from one end to the other, twisting and turning with many offshoots and dead ends. Boldred went in front, leading them out into brilliant morning sunlight on the other side of the mountain.

Martin blinked after the dark tunnel, taking his bearings. The slope on this side was much gentler, with areas of woodland and grassy glades dotting the warm stillness. Hardly a breeze swayed leaf or flower.

Grumm breathed deeply. "Hoo urr, et do almost smell loik 'ome!"

Pallum took an experimental sniff. "I can't remember ever having a home. What does it smell like?"

Rose patted the hedgehog's paw fondly. "You'll know when we get to Noonvale. That will be your home."

They descended at a leisurely pace, stopping to pick wild plum, damsons, pears and apples, which grew in profusion on the sunny slopes. Sometimes Boldred would fly off, but she always returned after a short while.

"I've been giving instructions to some birds I know. They're flying ahead to let the otters know you're coming."

Martin wiped at the berry juice that was staining his chin. "Why would otters want to know we're coming, Boldred?"

"To save your paws, they'll take us part of the way down the Broadstream in their boat."

Grumm looked slightly nervous. "Only part o' way? Do us'ns 'ave to swim'ee rest o' way? Oi carn't swim, marm. Water be bad as 'igh mountings."

"You won't have to swim, Grumm," the short-eared owl explained. "The otters will pass us on to the stream shrews, and you'll have to travel on their logboats. Not as comfortable as the otter boat, but considerably faster."

Rose found a clump of purple saxifrage. She wove some into a wreath and placed it on her head. Then they

266

came to a shallow stream weaving its way between the rocks and trees. Boldred perched in a rowan ash, watching them as they skipped downhill, splashing and laughing through the sun-warmed water. She shook her head, remembering the visit she had paid to Polleekin's tree house the day after the travellers had been there.

"If Polleekin's visions are true, it's a long hard road ahead for you, little Warrior. Enjoy a happy day while you can."

30

Cap'n Tramun Clogg woke feeling tremendously braced. He drank a flagon of seaweed ale, devoured a huge platter of pickled whelks and cockles, then sat back rebraiding some plaits on his chest. There was a gentle knock on the longhouse door.

"Is that you, Crosstooth?" Clogg called out without looking up from his task. "Any sign of Badrang yet, matey?"

The door creaked open and Badrang stood framed in the doorway, sunlight pouring in around him. "Get your braided behind off my chair, Clogg!"

The corsair was so surprised that the chair fell over backwards as he tried to lurch up. Dust rose in a golden shower of motes around him as the Tyrant of Marshank strode across and placed a none too gentle footpaw firmly on his bloated stomach. "Go on, Clogg. Ask me how I got here."

"'Ow did you get 'ere?" the corsair spluttered from his position on the floor.

Badrang smirked, pressing down harder on Clogg's stomach. "If you had as much brain in your head as you had fat in your gut, you'd know. I came in through the tunnel that the slaves escaped from. You can go both ways through it, in or out. Obviously you didn't think of that, swillhead!"

With a sudden move that belied his bulk, Clogg wriggled free of Badrang's paw and ran for the door shouting, "Crosstooth, Gruzzle, Boggs, arm the crew. Badrang's 'ere!"

The Tyrant stoat righted the fallen chair and sat in it, smiling. "Shout your thick head off, bucko. You'll get no help."

Clogg stood for a moment glaring at the horde soldiers surrounding the longhouse, then he whirled to face Badrang. "You foul 'earted blaggard, you've murdered all me lovely crew!"

Badrang sniffed the empty seaweed ale flagon, wrinkled his nose in distaste and pushed it away from him. "Hardly, but I could have. It's no trouble tying up a crowd of idiots who've drunk themselves to sleep on beetroot wine and seaweed ale. As for those two dozy sentries you left posted on the walltop over the gate, they've got lumps on their heads the size of gull eggs. Did you actually think that you could take Marshank from me?"

Clogg's attitude changed like a breeze at sea. Throwing his paws wide, he grinned in what he hoped was a disarming manner. "Matey, who said anythin' about takin' yer fortress from ye? Why, I was only mindin' it until you returned after chasin' those pesky slaves. Me an' my crew was actin' duty bound as caretakers. Ho, by the bye, you didn't catch the slaves, did ye?"

Badrang shook his head coolly. "I didn't have to. Come with me and I'll show you why."

The corsair crew sat in ranks at a corner of the courtyard, tightly bound and closely guarded by the Tyrant's horde. Badrang led Clogg to the center of the courtyard. The pirate stoat was forced to stand silent and listen to Badrang's announcement as he addressed the crew.

"Pay attention, you corsairs. You have three simple

choices. One is slavery. I have no slaves to serve me at the moment. Two is death. You can stay loyal to Clogg, and for that you will be executed. The charges are attempting to steal Marshank from me and siding with my enemy. The third and final choice is that you swear allegiance to me and join my horde as soldiers. Well, what is it to be?"

The fox Crosstooth struggled upright. "Cut these ropes from me, I'll serve under Lord Badrang's colors!"

It did not take long for the others to follow.

"Aye, set me loose, I'm with Crosstooth!"

"Me too, matey. I'll be an 'ordebeast!'"

"No point in bein' a corsair without a ship!"

"Better'n bein' a slave or gettin' executed!"

Clogg shook his head sadly. "Harr, 'twas an evil day when I landed up on this coast. Boggs, Gruzzle, Crosstooth, was I ever a bad Cap'n to ye?"

"No, Cap'n, you was a good un. We had some rare ol' times together."

"You just made too many mistakes, Tramun Clogg."

"Aye, when it's sink or swim, a creature has to look after hisself, Cap'n. No 'ard feelin's."

While the new horde members took the oath and signed articles with Badrang, Clogg was led off to the prison pit by two soldiers. He stared down into the hole miserably. "So it's come to this, bein' slung in an 'ole like a worm."

They nudged Clogg towards a barrow with a spade in it. "You're not goin' in it, Lord Badrang's orders are that you must fill it in. Think yerself lucky. Instead of execution he's givin' you the chance to become an 'onest 'ardworking slave. And don't fret, there'll be work aplenty for you!"

Felldoh was training an army to attack Marshank: the Fur and Freedom Fighters. Their flag waved proudly over the camp on the cliffs, a green banner with the representation of a flying javelin severing a chain.

Rowanoak shook her aching paws. "I hope they don't want uniforms as well. It took me hours to make that flag, rummaging through our costume box and sewing this bit to that. It does look rather good, though."

Ballaw broke off from drilling a marching column. He swaggered jauntily across and threw Rowanoak an elaborate salute. "All present an' correct, marm. What time are you servin' us stout creatures some jolly old luncheon, wot? An army marches on its stomach an' all that, y'know."

The badger turned her eyes skyward as if seeking help. "It's a wonder you can do any marching at all with that stomach of yours, you great flop-eared feedbag. Don't ask me, go and see the cooks."

Ballaw marched off, a blaze of military colour in the uniform he had designed for himself from the troupe's wardrobe. He sang to keep himself in step.

"All the ladies smile at me, lookit there, lookit there,
He's a fine dashin' figure of a hare, of a hare.
He'd fight off a horde alone, he's a warrior to the bone.
Feed him plenty an' you'll never have a care, have a care!"

Felldoh laid a lance on his throwing stick. The group he was training followed his actions, laying lances on their sticks as he instructed them.

"Arm right back at shoulder level, paw gripping stick firmly, lean your head in, take sight at the target along the javelin shaft, weight on the back footpaw and throw!"

The small hillock daubed with a likeness of Badrang was pincushioned by eighteen lances.

Keyla picked up a pebble, demonstrating to his group. "See, an ordinary stone, but it can become a weapon. In

271

paw-to-paw combat you can use it held tight as a club. Hit the foe with it as hard as you can. Or you can throw it. Watch!" He hurled the pebble and struck one of the lances on the hillock.

The mouse called Juniper held up a sling. "Look what old Barkjon gave me. What is it, Keyla?"

The otter took the tough vine thong, shaking his head in admiration as he fitted a pebble to the tongue at its middle. He swung it experimentally, testing its balance. "This is a fine sling. Give me a target to throw at."

Juniper pointed to the hillock. "Hit one of those lances like you did when you threw the pebble."

Crack!

No sooner had the words left Juniper's mouth than Keyla sent the pebble whistling from its whirling sling. It struck a lance, snapping it near the point with a cracking impact.

Keyla wound the sling round his paw with a happy smile. "I'll go and see if Barkjon can make us more of these!"

Gauchee and Kastern had a good number of long poles, sometimes used by the Rambling Rosehip Players when they were erecting an improvised tent. Trefoil had suggested that they would make good pikes, using the pointed ends which had served as tentstakes.

Buckler, his injured shoulder still bandaged, drilled a group in the uses of the pike. "Poikes up! Poikes daown. Points for'ard . . . Charge!"

Celandine sat dabbing her paws in rosewater. "Silly creatures, you'll either get hurt or have nasty rough paws from using those great long things!"

She found herself looking down the point of Gauchee's pike. "Off to the cookhouse and help out if you don't want to train as a fighter, little missy fusstail!"

Ballaw waggled his ears at Tullgrew, Purslane and Geum in a very persuasive manner. "Top o' the mornin', cooks. When does a chap get some fodder round here?"

The baby Fuffle was dressed in an oversized apron tucked up twice at his middle. He was spreading honey on scones with a wooden spoon.

Tullgrew pointed in his direction. "Don't ask us, Ballaw. Put in your request to Quartermaster Sergeant Fuffle over there."

The tiny mouse waved the spoon sternly at the hare. "Fuffle say back t' work, or I chop y' tail off!"

Ballaw backed away from the sticky spoon-wielding infant. "Nuff said, old lad. Nod's as good as a wink to a starved warrior. I say, Purslane, you've got a very violent offspring there!"

Lunch was a simple affair, leek and cabbage soup, summer salad, followed by honeyed scones and strawberry cordial. The midday sun was tempered by a gentle breeze from the sea as the newly formed Fur and Freedom Fighters sat about, eating and taking their ease. Rowanoak, Ballaw, Felldoh and Barkjon held an open discussion on the merits and drawbacks of going into battle. Barkjon and Rowanoak were not convinced that it was a good idea.

"Felldoh, you haven't got a tenth of the force that Badrang commands," the old squirrel cautioned his son. "We're not strong enough yet, lives could be lost needlessly in an attack on Marshank."

The strong young squirrel put aside his food. "I'm not talking about pitched battle, Father. Lightning attacks are what I plan. Hit hard and fast, then vanish. What's the matter with you? I've seen the days when we were slaves that you would vow vengeance on Badrang and all his kind."

Rowanoak intervened. "You both have valid points, Felldoh, but I agree with your father. We are not warriors, nor have we been into battle before. Granted that Badrang is evil and Marshank needs destroying, but you must realize that his horde are all seasoned killers and trained fighters. All that you have at the moment is a small bunch of freed slaves and some strolling players."

Ballaw finished off a scone, licking honey from his paws. "But we freed the slaves, didn't we? Brome walked right into old Badbottom's fort and bluffed it out. Who's to say we can't become a first-rate fightin' force and whack them for good. What d'you say, eh, Brome old feller?"

Brome avoided Felldoh's eyes. "I can't say much. I may be good at bluffing, but I'm not a warrior. I know that now. I don't want to see creatures killed, particularly our own."

Felldoh ruffled his young friend's ears. "Then you can become a healer, one who cares for the wounded. It takes a brave beast to dash about in battle doing that."

Old Geum dipped a scone in her cordial to soften it. "All this talk of fighting and killing, why don't we just find another place far away from here, where we can enjoy life. Leave Badrang to his own devices and forget about the whole nasty thing, Marshank and these shores."

Suddenly Purslane was up, her eyes blazing. "I'll tell you why, because if Badrang is still there and Marshank still stands, then other creatures will be captured and taken as slaves. I have a little one, and I would fight with my life so that he could grow up a free creature!"

Keyla sprang up applauding her brave words. "Well said, marm. We know what it's like to live under the whips of a tyrant. It's not life, it's living death!"

Felldoh turned to his father and Rowanoak. "These creatures have said it all. I could not have spoken more strongly. I will lead the first attack tonight."

Barkjon looked up at his strong fearless son. "It has been in you to do this thing since you were a little one in the quarry, helping me to haul rocks. May the seasons and good fortune aid you, Felldoh, and keep those under you safe."

Rowanoak shrugged, knowing protest would be useless. "What can I say except, break a leg!"

Felldoh looked puzzled until Ballaw explained. "In the actin' game it's our way of sayin' good luck to a chap."

The baby Fuffle waved his wooden spoon. "Break bofe legs!"

There was laughter and applause for the infant's wisdom.

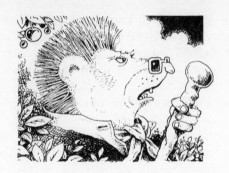

31

Travelling with Boldred was a real delight for Martin. The owl chose the prettiest paths and was friendly with every creature who dwelt beside them. They stopped often to eat the abundant fruits that grew everywhere. At one place Boldred showed them a tree laden with shiny dark red cherries. The temptation was too great to resist. They stood beneath the low hanging branches, plucking the juicy cherries and gobbling them down.

"Wonder, cudd oi make cherry zoop out'n these yurr?" Grumm ruminated.

Boldred spread a wing. "There's lots of cherry trees round here. Take your time, enjoy them. I'll be back in a short while." She flew off to map new features and talk with other creatures.

They lay beneath the tree, devouring cherries and seeing who could spit the stones furthest.

Pallum plucked a cherry off one of his spikes and popped it into his mouth. "Ah, this is the life for us, pals!"

Without warning, an incredibly ancient hedgehog came crashing through the undergrowth towards them, waving a knobbly blackthorn stick. He was completely grey and quite shaky on his paws, but it did not diminish his temper.

"Get ye gone, ye rascals, ye cherry thievin' wastrels. Be off with ye, or I'll lay this stick across your robbin' backs!"

Pallum stood upright, holding out his paws in peace. "Here now, hold hard, Father. We're not robbers!"

The ancient beast swung his stick at Pallum, but he did it so slowly that the young hedgehog had no trouble avoiding it. "Don't call me Father, ye young brigand. I wouldn't be thy father for a whole plum orchard!"

The old hedgehog wore tiny square spectacles on his snout end, and as he swung the stick they fell off. He groped about, still whacking out feebly. Rose dodged under the stick. Retrieving the spectacles, she held the blackthorn tight as she resettled the glasses on the grey-snouted creature.

"There, that's better. We're not thieves, sir. We didn't know the cherry trees belonged to you."

He tugged fitfully at the stick that Rose was still holding. "Let go of my stick, damsel. You're no better than ye should be!"

Martin sat up. There was no danger from the old one, but he was becoming very tiresome with his insults and rantings. The young mouse spoke sternly to him.

"Keep a civil tongue in your head, old one, and stop waving that stick about—or I'll take it from you!"

The hedgehog managed to get the stick loose from Rose and adopted a fighting stance. "Hoho, ye bold-faced mouse. So ye want to fight me now. Then so be it. Come on, have at ye!"

He raised the stick just in time for Boldred to swoop in and pluck it from his paws. She landed, shaking her head. "Aggril, stop this. How many times have you been told the cherry trees do not belong to you? They are here for all creatures, not just for you!"

The old hedgehog Aggril knocked the heads from some daisies with his footpaws, muttering rebelliously, "Young uns today have no respect for age. Yon mouse with the sword offered me combat, 'twere no fault o' mine."

Grumm stood up indignantly. "Oo, 'ee gurt fibber. Marthen dood no such a thing. You'm a crafty ole beast, zurr, beggin' yurr pardon, iffen oi do say so."

Immediately Aggril's mood changed at the sight of Grumm. "Oh, a moley creature. Do accept my 'umble apologies, friends. Moleys are the nicest an' wisest beasts alive. Do ye an' thy companions have a liking for cherry cordial? Follow me!"

The four travellers looked at each other nonplussed.

Boldred shook with silent mirth. "Go on, follow him. He's harmless really, just a touch eccentric. I'm mapping a stream course—see you later." She winged off high above the trees.

Grumm started following Aggril, calling to the others, "Coom on, oi dearly wudd loik t' taste cherry corjul!"

The old hedgehog lived in a hollow oak, long dead but still standing, with a small door over a hole at its base. They followed him in. It was cool and dark. Stacked all around its walls were kegs, flasks and gourds of cordial. Aggril was very proud of his stock. He adjusted his glasses and peered closely at the labels on each receptacle.

"Mmm now, here be a cordial fit for kings an' queens, a score of seasons old, I lined the cask with honey myself to sweeten it."

There was pure white cheese and celery wafers to go with the drink. They sat on upturned casks as he issued them with wonderfully carved cherrywood bowls to drink from.

"Cherrywood be the best of all trees to make bowls from. Taste this and see what thee think of my art."

It was absolutely delicious, dark, cool and sweet. Before they had finished he was opening a large gourd.

"This was made by my mother, or 'twas made by my grandmother, I'm not sure, 'twas so long ago. Notice, 'tis a brighter red and a fizzy taste, more suited to eat with salads."

Gourds were opened, casks unbunged and flasks broached. Martin and Rose sat together in the cool dimness of the hollow oak, eating cheese and celery wafers and sipping so many different cordials, each with its own history, that they lost count. Aggril's voice droned on like a bumblebee hovering round apple blossom, while outside the sun made leaf patterns in the still woodlands. Martin had never known such peace and happiness in all his life. He lay back and closed his eyes, the heavy fragrance of wild cherries scenting the air about him.

It was night. Rose came slowly awake with the sensation that she was drifting, floating under the soft dark canopy of the sky, star-pointed and centered with a waning moon. The mousemaid lay at peace, feeling the swirl of water against silent paddles, hearing the gentle creak of timbers . . .

She was on a boat!

"Be still, liddle shipmate, an' take yer ease."

The strong cheerful face of a big male otter appeared before her. Rose sat up slowly, trying to shake off the feeling of unreality.

"Where am I?"

"Aboard the good craft *Waterlily* an' travellin' on the great Broadstream. Lay back an' sleep now, yore in safe paws, miss."

Martin, Pallum and Grumm were curled up nearby, their contented snores blending with the slight noises of the boat. The otter plied his oar with a hefty tattooed paw as he chuckled, "Ole Aggril certainly slipped you an' yer pals a good measure of his special sleepin' potion. Them three won't know nothin' about it until way into mornin' light."

Rose felt helpless, a pleasant inertia stealing over her

as she slumped gently back. "You mean to tell me that Aggril drugged us?"

The otter grinned and winked at her. "Sure as my name's Starwort. That ole hedgepig don't like young uns noways. He reckons the cherry trees are his, an' it's good night to any beast that messes wi' them. Lucky you was with Boldred, or Aggril might've sent you into a sleep you'd never wake from. As it was, he just popped you off temp'ry so's Boldred could get you out of the way. We 'ad to sling you an' yer pals into 'ammocks an' carry you a fair way to get you aboard *Waterlily*."

Rose half tried to keep her eyes open, murmuring drowsily, "Where is Boldred?"

The short-eared owl's voice came from somewhere above her. "Perched nice and comfy up here on the masthead. Do as Starwort says, Rose. Go back to sleep."

The mousemaid could hear her own voice as if from a distance. "Back . . . to . . . slee . . . p."

The sun was up, and birds serenaded the new day from the thick foliage bordering Broadstream. The travellers sat with their paws through the midship rails, letting the water run through them. A crew of two dozen otters hauled the single square sail to catch the mild breeze, singing lustily as they heaved on the ropes.

"Oh, the Broadstream comes from who knows where,
It flows to who knows whither,
And I sail with it here an' there,
Wand'rin' yon an' hither.
The place of waters is my home,
For I'm a fearless rover.
Through calm an' storm I'm bound to roam,
Until my days are over.
Roll, roll and flow, and let the seasons goooooooooo."

As the last deep bass notes died, a triangle's discordant jangle rent the air.

Grumm sniffed. His homely face lit up. "Hurr, 'tis zoop!"

Small otters poured out of the forecastle cabin, leaping, somersaulting and banging ladles on wooden bowls. Starwort's wife Marigold issued the four friends with bowls and ladles.

"Were I you, I'd 'urry. Those nippers'll lick the pot dry. They're nought but stomachs on paws!"

Over a charcoal brazier on the afterdeck, a fat otter called Stewer was dishing out soup, loaves of barleybread and a concoction the otters drank called scupperjuice. Stewer filled their bowls to brimming, cautioning them cheerfully, "Watershrimp, bulrush 'n' hotroot soup, mates. It'll give you fur like velvet an' put a sparkle in yer eye. But drink plenty o' that scupperjuice to cool yer gills!"

Pallum's eyes watered. He fanned his mouth with both paws and gulped scupperjuice greedily. "Phwaw! My poor mouth's on fire. I never knew soup could taste so hot. Oh, my burning tongue!"

Martin and Rose were suffering equally. The soup was delicious, but the hotroot pepper must have been ladled into it.

Tossing aside his spoon, Grumm drank his soup with gusto. The heat of it did not seem to bother him. "Gurr, this be wunnerful zoop, ho aye. Furst clarss! Yurr, you uns 'ave moi bread an' moi drink. Give oi yurr zoop."

Willingly they exchanged their soup for the mole's bread and scupperjuice. Grumm slurped away merrily, watched by the entire otter crew and their families.

Starwort shook his head. "I ain't never seen a creature enjoy our soup so much in all me born days. We can't even take it without drinkin' scupperjuice to quench the burnin'. Grumm, matey, are you sure you've never 'ad this soup afore?"

The mole wiped a bead of sweat from his snout tip. "No zurr, never, tho' oi wisht oi 'ad. Think wot oi been a-missen all these seasons, hurr!"

Streamsailing was a novel experience for the travellers. Under the otter crew's helpful paws they learned to reef and tack, scull, row and steer. Boldred had flown on ahead to contact the shrews. The otters reckoned to meet up with them sometime in mid-evening.

Grumm and Pallum took instantly to the nautical life. The *Waterlily* was so large and flat-bottomed that they forgot their fear of the water. Both the hedgehog and the mole adopted the otters' rolling gait and streamslang.

"Ahoy, Grumm matey. 'Tis a fair day on an even keel."

"Ahurr, Pallum me 'earty, coom an' sit yurr midships an' drop anchor 'longside oi, you'm ole streamdog!"

Martin and Rose clapped paws to mouths, stifling their giggles at the antics of the pair.

Roach, tench, perch and the odd pike could be seen through the clear running stream, following the *Waterlily* for the scraps that were thrown overboard. Sometimes they would cruise where the bank was deepsided, enjoying the shade of the trees. Other times they would ride out on the broad swell, catching the breeze. Rose watched Martin waving at a kingfisher which hung over an inlet, whirring its wings in a ceaseless blur as it watched the water for small fry. It was an idyllic day.

Early evening passed, coloring Broadstream's banks a limpid green that gave way to gold-flecked cerise in midstream.

They heard the chattering and squabbling of small gruff voices from around a sharp bend in the watercourse. Starwort shook his head despairingly as he manoeuvred the tiller.

"Them Broadstream shrews, never stops arguin' an' disputin', they don't. I once saw two of 'em jump in the water an' climb out to argue over who was the wettest. Reef yer sail, you two streamdogs. We're roundin' the point!"

Pallum and Grumm attempted an otter's footpaw salute.

"Haye aye, steady as she goes. Reefin' an' furlin' wi' all paws!" Pulling smoothly into the bank, they disembarked into a noisy chaos. The Broadstream shrews were odd little creatures, raggledy-haired and clad in baggy pantaloons. They all carried short rapiers, which they constantly drew and jabbed the air with when making a point. Boldred perched by their campfire, checking the charts and maps she had revised. The travellers sat alongside her, surrounded by a horde of curious shrews. She squinted her large round eyes in exasperation.

"Shrews! They don't even have a leader of this tribe, but each one thinks that they are in charge of everything. Listen to them!"

"I'm not sailin' tonight, we've been on the stream all day!"

"I want to sail tonight, it's the best time for voyagin'!"

"We've done enough. I say we don't sail for the rest of the season!"

"Who asked you? Keep your opinions to yourself, rushmouth!"

"Hah! Rushmouth is it? When was the last time you put paw to paddle, boatbottom!"

"Boatbottom yourself. I vote we run the logboats ashore an' careen 'em. The hulls are filthy with moss!"

"A good voyage'd take the moss off 'em. You take my word!"

"I won't take your word, but you'll take the back o' my paw if you step on me tail again!"

The otters stayed on the *Waterlily*, shaking their heads sternly at the bad behavior of the little squabblers.

Grumm had been nosing around the fire, tasting the food from the various pans and cauldrons. He pulled a wry face, whispering to Rose, "Gurr, no wonder they be ill-tempered. 'Ee food tastes turrible, Miz Roser. Oi wouldn't feed et to a dead frog, burr no!"

The mousemaid took the foodpack from Martin's

shoulder. "I've just had an idea. Here, do as I do!" Breaking one of Grumm's sweet invention cakes, she gave them a portion each and began eating her own piece with huge enjoyment. "Mmmm, this tastes good!"

The others followed her example. Boldred snaffled hers in one bite and began pecking crumbs from her talons. "Delicious, can't afford to waste a single crumb!"

"Hoo aye, 'tis vurry scrummy, 'seedin'ly noice!"

"Absolutely delightful, best I ever tasted!"

"Oh yes, this is the stuff, pals. Great!"

Gradually the shrews became silent, turning their attention to the friends as they praised the cake to the skies.

A shrew stabbed the air with his sword. "Gimme some, I want to try that stuff!"

Martin eyed him disdainfully. "Watch yourself, shrew. Don't wave that sword in my face and make demands of me!"

Rose wagged a stern paw at the offender. "Put that weapon away this instant and ask properly. Didn't your mother ever teach you to say please?"

The shrew was dumbstruck for a moment, then he put down his sword and lowered his voice. "Can I try your cake, please?"

Pallum took a reflective nibble and turned to Grumm. "What d'you think, is our cake too good for the likes of these?"

The mole licked a crumb from his chin. "Moight drive they'm mad, they'm on'y use to eatin' dreffle swill."

Several of the shrews looked beseechingly to Boldred. The owl looked as if she were about to say yes, then shook her head. "No, I don't think so. I would have given them all the cakes from our pack, but they've made up their minds not to sail tonight. You can't make creatures go on the stream voyaging if they're afraid of the dark."

The owl's statement created uproar. Fights, scuffles and arguments broke out all over the shrew camp. Starwort bounded through the mêlée. Giving the friends a huge wink he roared out, "Ahoy, you can't talk about river creatures like that. My mates the stream shrews'll sail anywheres at anytime, ain't that right, lads?"

Immediately, the shrews stopped fighting and waved their swords. "Aye, we'll sail anywhere, day or night!"

Rose put her head to one side and imitated a gruff shrew voice. "Give us the cakes and it's a bargain!"

Boldred tossed the foodpack into a long shrew logboat. "You shrews drive a hard bargain. Those are the last of our cakes. But so be it, you've won the argument. Let's go!"

The short-eared owl had to take to the air to avoid being swept into the logboats with her four friends. In a very short time they were out in midstream, the shrews poling their canoe-shaped treetrunks hard, competing in a race between crews. The travellers barely had time to turn and wave at the cheering otters before they were swept out of sight. Water rushed by the bows of the six logboats as night fell. Grumm and Pallum gripped the sides tightly as the narrow craft shot along on the swift current, shaking and rocking from side to side. Rose held Martin's paw, her face shining.

"We're travelling downstream. I recognize this part of the water. If we take a turn off to a side channel on the right we can be in Noonvale tomorrow afternoon!"

As she spoke, the shrews backed water, wheeling their craft into an inlet and down a sidestream. It was narrower than the main water, but just as fast-running.

Rose laughed aloud with joy. "Ha, ha! See those knotty old willows drooping into the water? I sat under them when I was a little one. I knew it, we're going home to Noonvale!"

32

Cap'n Tramun Clogg had finished filling in the prison pit. His paws ached with weariness and his tawdry finery was coated in dust. Pushing the barrow to a corner of the courtyard, he lowered himself gently into it and let the enormous wooden clogs slip from his footpaws as he heaved a melancholy sigh.

"Harr, 'tis an 'ard life an' no mistake, but at least Badrang ain't got me stannin' guard up on the wall like those fellers."

Clogg lay in the barrow, watching the guards on the walltop silhouetted against the early night sky, ruminating to himself. "Aye, 'is 'igh 'n' mighty Lordship will be drinkin' wine an' dinin' off fish an' roasted fowl in that long'ouse, while I've got to bide 'ere til mornin', waitin' fer a crust an' some water."

The corsair heard the thwock of the slingstones as the two wall sentries fell in a heap. He smiled wickedly in the darkness. "Hah, them slaves is learnin' fast. Now iffen me an' Badrang was still partners, I'd raise the alarm. But we ain't, I'm only a slave, an' raisin' alarms is nought to do with slaves!"

A volley of flaming javelins whooshed in over the walls. Clogg was well out of their range. He watched with great interest as they hit the longhouse, two or three missing, some falling flat on the roof. But the majority thudded into the timber walls, blazing merrily. Another wave of burning javelins streaked through the night sky like comets, finding the wooden palisade fence of the slave compound. A mighty roar rose from the shores outside Marshank.

"Fur and freeeedoooooom!"

Badrang came tearing out of the longhouse, stood on a lighted javelin by accident and hopped about on one paw yelling, "Attack, attack! Stand to arms! Walltop stations!" He grabbed two scurrying half-asleep soldiers. "Put that fire out, quick!"

They stood undecided. "But we ain't got water, Sire!"

The enraged Tyrant knocked their heads sharply together. "Addlepates, use sand, earth, dust!" He dashed off to the walltop, drawing his sword as he shouted orders to the horde milling in the courtyard.

"Archers, slingthrowers, follow me!"

Ballaw and Felldoh doused the fire they had used to ignite the javelins. They split up, each taking half the force, Ballaw to the back of the fort, Felldoh to the left side.

Felldoh's attackers flattened themselves against the earth and lay quite still. The squirrel passed the order along to his group. "After Ballaw's troops send their javelins off, be ready!"

Badrang peered out across the deserted shore. The archers and slingthrowers stood ready for his command.

Crosstooth stood beside the Tyrant, watching. "They'll be hidin' behind those rocks on the shore."

Badrang could see what the fox said was true. He raised a paw. "Archers, put a volley or two over the back of those rocks. That should flush them out. Ready, fire!"

The shafts clattered harmlessly off the rocks, leaving

the beach still silent. There was a hissing noise in the air. Instinctively Badrang threw himself flat on the walltop. "Down! Get down!"

Too late. Three hordebeasts fell to the javelins that sped in over the back walls. Propelled by the throwing sticks, they smashed and splintered on the fort side of the walltop.

Badrang was up and running around the rampart. "The slimy tricksters, they're round the back. Come on!"

Felldoh crouched low, watching the walltop, his javelins and slings ready. "Here they come. Wait for it now, let them get to the middle of the wall. Wait for it, steady, steady. . . . Now!"

The javelins and sling stones whirred off into the night, wounding three and slaying a further two. Felldoh's troops immediately fell flat, blending with the landscape in the night.

As soon as they had launched their javelins, Ballaw's command dashed off to the right side wall and lay low. Badrang had left half his archers to fire at Felldoh's fighters, leading the other half around to the back, only to find the rear landscape deserted. He banged his sword handle hard against the wall.

"The scum, they've probably backed off into the marshes. Cringing curs, why don't they show themselves and fight!"

Boggs the ferret had served long in Clogg's crow's-nest. He had the keenest eyes of any beast. Peering hard into the darkness, he stood stock still, straining his eyes. "There's creatures out there. I'm sure of it, Sire!"

"Where, Boggs? Can you see 'em?" Badrang's voice was low and excited.

"Aye, I can now, Sire. They're a good distance off, but comin' this way. Looks to be about six, no, five of 'em!"

Badrang took a bow from a nearby rat. "Give me your arrows. You there, give Boggs your bow and arrows.

The rest of you archers, notch up your shafts and lie low. Don't fire until I give the word!"

Plastered with mud, hungry and boneweary after trekking the country, lost since emerging from the marshes, Hisk and four survivors staggered through the darkness. The weasel Captain rubbed dirt from his tired eyes. Peering at the shape that loomed ahead in the night, he gasped in sheer relief, "It's Marshank! The fortress! We're safe. Come on!"

They broke into a shambling run, cheering hoarsely.

To Badrang it appeared that the five figures were charging. Mistaking them for enemies, he drew back the shaft on his taut bowstring. "Let 'em get a bit closer. Wait!"

Ballaw and his throwers released a salvo of javelins from over the right side of the fort.

The force on the left walltop had an idea where Felldoh and his troop were lying, they kept them well pinned down with arrows and slingstones. Ballaw's javelins caused disarray among them, and a weasel shrieked as he was struck in the side.

Young Juniper leaped up calling triumphantly, "Haha, that stopped 'em, they aaaargh!"

He fell with an arrow protruding from his chest. His friend, a young mouse named Yarrow, stood up, completely in shock. "They got Juniper. Look, there's an arrow sti—"

Keyla tackled him low around the footpaws. Yarrow fell, staring in amazement at the arrow that pierced his paw right through.

Felldoh was grim-faced as he dragged Juniper's body to him. "Keep your heads down! Keyla, we've got to get out of here. Help Yarrow, I'll carry Juniper. Now all of you, crawl fast and stay low. Follow me!"

Badrang crouched below the parapet, straining the

arrow against his taut bowstring as he watched Boggs scanning across the walltop. The ferret dropped down by the Tyrant's side and nodded.

"They're very close now. We can pick 'em off like daisies!"

Badrang glared along at the archers ranged in a crouching row. "We're not taking any prisoners. Kill them. Now!"

The five creatures went down like stones as the hail of barbed shafts hit them. Two more volleys followed, thudding into the bodies to make sure they were truly slain.

Badrang was shaking with exhilaration. "I only wish it had been day, then I could have watched the looks of surprise on their stupid faces!"

Ballaw took his fighters around the front and along the beach, meeting up with Felldoh and the others at the foot of the cliffs. The hare was in high good humor. "Top hole, wot! I think I could get to like this soldierin' life. We gave them a bally good lesson an' not one of us was harmed. How did it go with you, squirrel m'lad?"

Felldoh nodded towards the limp form on the ground. "Juniper was killed, Yarrow is wounded."

The exhilaration of victory left Ballaw and his command. "Poor little chap. Here I'll carry him."

It was a sad procession that made its way along the clifftops back to camp.

In the dawn light a group of horde soldiers gathered round the five carcasses shot full of arrows. Clogg watched the venomous look on Badrang's face and laughed humourlessly.

"You did well last night, matey. Slayed Hisk an' four of yer own. Still, you could be forgiven fer the mistake. They're so covered in marshmud they could've been anybeast."

The Tyrant's paw shot to his sword, but then he

thought better of it. Turning on his paw, he barked out an order as he stalked off. "Fleabane, Wulpp, make that slave dig five separate graves and bury that lot. Don't spare the rod, keep him busy!"

Rowanoak stood over the small grave that Felldoh and Ballaw had dug, as near to the cliff edge as the rocky ground would permit. Brome put the finishing touches to a herbal dressing and bandage on Yarrow's paw.

"There, as good as new. How does that feel?"

Yarrow lifted his paw up and down, wincing slightly. "Thank you, Brome. It still hurts a bit, but I'll live with it. Not like poor Juniper." He wiped away the bitter tears that flowed afresh on the bandage.

Brome threw a comforting paw around the young mouse. "Come on, let's go and say our farewells to him, Yarrow. Ballaw and Felldoh made him a nice resting place that will always stand free to the sunshine and wind, in sight of the sea."

The entire camp gathered round the grave. After a short ceremony, summer flowers were placed on the fresh filled-in earth and Barkjon said some words.

"It is always sad when a young one who has not seen many seasons is taken from us. Juniper was such a mouse, cheerful and well loved by all. But he did not die in vain. This young one gave his life fighting tyranny, so that others in the seasons to come may live in peace and freedom. That is all I have to say. Would anybeast like to add a word or two?"

Felldoh stepped forward. He laid Juniper's sling and stones amid the flowers. "You were a brave fighter, Juniper. We will never forget you. Badrang and his horde will pay tenfold for your death!"

As the Fur and Freedom Fighters drifted away from the grave, Yarrow sat alone by the flowers, gazing numbly at the resting place of his friend. Brome caught up with Felldoh and motioned him to one side.

"That was not a goodbye to Juniper, it was an oath of vengeance. How many more must die before you're satisfied?"

Felldoh's eyes were like rainswept pebbles as he answered, "As many as fate decrees, myself included. I will not rest until Badrang is dead and Marshank brought down!" He strode off in search of fresh lancewood.

Kastern watched them parting before going across to Brome. "Do not blame Felldoh, he feels for Juniper as much as you, Brome."

The young mouse shook his head. "No he doesn't, all he feels is that he must take revenge and carry on killing. He was my hero once, but now it's like talking to a strange beast. I don't know him any more."

Kastern watched the lone figure of Felldoh in the distance. "He is a warrior, and that is the way of warriors, just like the mouse Martin you are always talking about."

Brome shouldered his healing kit. "If Martin is a warrior like Felldoh, then may the seasons help my sister Rose if she is still with him!"

33

It was as if the very air were enchanted. Martin, Grumm and Pallum followed Rose through serene woodlands quiet and high in the sun-warmed afternoon. They had thankfully left the shrews in a backwater tributary of Broadstream. The creatures were arguing and squabbling over the remainder of the food and drink which Rose had given them because she wanted to travel fast and light. It was a forest as old as time, with a special feel about it, cool in the dark green shade, carpeted with a many flowered floor, shafted with golden rays casting their light on fern and bush. Velvety green moss was soft underpaw, and melodious birdsong was the only sound to filter through the variegated canopy of emerald and viridian green. Rose halted by a conical timeworn rock.

"Rose, what is it?" Martin felt his own voice ringing strangely in the stillness.

She stroked the monolithic stone and pointed downwards.

"Noonvale!"

Through the trees, Martin saw the land dip down into a huge valley. The blue smoke of cooking fires rose in a lazy spiral above the foliage, and small thatched rooftops could be seen here and there. An aura of time forgotten hung over the beautiful scene. The softly colored patches of flower gardens mixed with the unmarked boundaries of brightly hued orchards, while the light and sparkle of a stream cascaded into full bloom of a waterfall below. High above them, Boldred circled and wheeled on the thermals, casting her great wingshadow over them as she soared gracefully downward.

"See you in Noonvale, friends!"

They stood looking at one another for a moment, happiness brimming between them.

Grumm waved his ladle. "Hurr, we'm made et. C'mon!" He broke into a run, went head over paws through the loam and rolled down the valley side chortling happily, his three companions' paws thrumming the ground as they took off in a dash after him.

Urran Voh was not an old mouse though he was completely grey and wore a beard. As the Patriarch of Noonvale he was an impressive figure, dressed in a flowing green robe with a thick cream-colored cord at its middle. His wife Aryah stood beside him, beautiful and motherly in a lilac gown embroidered with green leaves. Rose threw herself into their welcoming paws breathlessly.

Both mice hugged their daughter affectionately. Aryah's welcome for Rose was interspersed with anxious enquiries about her son.

"Oh, Rose, my Rose, you're home. Did you find your brother? My, you've grown taller, slimmer too. That rascal Brome, did you see him? Did he mention his mother and father? Noonvale has been quiet without your singing, Rose. Is Brome following along? Will he be here soon?"

Rose's heart sank. Brome and Felldoh had not found their way to Noonvale! She could only hope that they were safe, somewhere . . .

Rose began gasping out her story, but Urran Voh held up a paw. "Later, it is enough for now that you are

294

safely home, Rose. No doubt you've risked life and limb several times to help your brother. You must realize that Brome is a born wanderer, never content and stubborn to the last word. Well, that young mouse is getting big enough to look after himself. But if you've agreed to meet up here, I expect he'll turn up sooner or later. Maybe someday he'll have sense enough to stay in Noonvale and not go dashing off every time the mood takes him. Ah! Grumm Trencher, you good mole, greetings. Who are these two young creatures?"

Grumm introduced them. "Yurr be Pallum an' Marthen 'ee Wurrier, zurr. They'm wunnerful gudd friends to oi an' Miz Roser."

Rose's mother Aryah cut short the introductions busily. "We can talk later. You must be starving. Rose dear, show your friends where they can wash and find clean robes, then bring them to the Council Lodge. I must prepare a homecoming party for you!"

Sometime later Pallum and Martin stood at the entrance to Council Lodge. It was an immense, homely old thatched building, its foursquare banquet tables dominating the centre beneath smoke-darkened rafters. Rose and Grumm led Pallum and Martin in. Bathed in blossom water and clad in a clean faded purple tunic, Martin held Rose's paw, standing slightly behind the mousemaid. The Lodge was packed with the inhabitants of Noonvale. They stood, cheering Rose and Grumm heartily.

Rose tugged Martin's paw. "Come on, take a bow, Martin."

The young mouse bowed formally amid the applause. Urran Voh waved him up with the other travellers to their places at table. Everybeast stood as the Patriarch raised his goblet. "Good food, good friends and peace for ever in this place!"

"May the seasons always be kind to Noonvale!" a multitude of voices answered as one.

They sat, and the welcome party began.

Throughout his life the memory of that happy day stayed locked secretly in Martin's heart.

He sat with Rose between her parents, speechless at the sight of the abundant tables. Flowers trailed everywhere, from the rafters, walls, windows and table edges. Roses, lilies, vines and blossoms festooned the whole place, twining around the urns of strawberry cordial, dandelion and burdock cup, mint and lavender water, chestnut ale, blackcurrant wine and cider. Platters and trays were heaped high with salads, cheeses, breads and pasties whose contents he could only guess at. Babies and little ones seated on their parents' laps gazed longingly at the array of trifles, flans, puddings, pies and tartlets, each with its honey-covered contents peeking through mounds of cream.

Grumm chose a deep slice of cherrycake glazed with candied nuts. Allowing the tiny mole sitting with him to take a huge bite, he chuckled. "Burr hurrhurr, doant boite off more'n you'm can chew, Bungo!"

It took a while for the infant to swallow it all. He tugged at Grumm's snout. "Hurr, then get oi some stawb'rry drink, Nuncle Grumm. You'm wouldn't loik oi to purrish o' thirst!"

A friendly hedgehog maid sat next to Pallum, offering him various savoury delights. "Try our leek and chestnut pastie. Here, let me pour some thyme and radish sauce on it for you."

Pallum dug in gratefully. "Thank you, marm. Most kind of you, marm."

"Marm? What do you think I am, some old spikemaid?" she laughed. "My name is Teaslepaw. Have you tasted our chestnut ale? My family brews it."

Pallum flushed beneath his spikes, burying his snout in the beaker. "It's very tasty, marm, er, Peasletaw, Pawseltea, er, marm!"

Martin and Rose chose a damson and hazelnut flan

topped with mintcream. They attacked the plate from both sides, meeting in the middle of the platter. Rose wiped cream from Martin's nose with a napkin.

"What'll we try next, cherrycake?"

Martin shook his head vigorously. "No thanks, I don't want to go to sleep yet!"

They both laughed, remembering the sly Aggril.

Boldred was slightly too large for any seat. She perched on a windowsill, demolishing a wild plum and apple pudding, watched by a group of admiring youngsters.

"Can you eat all of that by yourself, Missus Boldred?"

The owl raised a large talon. "I can eat three of these without stopping. This is excellent!"

The onlookers' eyes grew even wider. "Three plum 'n' apple puddens. Great seasons!"

The party went on until late into the night. Nothing was stinted, there was an abundance of everything for every creature. The guests sat back, sipping mint and lavender water as a quartette of otters performed an acrobatic dance, while a band of mice and moles accompanied them, playing a lively slipjig on reed flutes and drums. At a nod from Rose, Martin excused himself quietly, and followed the mousemaid and her parents to their cottage.

Urran Voh relaxed in his favorite chair. Aryah took out her embroidery. She sewed slowly as they listened to Rose tell of their adventures.

Martin sat at a window seat, letting Rose do all the talking. As Rose described the evil and cruelty of the slaves' lives at Marshank, her parents' faces became more and more grave.

Rose came to the end of the tale. Her father nodded, "You did well to return home, Rose. While there is such evil you should be here with your family. If only Brome could see this too. I am sorry that he and his friend Felldoh are not here safe, as you are. Let us hope he has the good sense to see that the outside world is not for him and he returns to us before the autumn."

Martin took a deep breath. "Sir," he said, "I agree that Noonvale is a haven of peace. Would that we could all live in such. But outside there is evil, and I cannot rest here knowing that those I lived with in slavery are still under the heel of Badrang. I came here for help. Will you allow me to ask for that help among the folk of Noonvale? There may be some here who would join me in a quest to free my friends from slavery."

Urran Voh's face was serious. "You ask a great deal. Our creatures have never seen war, they are dedicated to our life of friendship and peace."

His wife said quietly, "But my dear, where there is such pain and hardship for so many innocent creatures, surely we could let Martin speak to our folk. Any who wish to help can decide for themselves."

Urran Voh turned to Martin. "My wife speaks wisely. I do not wish for evil to become part of our lives here, but maybe we can prevent the wickedness from spreading. Very well, Martin, ask my creatures for help—and good fortune go with you.

"I see that you carry a blade. We do not have such things here. For the time you are with us you must not stay armed. Give me your sword, Martin."

The young mouse placed a defensive paw on his sword handle. "I am sorry, sir, I cannot do what you ask."

Urran Voh's eyes were stern in the awkward silence that followed.

Aryah intervened between the Patriarch and the Warrior. "Martin, I know my husband's feelings, but I think I also know yours too. You have seen suffering and evil in your life. There is none of that to be found at Noonvale. Would you do something for me? I am not asking you to give your sword to Urran. Take it and hang it on the peg by the door. Do this yourself, no one else will touch your blade."

Without a word Martin drew his sword. Going over to the door, he hung the weapon upon a peg protruding from the wall, balancing it by the hilt. It hung there, small and lonely-looking. The young mouse could not help thinking of his father's blade, big and worn, but a proper warrior's weapon, now in the paws of the Tyrant. He would take it back someday . . . somehow.

Rose smiled happily at him. "Good, come and I'll show you to your room."

At a glance from Urran Voh, Aryah intervened once more. "No, Rose, you'll have Martin up half the night talking. I'll do it. Follow me, young mouse."

When they had gone, Rose's father put his paw about her shoulders and sighed unhappily. "Rose, listen to me carefully, daughter. What I tell you is for your own good. This Martin, he is a warrior, and death walks alongside such creatures. You must never let yourself grow too close to him."

The mousemaid smiled. "Father, you're not a warrior, you're a worrier. Martin is my best friend in the whole world, he would never hurt me or let me be hurt. I'll change him, you'll see. One day he will be the most peaceful creature in Noonvale!"

Urran Voh rose from his chair slowly. "You and Brome are alike, both strong-willed. I only hope that you are right, Rose, though I think no good will ever come of your friendship, because I can tell that Martin has a will and determination far stronger than any I have ever come across. Good night, my Rose. Before you sleep, think on what I have said."

Rose ruffled her father's grey beard. "Good night, you great fusspot. There's nothing to think about except a much needed night's rest. When you come to know Martin the Warrior as well as I do, you'll understand."

34

Felldoh had planted caches of javelins all around Marshank. In the half-shadowed world of twilight he was like a phantom. Two sentries hung over the wall, slain by his accurate throwing. Inside the fortress another one had been slain and three lay wounded.

"More pesky buryin' fer me to do in the mornin'," Tramun Clogg snorted as he peered out from under his wheelbarrow. "Stripe me, iffen I waits long enough I'll 'ave Marshank alone to meself, 'cos I'll be the only beast left livin' 'ere!"

Badrang paced the floor of his badly charred longhouse. Several prominent horde figures sat in silence as he ranted angrily.

"We're not dashing out into the night to get picked off like flies. That's what those slaves want. I'm not going to fight on their terms, I'll do it my way when the time's right!"

Crosstooth played with a dagger, twirling it deftly. "Yore right, Sire. I've told everybeast to keep under cover. Them that gets 'urt or slain, 'tis their own fault."

Slamming himself down in his chair, the Tyrant gulped wine.

The weasel Lumpback unwisely voiced an opinion.

"But if we don't fight back, they've got us pinned down. They'll start thinkin' we're frightened of 'em an' begin attackin' 'arder!"

Badrang hurled the wine jug. Lumpback scarcely had time to duck as it smashed on the wall behind him, covering the hapless weasel with pottery shards and damson wine. Badrang's teeth were bared as he hissed at Lumpback, "Who asked you, dirtbrain? I don't need the thoughts of idiots and halfwits to do my planning for me. Maybe you'd like to get out there and face them yourself!"

Boggs felt sorry for Lumpback. He could see it would only take a sudden whim for Badrang to send the weasel out on the shore alone. "Go easy, Lord. He was only sayin' —"

"Easy?" Badrang's face flushed dark with rage as he stood and threw the chair over. "Go easy, you say, while a stinking pawful of slaves are holding Marshank and an entire horde under siege . . . !" Whipping out his sword, he leaped at the group. "Get out of here! Go on, out of my sight, you mindless mud-crawling morons. You're about as much use as a one-winged gull!"

Yelling and shouting, they scrambled over each other to avoid the flailing blade and get out of the door.

Felldoh came out from behind a rock, his keen ears twitching as he pinpointed the sounds of the scuffle. With remarkable precision he quickly sent off two javelins, one after the other.

Lumpback was last to leave, he had been dodging the swordplay as Badrang chased him. With a yell he dived out of the open door, straight into Felldoh's first javelin.

Badrang slammed the door shut quickly.

Thruck!

Felldoh's second javelin pierced the half-burned timbers. The weapon came right through, stopping a hairsbreadth from the Tyrant's bloodshot eyes. Badrang

301

slashed with his sword, chopping the javelin in two pieces. Flinging back his head, he roared out into the gathering night, "Sneaks, cowards! I'll chop you into fishbait if I catch you!"

"Come on out then, stoatface," Felldoh's deep voice boomed back from the shore. "Two can make fishbait!"

"Scum!" Badrang yelled back at his unseen foe. "I'll fix you good and proper when the time is right!"

Felldoh's harsh laughter rang out in reply. "Hahahah! Scum yourself, yellowbelly. Hide in your fort. I know you're scared!"

"Scared, me?" Badrang's voice went shrill with spleen. "I am Badrang, Lord and Tyrant of all these lands. Nobeast can stand against me. I was killing and fighting while you were still clinging to your mother's tail!"

Felldoh had got a fix on the voice. Three javelins in swift succession burst through the longhouse door, another one thudded into the roof. Badrang lay flat behind his upturned chair, gripping the wood tightly to stop himself trembling.

"Hahaha, missed me," he managed to laugh back. "Pity you can't throw those things straight!"

Felldoh's reply came deep and confident. "Don't worry, I've got all night to practice. Don't go to sleep now!"

Gathering his javelins, Felldoh slid off into the night, leaving behind a very worried stoat.

Peering through a crack in the gate, Tramun Clogg saw the shadowy figure hurry off south toward the cliffs.

"Harr, 'twere as I reckoned—only one beast. Well, I'd best get me sleep. No use tryin' to tell 'is Lordship he's safe to 'ave a bit o' shuteye. He wouldn't take the word of a slave."

Away in the safety of the clifftops, Ballaw sat watching the gloomy little groups of creatures sitting around the campfire. All day long the mood had been heavy among

302

them. The hare finished sipping cider from a scallop shell and made his way over to where the Rambling Rosehip Players lounged about by the cart.

"Evenin', chaps an' chapesses, wot! My my, you lot look like a pile of frogs that've been to a rock-swallowin' party. No wonder our chums are lookin' glum if an entertainin' troupe can't smile."

Brome smiled wanly at the garrulous hare. "What do you want us to do?"

Ballaw twiddled his long ears cheerfully. "That's the spirit, young Brome me laddo. I'll tell you what I want you all to do. Bring a bit of cheer into those creatures' sad little lives, a laugh, a smile and a song. Let's do a show!"

Celandine fluttered her eyelids and cooed. "What a lovely idea. You'll have to wait until I've got myself ready though, Ballaw. Dearie me, I must look an absolute fright!"

"Fright?" Ballaw tickled her under the chin. "You, me pretty one, never. You look absoballylutely gorgeous. Come on, you apprehensive actors, the show's tonight!"

The audience sat shaking with laughter, their eyes shining in the firelight, the day's troubles temporarily forgotten as they watched the antics of the Rambling Rosehip troupe.

Rowanoak braced her huge back as Gauchee, Kastern, Trefoil and Buckler formed a pyramid on it. Buckler stood highest, on top of Trefoil's head.

Ballaw swirled a floppy cloak as he placed a scrap of material on the ground and called to the audience, "Pray silence. Please, no tittering or throwing objects whilst this dangerous trick is in progress. Malcolm the Magnificent Mole will dive from a very great and perilous height on to this damp cloth. Ladies an' gentlebeasts, I present Malcolm the Magnificent Diving Mole!"

There was a round of applause. Buckler, dressed in a baggy costume and wearing a curly black moustache, took a wobbly bow from on top of the pyramid and announced dramatically:

"Oi be ready an' willin' to die,
An' moi wages be a custard pie!"

Dressed in a spangled gown, Celandine paraded, showing the audience a huge custard pie.

"Oh, dive, my loved one, my dear.
I have your wages here!"

"Well, hurry up, my back's killing me!" Rowanoak roared out in mock agony.

Ballaw did an elegant bow in the badger's direction. "Do not worry, madam. Your face has been killing me for years, let alone your back. Keep quite still now. Malcolm, are you ready?"

"Oi be ready t' dive frum this gurt 'igh place on to 'ee damp cloth!"

Ballaw drummed his footpaw on a small tambourine. "We will not be responsible for small infants an' nervous folk who faint durin' this death-defyin' performance!"

Fuffle leaped up and pulled Rowanoak's stubby tail. "Ho, gerron wivvit!"

"Yaaaaaaaahhhhhhh!"

Rowanoak tried to stand up and the pyramid collapsed. Amid loud laughter the troupe lay on the ground pretending to be stunned, while Buckler appeared with the damp cloth balanced on his nose. He struck out as if swimming. "Oi did et, oi did et! Oh, 'elp, somebeast, afore oi drowns. Oi carn't swim!"

Celandine ran forward holding the custard pie and calling sweetly, "Oh, save him, someone. Don't let poor Malcolm drown before he's had his custard pie!"

"Fear not, fair maid, I will save the poor lad, for I can dive like a duck and swim like a rock!" Ballaw ran to the rescue. Celandine tripped and fell beautifully. The custard pie sailed through the air, and Kastern caught it just as Ballaw whipped the damp cloth from Buckler's nose. He waved it dramatically. "Saved, saved from a fate worse than tummyache!"

The flapping cloth hit Kastern in the face. She let go of the pie and it splattered all over Buckler's head. The audience fell about, holding their sides and hooting with laughter. Buckler bowed.

"Yurr am oi, Malcumm, cumpletely disgusted,
'Stead o' water oi bin drownded in custed!"

From the edge of the firelight Felldoh watched the performance. Barkjon suddenly noticed his son sitting next to him. "Ha ha, oh hohoho! What a good show. Felldoh, where did you come from, son?"

Felldoh kept his gaze on the performers, smiling as he clapped his paws together. "I've been here all the time. Funny, wasn't it? Cheers you up to see somebeast taking a tumble, eh Dad!"

His father was about to reply when Felldoh pointed. "Oh, look out, here comes young Brome. I wonder what he and Ballaw are up to?"

As they began the next act, Barkjon looked strangely at his son and murmured in his ear, "Yes, and I wonder what you've been up to."

Brome sat banging a large drum.

Boomboomboomboom!

Ballaw appeared from behind the cart in a long night-gown and a tasselled nightcap. He yawned, stamping his paw bad-temperedly. "I say, what d'you think you're doin' bangin' that thing all night, you young rip. I'm tryin' to sleep!"

Brome continued to bang the drum vigorously.

Boomboomboomboomboom!

"I'm practicing for the Periwinkle Parade!"

Ballaw wriggled a paw in his ear over the drum noise. "The whatiwinkle hooray, did y'say!"

305

Brome banged the drum louder as he shouted, "The Periwinkle Parade, you silly fool!"

Ballaw wriggled paws in both ears as if to hear better. "The pretty pinksnail in a slippy pool?"

Brome continued banging as Ballaw turned to the audience. "What did he say?"

"The Periwinkle Parade, you silly fool!" everyone yelled aloud.

Ballaw nodded. "Oh, I see. The gritty pigstail of a swilly cool!"

The audience roared out as Brome banged even louder.

Ballaw shook his head. Grabbing Brome's paw, he halted the noise. "Listen, you young rogue, I'll give you a cream pudden if you stop that bangin'. Is it a bargain?"

Brome smiled foolishly. "Done! Where's the cream pudden then, flopears?"

Ballaw produced a big knife. "Inside the drum. It's all yours if you stop that beastly bangin'."

Still smiling foolishly, Brome cut the drumskin wide open and poked his head inside. There was a moment's silence then he called out. "Hey, lankypaws, there's no cream pudden in here!"

Ballaw did a huge wink at the audience and grinned wickedly. "Oh, isn't there? What a jolly old shame. Ah well, I'm off for a nice long sleep, 'cos I'm playin' my drum tomorrow in the Periwinkle Parade y'know. Good night!"

Gauchee walked up holding a lantern. "Goodnight Mr. Ballaw!"

Ballaw shuffled past her. "Good night, Mrs. Gauchee. Oh, don't forget and leave my big drum out for me in the morning, I'm playin' in the Periwinkle Parade."

Gauchee threw her paws up. "Oh corks! I'd forgotten all about that, Mr. Ballaw. I'd better go and get your drum back off young Master Brome. I lent it to him to practice on!"

Ballaw clapped a paw to his head and collapsed in a

faint. Gauchee turned to Brome. "Leave that silly old drum with Mr. Ballaw and come in for your supper. I've made you a nice cream pudden, Master Brome!"

Tullgrew, Keyla and Baby Fuffle leaned on each other, the tears coursing down their cheeks as they tried to stop laughing. Purslane was shaking with laughter herself as she swept Fuffle up in her paws. "Come on, mischief. Time for bed. Are you coming, Groot?"

Purslane's husband Groot was saying his good nights to the others. He passed Felldoh at the edge of the firelight. "Good night, Felldoh. It's nice to see you smiling again."

The strong squirrel patted Groot's back as he passed. "Yes, it was very good night altogether!"

Brome had been watching Felldoh. He was rather puzzled by the squirrel's jolly mood. The young mouse lay down to rest near the campfire embers, next to Keyla and Tullgrew. The three lay staring at the myriad hosts of stars piercing the velvet cape of night.

"Felldoh is up to something," Brome said softly to the two otters. "I can't quite put my paw on it, but I'll swear he's hatching some plan or other."

Keyla half sat up. "Funny you should say that, Brome. I couldn't help watching Felldoh tonight myself. He's being far too smug, sort of secretive. Have you noticed anything, Tullgrew?"

"About Felldoh? Well, he's been going about patting backs and shaking paws, grinning like a demented frog. That's not like him, he's usually a dour creature these days."

Brome listened to the guttering fire crackle gently. So, it was not only he who had observed Felldoh acting oddly. "Listen, you two, I don't like it one little bit. In fact, I've been thinking. I'm going to follow that squirrel tomorrow and see what he's up to. Fancy coming along?"

Keyla and Tullgrew both nodded silently. Brome clasped their paws. "Good, as soon as it's light we stick to him like limpets!"

The campfire burned down to a tiny glimmer of light on the clifftops. Ballaw and Rowanoak snored gently in the cart, and a soft summer wind rippled the grass. The encampment slumbered peacefully in the calm night. Only Felldoh was still awake. He sat with his back against a rock, planning.

35

Dawn light crept over Noonvale in a golden haze. Unused to sleeping in a bed under a roof, Martin was up and about, feeling strangely light without the short sword tucked snugly at his side. He wandered about the settlement, marvelling at the beauty and proliferation of fruit and flower, a tribute to the industrious inhabitants. Sitting beside the waterfall, he enjoyed the cool atmosphere. Perch and trout could be seen gliding lazily in the crystal depths of a pool at the base of the falls. The young mouse stared at his reflection in a shadowed inlet. The marks of the deep scratches on his cheeks were still there, and his face was thinner, though the resolute jaw was firm and the eyes that stared back at him shone with the light of determination.

He was not surprised to see Aryah appear beside him. She placed her paws on his shoulders, watching his image in the water. "You are an early riser, Martin."

"I could not sleep, but I see you are up early too."

"Yes, I have spoken to Boldred. I have asked her to seek out Brome. What is the matter, Martin? Are you not happy here?"

"It is a beautiful spot."

"But you must soon return to Marshank?"

The young mouse flicked a pebble into the pool and

watched it sink. Aryah sat down beside him and patted his paw. "You and my husband Urran Voh are both alike in many ways, warrior and peacemaker, both walking different paths, but both stubborn and immovable. The world needs such creatures. Rose told me that the Tyrant holds your father's sword. Is that the reason you must go, to take the sword back from him?"

Martin stood up. He helped Aryah on to her paws. "Yes, the sword belonged to my father, Luke the Warrior. I swore a warrior's oath to him that I would never let another beast take it from me. I was little more than an infant when Badrang stole my sword, but now the seasons have given my paws the strength to take it back. You understand, I must do this, and I must free Marshank of slavery."

Martin thought he saw the glimmer of a tear in Aryah's eye.

"I understand, young warrior. The thing that grieves me is that Rose will go with you, no matter what I, or her father, may say."

Martin reached out, wiping the teardew from Aryah's cheek. "I will take far greater care protecting her life than I will my own."

Grumm ladled creamy pale batter on to a heated stone, grunting eagerly as he watched it cook. "Gurr, pancakers. Oi dearly do luv pancakers wi brekkist."

His tiny nephew Bungo stirred a cauldron furiously. "Hurrhurr, an' zoop, Nuncle Grumm. Doant furget 'ee zoop!"

Grumm turned the pancake over. "Gurrout you'm darft liddle moler. 'Ow could oi furget zoop! Yurr, doant stir et too farst, you'm ull spoil et."

Bungo's tiny paws were a blur as he stirred faster and faster. "You'm doant tell oi 'ow to stir zoop, oi been doin' et since oi were nought but a liddle un. Pay 'tenshun to thoi pancakers!"

Tables and forms had been set out under the trees in the sun-splashed shade, and creatures bustled to and fro with breakfast items. Rose dashed by Martin. She was carrying a tray of hot pancakes spread with honey and decorated with pear slices and raspberries. "Out of my way, sir, or you won't get breakfast today!"

Martin sprang nimbly aside and bowed low. "My apologies, marm. Nothing should get in the way of good food!"

"Then don't get in the way, lend a paw over here!" Pallum shouted across as he staggered under an immense beechwood bowl of fruit salad.

Mice, hedgehogs, moles and squirrels called out their morning greetings to each other as they went about their chores. Every creature helped until the tables were ready. Little ones scrubbed from tail to eartip and freshly besmocked clambered up on to familiar laps. Young ones, giggling and gossiping together, sat next to their closest friends. Old ones and parents made sure their families were comfortable before perching in their time-honoured positions at table. When every creature was settled, Urran Voh recited the grace and the meal began in earnest.

"Pass the barleybread, please!"

"Ooh, it's hot! Mind your paws."

"We'm bain't 'ad a gudd pancake since Grumm been away. Parss they yurr, Gumbler!"

"Martin, would you like some fruit salad? It's very good!"

"Thank you, Rose. Here, try some of this maple and buttercup wafer."

"Oh yes please. Auntie Poppy baked them—they're my favorite. Teaslepaw, can you stop baby Bungo dipping those pancakes in the soup!"

The hedgehog maid put aside her maplescone and tried to prevent the infant mole from dipping a pancake that oozed honey into the leek and mushroom soup.

Bungo eyed her indignantly. "Keep thoi spoiky paws offen oi an' eat thoi own brekkist, mizzy."

Grumm nudged Pallum as the hedgehog finished off a heavy slice of nutbread. "That Bungo be a liddle savage. He'm rooned a gurt pot o' zoop sturrin' et loik a wurlywind. Oi maked a speshul pot, jus' fur you'n oi. Do 'ave some."

Pallum ladled the broth into his bowl.

"Thankee, Grumm. Mmm, smells nice!"

"An' so et should, hurr. Oi maked et wi' roses an' onions an' daisies an' carrot, an' plums an' turnip too, ho aye, gudd zoop! An' oi sturred et slow, not loik some villyuns not arf a league from wurr oi sits!"

After breakfast, Rose showed Martin round the orchard. Plums, greengages and damsons, hung red, yellow and purple amid other trees bearing pears, apples and cherries. Neat rows of raspberry, blackcurrants, bilberry and redcurrants provided a border between the orchard and the vegetable garden. At the far end of the orchard a crew of moles was digging around a gaunt dead sycamore tree. Grumm was helping. He greeted them with a wave of his huge digging paw.

"Hurr, look at oi, not 'ome a twoday an' oi'm back at work!" He explained that they were digging to bring the dead sycamore down. It would be cut up and used as stump seats around the waterfall pool. Martin immediately rolled up the sleeves of his smock and began to help. Rose watched for a while, then tossing off her headband of woven flowers, she jumped into the hole alongside Martin.

All through the day they toiled. Six holes had been bored in and around the base of the dead forest giant and still the sycamore refused to budge. A crowd of Noonvale creatures who had finished their chores gathered round to watch. Grumm and several other moles shook soil from their digging claws and wiped perspiring snouts.

"Gurr, that thurr old tree doant want to budge, Grumm!"

"Hurr no, Gumbler. Nor wudd you'm iffen thoi roots 'ad been thurr for all they long seasons."

"Hurr, us'ns be yurr till winter shiften this'n!"

"Wot's 'olden et up? We'm digged deep all round et?"

Grumm vanished down a hole and reappeared, spraying earth about. "Taproot, gurt fat un. Et ull 'ave to break afore she moves, hurrr!"

Martin took a small mole axe and climbed into the hole. "I'm going to have a go at that taproot. Rose, take all these spectators and find the longest, thickest piece of wood you can. Bring it over here and give me a shout when you do."

Rose and her party scoured Noonvale. The only thing they could come up with was a long thick rowan trunk, forked at one end. Urran Voh watched them rolling it away.

"Where are you taking that? We were going to reinforce the ridgepole rafter of the Council Lodge with it."

Rose tugged her father's beard playfully. "Martin wants it to move the old sycamore. Don't worry, we'll bring it back."

Urran Voh snorted. "I should hope you will, though how you plan to move that big sycamore with it is beyond me."

Baby Bungo took the Patriarch's paw. "Hurr, then coom an' watch. You'm never too seasoned to lurn, zurr!"

Martin tossed aside the axe. He had cut as deep into the taproot as the limited space in the hole allowed. Climbing out of the hole, he directed the group rolling the rowan trunk into position.

"Push it over here. That's it! Let the forked end down towards me. Grumm, build up some earth and stones at

313

the edge of the main hole here. Watch out! Let the rowan slide down. Good!"

The rowan trunk stood at an angle down into the main hole, its twin forks buried in two more holes at the sycamore's roots.

Martin climbed from the hole and inspected it.

Urran Voh nodded. "A lever. Don't you think it's a bit big, Martin?"

The young mouse shook his head. "The bigger the better, sir. Right, come on, everybeast climb up it and perch on the high end. You too, Bungo. Every little helps."

Amid much merriment and whooping, the crowd climbed up the rowan trunk. They balanced precariously at its tilted top, hanging on to each other.

Urran Voh looked up at them. "There's too few. Not enough room for all up there. Get some ropes."

It was not long before Aryah and the otters who had sung in quartette came hurrying along, carrying coils of stout vine rope. "This is all we could find, dear. Will these do, Martin?"

The young mouse threw a rope up to the creatures balanced on the end of the rowan. "Perfect, marm! Tie those ropes fast up there, the rest of you swing on the ends for all your worth. You on top, when I give the word, jump up and down. Ready!"

Every creature waited on Martin's word.

"Right, jump up and down, now! Swing hard on the ropes. Swing!"

The rowan dipped and bent slightly, then loud crack was heard from beneath the sycamore. Martin and Urran Voh threw themselves on the ropes, yelling aloud to the others crowding above and below.

"Jump! Swing! Jump! Swing!"

There was more rumbling and cracking from beneath the base of the sycamore. It began to tipple as the rowan bent under the strain.

Rose and her mother laughed aloud as they swung on the ropes. "It's going, see, it's starting to topple!"

The sycamore could take no more. With a groan of creaking and splitting wood it crashed slowly over.

Krrrraaaaakkkkk!

The end of the rowan lever had dipped so low that it almost touched the ground. Loud cheers rang through the valley, Martin and Urran Voh pounded each other's backs. "We did it, hooray!"

The moles were quite carried away, and went into a wild stamping dance. Rose and her mother kicked up their paws happily at its center. Soon everybeast was dancing, singing and cheering. The great sycamore stood nearly as high as Council Lodge at its upturned base, a forest of roots, soil and rocks.

By evening a sprawling picnic had broken out along the fallen treetrunk, and strawberry cordial and waterfall-cooled gourds of cider flowed freely. Singing lustily in chorus, the moles brought out ten of their deeper 'n' ever turnip 'n' tater 'n' beetroot pies, huge, deep, hot and satisfying, made in traditional mole manner with massive patterned shining piecrusts topping each one.

"Give 'ee, give you, give them'n give oi,
Turnip 'n' tater 'n' beetroot poi,
Gurt platters each morn, an' more at 'ee noight,
Fill oi a bowlful, et tasters jus' roight.
An' iffen 'ee infant wakes, starten to croi,
Feed 'im turnip 'n' tater 'n' beetroot poi.
Et's gudd furr 'ee stummick, et's good furr' ee jaws,
Makes' em grow oop wi' big strong diggen claws.
Nought gives us molers more pleasure 'n' joy
Than turnip 'n' tater 'n' beetroot poi!"

Pallum, Rose, Martin and Grumm lay back exhausted, picking idly at half-filled bowls and sipping their drinks, contented after the long hard day's work.

It was then that Boldred dropped out of the sky like a thunderbolt with her news.

36

Three pairs of eyes watched Felldoh set off silently into the rosy dawn that tinged the clifftops. Brome nodded to his two otter companions. "There he goes, laden with enough javelins to stock an army. Come on, let's follow him!"

Felldoh's mood was light and carefree now that he had set out to complete his lone mission. With a bundle of javelins beneath each arm and his thrower strapped across his back, he hummed a cheerful little tune. What need of armies and hordes? He could rid the world of Badrang by himself. Once the Tyrant was dead, Marshank would be a snake without a head.

White-crested rollers boomed in over the shore, the sun seemed to smile out of a cloudless sky of powder blue, and a cooling breeze drove the thin layer of sun-warmed sand aimlessly around the foot of the cliffs.

For the first time in many seasons Felldoh's heart felt light.

Cautiously the gates of Marshank creaked open, and a phalanx of hordebeasts, armed to the fangs, filed outside. Crosstooth looked all around to reassure himself there was no immediate danger of attack.

Badrang appeared on the walltop with scores of archers and slingers. He shielded his eyes against the sun's glare as he issued orders. "Search every rock, hollow, dune and outcrop from here to the sea!" He stood enjoying the morning's warmth, the light wind blowing his cloak playfully about as he watched his soldiers scouring the beach.

Crosstooth was near the tideline. He waved his spear from side to side, calling aloud, "All clear down here, Lord. No sign of anybeast!"

Badrang cupped paws about his mouth, shouting a reply. "Get those beasts dug in where they can't be seen!"

Crosstooth ran back and forth, placing the soldiers in position. Some were behind rocks, others lay flat on the seaward side of low dunes, the rest dug shallow trenches above the tideline.

Tramun Clogg rested one clogged paw on his spade, cackling as he called up to the Tyrant, "Haharrharr, you got those beauties diggin' their own graves. That'll save me some work, matey!"

Nipwort and Frogbit, the two rat guards who had been left in charge of the corsair, prodded him with their spears. "They're diggin' slit trenches to keep themselves alive in case of attack. You get on with buryin' the dead."

Clogg dug with ferocious energy, muttering to himself, "Haharr, wait'll ole Tramun's diggin' yer grave, Badrang. I'll dig it deep an' 'andsome. Aye, an' put a great rock atop of it so's you won't be a-climbin' out again. Ho, that'll be a glorious day in the life of Cap'n Tramun Josiah Cuttlefish Clogg, to give me my full title. Ye won't be able to badmouth me when I'm throwin' spadefuls o' good earth in yer ugly gob, Badrang!"

Boggs stood atop the battlements, peering southward. He leaped down and ran to make his report. "Onebeast comin' along the cliffs in this direction, Lord!"

Badrang was slightly taken aback. "Only one?"

"Aye, just a loner, still a fair way off, but I spotted 'im."

The Tyrant pulled the closest two archers to him. "Rot-nose, Wetpaw, get down there as quick as you can. Tell Crosstooth to hide with the others. You two do the same. When I shout the word Marshank aloud, break cover and capture this one. Hurry now. Tell everybeast to be totally silent. If he sniffs a trap he'll be off!"

Once the two messengers had departed, Badrang turned to his archers. "Down, all of you. Be quiet and keep your heads low. Remember, the word is Marshank. You, Wulpp, go and shut the front gates."

As Felldoh trotted along from the cliffs to the shore, he hardly noticed the unusual silence that hung over the fortress. Had he been more vigilant he might have noticed the telltale signs that the foe were lying in concealment on the beach. But the squirrel's vengeful eyes were riveted on just one thing, Badrang, standing out bold and alone on the walltop over the gates. Felldoh's paws gripped the javelins like vices and his teeth made a grinding noise as his jaw muscles bulged, the breath hissing fiercely from both his nostrils. Now he broke into a run, his paws pounding rock and dry sand as he sped along, oblivious to all else but the figure of his most hated enemy.

At the edge of the cliffs, Brome threw himself flat with Keyla and Tullgrew either side of him. "Is he mad? Look at him!"

They watched the javelin-carrying squirrel skid to a halt within earshot of Badrang.

Tullgrew bit her clenched paw. "He's going to be killed, I can feel it in my bones. Surely they wouldn't let a lone escaped slave run up to the place like that in broad daylight?"

Keyla watched in horrified fascination, unable to tear his eyes away from the scene. "You're right, I'll bet my rudder he's walked into some sort of trap. Maybe we can shout a warning."

Brome was doubtful. "I think we're too far away, but let's give it a try. Shout his name. One, two, three. Shout!"

"Felldooooooooooh!" The three voices rang out as one.

Tullgrew struck the clifftop with her clenched paw. "I don't think he heard us, or even if he did he isn't paying any heed to us. What in the name of thunder is he doing down there?"

Keyla shook his head. "I don't know, but something awful is going to happen, I'd take my oath on that. I think one of us should go back to camp and bring help quickly."

"I'll go!" Brome cast off his healing bag and began wriggling backwards.

Keyla went into a low crouch, dashing past Brome. "You stay here, mate. I'm the best runner in these parts!" Leaping upright, he took off with dust spurting from his heels.

Wordlessly Felldoh dropped his bundles of javelins. Taking the throwing stick, he fitted one along it. Bending his whole body back, he sighted along the shaft and hurled it with tremendous force at Badrang.

The Tyrant was a fair distance away. He saw the javelin launched and leaped to one side, watching it as it sped harmlessly by. Leaning on the wall, he called out scornfully, "Try another one, squirrel!"

Felldoh did, this time with a short run and skip to give his javelin impetus. Badrang had dropped below the wall as the missile was thrown. He heard the thin whistle of wind as it passed overhead. Smiling, he stood up and shouted at the squirrel, who was just about within earshot, "Best you can do, slave?"

"I am not a slave of yours," Felldoh's voice roared back at him. "My name is Felldoh and I've come here to kill you, Badrang!"

Another javelin came hurtling through the air. This time Badrang jumped back to his former position, shrug-

320

ging expressively as the pointed wood sailed off towards the back wall of the fortress. "Tut, tut, missed again. You'll run out of those things soon!"

Quivering with rage, Felldoh held up a javelin in both paws. He broke it as if it were a straw. "I could break you like that if you weren't such a mud-sucking coward. Come down and fight me, paw to paw, beast to beast!"

Badrang swept his paws wide. "No doubt you have laid a trap for me. Those cliffs will be swarming with your friends, ready to leap up and come running to the attack at your signal, the same group you had with you last night, treacherously slaying my creatures in the darkness. Do you take me for a fool?"

Felldoh moved closer to the fortress, as Badrang hoped he would. Throwing caution to the winds as his temper got the better of him, the squirrel curled his lip contemptuously.

"You are both a fool and a coward! Last night there was only me out here. I am as you see me now, without any army or horde and without a fortress wall to hide behind like you have. So come out and fight. Poltroon, craven cur! Dithering idiot!"

Suddenly the positions were reversed. Badrang could hear his archers below the wall sniggering. Stung by Felldoh's insults, the Tyrant drew his sword.

"Nobeast uses words like that to me. I am Lord Badrang. Get ready to die, squirrel. I am coming down!"

Even in his rage the Tyrant was still playing the odds. Armed with a sword, he was sure he could defeat the squirrel, who had only some short wooden stakes to defend himself. As a last resort he could always call in his soldiers; they had his adversary surrounded. As Badrang pushed past the grinning archers, he swore silently to himself that he would slay the bold squirrel, wiping away any doubts in the minds of his horde that he, Badrang, was a leader to be feared and respected.

Brome gasped in amazement as the fortress gates

swung open and Badrang walked out alone to face Felldoh.

Tullgrew shook her head. "I don't believe it. Whatever Felldoh's been saying must have stung Badrang into action. Look, they're going to fight!"

Brome stared at the lone figure, and all his hostility to Felldoh evaporated. He remembered the squirrel's words, that he would die if it was necessary to bring down Badrang and Marshank. The young mouse found himself wishing that he possessed the bravery to be a warrior and help his friend by standing alongside him.

Badrang leaped at Felldoh, cleaving only empty air with his sword as his adversary skipped back nimbly. Gripping the sword tight in both paws, the stoat rushed in, swinging wildly, hoping to overwhelm his foe with the ferocity of the attack. Felldoh was like a stinging hornet. He weaved in under the flailing blade, jabbing at the Tyrant's face with his javelin as he flashed by. Badrang turned, drawing in his breath sharply as he felt blood trickle from a small wound on his jaw. Balanced lightly on his footpaws, Felldoh grinned insolently, threw himself into a swift roll and whacked his adversary hard on the shin with the wooden shaft. Badrang yelped with pain, spinning fast and chopping down with his sword. He chopped only sand, arching his back as the wicked javelin point raked a long scratch on it. Breathing heavily, he held the sword point forward and low, shuffling slowly towards the squirrel, watching for a sudden move. Felldoh stood his ground, eyeing the sword carefully as it rose fractionally, guessing the exact moment Badrang would choose to thrust. The stoat lunged! Felldoh skipped sideways, bringing the javelin down with numbing force on his opponent's left paw. Tears sprang unbidden to the stoat's eyes as he held on to the sword with his right paw, the left stinging and throbbing as it hung limp at his side. Felldoh was still smiling, adding insult to injury. Badrang feigned helplessness for a moment, trying to move his deadened paw. Suddenly he dropped flat, rolled over and swung out wildly. Felldoh was taken by surprise. The blade cut deep into his footpaw. Badrang moved in for the kill, swinging the sword in his good paw. The butt of the javelin struck him hard in the stomach, knocking his breath out in a sharp gasp. He doubled over, fighting for air.

Thwack!

The wooden haft struck the sword into the air. It curved in a shining arc, landing point down in the sand as Badrang's right paw fell numbly to his side. Holding the javelin in both paws like a quarterstave, Felldoh knocked his enemy flat on the shore. Ignoring his injured footpaw, the squirrel raised the javelin. He brought it down with punishing force.

Tullgrew clapped a paw across her eyes. "Has he killed him? I can't look. Is Badrang slain?"

Brome shook his head in astonishment. "No, Felldoh is beating him with the javelin as if it were a rod!"

Tullgrew uncovered her eyes, smiling with grim satisfaction. "Aye, just as he used to have slaves beaten. Lay it on, Felldoh!"

Badrang tried to curl up into a ball, yelping as he rolled about on the round. The javelin rose and fell across his back, each stroke punctuated by Felldoh's harsh shouts. "How does it feel to be beaten like a slave, O mighty one? Feel this! And this! You had me beaten when I was little more than an infant! My father was beaten with the rod because he was old and slow! You never made me cry out! Why are you wailing! Can't you take your own medicine!"

Tullgrew covered her eyes again, but Brome watched in horrified fascination. "He's going to beat Badrang to death, I can hear him yelling from here!'"

323

But the Tyrant was not crying out needlessly.

"Marshank! Marshank! Marshank!"

37

Boldred perched on the fallen sycamore as she related all she had seen.

"The first place I stopped at was a camp on the southeast cliffs. There were many creatures there. A hare and a badger seemed to be in charge, Ballaw and Rowanoak."

"I have not heard of these creatures," Martin interrupted.

Boldred held up a talon. "Let me continue, it will soon become clear. I spoke to them of Brome, and they assured me that he was alive and well. When I told them of you there were many there who knew the name of Martin. One, an old squirrel named Barkjon, sends you a message." Martin leaped up, unable to constrain himself. "Barkjon, old Barkjon! He's Felldoh's father. What did he tell you, Boldred?"

"He told me that his son has gone alone to face Badrang. Every able-bodied creature in the camp was armed, and they are planning to go to Felldoh's rescue—that is, if he still lives. Either way they will attack the fortress called Marshank, where the evil one rules with his horde of vermin."

Martin's eyes shone with the desire to be in the midst of battle. "The creatures in this camp on the cliffs, are they a great army?"

"Alas, no." Boldred shook her head. "I have seen the comings and goings at Marshank before. Badrang's horde is far too vast to be opposed. The creatures at the camp are brave, but pitifully few compared to the horde."

"I must go now!" Martin jumped down from the sycamore trunk.

Boldred nodded. "The old squirrel Barkjon is a shrewd beast, he said that you would act thus, and here is his message to you. Tell Martin if he is coming to travel with all speed and bring plenty of help!"

Aryah looked at Boldred anxiously. "Did you see my son Brome? Did you speak to him?"

Boldred spread her wings wide. "There was no time, I had many things to do. The hare Ballaw assured me that Brome was lively as a grasshopper and fit as a flea. The badger Rowanoak confirmed this. She seemed like a wise and sensible creature. Badgers usually are."

Aryah climbed down from the sycamore and took Martin's paw. "Bring my son back to me, please, Martin. I beg you!"

Rose leaped down to join Martin and her mother. "We will Mama, don't worry."

"Rose, how can you go?" Urran Voh gazed sternly at his daughter. "Is it not enough that we have Brome caught up in a war far from home!"

Rose faced her father resolutely. "I must go. Martin and I are the only ones who would stand a chance of bringing Brome back to Noonvale."

"Hurr, you'm not leavin' us'ns yurr, mizzy!" Pallum and Grumm joined paws with Martin and Rose.

Another little paw sneaked in to clasp theirs. "Hurr, say 'ee wurd an' Bungo's with you'm!"

Grumm ruffled the dark velvety head of the infant. "Gurr, you'm gotter stay yurr an' chop up'ee gurt tree. Oi wants t' see et chopped oop small when us'ns coom back."

Martin looked at Urran Voh, who nodded. Then he

raised his voice so that all could hear. "Is anybeast with us? You heard Boldred, we need plenty of help!"

The otter quartette, several moles and a few hedge-hogs stood forward. Martin counted, sixteen in all including his three friends.

"I am sorry, Martin," Urran Voh said, his tone more kindly, "but we are not warriors, my creatures do not have any knowledge of battle. Many have families to care for. Those who have volunteered to go with you are few, but brave. None of them have ever used a weapon, yet they are prepared to go and help you with their very lives."

Martin bowed to his small army. "I thank you with all my heart."

Boldred tut-tutted slightly and shook her head. "I've always said that the trouble with young creatures is they never listen properly, especially hot-headed warriors. Did you not hear me tell Aryah that I never stopped to search for Brome because I had things to do?"

"Things, what things?" Martin looked nonplussed at the owl.

"Things that only a wise owl would think of, like getting an army together for you. But let's deal with first things first. We've got to find the shortest route to Marshank and get you there as quickly as possible. Now I don't wish to preen myself on this matter, but I am the foremost pathfinder, mapmaker and researcher of this whole country, from beyond here to the Eastern Sea. Find me a clear space, somebeast!"

The moles patted a bare patch of soil flat as Rose went off with Aryah and Urran Voh to gather provisions for the journey.

Boldred crooked a claw at Martin. "Come here, War-rior, and pay attention!"

Martin sat and watched, fascinated as the owl's skilful talons marked out the route.

"This is the Broadstream here. You came the long way round to Noonvale, probably because you were washed up down the far south coast. Marshank is further north, facing the Eastern Sea. There is a much simpler way back to the coast. I know this, and so does Starwort. At this moment he will probably have just arrived at a wide tributary two hours' journey from here, to the north of Noonvale. So the sooner you get going, the quicker you'll be able to join him and get under way."

Martin stood upright. "What happens then, Boldred?"

The owl blinked impatiently. "Leave that to me, I'm coming too!"

Rose and her parents had just finished putting together some food and drink in packs when Martin strode into the cottage. Rose took the small shrew sword from its peg behind the door and held it out to Martin.

"You gave this up freely, now I give it back to you."

The Warrior thrust the sword into his belt. "I'm ready!"

"Fur and Freedoooooooommm!"

The cart rattled and bumped, leaping off the ground as it struck humps and clumps on the clifftop. It roared forward with Ballaw and Keyla holding to its jolting bed as they waved the streaming banner aloft. Rowanoak pounded along. Sinew and muscle bunching and stretching, she towed the careering cart. The Fur and Freedom Fighters pushed as they pelted madly alongside.

Brome could not stop himself. At the sight of Felldoh going down fighting amid a welter of horde vermin, he dashed forward down the cliffside, sobbing and calling his friend's name aloud, "Felldoh! Oh Felldoh, I'm coming!"

But Felldoh did not hear his young companion. He lay with a calm smile on his face, surrounded by a score of slain hordebeasts who had died trying to defeat him.

Badrang rushed back to the fort, away from the carnage and the broken javelins, the memory burned into his beaten skull of the roaring, laughing squirrel who had died with a shattered piece of timber in each paw, still taking ferrets, rats and weasels with him as he went.

As Marshank's gates slammed shut, the cart sped by Brome. Scattering the last few venturesome horde members, it ground to a halt next to Felldoh's body.

Rowanoak leaped from the shafts as the first wave of arrows flew from the walltops. "Dig in, turn the cart on its side, get to cover quick!"

Ballaw assembled his throwers behind the cart. "Take your range, chaps, and drop those javelins in just over the walltop. You others, pick up any weapons you find lyin' about. That's the ticket! Slingers, get those stones from the cart. Look lively now, lads!"

Brome staggered up, tears streaming from him as he undid his healing bag and pulled out herbs and bandages. Barkjon sat with his son's head cradled in his lap, dry-eyed.

"He won't be needing those, young one. Save them for the living. My son has gone to the silent forest where he'll always be free."

Brome sat with Barkjon. The old squirrel wiped away the young mouse's tears. "It is good to grieve for a friend who has gone. He looks so happy and peaceful."

Brome shook his head. Placing a paw about Barkjon's shoulders, he said, "I've never seen anything like it; he was laughing aloud. It took a score and a half to get him down, and he still slew most of them. It was as if he knew his fate."

Barkjon nodded. "Never afraid, always a true warrior—that was Felldoh's way."

The side of the cart was thick with quivering arrows. Ballaw barked out a sharp command: "Up an' at 'em, javelins!"

The line of throwers leapt up, flung their weapons off and dropped back down.

Immediately Ballaw called to the slingers, "Quick as y' like, one volley of stones. Go!"

The slingers stood, threw and dropped back down.

Howls and screams greeted the wave of javelins that dropped in on the archers at the walltop. They stood up to retaliate, and met the volley of slingstones zinging up hard on the heels of the javelins.

Crosstooth grabbed Wetpaw and Fleabane. "Take fifty fighters apiece over the back wall, an' spread out left an' right, advance along the shore an' dig in. We'll have 'em cut off at both sides, with the fort in front of 'em an' the sea behind. They'll have to surrender, or die!"

Buckler saw the hordebeasts pouring out either side of Marshank. He found Rowanoak. "Lukkit, us'ns all 'ave to proteck 'ee flanks!"

Kastern, Gauchee, Trefoil and Celandine helped to shore up two long hillocks of sand either side of the cart. The slingers were split up and detailed to both sides, while the javelin throwers concentrated on the front facing the fortress.

Inside the fortress, Badrang lay on the longhouse table while Boggs and Growch dressed his wounds. The Tyrant had been beaten black and blue before his soldiers got to the rescue, and his head, face, shoulders and back were a welter of ugly lumps and long bruises. He arched his back painfully as Boggs treated the long javelin scratch.

"Haharr, matey, I thought you'd run into an army, but they tells me 'twere on'y one 'ard-nosed squirrel. Scorch me sails, but 'e did a right good job on yer. Haharrharrharr!"

Badrang glared at Clogg through puffy eyes. "Get out of my sight. You're bad luck to me, Clogg!"

Boggs applied a dock leaf poultice to Badrang's shoulder. "Stay still, Sire. 'Ere, 'old that in place."

Clogg did a little jig in the doorway. "Aye, you 'old still, yer mightiness, lest yer ugly 'ead drops off, haharr!"

Badrang made as if to rise and grab his sword. Clogg scuttled off, chuckling to himself, "I'll 'ave the last laugh yet. Now, where's the galley round 'ere? I might as well eat an' drink me fill, seein' as all the rest are too busy warrin' an' fightin' fer glory!"

Ballaw gave a sharp gasp. He plucked out the arrow sticking from his paw and snapped it. "Ruined me best eatin' and gesturin' paw. Rotters!"

Brome sat down behind the cart. Cleaning the wound, he applied a comfrey poultice and bound the paw with a clean linen strip.

"Good as new, eh wot!" Ballaw held it up, admiring the dressing. "I say, Brome old lad, you're gettin' to be a bit of a dab paw at this healin' lark!"

Wordlessly the young mouse crawled off to the next casualty.

Noon brought a lull in the fighting. The sun beat mercilessly down on the beach, and there was not even a welcome breeze. Behind Rowanoak's back, the sea shimmered, showing hardly a wave. The badger dusted sand from her paws as she gratefully accepted food from Keyla.

"It's only a mouthful of water and a scone. We don't know how long we'll be stuck here."

Trefoil nibbled at her scone. "Stuck is the right word, Keyla. We're boxed off on three sides, with the sea behind us if we fancy drowning ourselves."

Celandine sipped daintily at a scallop shell of water. "Drown ourselves? Ugh, how horrible! It'd ruin my tail!"

Kastern was making a bow with some springy wood and a cord. "Well it's either that or carry on fighting a horde about thirty times greater than us. I should think that'd ruin your tail in the long run, Miss Fussbudget."

Buckler came to sit by Kastern. "Hurr, wot be you'm a-maken a bow furr?"

"Well, there are so many arrows lying about and sticking out of everywhere, it seems a shame to waste them."

Rowanoak shook her head in admiration. "What an efficient trouper. Hey, Groot, see if you can make a few bows and help Kastern to use all these arrows messing the place up!"

Yarrow looked at Rowanoak strangely. "You Rambling Rosehip Players, you seem to make a joke of everything. Don't you realize we're in the middle of a battle, fighting for our lives?"

Ballaw patted his head with a bandaged paw. "What d'you want us to do then, laddie buck? Break down an' weep? Make the best of the situation, m' boy. Smile!"

The cart shook under a rattle of arrows, several piercing the wood by half a shaft-length.

"Ah well, back to work, wot wot?" Yarrow yawned, fitting a stone to his sling.

Ballaw launched a javelin and ducked low. "Cheeky blighter! Catches on fast, though."

Badrang was up and about, looking much the worse for wear but still bad-tempered and active.

"Crosstooth, tell the horde to hold back their weapons a bit. I want to parley with that lot on the shore."

Archers and slingers stopped. Badrang's jaws were aching from Felldoh's blows, so he got a rat called Nipwort, who possessed a high squeaky voice, to call out his message.

Nipwort funnelled both paws around his mouth and shouted, "Parley! Cease fire, we want a parley!"

"Then parley away, pipsqueak. What do you want?" Rowanoak's readily identifiable roar came back at him.

"My master, Lord Badrang, can keep you pinned down there and slay you at his leisure. If you surrender you will not be killed!"

This time it was Ballaw who answered. "Tell me my good chap, what happens to us after we surrender?"

"That will be for Lord Badrang to decide!"

Ballaw's head popped up over the cart. "Blinkin' nerve o' the rascal! Listen, rustyhinge, you tell old Badtrousers that the Commander-in-Chief of the Fur and Freedom Fighters said that he can go an' boil his scurvy head, wot!"

The reply was accompanied by a healthy hail of slingstones, one of which knocked Nipwort senseless. Badrang crouched beneath the parapet, massaging the numbness from his paws. "Get a fire going, use flaming arrows on that cart. We'll burn them out into the open!"

38

Guided by Boldred, Martin and his party made it in good time to the Broadstream inlet. They were greeted by Starwort's cheery cry as they came in sight of the water.

"Ahoy, mates, come on aboard!"

The big otter boat *Waterlily* was packed with tough-looking otters, and in tow she had a flat-bottomed barge, also filled to the gunwales with more otters. They made room for Martin and his contingent.

Starwort grinned and held up a thonged sling. "Mainly uses these for sport an' fishin', but we've all got one. Miss Rose, good to see yer pretty face again. Still keepin' this Warrior of yours in check, I 'ope. Pallum an' Grumm, well, shake me rudder yer lookin' plump an' fitter'n ever!"

A flotilla of shrew canoes came racing round the bend and hit the bank with a loud damp thud. Starwort winked at Boldred. "Ho, look out, 'ere comes trouble on the tide!"

Boldred blinked at the teeming arguing masses of shrews, yelling and waving their swords angrily. "What are they doing here?"

Starwort flexed his powerful paws. "I thought we might need extra 'elp, so I told 'em they weren't allowed to follow us an' I forbid them to take part in any fight. You know the shrews, mate—never do as they're told." The otter waved at his deck crew. "Cast off for'ard, cast off aft, cast off midships. Away we go! You shrews, stop 'ere, you ain't comin', see!"

Rose and Pallum chuckled at Starwort's ruse as a veritable armada of craft pulled out into the stream, with *Waterlily* in the vanguard.

Martin stood in the bows of the otter boat as if willing it to travel faster. Worry etched itself across his brow. Boldred perched on the for'ard rail. "Rest, Martin. Nothing you can do will make the river flow swifter."

Grim-jawed, the young mouse pawed his sword hilt as he paced back and forth, heedless of the glorious sunset on the water. "I'll never forgive myself if we're too late. Travelling to Noonvale was a mistake, I should have stayed on the coast and sought Brome out, Felldoh too. Things might have been different."

Boldred folded her wings, shifting from claw to claw.

"Aye, you could have all been slain, then what help would you be? This way you are returning to Marshank with an army at your back. Many more are coming to aid your cause. I have made sure of that."

Martin watched the stream slip by, gurgling and eddying. "Forgive me, friend. I must seem very ungrateful after all you have done to help."

"It is natural to worry when friends are in danger, Martin. Don't think about what you could have done, concentrate on what you plan to do; it is more useful." Boldred spread her wings, preparing for flight. "I must leave you for a while now. There are more things that I have to do. I'll see you at Marshank, Warrior mouse. Good seasons and fair winds go with us both."

Martin watched his feathered friend winging off downstream into the evening treetops, silhouetted against a sky of lilac and gold.

"Move yer stern a touch, matey, and let me get at the

drum!" Starwort's wife Marigold opened a locker and rolled out a big flat drum. She placed it on a coil of rope and began whacking it slowly with her rudderlike tail. The deep boom cut through the twilight stillness as Rose came to join Martin in the bows. They both looked on perplexed, until Marigold explained, "Just drummin' up a little more 'elp. My Starwort always says that willin' paws are welcome ones."

A rolling drum answered Marigold's summons. Rose pointed upstream. "Look!"

Waiting to join them was a sprawling flat raft with a rickety shed built at its centre. Lines of otters and burly hedgehogs stood by their long poles, waiting to join the fleet.

Starwort sprang to the bowsprit, waving at the newcomers. "Yoho, Gulba, me ole mucker, come to join in the fun?"

The biggest of the hedgehogs was a female. Colored tassels hung from her headspikes and she brandished a formidable warclub studded with chunks of crystal.

"Yoho, Starwort. Yore gittin' fat an' sleek these days. Wot's Marigold bin feedin' ye on?"

Starwort grinned mischievously as he ducked a swipe from his wife. "Hard words an' hotroot when she's not bullyin' the babies!"

Gulba's husband Trung was small and fat. He emerged from the shack eating a watershrimp pastie and twirling a thong with two stones clacking on its split end. "Who are we fightin' an' when do we get at 'em, Marigold?"

Martin came alert as he listened to the information.

"The vermin in the big place by Eastern Sea. With a followin' breeze an' no stream blockages, we should get there by noon on the morrow. Are you game?"

The raft pushed off as they passed, bumping several shrew longboats and following the *Waterlily*'s wakeswirl.

Gulba leaned on her warclub and scowled. "We're with you. 'Tis only a matter o' time afore that scummy stoat takes over the whole coast an' starts foragin' inland for slaves. I say we put a stop to him smartlike!"

Throughout the night Martin's piecemeal slumbers were broken as the drums sounded and more woodland tribes joined the swelling ranks. Rose slept through it all. Waking at dawn light, she was amazed and delighted to see the stream packed with boats and craft of all shapes, each one low in the water with creatures ready to fight at their side. Along the banks she could see others, squirrels and mice, keeping pace with the vessels at a swift lope. Starwort dashed past her and leaped up on the rail. Steadying himself on a rope, he put a paw to his brow, scanning the mist-wreathed waters ahead.

"Steady on, backwater buckoes, the outlet's in sight!"

Martin left off opening a food pack. "What's the outlet?"

Suddenly the *Waterlily* picked up speed as if she were being sucked along on the current, and a rushing noise became audible.

Starwort winked at Martin and Rose. "Best 'old tight, the outlet's where we join the main Broadstream again. Nothin' t' worry about, it's only rapids."

The whole craft gave a lurch, and it began to buck and leap. Timbers groaned crazily as Marigold shouted forward. "Starwort, get yer hide aft an' do somethin' useful. I can't manage this tiller single-pawed!"

There was no time for more talk. Rose hung grimly on to Martin. Winding a rigging rope about his paws, the young mouse took a deep breath as the otter boat tilted into the rapids. A huge rainbow appeared through the mist of boiling spray as water engulfed everybeast aboard, and the craft stood almost on its end as it flew helter-skelter down the sickening drop. Ragged rocks rushed by. Grumm opened his mouth to yell, but it was filled with water. He clung to Pallum, ignoring his friend's spikes. The world seemed to turn upside down for several perilous moments, the drum rat-tatting as rapid water beat at it.

Starwort and Marigold laughed with wild exuberance as they fought the swivelling tiller. Together they roared above the mêlée, "Down weeeeeee gooooooooo!"

With a loud flat splash, the *Waterlily* landed in the Broadstream. Starwort was immediately up on the stern, bawling orders. "Ship out, ship out, mates! Pull 'er clear, make fast that raft an' get 'er in midstream!"

The otter crew worked furiously as other craft dropped in behind them. Two shrew longboats collided in midair and overturned. Gulba and her husband Trung, the two hedgehogs who steered the ramshackle craft, together with their otter friends managed to make a perfect flat landing in an immense cascade of water. The hut at the center of the big raft half disintegrated under the impact, but Gulba paid it no heed. She was yelling sternly at the shrews.

"Hoi, shrewheads, don't ye know the meanin' of the order to backwater. Yore mad as scorched frogs, you lot!"

As if to prove her point, two shrew boats flew overhead, packed with shouting and arguing creatures. They sailed right over the raft. Gulba ducked as they flew by in midair.

Splash! Crash!

Both boats hit the water, miraculously staying upright. A shrew stood up, waving his sword at the hedgehog. "Tend to yer own raft, spikedog. We know what we're doin'!"

As boats were righted and soaking creatures hauled from the water, the fleet gradually got itself back on to an even keel.

Rose shook Starwort and his wife by their paws gratefully. "Oh, you were so skillful, both of you, the way you took command and knew just what to do, steering this great boat right the way down those dangerous

338

rapids. Only two creatures such as yourselves would know how to navigate that terrible drop in safety . . ."

Marigold bobbed a comical curtsy. "Well, thankee now, pretty one. That was the first time we've ever been down those rapids!"

Bump! Grumm fainted.

Swifts darted and wheeled over the water in brilliant morning sunlight as it burned the mists away. Martin finished breakfasting and went to stand up in the bows next to Starwort. The sturdy otter leaned confidentially close. "Listen, matey, while I tells yer three words you've wanted to 'ear . . . Next stop Marshank!"

A tremor ran through the Warrior's body. He clasped the sword handle tight, his eyes shining like flints in firelight.

"I'm coming, Badrang!"

39

The cart was a charred, smoking thing, but it still stood. All night the fighting had been furious, with no let-up.

Fur and Freedom Fighters had battled against flaming shafts with their bare paws and sand. Four lay dead and three wounded. Smoke-grimed and bleary-eyed, they had plucked burning arrows from the wood, strung them on their bows and returned them to stick blazing in the gates of Marshank. The javelin supply was depleted, one shaft being retained for each creature in the event that paw-to-paw combat would be their final stand. There were still plenty of rocks to sling, Keyla and Tullgrew taking charge of the slingers while Ballaw managed a frugal breakfast. The hare sat wearily against one of the sandbanks that had been shorn up either side of the cart, Rowanoak slumped beside him. Both were singed and smoke-grimed.

Rowanoak drank half her water, passing the rest on to Brome, who distributed it among the wounded. The badger wiped a sandy paw across her scorched muzzle. "Well, Ballaw De Quincewold, what's to report?"

The irrepressible hare wiped dust from his half-scone ration and looked up at the sky. "Report? Er, nothin' much really, except that it looks like being another nice sunny day, wot!"

A flaming arrow extinguished itself in the sand close by Rowanoak. She tossed it on to a pile of other shafts waiting to be shot. "A nice day indeed. D'you think we'll be around to see the sunset?" Without waiting for an answer, she continued, "I wonder if that owl—Boldred, wasn't it—I wonder if she ever managed to get through to this Martin the Warrior creature."

Ballaw picked dried blood from a wound on his narrow chest. "Doesn't look like it, does it? No, old Rowan me badger oak, I think the stage is all ours and it'll be our duty to give the best performance we can before the curtain falls for the last time."

Groot plucked a pawful of arrows from the sand. Tossing them behind the smouldering cart, he took his bow from Buckler. Together they notched up their shafts, nodding to each other.

"Watch the cart, it's roasting hot. Right, fire!"

Swiftly they stood and released the taut bowstrings, throwing themselves flat immediately. A hail of arrows hit the cart and the surrounding sand in reply. Groot scratched a mark in the sand next to a line of others.

"Got one, big weasel type wearin' a red jerkin!"

Buckler shook his head in disappointment. "Oi been arfter that vurmint all noight moiself, hurr!"

They notched up another two arrows. "At least the little ones'll be safe with Geum and Purslane," Groot sniffed. "Maybe they'll take off south and find some place where they can live in peace. Pity, I would've liked to see my little Fuffle grow up and take care of his mother when she's an old un."

Buckler wrinkled his homely face into a smile. "Ho urr, he'm be a right liddle roguer, that babe o' thoin. Doant you'm give oop 'ope, Groot. We'm bain't finished yet, burr no!"

Badrang sat in the courtyard. Shaded by the wall, it was the only place where missiles could not fall. He took a

341

leisurely breakfast of smoked herrings and dandelion water.

Boggs came down from the walltop and saluted with his bow. "That cart's still there, Lord, though it can't be much more than splinters an' ash by now. A good breeze'd blow it over."

The Tyrant delicately plucked a fish scale from his upper lip. "Keep those archers firing until I tell you to stop. Have we lost many through the night?"

"Twelve, maybe thirteen, Sire. There was quite a few wounded tryin' to put the fire out on the gates."

Badrang nodded thoughtfully and beckoned to a passing ferret. "You there, Stumptooth. Get the rest of the horde on their paws. Issue the long pikes and spears, have them stand by."

Boggs brightened up a little. "Are you goin' to start the charge, Lord?"

Badrang poured a beaker of dandelion water and passed it to Boggs. "Not yet. Drink that. It's cool, isn't it? Also we've got plenty of food, solid walls around us and plenty of shade. Those wretches out there have only sun, sand, a few drops of water and hardly any food by now. They've not been able to sleep all night, while we've had archers relieving each other to take a rest. I think I'll leave it a bit yet, keep them in suspense, make them suffer. Who knows, we might yet save a good number of slaves. Go and ask them to surrender again."

Tramun Clogg was digging graves in the soft ground near the corner of the wall. He leaned on his spade and eyed Badrang. "You never could go fer the clean kill, could yer, matey? Ho no, you likes pullin' the wings off butterflies an' watchin' them crawl round 'elpless, as I recall. Though maybe yore worried that if yer did charge now, they'd put up a good fight."

Badrang held the dandelion water out to Clogg. As the corsair reached for it, he upended the jug, pouring it out on the ground. "You're right, of course, Clogg. That's why I like to keep you as a slave—it reminds me that once you tried to be my equal, or even my better, and now you have to take orders from the lowliest of my creatures. You are lower than a worm, Tramun Clogg!"

The corsair dabbed his paw in the wet sand and sucked it. "Haharr, I never was 'igh an' mighty like you, Badrang. I'll just go back to buryin' yer dead an' wait fer you to turn up as a customer."

With his head wound in a bandage, Nipwort shrilled the message across to the creatures barricaded behind the sandbanks on either side of the burned-out cart.

"My Lord Badrang is still merciful, he gives you a second chance to surrender and keep your lives. What is your answer?"

"Tell old Badthingy it is beneath our dignity to surrender to scum!" Ballaw's voice came back insolently clear, this time accompanied by many others.

"Stinky, slimy scum!"

"Gutless, wet-nosed crook-tailed scum!"

"Yurr, gurt fat-bottomed vurmint scummer!"

Nipwort's high-pitched squeak cut across the insults. "Is that the answer I must take to my Lord Badrang?"

A good-sized, well-placed slingstone from Rowanoak knocked the rat backwards from the walltop to the courtyard.

"Tell him he can chew on that for free!"

Badrang had heard the exchange. He rolled the stunned form of Nipwort over with a kick. "Boggs, redouble the archers on the walltop and continue without halting. I'll make those fools think it's raining arrows!"

Ballaw helped to shore up the banks, and Rowanoak piled sand against the flimsy burnt cart. Brome kept his head down as he bandaged Keyla's injured tail under a pelting hail of arrows.

The young otter gritted his teeth, forcing a tight smile

as he gasped through a wave of pain, "D'you think it's somethin' we've said that's offended him?"

Brome ducked an arrow and continued with Keyla's dressing. "Brave words. Slingstones and arrows is all we've got left, that's the last of my herbs and bandages."

At midday the arrows ceased. There followed a lull. Ballaw went around doling out the last of the food and water. Groot nodded to the trenched ranks on the south-side. "Any chance we could charge them and break through? We could make it to the cliffs if we could."

Rowanoak patted his head lightly. "No chance at all. See, they're all still standing ready on the walltop. We'd be cut down before we got halfway."

Groot shrugged. "Just a thought."

Ballaw took Rowanoak to one side, out of the hearing of the others. "This silence, I don't like it one bit!"

Rowanoak watched the still fortress and nodded. "They're definitely planning something. A charge, d'you think?"

Ballaw picked up a javelin. "Right, that's exactly my thoughts, old thing. Issue the javelins!"

Each creature took a javelin in silence, knowing what it meant. Ballaw dusted himself down and stood to attention. "Listen up now, chaps. I'm not given to makin' jolly great speeches an' all that—"

"Oh you dreadful old scene-stealer," Celandine tittered. "You've never made a short one in your life!"

The hare glared at her as Rowanoak took over from him.

"All that can be said has been said. I'm sure you know what I mean, but let me add this. For myself, it has been a pleasure to know you all and to serve with you in this great battle. May the seasons remember us kindly and what we tried to do here."

There was an embarrassed silence, then Brome held out his paw. "Give me a javelin too. I will try to be a warrior like Felldoh!"

A wild yell arose from the fortress as Marshank's gates swung open and the horde poured forth fully armed, racing across the sands towards the beleaguered little group standing behind the ruined cart.

40

Martin drew his sword and leaped into the shallows. Splashing ashore, he watched the other boats empty out as he called to Starwort, "Which way to Marshank?"

The draught from Boldred's wings nearly knocked Martin over as the owl landed at his side. "Over that hill. Follow me!"

Rose saw Martin stop at the hilltop. She ran to catch up with him, Grumm and Pallum following close behind her. "Martin, wait for us!"

When they reached him, the young mouse stood staring open-mouthed at the scene below. Boldred ambled up, smiling. "Now you have a horde too!"

Queen Amballa stood at the head of her mighty army of pigmy shrews, and behind them the Warden of Marshwood Hill could be seen stalking among the crowds of Gawtrybe squirrels as they waved their axes eagerly, wanting to play a new game. Otters, hedgehogs, mice, squirrels, moles and vast numbers of shrews stood surrounding the hill.

From his vantage point on the hilltop, Martin looked to his left. There in the distance he could see the north-side wall of Marshank. Rose stared at Martin; it was as if she were looking at a strange creature. He was still as a rock, the blood rising behind his eyes as his paw

346

whitened with the furious grip he had on his sword handle. The blade rose above his head and fell in a straight line, pointing at Badrang's hated fortress. The horde went silent, staring up at the Warrior mouse, waiting on the word which rolled from his lips like steel striking stone.

"*Chaaaarge!!!*"

They went in a rush like a giant tidal wave covering the land, but none was more fleet of paw than the mouse Martin. He was out in front, teeth bared, sword still pointing as he tore through dune and foothill. Rose was swept along in the midst of the howling horde with Pallum and Grumm. Now and then, through the forest of spears, lances and swords, she could see him, a lone figure ahead of the rest. Her heart went out to him as she remembered her first sight of him, bound between two posts, left to die on Marshank's walls, and recalled the words he had shouted into the stormy night. Now she heard those words as in a dream:

"I am a warrior! Martin son of Luke! I will live, I will not give in and die up here! Do you hear me, Badrang? I will live to take back my father's sword and slay you one day! Badraaaaaang!"

Javelins stuck in the sand at their sides, the archers knelt and drew back their bowstrings full stretch. Ballaw strode the line, holding up his paw. Bowstrings trembled with the tension as the screaming horde dashed across the shore in a mass, bound straight at them.

"Wait for it, chaps. Steady on, wait'll you see the scum on their snouts. . . . Now!"

The hail of arrows struck, hordebeasts fell and were trampled underpaw by those behind, but the horde kept coming.

"Load and throw!" Rowanoak cried to her line of slingers as the archers dropped back.

The stones hit true, but not well enough to halt the relentless charge. Spears from the horde ranks cut down several of the Fur and Freedom Fighters. They backed up, retreating towards the sea as the horde pressed forward.

Badrang stood on the walltop, unable to contain a thin smile of triumph as he watched the little army being battered remorselessly back to the Eastern Sea. He turned to Boggs. "Wait and see, we'll get a few slaves out of this yet—those that aren't drowned."

Boggs looked up at the sky. "Strange, I thought I could hear thunder."

Badrang also looked up. "Fool, how could you hear thunder when there's not a cloud in the sky!"

Boggs cupped paws around both his ears. "I'm sure it's thunder, Sire. Comin' from over there . . ." Speechless with terror, he pointed at the thundering horde breasting a low hill to the north, heading directly for them.

Even though he was practically numb with shock, Badrang found himself automatically giving out orders. "Call the horde back, Nipwort. Boggs, get the archers on to the north wall. I'll hold the gates open until they're back in!"

Yarrow tripped and fell in the shallows. The front runners were in the water, grappling with Fur and Freedom Fighters, when Crosstooth began shouting, "Retreat! Retreat! Back to Marshank on the double! There's a horde headed to attack the fort. Hurry!"

Ballaw sat down hard in the shallows and blew water from his nose. "Hold up, where are they bally well goin'? Great seasons, relief's arrived! Hurrah! It's a horde! A flood! A mob! A bloomin' tidal wave of warbeasts attackin' the fort!"

Ballaw's fighters let out a loud cheer of delight, leaping about in the shallows like mad creatures.

The horde were streaming back to the fortress, leaving a bare dozen fighting in the sea. Swift javelin thrusts and throws found their way around pikes and spears, laying the hordebeasts low. Brome found himself standing, javelin poised, over a searat who lay wounded in the surf. He was trying to force himself to stab and slay the foebeast when the rat whined out pleadingly, "It's me, matey, Wulpp. Don't kill me!"

Brome gasped. It was Wulpp, the searat whose injured paw he had treated when, disguised as a corsair, he had gained entry to Marshank. Brome thrust the javelin into the sea close to Wulpp's neck. Leaning down, he muttered to the terrified rat, "Lie still. When we've gone, take off south down the beach. I never want to see you again. Good luck!"

Turning, Brome picked up a spear and followed the triumphantly shouting fighters who were running towards Marshank.

Now the battle was joined! Horde fought horde that day by the Eastern Sea. Martin's army flooded around Marshank, surrounding its walls on all four sides. Slingstones, javelins, arrows and spears were loosed up at the walltops as roaring warcries rent the air.

"Fur and Freeeedoooooom!"

"Broadstream for eveeeeer!"

"Amballa Amballa! Kill kill kill!"

"Maaaartiiiiin!"

Badrang was everywhere at once, waving his sword as he shouted encouragement to his fighters massed thick on the high walls. "Crosstooth, more archers at the front. See the gates are defended! Boggs, tell those spears to stand ready on the northside. Slash any ropes and grapnels—don't let them over! Frogbit, get boulders and rocks to the back wall. Crush them! Bluehide, take the south wall. Use long spears and pikes—throw fire down on them!"

Badrang was an experienced battler. He found his confidence and shrewdness returning as the horde looked to him as their leader. Grabbing a passing ferret, he rapped out more orders.

"Stumptooth, take thirty wounded, four groups of five

to supply the walls with arrows, spears and slingstones. Get the other ten to carry the big fishnets to the walltops and drop them over on any large groups. That'll slow 'em up. Come on, you fighters and hordebeasts, this is our chance to rule the whole country. Slaves, land, plunder, we'll have it all!"

Ignoring his sore and bandaged paws, the Tyrant snatched a spear from a searat, hurled it coolly and slew a shrew who was trying to climb the gates. "See, it's easy. They die like other creatures. We'll make the sands run red before nightfall!"

Arrows zipped down from the walltops in dark clouds like angry wasps, tearing into the packed ranks that charged Marshank. Slingstones whirred like flights of small birds, clanging on armour and blade alike in their upward flight.

Rose found Boldred and the Warden on a hillock out of weapon range. The two great birds stood waiting their chance. Boldred greeted the mousemaid.

"We'd be shot out of the air in the middle of that lot. When it gets dark and the pace slackens, my friend and I will be able to fly in."

Rose looked out over the mêlée of battle. "Where's Martin? I lost sight of him in the charge."

The grey heron pointed his beak towards the front gates. "He is over there with otters and hedgehogs. They have a piece of timber to batter the gates, but it is not big enough."

Ballaw came panting up with the remnants of his gallant force. Weary and battle-scarred, the brave hare slumped down in the sand. "Phew, what a day, chaps! Rowanoak and m'self pulled our little army out for a breather, wot. Let those other creatures have a crack at the foe, they're a lot fresher than my gang!"

Rowanoak sat with the owl and the heron, shaking her head. "You arrived just in time to save us from being slaughtered on the tideline; thank you. But your charge has been too furious. I am not a warrior or a commander, but I can see that they will never breach those walls by throwing themselves at them."

The owl blinked as she watched the assault on the fortress. "You are right, Rowanoak. Martin seems to be the only one who has any kind of plan, but he is unaware of others when his warrior blood is roused. We need a plan of attack. Badrang is not stupid, he has the advantage of the walls and is using them well. Other creatures less shrewd might have been panicked by our charge; not him, though. He is a cool one in a pinch."

Ballaw brightened up. "That's it, a plan. Capital! What d'you suggest, marm?"

41

Martin let go of the shattered remnants of the inadequate chunk of driftwood he and his allies had been using as a battering ram. Drawing his sword, he attacked the gates in a wild rage.

Starwort and Gulba ducked into the shelter of the gates as missiles rained down from above. They tried to restrain Martin. "It's no use, mate, the gates are too strong. Come away!"

Martin hacked and hammered at the stout timbers, oblivious to everything about him. Rose pressed through the chaos, sided by Grumm and Pallum. They forced a way through to the gate. Martin halted at the sight of her, deflecting a broken spear haft with his short sword. "Rose, get out of here. It's too dangerous!"

She picked up the sharp pointed end of the spear boldly. "Not without you, Martin. Come with us, you are needed. Starwort, Gulba, you too. We need a proper battle plan, too many creatures are being killed needlessly. We won't get inside Marshank by charging and milling about willy-nilly. Come!"

It had turned noon when otter drums sounded over the fray. The attackers broke off their charging and retreated back to the sands around the low dune.

Crosstooth shook his spear in the air jubilantly. "Yah, they've turned tail and run!"

Badrang knew better. He had seen Ballaw's fighters contacting the leaders—it was a calculated retreat. However, the Tyrant said nothing of this. Imitating Crosstooth, he waved his sword. "See, I told you it was easy. Look at them, running like frightened babies now that they've had a taste of real fighting from warriors like us, eh lads!"

Gesturing and prancing on the walltops, the horde took up his cry. "Haha, had enough, have you? Cowards!"

"Come back and fight me, I only slew ten!"

"Ten? I slew two score and I'd have got more of 'em if they hadn't scurried off in a fright!"

Tramun Clogg left off his grave digging and clambered to the walltop. He sized the situation up immediately. "Burn me clogs, buckoes. Yore a bunch of strawheads iffen you think those fighters are runnin' away. I'd save me breath fer more action iffen I was you lot!"

Whock!

Badrang dealt Clogg a ferocious blow across his head with a long pike he had snatched from Gruzzle. The corsair fell senseless in a heap. Badrang kicked him from the walltop, and Clogg's unconscious form fell with a thump on to a heap of sand he had excavated. The Tyrant stoat leaned on the pike, dismissing his former partner. "Don't listen to that old fool, his brains are all in his clogs. Crosstooth, see that everybeast has extra rations. Stay awake, lads. Maybe they'll get brave enough to give it another try. I certainly hope so, eh?"

This announcement was greeted with raucous cheers.

While the wounded were treated by Rose and Brome, food was divided up among the groups of creatures seated around the low hillock. Martin sat with the Council of Chieftains as they laid war plans. Rowanoak and

Boldred were rocks of good sense, rejecting the wild schemes of hot-headed beasts, considering the suggestions of cooler and wiser creatures.

Queen Amballa had several of her pigmy shrews drag a large square fishing net to the hill. It was made of strong woven kelp. "See, Martinmouse, wallbeast throwthis, snarl us up plentygood!"

A Gawtrybe squirrel laughed scornfully. "Hehee, good game. They di'n't catch squirrels, Gawtrybe's too fast for nets. Heehee!"

Martin sat up alert, the light of idea dawning in his eyes. "That's it! We go in over the walls on two sides when night falls, and use the nets one side, say on the north, while the squirrels take the south wall!"

Starwort's wife Marigold put down the pitcher she had been drinking from. "An' what's Badrang's crew goin' to be doin' while all this goes on, 'cos they won't be sleepin' or pickin' their claws."

Martin pointed across to where the old Rambling Rosehip troupe's fire-charred cart lay half buried in the sand. "Will the wheels on that thing still turn?"

Ballaw shrugged. "What d'you think, Buckler old lad?"

The mole gazed at it for a while before giving his verdict. "Ho urr, 'twere a gudd ole cart that'n. Oi wager oi'll get 'er goin' tho' et woant go furr, Marthen."

The Warrior mouse shook Buckler by the paw. "It won't have to go far, friend. Only from here to those gates, loaded with burning grass and wood, just to create a diversion!"

Boldred blinked excitedly. "It could work! Hold back the attack until before dawn; that's when they'll least expect it. The Warden and I will fly the net and drop it over the north wall. Who'll be going over there, Martin?"

"Queen Amballa with her warriors and the big hedgehogs."

Trung thumped his loaded thong weapon gleefully into the sand, grinning at his wife as she nursed her immense warclub. "Y'hear that, me dearie? We'll go over paw in paw!"

"The Gawtrybe squirrels will help the otters to scale the south wall," Martin continued.

Starwort winked at a nearby squirrel. "Eat plenty, mate, an get yer stren'th up. I'm no featherweight."

Martin eyed the cart grimly. "I'll be in charge of that. All our hopes hang on it. Right, any more suggestions?"

Grumm held up a digging paw. "Aye, Marthen, thurr be other molers yurr. Us'ns tunnel round 'ee back wall, gurt woid 'ole, given everybeast a chance to get insoides."

Old Barkjon stood up, dusting himself off slowly. "I'll go with Buckler and the others to fix the cart up, then I'll bury Felldoh."

Martin put his paw about the old squirrel's shoulders. "We'll come with you, Rose, Pallum, Brome, Grumm and myself. We all started out together, so we'd like to help put our friend to rest."

The Rambling Rosehip Players voted to accompany Barkjon too, all wanting to pay their last respects to their friend.

Fleabane laughed against the walltop. "Boggs was right, mate, I can see them tryin' to fix up that burnt cart. Betcha they'll be gone by mornin'."

Rotnose peered out into the gathering evening. "Well, I won't be sorry to see the back o' them. They fought like madbeasts, an' as fer that big squirrel, Fellow or whatever 'e was called, that one was a real madbeast. I never seen nothin' like it!"

Fleabane nodded. "Aye, well 'e won't do no more slayin'. They buried 'im where 'e fell. I never want t' be within a league of a warrior like 'im fer the rest o' me days!"

Badrang passed by them as he inspected the walltop troops. "Cut the gossip and keep your eyes peeled. No sleeping while you stand at stations."

When he had passed by, Fleabane muttered to Rotnose, "That stoat's gettin' to be a right ole worrywart, mate. Take it from me, they ain't comin' back fer more of what we give 'em t'day."

Rotnose propped his chin on a battlement. "Y'right there, matey. Listen, we only got a few hours shuteye last night an' we been fightin' all day. Now I'm gonna take a liddle snooze. You keep watch then you can 'ave second nap."

Badrang descended from the walls and went in company with some of his Captains to take supper in the longhouse. Boggs rubbed his paws together in anticipation as he walked with them. "I'd give me whiskers fer a good beaker of kelp beer!"

A cracked voice came out of the shadows. "Badrang is the great Evil One, mates, leadin' you all to yer doom. Steer clear of 'im. Foller me an' dig graves—deadbeasts can't 'arm yer!"

Boggs shuddered. "Sounds like Clogg, though I don't see 'im."

Crosstooth laughed harshly. "Ole Clogg isn't right in the brainbox no more. May'ap it was that crack you give 'im with the pike, Sire. The daft ole beast's been goin' about like that since 'e came to, rantin' an' ravin'."

Clogg's crazy laugh seemed to come from nowhere. "Haharrharrharr! Stay with Badrang the Evil One an' yore all dead meat. Come an' dig nice graves with me, mates!"

Badrang paused with his paw on the longhouse door. Staring out into the gathering gloom he called aloud, "Stay clear of me, you crazy old coot, or I'll let daylight through your hide, d'you hear me?"

"Haharrharr, ye can't see me 'cos I'm invisible. I've got a nice dark hole waitin' for ye, Evil One!"

The Captains hurried inside. As Badrang slammed the door, the upturned wheelbarrow over a freshly dug grave moved. Clogg peered out from under it.

"I'm arf a stoat an' arf a mole,
An' I'll bury youse all in a nice deep 'ole,
Down, down where it's still an' cold,
An' y'never live to get old!"

Every fighter had been fed. No fires glowed in the still summer night. It was warm and heavy. Martin sat awake with Rose as the camp lay in slumber. The mousemaid stared up at the stars which twinkled with pale fires in the midnight heavens.

"Strange isn't it, Martin, the same stars that shine on this terrible place with all its death and war, those same stars are shining over Noonvale, where all is at peace and war has never been. What are you thinking of, Warrior?"

Martin smiled, nodding at the sight of Grumm, his small fat stomach rising and falling gently. "I wasn't thinking of anything, Rose, I was just watching Grumm, flat out and snoozing with his ladle clutched in both paws."

The mousemaid relieved the sleeping mole of his ladle, placing it close to his side where he would find it on waking. "He's the most friendly and loyal mole anybeast could wish to know. Grumm has always looked out for me, ever since I was a tiny mousebabe in Noonvale. When we go back there you'll make lots of friends among our moles—you're a hero to them."

"Me, a hero? What for?" Martin laughed softly.

"For bringing down that great dead sycamore. They've been at it for seasons, on and off, without much success. Then you came along and in a single day it was uprooted and fallen."

The young mouse passed her a cloak Trung had given him. "You look tired, Rose. Better get some rest. Go on. I'm not sleepy, I'll sit here close by."

Rose draped the cloak lightly about her, and she was soon asleep. Martin sat up, thinking of many things as he felt the night hours slip slowly by.

42

Ballaw was wakened by a shake from Martin. It was still dark, though the night was on the wane.

"Come on, it's time!"

The camp was stirring quietly into life. Grumm had taken off with Pallum and Rose and a lot of others; they travelled in a wide semi-circle, round to the back walls of Marshank. Boldred and the Warden stood ready, the big kelp net clutched tight between them. Queen Amballa and her pigmy shrews grouped with the big hedgehogs on one side, while Starwort and his otters mingled with the Gawtrybe squirrels. Martin, Ballaw and Rowanoak inspected the cart. It was flimsy in the extreme and wobbly on its wheels, piled high with grass, driftwood and brush.

Buckler patted it fondly. "Hurr, she'll do a gurt last run, oi'll stake moi name on et."

Amballa raised her paw to Gulba and their joint forces moved off. Starwort gave the squirrels a stern nod to set them on their way. Now there were only fifty archers under Martin's command left in camp. At his signal, Buckler set flint to tinder and Rowanoak braced herself in the fire-blackened shafts.

"Nearly curtain time, chaps," Ballaw whispered. "Here we go!"

Gruzzle was dreaming. In his dream he was back on board his old ship. Someone had lit a fire on the deck and creatures were dancing around it shouting. The searat felt drowsily happy. He wanted to join in with them and dance around the flickering flames. He moaned luxuriously and shifted. Slipping off his spear-handle, Gruzzle cracked his chin hard on the battlement, thrusting him into wakefulness and horrifying reality. The blazing cart plunged madly over the shore towards the fortress gates.

"Owch! Wha, er, 'ey, y'can't do that! Fire, fire, 'elp!"

In seconds all was chaos and mad confusion. Most of the soldiers on the walltops were sound asleep. They came awake tripping and bumping into each other. The longhouse door flew open and Badrang dashed out with his Captains stumbling behind. Hearing the shouts and seeing the bright glow against the darkness, the Tyrant drew his sword and yelled mightily, "Front wall! The gates! Hurry!"

He raced up the wall ladder, with Clogg's voice ringing over the alarm shouts. "Haharr, 'tis the ghost of me burned ship come back to take revenge on ye, Evil One. You should 'ave listened t' me, Badrang!"

The heat of the roaring conflagration scorched Rowanoak's cheeks as she pushed the blazing cart along. Martin and the others ran after her, having been driven from the sides of the cart by the searing flames. At a sharp shout from Rowanoak they halted, notching arrows to their bows. The badger continued running with the cart. Putting her every last ounce of strength into the act, she gave one mighty final push and fell flat. Crackling and hissing with tails of flame like a massive comet, the cart careered madly into the gates of Marshank.

Whoom! Crumph!

It struck the gates, blossoming like a monstrous fiery flower as the whole thing burst on the timbers, sending showers and cascades of angry red sparks upwards in a mushroom of smoke.

Ballaw already had the archers in three lines. He was in his element, ears quivering as he rapped out smart commands.

"First rank, shoot and drop!"

A volley of shafts hissed through the night.

"First rank, reload! Second rank, shoot and drop!"

Another hail of death followed in the wake of the first.

"Second rank, reload! Third rank, shoot and drop! Ready, first rank!"

Unable to see because of the bright light burning in their eyes, the walltop troops were hit hard. Amid it all Badrang was knocking the bows from fighters' paws. "Slopheads! Never mind shooting arrows, the doors are burning. Get sand, get water, put that blaze out!" He grabbed hold of Rotnose. "Did you hear me, muckears. Put the fi—"

The weasel slumped forward with a barbed arrow in his skull.

Boldred and the Warden released the net. It fell accurately, draping one end over three battlements while the rest of it trailed down the wall. Queen Amballa gave it a quick tug to make sure it was secure.

"Allbeast gonow, upupupupup!"

Gulba and Trung were alongside her as the net suddenly became alive with hedgehogs and pigmy shrews.

Ten Gawtrybe squirrels had made it to the top of the south wall. Six stood by on the narrow catwalk, fighting off hordebeasts as the other four let down ropes with sticks tied across them ladder fashion. Starwort wound his sling about his waist and grabbed one of the ropes.

"Come on, mates, just like climbin' up the riggin'!"

Grumm and the moles waited until they heard the

screams and shouts of combat on the other side of the wall.

"Roight, molers. Show'm 'ow to go a-tunellen!"

Powerful digging claws tore at rock, sand, earth and grass as the hole began to sink deep and wide.

Pallum stood close to Rose. "I never was in a war, is it always this complicated?"

Rose shrugged as she twirled a sling. "Your guess is as good as mine, Pallum. I was never in one either!"

Standing on the darkened beach, Martin could see the confused figures in the light of the gates. He fired off his arrow, seeing a searat fall with it in his throat, as Ballaw bade his rank drop and reload their bows.

The firecart had done its work well. Despite copious doses of sand and inaccurately thrown water, the flames licked hungrily up the woodwork, eating into the timber until they were well established.

Rowanoak came crawling, belly down, across the sand to Martin and Ballaw, joining them in time to see a ferret on the walltop beating wildly at his burning cloak.

"One badger reporting back. Mission successful—what's next?"

Martin cast aside the bow and drew his sword. "I'm going round to climb that net on the north wall!"

Ballaw and the others went with him. Rowanoak heaved a sigh and sat down with a bow and arrow. "I'll stop here and practice my archery. I could've climbed that net though, when I was younger, and slimmer!"

The burning gate was a lost cause. Badrang sent a platoon of long pikes to stand in the courtyard and repel anybeast that tried to gain entrance once the gates fell. Dividing his walltroops into two groups, he gave charge of the north wall to Crosstooth and the south to Fleabane. Dashing down from the walls, he ran into the longhouse. For the first time in his life the Tyrant felt the icy claws of terror grip him. With an awful certainty, he knew he was defeated: Marshank would fall. He stifled a sob of fear in his throat as he looked around frantically.

What to do?

He was trapped inside his own fortress, surrounded by a determined horde of fighters. Some of them had been slaves of his, slaves that he had starved, beaten and ill-treated. His paws began to shake. Suppose he was captured by those same slaves? Striving desperately not to think what they would do to him, he climbed out of the back window of the longhouse. He was facing the north wall, and the sounds of fighting above him were loud and furious. Badrang looked up. In the red glow from the blaze he saw his troops being pressed back by a growing multitude of small shrews and large fearsome hedgehogs. Bodies hurtled from the walltops amid wild battle shouts and war cries.

Suddenly the Tyrant's blood chilled, his mouth went dry with fright. There illuminated in the light from the burning gates stood a warrior on the battlements. Badrang recalled him in a flash. This was the one called Martin, the young mouse who had defied his authority, the one he had tied over the gate and imprisoned in the pit. The mouse warrior fought like ten beasts. Reckless of caution, he was everywhere at once, teeth bared, eyes glittering as he threw himself into the fray. Hugging the wallshadows, Badrang whimpered and ran for his life, before he was seen and identified by the fearless avenger.

Starwort and Marigold left the savage Gawtrybe squirrels to deal with the troops on the south wall, laughing crazily as they wielded their stone-headed axes against sword, spear and dagger. Heading their contingent of Broadstream fighters, the two otters descended the wall ladders to the courtyard. They charged straight into the platoon of pikebeasts who had been left to defend the burning gateway. With lightning agility the otters were in under the pikeshafts before the surprised foe had a chance to retaliate. Swinging stone-loaded slings, the fighting otters battered their enemies to the ground with startling speed. As the last one fell, there was a sagging and creaking of timbers, and the gates began caving slowly inwards.

"Gangway, the doors are openin'!" Marigold yelled out urgently.

Otters scattered left, right and back, as the gates buckled and groaned, collapsing inwards with a crash of dust, fire, smoke and sparks.

Starwort picked himself up from where the scorching air had bowled him over. "Stan' aside, mates. Badger comin' through!"

Rowanoak came at full tilt, sand flying from her paws as she galloped straight at the inferno. With an ear-splitting roar, the big badger leaped over the fallen gates. It was an awesome sight. Sailing through the flames, she landed square on all four paws inside the courtyard. The otters crowded round her, beating out the smouldering patches on her fur.

"There now, I wasn't as old as I thought," Rowanoak laughed, shuffling her paws to cool them on the ground. "Still life in the old stripes yet!"

Crosstooth fought his way along the north wall to the rear, hoping to reach the back wall, which offered quietness and a chance of escape. The fox was a seasoned battler, and cut his way through several pigmy shrews with the long-bladed spear he carried. Thrusting hard, he sent a shrew spinning from the walltop, knocking another flat with his spearshaft as he did.

Queen Amballa wriggled away from the questing spearpoint as the fox sought to skewer her, striking out valiantly with her small shrew sword. Martin came in with both footpaws first, catching Crosstooth in the lower back and sending him sprawling. Amballa was quick; she dispatched the foebeast with a single thrust as he fell forward upon her. Pushing her way free of the body, she leaped upright.

"Martinmouse save Ballamum!"

But Martin was not listening. He ran past her, along the walltop to where he had caught sight of Badrang down below, scurrying from the wall shadow to the burnt-out slave compound.

Lying low, the Tyrant peered through the ash-blackened stakes of the compound to the base of the rear wall. Moles, squirrels and mice were climbing out of a sizeable tunnel which had been dug through from the outside. Badrang saw his one chance of escape.

"Badraaaang, I am here!"

The Tyrant heard the challenge over the mêlée of battle. Casting a swift glance over his shoulder, he saw Martin dashing along the walltop. It was now or never. Badrang broke cover and ran for the tunnel, slashing viciously with his sword at anybeast who barred his way. Brandishing a ladle, a mole leaped growling at him. Badrang swung his sword. It caught the side of the ladle, sweeping Grumm away as his own ladle was smashed against the side of his head. A mousemaid threw herself on him, battering at his face with a pebble loaded in her sling. Once, twice, thrice she struck. Taken aback by the ferocity of the attack, Badrang tasted blood from a mouthwound. The loaded sling caught him hard in his left eye. Snarling with pain and rage, he grabbed the mousemaid. Lifting her easily, he flung her savagely from him. Rose's head struck the wall heavily, and she slid down like a broken doll.

Roaring and screaming like a wounded wolf, Martin threw himself from the walltop. Badrang leaped into the hole, only to find Pallum in a needletight ball blocking his way. The burned palisade of the slave compound saved Martin, breaking his fall as it exploded in a cloud of black ashdust to the dawn-streaked sky. Badrang had time to hack at Pallum only once before the Warrior was on him. He was heaved bodily from the hole, arching his back in agony as the flat of Martin's small sword whipped him.

"Get up, you scum! Up on your paws and face me!"

Badrang scrambled up. Holding the long sword of Luke the Warrior before him with both paws, he rushed Martin. The onlookers gave a cry of dismay as the sword raked Martin's chest. Heedless of it, the Warrior began striking back. Steel clashed upon steel as the young mouse with the short sword battered Badrang round and round the ruins of the compound. Badrang flailed out in a panic, catching his enemy on the shoulder, arm and paw. They locked blades and stood with their noses touching, Badrang's eyes wide with horror as he stared into the face of the snarling, unstoppable Warrior who was forcing him backwards as he gritted out, "I told you I would return someday and put an end to you!"

Wrenching his face away, the stoat bit deep into his foe's shoulder, only to find himself lifted bodily and hurled hard against the wall. Martin flung the shrew sword from him, locking both paws around Badrang's grip on the sword. The Tyrant wailed as he felt the Warrior's inexorable power turning the weapon until its point was hovering close to his heart.

Badrang's nerve deserted him. "Don't kill me," he sobbed. "You can have it all, the fortress, everythi—!"

The Tyrant of Marshank's mouth fell open and his head lolled to one side as he fell forward, carrying Martin to the ground underneath him. With his last vestige of strength, the young mouse pushed the slain foebeast from him and tugged his father's sword loose. Lying on his side with sand crusting the blood of his warwounds, Martin saw dawn's light beam across the face of Rose where she lay close to him by the wall.

The merciful darkness closed in on him as he murmured to her, "Rose, we could have chopped the sycamore down with this."

43

The sun rose in summer splendor as Starwort's drum beat out a victory roll. Unaware of certain events, a large crowd stood cheering in the smouldering gateway that lay open to the sun-warmed shore and the sparkling sea. Rowanoak strode slowly up, placing a restraining paw on the jubilant otter Chieftain. "Silence the drum, friend. Our battle was won at a bitter price."

Brome worked away dry-eyed on the wounds of the unconscious mouse warrior, binding and staunching as he applied herb poultices, all the time talking to himself. "It was all my fault, if I had stayed at Noonvale and not gone wandering I would never have been captured by Badrang's creatures and none of this would have happened. I am to blame!"

Ballaw sniffed. Bending down one ear, he wiped his eyes. "There, there, old lad. There's only one beast t' blame for all this and that's Badrang. Martin settled the score with him for good; the evil has gone from this land for ever."

Grumm stumbled up with a large dressing on the side of his face and neck. Deep rivulets carved their way down his face where the tears flowed constantly, and he made several small gestures with his paws before Buck-

366

ler sat him down with a large kerchief. "You'm 'ave to 'scuse Grumm, Maister Brome, him'n losed 'is voice through a-grieven. We'm puttin' fallen uns t' rest. . . . Wot abowt Miz Roser?"

Brome left off ministering to Martin's senseless form. He took a huge breath, letting it out in a shuddering sigh. "Thank you, friends, but I'm taking her home to Noonvale with me." Reaching out, he tucked in a corner of the simple white linen cloth that covered his sister's pitiful body. "Rose would have been alive today but for me, you know."

Buckler shook his head. "You'm not to blame, maister, nor Marthen, nor nobeast yurr."

Rowanoak looked bleakly around at the ruined, smoke-stained walls of Marshank, where not one foebeast had been left alive. "I don't know where we're all bound, but let's get away from this place!"

Boldred seconded the badger's wise words. "Rowanoak is right. There's been too much death and grief here, it seems to be part of the very stones. We'll leave what's left of Marshank standing as a reminder to any bad ones of what free and peaceful creatures can do when they're driven to it!"

Helped by Marigold, Brome placed Martin on a stretcher. He stood upright and addressed the multitude.

"Some of you, like the otters and the shrews of Broadstream, have homes to return to. Those of you who have no homes, listen to me. Noonvale can be your home, a place of peace to live happily in for all seasons. Put aside your weapons if you wish to go with me to Noonvale."

A pile of javelins, swords, daggers, bows and arrows lay at the center of the deserted compound that had once held Badrang's slaves. On the shore outside the fortress, comrades who had fought together now took their leave of each other. Like a stern father, the Warden of Marshwood Hill shepherded the wild and wayward squirrel tribe back to their mountain foothills beyond the marshes. Boldred watched them go. "He'll keep his eye on those rogues. Come on, let's get Martin away from here."

Bound to the stretcher, and still clasping his father's sword tightly, the unconscious young mouse was carried south along the beach by Pallum, Grumm, Boldred and Rowanoak.

Ballaw turned to the remainder of the Rambling Rosehip players, who stood alongside others bound for Noonvale. "Old Rowanoak'll join us once Martin's safe, wot! Right ho, Starwort, lead us to your vessel, my good otter!"

Queen Amballa stood with her pigmy shrews. They were the last to leave. One of the shrews had picked up the sword she had once given to Martin. Waddling behind Brome, she called out, "Waitmouse!"

Brome halted. He watched as the Queen of the pigmy shrews signalled the otters carrying Rose's bier to lower it. Placing the small sword beside the mousemaid's still form, Amballa spoke in her curt vigorous manner.

"Rosemouse bravemouse! We remember hername allseasons!" She waved to the pigmy shrews and they set off south along the shoreline for their own territory.

High noontide hung over Marshank. It lay open to the insects, birds and seasons. A breeze lingered there, swirling the dust and sand into miniature spirals, mingling it with ashes around the carcasses of Badrang's horde, which had been left for the gannets and scavenging sea birds to dispose of. The once proud fortress of the Tyrant now stood deserted and forsaken.

The first gannet to land was chased off by Cap'n Tramun Clogg, waving his spade as he trundled out of hiding from the grave surmounted by the upturned wheelbarrow.

"Garn! Gerroutofit, you robbin' featherbag! Leave my 'orde alone. I'm master 'ere now, just like I said I'd be one day, haharrharr!" The crazed corsair clumped about, turning first this one and then another, chatting amiably with the slain.

"Crosstooth, me ole matey, yore lookin' prime!"

"Harr, Boggs, sorry ye didn't join yer ole Cap'n to dig graves now, are ye?"

"Stumptooth, I allus said you should've sided with me. Never mind, mate, I'll find ye a snug berth. Leave it to Cloggo!"

He worked his way around until he found what he was looking for. "Badrang! Arr, where's yer fine dreams of empires now, you swab? Met a warrior who was more'n a match for ye, eh! Well, we're gonna be 'ere for ever now, you'n me, so let's not quarrel an' fall out with each other, matey. Tell yer wot, I'll dig ye a smart new grave, nice an' deep, aye, with rocks piled atop an' yer name carved all 'andsome like on one of 'em!"

The sea birds wheeled and soared over the lone figure below, sitting in the slave compound as he argued and gossiped with the dead stoat, who made no reply as he stared through sightless eyes at the unclouded blue sky of the Eastern Coast.

44

Days shortened, and the flowers of summer died one by one as leaves began turning brown and gold. It was on one such mist-shrouded autumn morning that Martin sat in the odd tree house, with the molewife Polleekin and his three friends, Boldred having long since departed for her mountain and her family.

All through the remainder of the summer Polleekin, Grumm, Pallum and Rowanoak had spent sleepless nights and restless days, nursing the Warrior back to health. Martin had come through it in silence, never speaking a word. He looked young still. Though healed in body and getting stronger by the day, his eyes still had a faraway look in them.

Grumm was about to speak when Polleekin silenced him with a glance. She nodded to the sword at Martin's side. "Oi be a-needen more foirewood, Marthen. Will you'm cut some?"

Wordlessly Martin took up his sword and went off, descending to the forest to cut wood. Pawing at the scar cut through his backspikes, Pallum got up as if to follow, but the molewife forbade it. "You'm set thurr, 'edgepig. They Wurrier garn off to shed tears!"

Rowanoak shook her head wonderingly. "I heard him

yesterday as I was walking through the forest. It must be very hard for him, he never mentions Rose."

Polleekin busied herself with breakfast. "No, marm, nor will him'n, oi doant think never. That liddle mousey-maid be locked in Marthen's 'eart, and thurr she'm bound to stay."

Grumm blinked and sniffed. "Marthen be a gurt brave wurrier, tho' him'n woant go back to Noonvale; too many mem'ries furr 'im thurr."

Polleekin's breakfast was good homely fare, oatmeal with honey, nutbread spread thick with strawberry preserve and a steaming pot of mint and dandelion tea. Martin ate automatically, neither tasting nor commenting on the food. When he had finished he made a simple announcement. "I am leaving today."

It was the first time he had spoken since the battle at Marshank. His friend waited for him to say more, but he sat silent, staring at his empty plate, face calm and resolute.

It was then that Rowanoak knew Martin had rejoined the land of the living. "Will you come to Noonvale with us? We will be leaving to go there today."

The young mouse sat, testing the swordblade against his paw, pressing so hard that he almost drew blood.

"I can never return to Noonvale. I will travel alone. South."

Grumm knew it was no use trying to change his friend's mind. "Whurr be you'm a-goen? Wot be you'm a-goen t' do, Marthen?"

They listened carefully, knowing that this would be the last time he would speak to them at any length. "One day maybe I will hang up this sword and be a creature of peace. Until then, I must follow the way of the Warrior; it is in my blood. Have no fear, I will never mention Noonvale, or any of you. Noonvale is a secret place untouched by evil. I could not forgive myself if I unknowingly sent trouble there. Nobeast will know from where I came."

Pallum stared quizzically at his stern-eyed friend. "But what will you say? We had such adventures together, maybe in another time and another place you will tell the tale."

"Never!" Martin shook his head slowly. "I will only say that I guarded my father's cave against searats while he was away. When I felt that he would not return I began my wanderings. How could anybeast understand what we went through together, the freedom we won and the friends we lost?"

The comrades sat in silence, each with their own memories. Polleekin rose stiffly and cleared away the remnants of their final meal together.

Soft autumn sunlight had cleared away twining wreaths of mist that hung over the still woodlands, leaves were falling in a crisp brown carpet, and a mild hoar frost melted to glistening dewdrops as the five companions took their leave of each other in the silent, timeless morning. Martin carried his sword slung across his back over an old cloak. Polleekin had made packs of food for them all. Grumm held his ladle in front of his face to hide the tears he could not stop from flowing. Rowanoak embraced the Warrior awkwardly, standing back as Pallum and Grumm did likewise. Polleekin kissed them all on the cheeks.

Rowanoak squared her broad shoulders and smiled. "We will never forget you, Martin the Warrior. Come on, let's see if we can make this place ring one last time with the old war cry!"

Birds flapped their startled wings as four voices yelled aloud, "Fur and Freedoooooom!"

Polleekin stood alone, watching as Martin was lost among the trees, a solitary figure going south. The ancient molewife slowly pawed her flowery apron, eyes clouding over as the destiny of the lone traveller stole unbidden into her mind.

"Hurr, oi told you'm 'twould be bad fate iffen you'm returned t' Marshank wi' thoi mousemaiden. Naow thurr be on'y you'm left, young un. Bo urr, you'm got some 'ard days to go yet awhoil, tho' 'appiness will be thoine in toime yet t' come. But furr all seasons everybeast shall amember thoi name, Marthen 'ee Wurrier!"

45

Down in Cavern Hole at Redwall Abbey, a night and a day had passed and the fire and wall torches had been replenished four times since the mousemaid Aubretia had begun her story. There was not a one who had fallen asleep throughout the whole epic tale, nor was there a creature who had not shed a tear.

Abbot Saxtus took off his spectacles and sighed in the silence that had reigned since Aubretia stopped talking. "Polleekin was right, of course. Martin did go on to find happiness. He forsook the Warrior's way and dedicated himself to peace, the founding of our order and the building of Redwall. But tell me, how did you know all this, who told the story to you, Aubretia?"

The big hedgehog Bultip put aside his tankard. "I can answer that, Father Abbot. Aubretia comes from the ruling line of Noonvale, though she and I have not been back there in a full season. The blood of Urran Voh runs in her veins—her great ancestor was called Brome the Healer, Brother of Rose. My great ancestor, far back in the mists of countless days, was called Pallum the Peaceful. I am a direct descendant of his line."

Simeon passed his sensitive paws gently over Aubretia's face. "You have inherited the beauty of Brome's sister."

The mousemaid undid a thong from about her neck. On it was a brilliantly carved locket of scallop shell. She opened it. "Every creature who sees this says the same thing."

Abbot Saxtus took the locket carefully. Inside was a picture painted with plant and vegetable dyes on a small tablet of polished cherrywood. It was a miniature portrait of Martin and Rose carried out in loving detail. Both their faces seemed to stare out at him across the dust and time of bygone seasons. "Martin looks exactly like his picture on the tapestry, though younger. You are right, Aubretia. You could have passed for Rose's twin sister. This is a marvellous thing, where did it come from?"

"It was given to the family of Brome by an owl called Emalet,"the mousemaid answered as she rummaged in her herb satchel. "Boldred her mother was a great artist, besides being a good mapmaker. Bultip and I left Noonvale early last summer. We had heard tales of Martin and Redwall from travellers since we were babes, so we set out to see the Abbey for ourselves. Here is something I brought with me for Redwall."

The Abbot took the gift. Donning his spectacles, he looked at it curiously, turning it this way and that. "Thank you very much, but please excuse my ignorance, what is it?"

Aubretia explained about the sprig with its attached wet loam bag. "Grumm planted a rose on the grave of Rose. It is a red rose. Sometimes it flowers later than others, and we call it Laterose. This is a cutting from the original bush. It is very sturdy."

Simeon felt the little shoot tenderly. "This spring I will plant it in our Abbey grounds. It will bloom and flourish in memory of the mousemaid. Laterose, what a pretty name. That was Rose's full title as you told it, Laterose of Noonvale, daughter of Urran Voh and Aryah."

Abbot Saxtus returned Aubretia's locket. "We thank you, my child, for everything. Laterose will remain precious to Redwall Abbey. Martin gave it strength, now Rose will give it beauty. Now I am tired, and you must be too, friends. Go and rest. Stop at our home for as long as you wish—you are both welcome."

The entire company walked together up the stairs from Cavern Hole to their rooms. Aubretia and the Abbot went paw in paw. "Thank you for your offer, Father Abbot. Bultip and I would love to stay here through winter, until the spring."

"There is always room for you and Bultip here, Aubretia. Our Abbey is a place of friendship. Anyone, young or old, who has read or heard of Redwall may come and visit us. If you are honest and of good heart, no matter what the season our door is open to you. Whether for the first time, or for the return of an old companion, you are welcome. Please feel free to visit us anytime you pass by this way."